ORBIS

a diversion

Edwin Ahearn

1.

It is as well, in a world which, with a living paradise within easy reach of its competence, perversely insists on lunging for ruin, that liars and known frauds, so long as they reassure, are acknowledged as prophets, while plain realism is dismissed as wild and pessimistic fantasy. Although self-destructive conscience or some unquenchable belief in happy endings won't let me stay silent, I might have a slender chance of survival, passing for one of those deranged doomsayers. Thus, solemnly, he begins his trifling tale.

Writing a brochure for an outfit offering summer cruises on the Great Lakes was my first professional contact with Orbis, so far as I know. The disclaimer is necessary; when hired for the job by Harry Yeats, who not only runs but virtually is Tintype Productions, I had no idea his client, Lynx Cruises, was part of the Orbis empire, so perhaps other things I've done handouts for in the past, airlines, hotels, restaurants, for example, or educational toys, pharmaceuticals, may have been Orbis offspring. There must be many a nine-to-fiver who doesn't know the company name appearing on each weekly or fortnightly paycheck long ago became part of a job-lot Orbis acquisition; divisions within Orbis buy out rivals, holding companies at the top make mergers; already a swollen conglomerate under a former name, with no internal logic but the quest for profit, the group had, a few years ago, outbid all competition to expensively subsume a further tangled corporate skein, vast by any standards except its own, at which time the name, Orbis International, and catchall logo, ORBIS, came into being. As its institutional ads say, over a murmur of

Mozart between segments of Sunday news shows, ORBIS
touches every life — a slogan I seemed to be alone in finding
slightly sinister. Through its electronics manufacturing
component, by the way, Orbis has controlling interest in one of
the networks, but is careful to distribute its advertising budget
impartially among all three, as also to compete with itself in
running a completely separate Cable TV operation. There are,
indeed, a number of fields — pet-foods, for example — where
two of the leading brands, locked in eternal rivalry, are in fact
both from the Orbis stable, while the cans they're rammed in,
like the labels on the cans, are likely to be made by Orbis
companies; at least one big supermarket chain selling those
cans is also owned by an Orbis subsidiary — it's hard to find
any species of pie without the Orbis finger inserted. Most of
this information can be found in *Empires*, that overhyped
exposé of the year before last, a missile that burst with the
destructive force of a jelly doughnut on its corporate targets,
brought out, as it happens, by the publishing house owned by
Elipse Communications (an ORBIS corporation).

  I made up that last part, which is merry satire. Some
light relief is needed from the knowledge, every watchful
minute, my life has become an erasable digit in the icy sums of
corporate greed.

  So the faceless monster. The conglomerate first
assumed some anthropoid characteristics on a crystal-innocent,
murderously cold day in early March last year, when I visited
Harry Yeats at Tintype to talk about a few added touches for
the cruise-ship brochure, and found him already showing our
dummy to a crisp-suited, smooth young man of about my own
age (low mid-thirties), named as Frank Lupin, publicity chief
for Orbis Special Projects. Harry's a wily old production man,
using a blue-collar bonhomie to camouflage both an
encyclopedic knowledge of how books and printed things in
general come into physical being, and eternal worry over a
cash flow that never gets more than a ripple ahead of

catastrophe. He was naturally anxious (exactly, anxious) for me to shine in this Lupin's esteem, and introduced me in terms that might have made genius blush; but we mediocrities are made of less shrinking stuff, and know how to milk overpraise with the modest smile that denies nothing.

Suavely, Lupin joined in, noting how gratified he and his employers had been by my deft counterpointing of contrasted cruise themes, adventure and luxury: Our Third Ocean, North America's Least Tameable Wilderness, against notions of guiltless, merited pampering, allusions to the old Orient Express, Cunard liners of the great between-the-wars years. Harry's creased face took on the proprietary beam of a successful matchmaker, but I didn't really take to this Frank Lupin, frigid beneath honed amiability; when I made the littlest joke about having steered well clear of the *Titanic* era, he shot me a quick, penetrating look from his coal-black eyes, as if actually trying to determine whether my commitment to Lynx Cruises was *sincere*, God help us. He spoke, nonetheless, of doing more to exploit Romance, as a feature to attract a younger crowd; by Romance I understood him to mean humid consummation, not the ductless yearning of *amor cortois*, but after his reaction to my *Titanic* joke didn't say what came into my mind, that we might promote Safe Romance, with complimentary gift-packs of rubber goods for all single cruisers. Instead I pointed out how, together with an illustration, all bikini and bicep, the existent reference to starlit nights on the Terrarium Deck could be made more explicit with a few well-chosen erotic adjectives. As Harry Yeats would say, did say when we were alone, the guy lapped it up like Dom Perignon.

As a result of this meeting, I was invited to visit Orbis Special Projects at its home in the angular and glassy Javelin Building downtown, where Orbis is both landlord and its own best tenant.

I've encountered corporate security before, with watchdog receptionists and buzz-in doors, but there must be missile silos more penetrable than Special Projects. For a start, I was told it was on the eleventh floor, but from ground floor I couldn't get there by elevator, being offered only the choice of floors 1-10, or 12-23 (there are other, loftier banks). As instructed, I rode to ten, and was challenged by a security guard within the redoubt of a large, high, horseshoe desk. When I gave my name and said who I'd come to see, he used the internal phone to relay this information; as I later discovered the closed-circuit camera trained on my face allowed Frank Lupin to make sure I wasn't some spurious Arthur Ames on a mission of sabotage or espionage. Approved, I was buzzed through a door otherwise opened only by key-card, and found it led to a short corridor, also looked over by the blinkless eye of a security camera, with no other egress except another pair of elevators. These had no indicators, and were in fact access solely to, and sole access to, the eleventh floor, or at least that fortress portion of eleven devoted to Special Projects. Emerging from my brief ascent, I was hindered by yet another desk, this one manned by an immaculate young woman with impersonal smile, who reconfirmed my identity before using her phone. Quite soon, Frank Lupin emerged from another card-key door extending a welcoming hand, and I was ushered into the fastness.

Really quite small, though that wasn't immediately apparent; no vistas were offered in a labyrinth of more than head-high partitions dividing off small cubicle-offices, though many of these, I noted, were internally separated only by waist-level portable walls, with connecting gaps. Though I had very inexact ideas about this enclave's function, it was oddly modest, out of scale with Orbis, like the pecan brain of a dinosaur, and cubicles appeared to outnumber employees, mainly youthful, by at least three-to-one; I glimpsed typewriters, a copier, terminals, drawing-boards, a coffeemaking station with the normal detritus of ozone-assailing cups, pouched sugar and synthetic sweeteners, teabags, a large jar of whitish powder for which wild claims were made. Then we'd arrived at a row of more substantial offices, the large corner one defended by another breastwork, with space, unoccupied, for a secretary-sentinel. If I'd considered it at the time that would have been my first hint of tormented vacillation here between two kinds of security; every vigilant human was also a potential loose-lipped risk to the secrecy Special Projects strove for — the absurd secrecy, I would have said then, convinced it shrouded itself about such concerns as being first to market low-fat shortening, for example, or a flatulence control food for elderly dogs. One recognizes the need to protect exclusive rights to such epochal advances, but I thought it made Frank Lupin's job as publicity chief an anomalous one: as he said himself at a later date, he had to maximize consumer anticipation in the small window of time between end of the secrecy thing and initiation of the marketing phase. Amused contempt was easier for me then, before I knew what depths of darkness were restrained under that lid.

The big, bright office belonged to Mark Worth, whose position as Director of Special Projects was confirmed by multiple phones and monitors, a fax machine, his own desk copier, a shelf of reference books. He was a large man, perhaps 45, with a golfer's tan and prominent, perfect teeth, a warm, brown voice and a firm handshake, yet when he told me how many good things he'd heard about me from Frank here, I sensed the conditionality of his command in the sidelong look he had for the slighter, older and better-tailored man half-sitting, half-leaning at the corner window. Brown hair silvering, eyes keenly intelligent behind slender-rimmed glasses despite a murky, nondescript color, a razor nose and straight, flat lips of a man who, in patient pursuit of some great goal, can indefinitely postpone personal gratification. Hurd Laxitter, introduced as Vice-President of Orbis

(Development), though I was to learn he held titles with half a dozen different divisions and component corporations, and most notably was on the board of Orbis (Holdings), nearest there is to a cortex for the whole sprawling organism.

Like Mark Worth he spoke in praise of the cruise brochure, but not with Laxitter could I miss the note of a man perfunctorily tagging up before coming home. "Orbis," he said, "deals in resources. We find it useful to think in those terms."

"When we say, resources," Frank Lupin chimed, taking his cue like a trouper. "We're not thinking only of raw materials, manufacturing capacity, financial assets. A man's, a woman's skill is a resource. What's in my head, your head, can be a resource. Orbis takes pride in its success at recognizing and developing human resources."

Under the last I could almost hear soft undulations of K.488, middle movement, while another PGA tour event waited to resume. Like me, Mark Worth might have thought this was laying it on a bit thick, as he ever-so-slightly cleared his throat. The corporation, he said, made use of regular ad agencies, and there were some fine creative people sprinkled throughout the divisions, but specific situations arose, he almost apologized, where to keep things within a small family circle was only prudent. You got a situation where you had, best scenario, a few weeks lead-time on a new idea, that few weeks could be all the difference between a million dollars and zilch.

"Innovation," Frank Lupin slid in. "Is also an important resource, and one that has to be defended. Once the cat's out of the bag — "

"He gets it, Frank," Laxitter suggested, closing the speechmaking he himself had first uncorked. Turning to me in a candid, man-to-man mode, he asked flatly whether, if I did a job for them, they could trust me to respect confidentiality.

The chance of finding an applicant who'd answer no to

such a question is, of course, near zero. Not being a stupid man, Laxitter knew that, and I judge that rather than hear what, he wanted to see how I answered. It must have been acceptable, as on my side was the pay-scale he proposed, nearly twice my usual top rate. After all the fuss, wondrously anti-climactic to discover the great secret concerned nothing more astounding than traveller's checks. Free traveller's checks.

"I know, you're going to say," Mark Worth, swiftly. "Other people already offer free traveller's checks. Only free, though, in the context of there being no charge for the check — the situation is, you lay out a thousand dollars and get a thousand dollars in checks. Ours are going to be *free*, up front; we give them to you, and you don't pay a dime till you spend them or cash them."

Not a bad idea, effectively an extension of the credit card system, to be available to all ORBISCARD users, maybe to recruit some new ones; the company issued one, five or ten thousand dollarsworth of the traveller's checks, and only amounts spent were to be added to the credit card account, from the date countersigned, at a trifling interest-rate of 18% or so. As Frank Lupin pointed out, the conglomerate having spent half a billion dollars worldwide to make the ORBIS logo more widely recognizable than an international No Entry sign, the checks would be negotiable practically anywhere, and especially useful for small purchases, or with retailers who didn't honor credit cards as such. "Like, if you were overseas someplace, and wanted to buy — " he began, and failed to find a ready example.

"A sling in Singapore," I offered, and started, couldn't stop. "A mule in Moscow, a rose in Tokyo, air in Londonderry, some sprouts in Brussels, ink in India — "

"Let's use that, Frank," Laxitter said, and Lupin, who'd begun a frown at my levity was slick to change gears, and see the possibilities of some cute illustrations. To me, it became clear in time the vigilance at Special Projects extended only to

Orbis ideas; my *jeu d'esprit* eventually became theme for an
amusing, immensely popular series of television commercials,
which used all of my examples, outentertained most programs,
and won several awards, for all which I received no jot of
either glory or payment.

Other, that is, than what I was paid for their first use, in
the eight-page brochure I found myself committed to
producing, for handout in banks and travel agencies, along
with a four-page abridgement for tucking in with the
ORBISCARD bills in May, and an insert card with order form for
that and other mailings. When I asked on the basis of the
glimpsed drawing board whether they had a staff illustrator in
mind, Lupin fumbled in his breast-pocket for a small slip of
paper, and said Harry Yeats had mentioned, um, Paula Leahy
as a possibility, did I know her?

Harry has a sentimental streak as wide as the Shannon,
particularly after a long steady evening of consuming brandy
in tiny, only slowly cumulative sips. "Yes, I know Paula,"
holding my voice steady with both fists.

Laxitter didn't miss much. "And you can work with
her? We have to know; there isn't much time to spare."

"We worked together on a piece for the opera," I
reminisced. "Yes, I can work with Paula. She's a fine
illustrator." She was also, to me, devastatingly attractive, and,
while giving my work all professional respect, classed me
currently, I believed, among lower invertebrates. Her
departure, alone and unwarned, between acts two and three of
the *Manon* we'd gone to together on freebees, part of our
reward for the anniversary booklet we'd done, was, I thought,
some indication, though she explained days after she'd had an
unignorable idea for a picture. Perhaps it's Paula's auburn hair,
but Harry, based on his long experience of life as depicted in
films starring Maureen O'Hara, was not-very-secretly
convinced it would take only some troglodytically aggressive
action on my part to convert self-evident incompatibility into

immortal passion, while I knew very well I'd remain
wonderfully polite.

With security clearance for me put in the works, my
promise to make contact with Paula and a vow not to carry
from these premises any documents or notes pertaining to the
project, it was settled I'd meet here Monday with one Bill
Fasstin, the Orbis executive most conversant with details of
the traveller's check plan. All was handshakes and affability,
and I was gratified, as always, at the prospect of some weeks
of assured income, yet there was a feeling of letdown after the
weighty build-up, as if trumpets and cannon had portended
arrival of the man who reads the meter. Then, as I reached for
my treed topcoat, Mark Worth, in what the others' expressions
instantly labelled as indiscretion, asked Laxitter, "What about
the other, the stirrup?"

"Later," Laxitter, with a palms-down gesture.

"We've got time on that," Frank Lupin agreed, and as I
turned, coated, resumed his welcome-esteemed-colleague
smile for me. A momentary wrinkle, no more, but enough for
me to understand. I was being given a trial run. At that time,
beyond the obvious, the word *stirrup* meant nothing to me.

Infidelities of prominent folk are normally no concern
of mine, and it's not easy to speak of one's own liaisons (or
singular liaison) with celebrity without seeming to boast. I
have, besides, more perilous secrets to bring out into the light,
and personal life, mine or anyone's, is only tangential: nothing
can be served by revealing more than what's germane to my
story. Born in the Upper Middle West, I began by wanting to
be a musician, my imagined career as pianist foredoomed by
an incurably weak left hand. I still review concerts and opera
over the radio and for minor publications, and sometimes do
program notes or synopses for a performance (I mean, at the
time we're talking about still did those things); I've always
enjoyed the company of musicians, as a class, contrary to
popular legend, the warmest, least envious people I know,
happy to be in service to a goddess they love (we're speaking

of real music, not the thump and howl of masscult hysterics);
the process that put me in bed with a renowned soloist noted
for her impassioned interpretations was, surely, ingrowth of
my admiration rather than any base desire to bask in reflected
glory. We met at a reception after she'd performed (on what
instrument I shan't say, or perhaps she's a singer) with our
proud orchestra, and when I alluded to a powerful but
relatively obscure work that should be in her repertoire (which,
as transpired, she already knew and loved) there was
immediate rapport; those post-concert affairs are always full of
cooing idiots to whom everything is equally lovely, and she
turned to me as to an oasis of understanding in a desert of
undifferentiated praise. At the time, her somewhat-less-
celebrated husband, a conductor of unimpeachable, aridly
predictable competence, was four thousand miles away as the
cuckoo flies, and they had, as I heard at about one a.m. in
moonlight filtered through hotel drapes, no fixed plans for any
reunion. But we soon had, Antonia and I (let's call her
Antonia); she possessed a mountain-lodge in the orbit of a
popular western, but not farthest western, ski-resort, where she
planned to spend some time in autumn; the countryside, she
plausibly attested, was at its best out of ski-season, and
weather in September ideal, golden by day, diamonded by
night, with edge enough to make log fires more than merely
romantic. Words were murmured about a sheepskin. Could I,
on the far side of summer, make time to join her there as she
rested (her bow-arm, fingers, vocal chords, embouchure) and
studied scores, between the end of her murderous schedule of
festivals and before the opening of the gruelling concert
season? Could I not, I greedily affirmed.

Perverse, seemingly, to fritter away precious rug-time
driving a thousand miles, but roads were good, weather better,
my car whimpering for some sustained exercise, and while in
snow-months the spot I was going has an active airport

reachable from half-a-dozen points, here in off-season it would have meant flying to the nearest major city and either waiting for a spasmodic bus, or renting a car to take me the rest of the way. As was, with a noon start I made excellent going on the prairie, spent overnight at a motel in the middle of a flat state, and in the morning, within always-stirring sight of what could no longer be banks of cloud on the horizon, called Antonia, to hear the numbing news that her husband, after giving a performance, doggedly authentic, I bet, of *Il ritorno di Ulisse in patria*, had been inspired to call her from Edinburgh, and was at that moment winging across the Atlantic and half a continent for a fresh go at reconciliation. All-too-readily doomed, she indicated, if there were any hint she'd done other than weave contrapuntal tapestries in his absence. She was dubious for herself, regretful for me, but convinced she owed him this retake. As for what I might be owed — well, I'll admit to having pored out-of-town newspapers, following her summer career, rejoicing in consistently ecstatic reviews, inordinately grateful to find a picture of her, however indistinct, in performance, looking forward fixedly to reunion, and there in the middle of corn country my responses to disappointment were appropriately trite; when Antonia, throwing a bone to my devastation, offered wanly that there might be another time, I said, perhaps, but I wouldn't dream of posing any threat to connubial harmony, a remark which I thought measured and temperate, till she muttered, "I guess I deserved that."

After carefully clearing ten whole days I couldn't go tamely back: my summerlong yearning for reunion with unexpected Antonia had been counterpoint to a — *tempestuous*, I think the word would be, a tempestuous juxtaposition with maddening Paula, with whom I was certainly in love at the same time as I was devouring inadequate news of Antonia in the *Cleveland Plain Dealer* or *Seattle Post-Intelligencer*. Why does this seem so much more discreditable than in the living of it? Putting my emotions into writing doesn't suddenly bind me to an unreal novelistic code for monomania; the one had nothing to do with the other. Others, I might say; if there was a gratifyingly dreamlike air about detached hedonics with elusive Antonia, there was bruising reality in everything concerning both the Paulas.

Even as artist she was two distinct beings. The commercial operative had all professional dodges at her fingertips, and not the slightest conscience; she could switch styles as easily as changing nibs, and her work was adroit and impersonal, effortlessly successful. As a serious artist she never had much luck getting shown, and her paintings had an almost painful lack of tricks; she was too accomplished ever to be exactly clumsy, but there was an open, vulnerable innocence about her work that couldn't be connected to the tough-minded illustrator. Bewilderingly, when it came to the personalities responsible for the two species, there was a counterchange: as my collaborator on the brochure for Orbis she was winning company, laughed at my jokes, accepted need for revisions with unfaltering cheerfulness, and over all had a wide-eyed quality, perpetually amazed by her own flair, readily huggable when a problem was solved, just as she herself was quick to touch when bestowing congratulations on one of my verbal triumphs, or we rejoiced together over a felicitous marriage between content and design. Whereas, in the apartment studio, working at her own stuff, she was quite often, in a daunted word, bitchy; she could attack a canvas full of pale spring flowers with a taut, combative intensity troubling to witness, and just thinking about serious painting (which she scrupulously avoided while illustrating) could pull back the soft lower lip into an agonized stripe, and cause her vocabulary to undergo a startling metamorphosis: I still recall my shock, not just at the first obscenity I heard her utter, but at the demonic anger it gave vent to. I never once saw her delighted by painting or by her paintings, as she could be so easily, so lovably, by a deft little vignette she drew in the flick

of a pencil. I can see some Movement authority nodding
recognition of the insecure male who couldn't cope with
female Paula's threatening talent, but life's more quirky than
those smug slogans: the Paula who evoked my choked surges
of admiring affection was, remember, not the manageable little
woman of legend, but a formidable pro, who made my skills
plodding by comparison, and could, by the way, easily outearn
me.

What didn't and couldn't work out was that I fell in
love and kept falling in love with that one, no matter how
often assailed, bitterly denounced or thrust away by the
tormented other, who could spin quarrels out of filaments
thinner than air, and maintain a wronged taciturnity far beyond
any conceivable, let alone actual, cause. I have no wish to
pose as saintly; though patient I am provokable, and
contributed, certainly, my own share of unforgivable
counterthrusts. It may have bearing that there was in her past a
devastation, when scarcely out of her teens, concerning a
drawing instructor, married, perpetually promising not to be,
in the end returning to the more elaborate precedent vows. A
commonplace tale, but bitterly particular for each lone liver of
it.

One of the many final breaks with Paula had put me
next to an empty seat at Antonia's concert in May, laying
groundwork for the western expedition in September. By
then, with our collaboration at Orbis long over, I had achieved
with Paula, though too soon to acknowledge it, an imperfect
misery; we could revel in bedding together, still find other
moments of joy, but if there's a technique for exorcising a
feeling of doom, I'd like to hear it; her healing smile, the light
coppery down on arms or neck, her voice when the demons
were absent, could renew all my first wishes, but not make me
unbelieve a systemic conviction it was all spoiled by
knowledge of too many repairs, too many fresh beginnings.
You never really come to the same place twice, because
human location is perception, and knowing it *is* a same place

changes it.

Paula never had any shrift at all for that sort of metaphysical argumentation; although she often wished aloud I'd relieve her from the burden of being my chief obsession, and claimed freedom, whether or not she exercised it, to "see" other men (which I think meant, take them to bed), she didn't buy any of my logically watertight explanations of why the tryst with Antonia must be kept, and when the time came my departure west partook of a defiance I would fain have avoided or denied.

The recollection of being on one's dignity is always anything but dignified, yet can we doubt emotional overinvestment in the abstract right to be away for a tennight was a large part of my inability to turn for home once my Antonia had melted into air? Just before leaving, with the thought we might ramble some uplands, I'd thrown my camping gear on the back seat, and now, within sight of mountains, a payphone cold and lifeless in my stricken hand, I made up my mind to do it alone. Coming about noon to a foothills metropolis, I laid in some fairly portable supplies, bought a map, and that night brewed my whisky and milk over a balsamic fire at about six thousand feet. The start of a week which could be made to sound idyllic, omitting any consideration of whether I was happy, and on the eighth morning I rejoined my ghostly, shrouded car off a dusty disused lane, and drove to where I could call Paula.

Protestant from a state more Nordic than Kelt (her mother was a Hansen), she began with one of her flashes of atavistic Irishness, asking sweetly if the concerto had turned out to my satisfaction, but I was too strong-armed in misery to respond in kind, and opened myself for a killing stab by simply confessing I'd missed her.

"Oh, by the way," after a sadistic silence. "Orbis has been trying to talk to you. Mark Worth called wanting to know where you were. I said you'd call him as soon as you got back your strength."

She hadn't said any such thing, and had no idea of what Orbis wanted. Queried what she should say if Worth called again, I answered both that and the unasked question by saying I'd be back tomorrow night, but would call him right now.

"Collect," she reminded me.

"See you soon," I said, epic inadequacy.

For one offering me another opportunity, however brief, to be overpaid, Mark Worth on the phone sounded inexplicably apologetic, finding it necessary to invoke the talismanic name of Hurd Laxitter. What they wanted, he said, was an update of the traveller's check brochures, in context of the resort season, which I instantly translated as more sun, palms and pesos at the expense of francs, culture and crockery. Once more, time was pressing; how soon could I start. Monday, I reassured him.

On Monday when I again penetrated the eleventh-floor keep, Mark Worth was in conference, and I did what everyone with experience there did, and went to see Fena Keller. It meant enduring the dense air of her cubbyhole office, where she chain-smoked short, unfiltered cigarettes, responsible, perhaps, for the rasp in her voice, but Fena, titled Special Projects Coordinator, effectively office manager, is that indispensable of large organizations, the executive who actually executes, occupying and controlling a middle ground between pure and manicured decision-maker and the lowly empowered only to follow orders; the company sergeant-major. Early forties, plain, a product of the New York office, she had what in relative ignorance I'd call a Brooklyn toughness, an assumed general scorn which preempted any possible idea of being conned, and in which, if you were lucky, you were implicitly invited to share. By curious contrast, she could become cheerfully rhapsodic on how several large, determined cats controlled and ordered her home life, and was an enthusiast, nay, a cultist, for the works of J.R.R. Tolkien; through blue haze above her desk a large

Frodo Lives poster could dimly be discerned on the wall behind, and she used a Middle Earth calendar for noting deadlines and the like. Since she was also the programmer who'd set up the computer system for Special Projects, Fena was thought to be a subterranean devotee of those pseudo-medieval sword-and-spell games which remotely (and bizarrely) derive from the world of Tolkien, but that remains sheer speculation.

"Hi, Ames," swinging from her terminal to face front. "You gonna be with us some more, right?"

I agreed that was my understanding, and asked if she knew whether Bill Fasstin was to be here. Bill was the young and painstaking executive from ORBIS/Orbiscard who'd been my authority for all I wrote about the traveller's checks.

Fena appeared surprised, then recollected I'd been away some months. Fasstin was gone, she told me. No, he hadn't been fired, and only in a manner of speaking had he quit. "The dumb shit had his hand in the till. Was into Orbis for about a hundred and forty thousand. We got him, though. He's not gonna go to the slammer, signed a restitution agreement, that keeps it low-profile. I hear we had trouble finding you," as if it connected. "Worth was about ready to get the mounties on it, he had Laxitter on his back."

A few days earlier as I scrambled in unpeopled sub-Rockies it had idly occurred to me that if I fell and broke something necessary it could be a very long time before any intentional help arrived: no one could say to five hundred miles or so where I might be, and my empty car, first possible evidence of trouble, was out of easy sight on a road altogether abandoned. With this in mind I smiled and told Fena the slogan of even the estimable redcoats might well have proved an empty boast this time.

"Oh, weda found you. Like Fasstin, he thought he could disappear, we got him. You gonna go anywhere, you're gonna use credit cards, right? Oh, sure, cash, how much cash you gonna carry? You try renting a car for cash, you're gonna buy a plane ticket for cash?"

I suggested if a personal check wasn't negotiable, one might repeatedly raid the money-machine, or else purchase a cashier's check, but Fena triumphantly riposted that merely by getting on the phone and talking about embezzlement, Hurd Laxitter could put an immediate block on an account with any major bank in the city, instantly depriving plastic of its power to call forth currency. National credit-cards, she admitted, took a little longer. "The first thing we did when his accounts didn't add up was pull his Orbiscard, naturally. But the guy had a couple of other credit cards, and a weekend's head start." She swivelled back to her computer terminal, cleared the screen, tapped in some numbers, and when the machine beeped twice, entered a further long string of characters, all from memory. Instantly, a three-color menu unrolled on screen.

Fena said, "Here, I can access the central file for all major credit-card transactions anywhere in the US and Canada, broken down by location, type of card, name, date, whatever you want. I can do Europe, the world, too, but that gets more complicated."

"Still," I said. "That would be quite a few transactions."

"Tell me about it, zillions. But we could narrow it down. See, Fasstin meant this to go on a whole lot longer, I mean, you're not gonna retire for life on a hundred and forty grand, huh? He had not an idea we were even close to him till that Thursday, the auditor asked him a question about the account he'd been tapping, innocent question, just wanting a small inconsistency cleared up. Fasstin never came in Friday, he couldn't have had any long-standing plans for disappearing, you know, like having a plane ticket ready, accumulating a lot of cash, renting a house in Belize or someplace. This was a panic thing. That meant I was looking at between Friday and Monday. I said to myself, he'd never use his Orbiscard, I knew the other cards he had, so I asked for charges to those two cards, in the city, between those two dates, airlines." As she recounted this, Fena's fingers mimed the needed entries, but didn't touch the keys.

"Nothing," she said. "Okay, what about car-rentals, same cards, same dates? Bam! William R. Fasstin rented a full-size, Saturday around noon. I found out it was a one-way, dropoff Pittsburgh — is that stupid? He coulda told them he'd turn the car back in here, and just ditched it in Pittsburgh — left it in the airport parking-lot, it woulda been a month before we knew about that. Because when I tried airlines, Pittsburgh, late Saturday through Monday, there it was. He was on the British Airlines Monday morning flight to London Heathrow, first class no less. After that it was a piece of cake; the British police picked him up at his hotel on Wednesday." She gave a barking laugh. "The same day the FBI told Laxitter they had a lead Fasstin had driven to Pittsburgh. Shit! I bet they dusted the steering-wheel for fingerprints."

I was properly impressed and dutifully acknowledged it, but noted Fena's slight exaggeration of Orbis's albeit considerable powers: according to her own timetable, Hurd Laxitter would have had no reason to exercise his influence with the city's banks before that Monday; the fugitive Fasstin could and no doubt did go on making use of his automated teller card till he headed for Pittsburgh, probably sometime Sunday. If he'd only said Pittsburgh and headed for St, Louis, he might have disappeared, Hannaylike, into the Scottish mists, before ever the Yard began to look for him. He would have had, it's true, not much money.

Fulfilling another duty, I murmured how impossible it would have been to guess from his diffident demeanor and company-man veneer that Fasstin, of all people —

After clearing her screen, she lunged for and lit a cigarette. "Fair speech may hide a foul heart," she quoted. "Huh?" Since discovering I'd read and enjoyed *Lord of the*

Rings she'd made a ritual of testing me with such scraps, but that one I couldn't place.

So, for a few days, the happier uncomplicated Paula was to be back with me at Orbis. On her own she'd done another small job for Special Projects since my first, and in a rare, flattering confessional moment said that without me there she'd really begun to get spooked by that walled-in place, which she called Paranoia City.

We differed on the subject of Hilde Konwitschny, who to me was the one above all to justify Paula's shivering sobriquet; each of the brief times I'd spoken with her Hilde had been darkly haloed in Mitteleuropa distrust, whereas Paula, on the basis of yet fewer encounters, thought her quite an elegant Continental lady. Both could, I surmised, be true; too short to be certifiably stylish, Hilde, distanced from the seductive pastries and *Schlag* of her native Vienna, had maintained into her forties a figure fuller than ideal only by tendentious standards of the aerobics-and-cardboard-food racket. Except for the frowning eyebrows her face might have been called doll-like, if dolls' eyes could be haunted by bad dreams (of prowling teddy-bears, perhaps, or sudden accidental amputations). As to Hilde's clothes, I could accept Paula's word they were anything but cheap, yet to me they exuded a mysterious quality: the skirt-and-jacket suits of classic cut were always murky checks, but with tiny squares of intense color burning in the depths, blood-red, the deep blue of cobalt imaginings. There was a fine-ribbed sweater, mustard yellow, till from another angle swiftly it switched to a dark brick-orange, and she wore olive green shot-silk scarves where purple ripples shimmered and rainbow-hued paramecia swam and vanished. Moreover, smiling, she proffered boxes of chocolate-clad marzipan, and every day made herself cups of strange tea, reeking Lapsang Souchong midmorning, lotus-land jasmine in the afternoon: need I say more? (Forgive me, Hilde, if you're anywhere you can.)

At her Lapsang-making when I emerged from Fena's
cloud-chamber that day recalled above, she asked whether she
could seethe another teabag for me. Her English was
excellent, with only entire absence of any accent betraying a
not-native speaker. Hilde was a translator, and, as such, a
sudden glimpse into the global reich that was Orbis; she did
nothing else. Somewhere an elegant Oriental lady did
Japanese and doubled as a receptionist, but Hilde had Europe
sewn up, fluent and literate in not fewer than nine major
languages, including impossible Hungarian but not counting
dialects; with the Slavonic group, where I am altogether
ignorant, she had a relationship I couldn't untangle, except that
besides Russian she managed in Polish, Bulgarian and Czech,
coped with Croatian, and once said she could translate from
but not into Lusatian, or Wendish, whatever that is. Not quite
true she did nothing but translate; she was looked to for
summaries of news, analytical reports of developments and
tendencies, especially in Eastern European regions. Her
security clearance had to be at the highest level, since she
often read very confidential communications before their end-
recipients did (or could), and it was puzzling she wasn't on
more cordial terms with the executive wing; her manner with
Worth or Laxitter was total deference in which I could detect
no trace of real respect. Her cloistered office, electronically
the most equipped of all, with telex, fax, computer terminal
and its own printer, two TV screens tuned silently whenever I
saw them to cable news, was two bends in the corridor away
from the imperial suite.

　　She was philosophical about my refusal of Lapsang,
which to me came somewhere in taste between Latakia
tobacco and charred bacon, and rued the latest tragic brutalities
in splintering Yugoslavia, speaking as if she might know
Slovenia and Croatia first-hand, not unreasonable, considering
their proximity to and historical connection with Austria. But
when I enquired, Hilde became instantly wary, and then almost

parodistically conspiratorial à la Bugs Bunny as she shot glances beyond me and behind her before asking, "You are to work on *Harness*, *Stirrup* as they now call it?"

"Not as far as I know," brightly, declining the contagion of her furtiveness. *Stirrup* I'd heard muttered before, in Worth's office, but *Harness*, while not otherwise mentioned at Orbis, somewhere chinked faint bells in my memory.

"If you do, ask to see all the files. All."

"Good." Here, obviously, the place where I was supposed to give an agreed password or make a secret sign, but not knowing any I nodded and moved on, leaving Hilde to her shadow-world and the plangent zither of Anton Karas.

All the same, she had it right. After Paula and I had swiftly completed our revisions to the brochure, I was summoned to Mark Worth's office, where, with Frank Lupin sitting silently by, we began with throwaway talk about baseball, the post-season playoffs drawing near. Worth had an inattentive expertise unnerving to me; he threw out a trenchant observation about the doubtful success of left-handed pitching against a largely right-hand lineup in a park notorious for its short left field, but wasn't listening to my reply, which wrested the name of Mel Parnell out of pre-natal memory. I've been known to speak of Hank Greenberg as if I could have seen him hit: colonized recollections from my father, who taught English Lit. in Ann Arbor, and was an unquenchable enthusiast, alike for Elizabethan drama and the Detroit Tigers.

Worth abandoned the gambit. "Hurd Laxitter wanted me to ask you what your immediate plans are. Let me clarify that." He sat at his desk, and drew the sides of a box with his hands. "We have a situation where we need somebody who'll definitely be available over the next, well, four to five months. It might be longer, but those are the foreseeable parameters — I don't say there's four to five months' steady work; what it is is, somebody who can produce on short notice, as the situation demands. We've had a chance to see your capacities there."

"Produce what?" barely acknowledging the butter-up smile.

"Well. Hurd Laxitter is going to have some input on this," Worth said, at the same time seeking support from the publicity man.

"Right," Lupin, as if returning abruptly from daydreams. "But we can tell you there'll definitely be a fairly extensive booklet, where you'll have to work closely with the people involved in the project. That would be ongoing, but there might well be times when you would have to put that on hold, to turn out, oh, maybe a pamphlet, maybe a position paper, it could be a rebuttal, this would be in a political context."

A Presidential year, and the campaigns, already battering at each other's shields, would be ready to open up with the photon torpedoes as soon as the World Series was done.

"What project?" I asked. Small question which side the corporation would favor, but it seemed unlikely they would be an overt part of Dwayne Hardy's attempt to succeed to Presidency; no candidate could survive such an identification with the voracious interests of Orbis. Nevertheless, with more than passing regret for what it meant to me financially, I vowed to have nothing to do with any job which even indirectly helped Hardy, whose nasty amalgam of callousness, ineptitude and suspect probity had been amply displayed in eight years as Vice-President. Not that Orford Lomax, his opponent, a Plains State governor, was one I'd be thrilled to die for, but I no longer expect that, belonging to a generation deprived of a past birthright, positive choice. In all my balloting life, I've never had a Presidential candidate to vote for, only a sad succession to vote against, most often by a hairsbreadth margin of distaste.

"This is going to be of critical importance to Special Projects and to Orbis at large," Lupin said. "Have you heard of the Stirrup Project?"

"I may have heard it mentioned," I equivocated.

"The successor to the Harness Initiative. Although that's a connection we're not necessarily anxious to stress."

With a fresh focus of fuzzed memory, I could see why. Though details were unclear, I recalled Harness was some sort of scheme for greatly increasing food production, using nuclear radiation; The Second Green Revolution was a phrase bandied about. Orbis had run a pilot project somewhere strange, Poland or Yugoslavia, and then, about two years back, there'd been a nine-day controversy over results; Vice-President Hardy for the administration had been an ardent supporter of the scheme, and had been obliged to blur his position when the affair became more complex and a Senate investigation had begun; in some way Palestinian terrorists and an assassination had been part of it, and above all I remembered the sudden advent of an exotic woman with a Bette Davis mouth and hair like licorice, Vera Sobieska, associate of the dead director of the project, who'd been heralded by its opponents as a whistle-blower, but in the end had offered only mild, heavily accented criticism of its procedures and results. There were mandatory imputations of a cover-up, but to judge by my own vague conclusions it had all petered out quite tamely.

"Because of some residual concerns about the safety situation," Mark Worth said, when I'd told as much as was tactful of what I recollected. "Which at the time were much exaggerated, but we would now concede were somewhat justifiable — "

"If only in the context of public perception," Lupin modified.

"Exactly. In that context, Orbis agreed to a second pilot project, which in fact had been envisaged from day one."

"We had already broken ground in southern Chile,"

Frank Lupin said. "And a decision was made at the highest level to go low-profile until we had conclusive results to show. At that time, the name Stirrup was adopted; we didn't want to get into the Edsel syndrome."

With small idea of what he meant, I made the derisive face the reference demanded.

"For your information," Lupin's severity was amiable, "and contrary to accepted myth, the Edsel was an excellent car for its time, excellent value, with some very advanced features. It was badly merchandised is all, its poor sales became a joke about the car itself, and now *Edsel* is a standard reference for *lemon*. It was a good car.

"I don't expect you to believe this," he appended, my face possibly having retained some skepticism. "Axiomatic, one mistake can destroy any positive image, but all the truth in the world can never erase a negative myth, once established. That's why negative political campaigns work so well."

"That's also why Orbis decided to call the Chile project Stirrup," Mark Worth said, firmly banishing digression. The name, by the way, not truly, as I was so often told, an acronym, ought to be written STiRRuP, just as Harness, no less barbarically, should be hARNeSs; in both cases workable sets of initials were extended into pronounceable words, in the earlier instance, as you say, with side-reference to the harnessing of otherwise waste energy.

According to Worth, every indication was, the project in Chile had exceeded all expectations, with any bugs remaining from Harness thoroughly swatted; Orbis was ready to launch its revolution on the world. It sounded like the apocalypse. As I was to learn at a later, more complicated meeting, with Hurd Laxitter and some science people also present, a system which, by extending the growing-season, would make double-cropping possible in temperate climates, permit intensive agriculture at higher altitudes and on more marginal soils, and to an extent defeat severe weather;

Canada's frontier of agriculture would be advanced seventy to a hundred miles northward, large areas of Siberia and Central Asia made productive, and the fringes at least of Greenland at last caused to live up to the name. This was to be achieved with the use of hybrids developed for their response to low-level radiation, successful strains which could never occur in nature, nor survive unaided on the sites for which they were destined (I should emphasize I have no competency to judge the scientific validity of what I'm writing, but am merely recording a lay understanding of what I was told). The radiation, said to be confined to a narrow spectrum and of smaller absolute quantity than emitted by a smoke-detector, came from small, capsule-like buttons of dull, porous-looking metal, which, notwithstanding the instant dark reminder of bodysnatchers, they insisted on calling *pods*. Since effective range of the radiation was small, many were needed, about five thousand pods to the hectare, but they could be manufactured very cheaply, largely as a by-product of nuclear power generation. Both radioactively and physically, the pods were said to decay relatively quickly, becoming part of the soil in which they were planted. I've held half a dozen in my hand, while being informed there would be ten to twelve different grades of pod made available, as suited to various crops and conditions of soil and climate.

Still at the earlier meeting, where I was spared all these technical details, Mark Worth said Orbis was very nearly ready to market Stirrup on a commercial scale, and was confident of bipartisan support in obtaining all necessary licenses and authorizations. Indications were, however, that Orford Lomax was going to make a campaign issue of Vice-President Hardy's original, uncritical support for the Harness Initiative.

"Which would mean," Worth expanded. "Dragging up the old charges, unfounded rumors, the little green men — all the same objections Orbis had to answer after Harness closed down."

"And did so, fully and freely," Lupin said. "In the best

of all possible worlds, we'd prefer that be the last word. But
we have a definite tip from inside Orford's campaign that
Harness is on his short list of hot issues, and if it does come up
the Vice-President must be fully prepared to rebut.

"Frankly," reading my reluctant face. "This isn't a
question of Orbis trying to get Hardy elected. The guy had a
forty-two point lead coming out of the convention, it was
down to around twenty points last time I looked, and if he
blows that, maybe he never was good enough for the job. Not
that critical; Stirrup has plenty of supporters within Lomax's
party, and some of them are going to be urging him not to
open up the Harness can of worms again."

Not unsusceptible to the headiness of this glimpse into
the world of hardball power-brokerage, I still managed the
logical demur, that if criticism of Harness helped elect Lomax,
predictably, as President, he'd oppose Stirrup.

"He's not necessarily critical of Harness per se," Worth
insisted. "Just digging for an issue to use against Hardy.
Either way, Orbis is going into the big push right after the
inauguration. Hurd Laxitter feels, Orbis feels, after the
election, if Lomax makes it, we can legitimately approach him,
we understand about politics, things are said in the heat of the
campaign, now let's get real — he'll have no difficulty
supporting Stirrup."

"Unless," Lupin came in. "Unless we get into the
Edsel syndrome. If he begins raking up these charges and it
starts to work for him, if they're not laid to rest right away, we
can get a situation where it's politically impossible for him to
sign off on Stirrup. You know how it is; a guy in authority
keeps saying he smells smoke, and when the crowd starts
yelling fire, he thinks it's the voice of the people."

"You could get a situation," Worth said, "Where
enough of the smear sticks, and in that context no President,
not Hardy himself, if he wins, can save Stirrup. Oh, in the
final analysis, the world is going to get the agricultural

revolution Stirrup stands for, if not now, in five years, or ten. We can't afford to wait that long."

"The world can't afford it," Lupin amended. "Sure, this represents a substantial investment in time, and money, corporate resources, very substantial potential sales, but beyond that, this is a program we believe in. Selective radiation is the future of agriculture, the future of a world without hunger."

This was eloquent enough, so eloquent I failed to see why Lupin wanted me, why he didn't write the stuff himself. A first, middle and last rule of freelancing is never to inform large corporations they already possess their own perfectly adequate resources. But if half what I'd been told was true, it was hard to find reasons not to take the job, and I'm only mildly shamefaced to report the last lingering reservations I had over political ramifications were swept away when Worth named a figure as my six-month retainer, more money than I'd ever made in any full year hitherto. Much more.

2

After all the forecasts of political cut-and-thrust we began innocuously with what would be a lavish thirty-two page booklet, *Century Without Hunger* (my title), copies of which would go to every member of the House and Senate, all cabinet-members, department and agency heads in the new Administration, no matter whose. For this low-security venture I could bring in Harry Yeats, whose expensive suggestions were approved without a murmur, coated stock, eight pages using color separations. Paula, after selecting a picture and roughing out lettering for the cover, abruptly told me I'd better find another illustrator, and went away to paint in preparation for a forthcoming show at a small gallery, which, while important to her, was inadequate cause for her defection. The manner of her defection, I mean to say. When, nevertheless, we had a meal together, prelude, I supposed on the basis of experience, to some lovemaking, she explained herself by making the mystifying charge I had humiliated her by my ostentatious dalliance with Dionne Theobald.

Dionne, with whom I'd been working closely, is, beyond argument, arresting. To call her black is an adjectival parsimony defensible only for narrow ethnic purposes; she was, with her taut, youthful fitness, many glowing tones; that she could be mother (unattached) of a sixteen-year-old daughter seemed hardly possible. I'd first met her at the gathering when I'd been given some of the technical details on Stirrup; her chief function there was to translate into lay terms some of the more obscure utterances of Gerhardt Fiori, a balding, gnomic man no one would ever take for anything but a rarefied scientist, overlord, indeed, of the experimental project in Chile. Dionne was, or had become, more scientific populariser than scientist; she made fairly frequent appearances on TV news or talk shows, either to hymn the implications of new wonders from ORBIS, or when brought in by the station to comment on a current story with scientific ramifications. The soft Jamaican voice together with her large-eyed beauty lent an unwonted grace to the problems of desalination, or the waste-disposal crisis.

At fund-raisers, premieres, she was sometimes seen, as the phrase goes, with one or another local sports, business or media star, and though Dionne was nothing like aloof when supplying data or checking my copy for scientific accuracy, Paula's notion such a soaring donna would descend from those glamoured eyries to the level where I made my prosaic perch was, as I protested, pure fantasy (but that no-less-unreachable Paula was with me now shattered the validity of the general principle).

"She flirts with you all the time," Paula complained. I very nearly replied I hadn't noticed, which would have been true unsaid, but disingenuous as spoken; once given verbal life self-evident; Dionne did flirt, I was there. I asked instead what, if so, I could do about it, and the answer was, nothing now, Paula no longer cared, but would have kept caring if I hadn't displayed such callous signs of enjoying the byplay.

If forced to choose among many imperfections, I'd say my salient defect is an incapacity for coping with illogic, and simultaneous inability to stop trying: I fail in the thrill of debate to rake away the tangles of manifest self-contradiction and attend to the underlying pain. The result in this instance was a cool parting outside Paula's door, with no set plans for resumption. Because of its ironic aptness I remember very well that twenty minutes later at the entrance to my own building I encountered Judy Fine, who shared an apartment a couple of floors above mine. Small, compact Judy with the frank face and smiling eyes, could, just for existing, easily have been another provocation to Paula's anxious animosity, and with more reason, I'll admit, than ever with remote

Dionne. Like me, a nocturnal, Judy had often tapped at my door past midnight, and come in to share talk and coffee, lemonade in summer, but then Paula had met Judy and, like everyone, liked her. Why that should absolve Judy of any charge of flirting (which she did), or our friendship from any suspicion of liaison (which was never out of the cards), is another of those riddles I lack equipment to answer.

Judy works in special education, but is a devoted hobbyist in the world of computers, spending all her income and testing the generosity of affluent parents in filling her half of the shared apartment with costly devices mostly enigmatic to me, and the fat packs of yet-untried software. I draw back from calling her a hacker, since she was altogether free of the hermetic strangeness that label connotes, but Judy was certainly an adept, who, at the hour of evening prayer, could with conviction point her rug at Silicon Valley. She'd helped me set up my own system, and from time to time assisted in subduing to my purpose what I regarded as a sometimes refractory tool. In my mood of mixed exasperation and sorrow, an hour or so of her straightforward company would have been balm, and I could easily have found an excuse for inviting her, faking some problem of procedure with my recently upgraded word processing program.

As I passed through the tiled vestibule and we exchanged glad greetings, it was distressingly apparent she was lingering by the door for someone else, for inexplicable Michael, who'd been parking his car; glancing behind I saw his tall, round-shouldered approach, and paused to wish him a specious good evening. He was a photographer with a bad complexion and a worse dearth of the social graces, as rudely inattentive to the interests of others as he was brutally bulldozing with his own. Other than f-stops and ASA speeds, that meant southern Mexico and Central America, where he'd spent a whole year in the middle of his college career, supporting himself with smalltime dealing in native crafts, pottery and textiles. He spoke Spanish quite fluently in the imperialist way of norteamericanos in those latitudes who make pillaging raids on the back-country from well-established yanqui communities, not actively mispronounced, but arrogantly disdaining the rhythms of native song. Michael fancied himself a connoisseur in the cuisine of the region: on this occasion, he held up the drooping plastic bag throttled in the hand not occupied with stuffing away car-keys, and announced it as a chicken, which on the morrow, Saturday, he meant to prepare according to a genuine Aztec recipe, in a sauce of unsweetened chocolate — perhaps one should say, *chocolatl.*

Indigenous ingredients don't certify authenticity; I believed in his chocolate chicken no more than I would butterscotch haggis, and had no qualms about inventing a prior commitment when invited to partake; it's possible I asked him to let me know when he used the same recipe for a winged serpent. I was far from unique in bafflement over why Judy tolerated repellent Michael; her roommate and long-term chum, the normally unconfiding Vickie, while conveying her own loathing, had also told me of the consternation in Judy's family when she announced she might be Michael's companion for an extended revisit of his old Central American haunts; why he chose always-amiable Judy was no mystery.

A poor week. My new artist, found by Harry, was Paul Merriam, competent enough, without Paula's goetic flair. A few years older than I, but with the threadbare appearance of a worn adolescent, he was extravagantly interested in theatre, painting scenery, of course, but also taking small parts and sometimes directing for a community group; my no more than civil interest encouraged him to give me a fat bundle of his flaccid plays to read, and because of his pale, damp eyes I never had the heart to tell him not to waste more time or typing-paper pursuing an antiquark of talent. Dionne Theobald arrived to look over my newest pages, and prompted by Paula's indictment I let myself begin to be stirred by her floral mouth, the cowled eyelids, long, glossy, keel-edged shins, and pretended to cure myself with thoughts of the tuxedos, limousines and flashcube occasions into any of which I could never fit. It is meet to speak frankly when death may come at any moment, and truth is there isn't any cure; all my life is filled with howling, ineradicable regrets for the women I couldn't or didn't collect, far exceeding any pleasure I could ever have derived from checkless consummation; it's the awakened *aesthetic* desire that can never be assuaged.

There was another fleeting exchange with Hilde Konwitschny, where I deliberately challenged her doominess by claiming uncritical enthusiasm for the Stirrup project. Mostly true; it's hard not to favor a world with enough to eat, but still there was a small chafe of doubt; it was all too easy, too painless. Even on a global scale, it might remain true there ain't no free lunch.

Hilde, today with a curiously fiery dark-emerald fleck in the otherwise drab tweed of her coat, said brightly and overloudly, "Ah, yes, I've heard about your work." Quick darting glances to and fro, and in a barely audible mutter between bottom teeth she gave the footnote: "They're mad. Someone must stop them. You must read the confidential Harness files — " and then, resuming the former volume as one of the young typists turned a corner and came near, "With pastries I prefer Earl Grey, with just a little milk."

When at weekend I was authorized by Hurd Laxitter and enabled by Fena Keller precisely to read the confidential files on Harness, it made me surer, not less so, that Hilde must be delusional. Her fear was general, but only with me, so far as I could tell, did she have this need to seek alliance against the forces of darkness. Flattering, perhaps, in an odd and unsought way, but it speaks for Paula's view of Special Projects as Paranoia City that I never mentioned Hilde's sibylline utterances to anyone there, never asked Mark Worth or Frank Lupin or even Fena whether any of them found Hilde as batty as I did.

Lupin hailed me at my desk on Friday morning and said (his words) that politically the excrement was about to collide with the rotary ventilating device. He handed me a sheaf of printout pages roughing out ripostes to various criticisms of the Harness project that fathered Stirrup, and asked if I could work it up into a coherent position-paper with clear subject-headings.

"As what?" riffling pages and seeing a hand, probably Lupin's, had already made pencil notes and emendations. "A handout, a press-release, a mailing?"

"Any of the above, could be. Something that could go into a press-kit, or the candidate could read as his statement at a press-conference. But clear, clear and simple, so he can learn it, get the main points down, anyway, if he has to field questions about his support for the project. It's coming, we know that, but Lomax might want to get it started by planting a question with one of his pals from the *Times* or the *Washington Post*. That way he can pick it up in the debates as an ongoing public concern, but if we can nail it, first time out, we won't have that situation to face. You better drop everything else," he said, as Paul Merriam returned from some photocopying and was waved away. "This is double-A priority. How soon can you have something for Laxitter to see?"

"I'll let you know," trying to count how many different headings would be needed. "Give me a couple of hours." As a freelance writer I'd learned long ago to greet the unfamiliar with a simulation of impassive confidence, but in this case I honestly was unexpectedly calm about my debut in the killing arena of politics.

"Those notes, likewise any notes you make, must not leave Special Projects — don't let them out of your sight. In fact — " he frowned around at eight-foot partitions enclosing us on three sides, as if he'd never noticed them before. "We better put you in a secure office with a door you can lock when you go out. I think Jane Plotnik's still in Europe, we can move you into her office, maybe. I'll get Fena on it right away. Brief, punchy, clear," he prescribed, and went off to find Fena.

So I was installed in a real office in the imperial suite, behind a large real desk with an intimidating console phone abounding with function-buttons, and a framed portrait of a real family, plain Jane, a bland husband and three outstandingly unattractive children, orthodontic disasters all, curls, frizz, yarmulka. There, in far less than a couple of hours, I saw this was an impracticable task. Either in haste or in their mania for confidentiality, the compilers of these pages had done no more than indicate general subjects for questions and objections the position-paper was meant to answer; not possible for me to determine whether the sketched responses were relevant, let alone accurate, coherent or complete.

Exasperatingly after all the urgency Frank Lupin had vanished leaving a message he'd see me around two. Mark Worth was still at a meeting on seven, and Fena said, "Typical," blew smoke and quoted me some Tolkien. Nearly one, and I shut the explosive notes up in a desk-drawer with resident emery-board and a tattered stump, only two left, from a roll of antacid mints. Using the key I'd been given, I locked Jane Plotnik's office, and went to lunch.

Tedious to detail all the meetings, re-meetings, proposals, disputes and unproductive expletives engendered by

my reasonable objection to answering questions I hadn't seen
("Whatja think this is, *Jeopardy*?" Fena demanded of Frank
Lupin at one point). Nothing happened to advance my urgent
task till Mark Worth returned from his meeting mid-afternoon,
and then nothing happened but a call to Hurd Laxitter,
elsewhere in the city, and his promise to be on the scene
forthwith. In the interim I was asked if I could stay late,
maybe come in tomorrow, and this began a new round for
Worth, Lupin and Keller, all in the Plotnik office, to which I
was merely inanimate appendage, subject-matter more than
participant. Mark Worth maintained that while tonight could
be cleared, opening the building tomorrow created problems
with insurance and with the security people, who required a
minimum of two days notice for weekend coverage. Unreal,
Lupin commented. That I was going to be allowed to see the
Harness source-material was already assumed, because when
Worth offered there could still be several hours work tonight,
Fena said, "Come on, Mark. It's gonna take him that long just
to read the bloody file."

"Skim it," Worth offered.

"That is skimming it," Fena insisted.

"All that later stuff, with the Palestinian situation — "

"Shit, Mark, he has to go through that," Frank Lupin
said. "What's it going to look like if some newsman brings
that up, and we let Hardy make up his own answer out of his
head? He might say he doesn't recall, like with that `middle-
class civil rights' speech; the media is just waiting for a chance
to find an Orbis-Administration coverup. The *Washington
Post* has a Yugogate headline all ready, set in type."

Like less-excitable Mark Worth, I found hard to
understand how it could be claimed Orbis had any reason to
conceal the activities of Palestinian terrorists, and paid only
marginal attention to what Lupin himself called the fantasy, or
Oy, vay scenario, in which, because of its secret favoring of
the Arabs in the Middle East peace negotiations, the State
Department had conspired with the Orbis office in Vienna to

ignore or dismiss a tip from Israeli intelligence about the planned assassination of the Harness project's director: I was unclear then what interest Palestinians could ever have in an agricultural experiment in the Balkans.

Still before Laxitter arrived, there was a further wrangle over deadlines, with Worth contending that if I read over the material tonight, I'd still have Monday to put the position-paper in shape, since the Vice-President's first possible exposure to questions would be no sooner than Tuesday evening in Des Moines, where the document could be faxed.

"Shit, Mark," Frank Lupin said once more, and pointed out the candidate had to have time to study the paper, and that he himself would want to go over it point by point with the Hardy handlers, to make sure there would be no misrepresentation of the Orbis position; he planned to join the campaign on Monday in Detroit and be aboard Air Force Two for the flight to Iowa.

"Fine, well, be sure you stay aboard until the motorcade gets under way," said Hurd Laxitter from the doorway. "We don't need a bunch of press-pictures with *Orbis exec Frank Lupin* in bed with the candidate."

"Goes without saying," Lupin muttered. The change in atmosphere with Laxitter's arrival reminded me of competitive sex-talk in a Catholic schoolyard petering out shamefacedly at the approach of a formidable nun. He removed the debate to Worth's office, leaving me to contemplate the Plotniks, and wonder which of the three gargoyles had crafted the free-form shiny black ashtray Jane used for paperclips, about eight pounds of clay hollowed out, baked, and painted to resemble a monstrous pitted prune.

After some minutes Fena came to my doorway, to ask, "Did you have any plans for the weekend?"

"Nothing special." Laundry, music, some brooding over Paula, with the phone near my knuckles.

"You got a modem, right?" I had, and she didn't need to ask about the rest of my equipment, having discussed my installation in fine detail when I first came to Special Projects, Fena offering critical comments on software, about which she had decided, not to say dogmatic views.

"Okay." She disappeared.

For me the next stage, after formal notification I would work all weekend, and be permitted access to the Harness file from my home PC, was a disquisition by Hurd Laxitter to be sure I was conversant with the *philosophy* behind the Orbis position. For this he borrowed Mark Worth's office; the first time I'd ever been alone in his presence, and subtly unnerving; the man sought to dominate and be liked all at once. Easily possible, if you assume there are those who prefer to be dominated and who love their masters, but that wasn't Laxitter's way; his manner was part quiet bullying, part plea for understanding, always with the certainty if it came to a choice, getting his way would supersede desire for friendship.

As Worth and Lupin had, he emphasized any aid the position-paper gave Hardy would be incidental, and was not an object of my brief from Orbis, which was only to keep the record straight. "When you see the files, you'll be looking at some information we wouldn't want to become public property. As you'll see, all the major original objections, the glitches in the project, have been taken care of to the satisfaction of any fair-minded person, which is precisely why we object to having them all raked over again. Well, you read it for yourself — " he became almost benign. "Read the whole story, make up your own mind."

Evidently to help me do that, he broke down the problems, real and alleged, into three main categories, of which the third, he said, loosely designated "shady business, scandal," was at the same time most trivial from the Orbis standpoint, and in many ways hardest to deal with.

"Orbis has used questionable political influence in moving forward with Harness, which is now Stirrup," he cited.

"Well, we have lobbyists, good lobbyists, you have to have, if
you're going to get anything done in today's Washington
climate. We've also spent a lot of money, and I mean a lot of
money, on publicity, and we've made some friends in various
departments and agencies — all of this is standard good
business practise in America; we've done nothing GM or
General Dynamics or Exxon doesn't routinely do, but if you
pick out some of the details without showing the big picture,
you can make it sound like some kind of unique conspiracy.
That's a situation we have to contain, but as you'll see there's
nothing in the total record that by itself is enough to do us in.
Taken in conjunction with doubts about the program itself,
unanswered questions about the validity and safety of
radiation-enhanced agriculture — then you're in a whole other
ballgame, you turn influence into corruption, and get into the *if
he didn't know, why didn't he know* game, who was paid off to
look the other way? — Yugogate, like Frank says."

Those, validity and safety, were his other two
categories, and he invited me again to weigh carefully the
entire record, and see no other conclusion was possible than
that Harness-Stirrup was potentially the agrarian revolution it
claimed to be, and Orbis had done everything possible to make
it safe in every way. "Some of the questions raised at the time
Harness was winding up have complex answers. Your job is
to simplify without distorting, to put those answers, those
reassurances, into language anybody can understand, cast them
in the terms of a political campaign. That doesn't mean I
expect you or anybody else to put a concept like half-life into a
sound-byte. Sometimes you have to cut corners a little;
Heisenberg's uncertainty principle makes a rotten lyric for a
show-tune. The bottom line is, Orbis. The stuff you can
generate may get the Vice-President past some awkward
moments, that's okay. For all I know it might be the straw that
gets him elected, we can't tell. If he makes it, fine, but that's
not the target, your target is, Orbis has to win, Harness, hence

Stirrup, has to come out without any of the mud sticking to it.
If Orbis wins — " he'd reached his punchline. "The world
wins. It's that simple."

Genuine belief was clear to me, though not in exactly
what; I was reluctantly impressed. Scared a little, but
impressed.

Lastly before leaving for my captive weekend I was
briefed by Fena, who told me in just-between-us derision Mark
Worth had wanted to know whether my home computer was in
"a secure location."

"I said, what the do-do, Mark, it's in the guy's
apartment," she recounted. "What do you want, Orthanc?"
Tolkien again.

No one, however, could have outdone Fena herself in
conspiratoriality when she explained the Harness file. It was
Read Only; I would be unable to copy it, print it, certainly I
couldn't edit it. "You'll have to make notes as you go. Bring
your notes in when you're done, and we'll shred them."

She started to give me a dial-in number, then changed
her mind and wrote down another. "That's the reserved
number, better use that, you'll be plugged in for a long time,
and somebody else might want to see a file. That number gets
you into the Special Projects system. You enter HARNESS, I'm
not writing any of this down, HARNESS, okay?"

"HARNESS," I said.

"Wait, now it's gonna ask who you are, and you have to
log on as somebody the program recognizes, otherwise it's like
trying to break into the Mines of Moria. There's a routine
built-in," proudly, "that records any unauthorized attempt at
entry, and identifies the source telephone number, date, time.
So get it right; you can log on as DIRTYSPY, like that, one
word, no space, no punctuation. After that, you'll see a menu,

you can find your own way around, you're free to wander.
DIRTYSPY, got it?"

"DIRTYSPY," I echoed. Not quite as good a joke as
Fena obviously found it.

Without a word, I swear, about the content of the file, I
outlined my task to Judy, who'd unforeseen come to borrow
my little camping stove. When told I intended to transcribe in
longhand lengthy passages, perhaps whole pages, from a file I
couldn't copy, she said that was ridiculous, and whatever Fena
had told me, my modem allowed me to capture anything
displayed on-screen with a simple command.

Good news, but having bragged to Fena about my
endless spare capacity, I found recent additions had shrunk
lordly megs down to a few hundred grudging *k*s, small margin
for safety, and was only rescued from deleting desktop
publishing by Judy's insistence I use her mobile disk. No
problem, she said, about my keeping it as long as needed,
since at dawn she was leaving for the northlands to inspect
autumn foliage with the Aztec Connection, and would be gone
the rest of the weekend. Actually, she amended, somewhat
embarrassed about her own insatiable acquisition of gadgetry,
she was lending me a spare, the eighty meg model she'd
purchased before finding out there was another version with
half again that capacity. An established neophyte having small
idea of what a mobile disk might be, I made the proper
marvelling noises over the mere idea of such spaciousness,
and refrained from asking for what she could ever need one
hundred and twenty million bytes. As a plain bookshelf, I
swiftly calculated, it would more than hold the Hundred Best
Books. I knew: as it used to be for the wattage of stereo
amplifiers, or with horsepower in my Dad's middle day, the
golden age of the Michigan mastodon, such figures were an
end in themselves.

That image of a forty-foot bookshelf groaning with its
own gravity recurred with extra force when I saw the device, a

box not much larger than the cassette recorder I often carried in a pocket of my duffel-jacket. This Judy swiftly attached by cable to a spare port at the back of my PC, and after switching on and manipulating a few keys, announced it was installed and ready, and would be identified as Drive E.

"If you want to keep what you save, and use it on another machine," she said. "Or if you were working, like, on hush-hush stuff, you could just disconnect it, here, and take it with you. It's great."

"As it happens, this is hush-hush stuff."

"Oh, wow," she said, a habit.

"How was the chocolate chicken?"

She remained quite earnest. "Good. You should have come to dinner. You didn't really taste the chocolate. It was a lot like chicken cacciatore. I gotta go, Michael's making gazpacho."

I thanked her, she thanked me for the stove and canisters of gas, and we touched lips lightly, a thing we did, wishing each other good weekends (I with Harness, she in the flaming wilds with dreary Michael). It occurred to me that if I could have taken this small box in to Special Projects, loaded up the Harness file and brought it home with me, I would have had no need to use my modem, or to learn access codes and authorized names. To have done so would have changed, and, as things stand, maybe lengthened, my life.

So, with a sandwich nearby and what I prided myself was cool skepticism in my heart, I launched into my great fatuity, dialing, requesting HARNESS, logging on as DIRTYSPY, arriving at a menu which was nothing more than a directory of chapters. My lingering suspicion I would be permitted to see only a carefully expurgated selection of documents vanished when I saw the dimensions: the OVERVIEW chapter alone ran to more than eighty pages, and could have been three times that, since it consisted only of text in English, portions identified as translated, while reproductions of original documents and newspaper columns, as well as many supporting maps, charts, diagrams, graphs, tabulated scientific data and statistical reports, were relegated to the far longer DOCFILE.

Harness, then, had begun nearly eight years ago, when, with the assistance of the State Department and a United Nations agency, what was to become ORBIS, at that time still ORH/Ilcom, had leased about 120 hectares in what was then northeastern Yugoslavia; the administrative offices in Zagreb, though the tract was in uplands to the east of a place called Jastrebarsko, marginal land that had with difficulty supported potatoes, low yields of barley, and some sparse grazing for sheep.

The director of the Harness Initiative was Emil Bieman, a German scientist with credentials in both nuclear physics and biology, who had been a prominent member of the ORH development team. As emerged from his own reports and the descriptions of others, he was a passionate advocate for the role of selective radiation in agriculture; with him the phrase, Second Green Revolution, had originated. The chosen site gave him opportunity to test the effectiveness of his magic pods in overcoming (or, as he insisted, moderating) limitations hitherto imposed by poor soil and, at higher altitudes, a short growing-season, but he would have liked other test sites, perhaps in the interior of Australia, believing a recalibration of the radiation spectrum, by improving plant-efficiency in the use of moisture, could extend usefulness to places where water was the limiting factor.

These speculations were summarily dismissed by the executive director for the project, one Rockforth Freer, based in New York (but staying in touch with Zagreb, often through a shadowy envoy named Helena Smitt) whose position was, succinctly, that Bieman had enough on his plate with the Yugoslav experiment.

An accurate prediction. I'm not going to attempt here a detailed encapsulation of the history, the cascades of reports

and blizzards of memos; enough to say no one had foreseen a
tithe of the problems there'd be in translating the use of
selective radiation from near-laboratory conditions in Port
Washington, Long Island, to the recalcitrant field in back-
country Croatia. The first season, after a late beginning,
produced acutely disappointing results; stony soil had claimed
seed before the pulsing pods had any chance to encourage
growth, sloping and undulating terrain changed all calculations
as to dosage, and a wet September made a muddy shambles of
what harvest there was. There followed a disaster with winter
wheat; after the first shoots (as I learned was standard) were
used as grazing in November, the wheat failed to reappear in
spring, and that acreage was only saved by a hasty sowing of
what Bieman, even in translation, always called maize, and
Freer's office routinely talked about as corn. That small
snatched rescue was the project's Dunkirk, not victory but a
halt to successive defeats, and from that point on, with an
increasingly Churchillian air, Bieman, whose faith had never
faltered, was able to proclaim mounting triumph; in view of
the implications for feeding the world, it was clear in all
history there could be found no precedent for the relative
numbers of the tiny research team and the multitudes indebted
to their efforts.

I spoof, but was genuinely stirred to read about maize
grown where no corn had ever been, to sense the enthusiasm
when some adjustment in procedures worked, till in the fourth
summer Bieman himself, as cautious about assessing gains as
he was confident of his theoretical rightness, was willing to
claim enough success to justify the public proclamation New
York was clamoring for.

As the record showed, Rockforth Freer was concerned
to minimize or altogether suppress any report which cast the
smallest shadow on the blazing success of the Harness
experiment, whereas Bieman, notwithstanding his personal
investment of time and conviction, was stubborn in his
determination to maintain scientific integrity, and publish a

complete and accurate final accounting. The Yugoslav
government's sudden, numbing allegation of significantly
higher levels of sterility, thyroid cancer and leukemia among
those who'd worked on the Jastrebarsko site, and a forecast of
birth defects and adult deaths to come, brought the internal
dispute to a head; Freer's office issued a statement calling the
Yugoslav findings "false and preposterous" and stating that the
corporation's own meticulous monitoring of radiation dosage
levels, their constant testing of workers themselves, had found
absolutely no ill-effects. Once more, Bieman demurred, and in
an interview with a German newspaper called the Freer
statement "premature," allowing that in the early days of the
project some accidental over-exposure may have occurred. At
the same time he took the opportunity to criticize New York's
claims of total triumph, saying much study and fine-tuning
was required before Harness could be marketed on a
commercial scale. The German journalist's snide hints that
Bieman, with his cautious reservations, was putting the best
face on unmitigated disaster, were picked up by *Newsweek*,
whose commentator thought it fair to suggest that when a
proud father is willing to admit disappointment with a favorite
child, it usually means the child has done very badly indeed.

Suddenly, Hurd Laxitter entered the picture, with a
confidential message to Freer, warning him the negative
effects of anything that smelled like coverup would be far
more damaging than an admission the Harness experiment had
fallen short of ideal success. Freer's answer was to fire
Bieman, flying to Zagreb, where he gave a press-conference
reiterating the roseate view, and again excoriating the Belgrade
government's "paltry" attempts to discredit Harness, and to
impugn Orbis's, and by extension, America's concern for
worker safety.

Laxitter himself noted wryly such a rebuke at that time
was tantamount to an endorsement of Croatian independence,
and Belgrade's angry response, including full publication of its

health survey, was predictable; they requested Orbis terminate operations forthwith. Meanwhile the dismissed Bieman announced his intention of giving a press-conference in Vienna, at which he would freely and without restraint answer all questions about Harness, and conduct of Orbis operations in Yugoslavia.

Just as Laxitter had predicted, there was widespread speculation the lid was about to be blown on an attempted coverup of catastrophe, but on the eve of the Vienna unbosoming Bieman was killed in the Schottenring by a car bomb.

This, plainly, could have been worse for Orbis than any dirty little secrets Bieman might have revealed; Laxitter again, in a caustic memo to Freer, observed there were plenty of people eager to believe big business, as in the movies, readily made use of assassination where the checkbook failed.

Fortunately, if that's the word, the Austrian police swiftly laid the crime at the door of Palestinian extremists, who assisted them by phoning to claim the kill. Bieman was revealed to have co-founded a Zionist organization in Vienna, and in discussing the potential for his selective radiation system in arid zones had angered the Palestinians by suggesting a large tract of the West Bank, unirrigated and so far undeveloped by its occupiers, as an ideal site for the experiment.

Here, the one figure I had remembered from the entire Harness business made her appearance, Bieman's long-time associate, exotic Vera Sobieska, who, though tearfully, gave what she said was the press-conference "dear Emil" would have wished, a flat, somewhat hedged claim of conditional success, with some points still to be reconsidered. For those many ravening after sensational exposé it had turned out to be as damp a squib as her later appearance in the US with the Senate committee, made yet more anticlimactic by the presence on the platform of Hurd Laxitter, who disavowed any attempts there might have been to conceal the very real though

certainly solvable problems Mme. Sobieska had brought to
light, paid warm tribute to Bieman, "a great scientist, a man of
rare integrity," and gracefully introduced the late researcher's
family (I had been, despite myself, touched by a Laxitter note
to the Vienna office immediately after the assassination,
asking "what can we do for his wife and son?").

Now, Laxitter had taken charge, and his inaugural
message to the Harness team was once more that nothing they
revealed could do more harm than trying to conceal flaws,
while for the incipient Stirrup project he wrote, "I don't care if
this takes five years, ten; it has to be right before we market."
Rockforth Freer still hung on, after he'd tried to make a
scapegoat of the unfortunate Helena Smitt, whom he fired,
though clearly she'd advised Freer against the disastrous
Zagreb press-conference, and attempted to make peace
between her boss and Bieman. I had to consult another file
entirely to find the end of that power-struggle; discredited over
Harness, Freer remained a major stockholder and an officer of
the corporation; there was a bitter boardroom battle before
Freer was pried into retirement by Laxitter's coalition, of
which Mark Worth was a staunch member. The change in
stock distribution when ORH/Ilcom acquired another large
conglomerate, and the ORBIS logo was born, had a part in
Laxitter's victory, and so had the start of the Senate
investigation into Harness. In a memo not among his more
diplomatic, Laxitter noted public interest in foreign activities
of US corporations is normally close to non-existence, and that
only the antics of Freer (then testifying), had escalated the
Harness affair into a near-scandal.

A separate file, SENATE, contained a great deal of
testimony, but I spent little time with it, finding it went over
the same ground as the Overview, only far more tediously. I
did notice the committee expended disproportionate effort on
the relatively minor question of State Department involvement
in the original overtures to Belgrade, and on an egregious

political red-herring about whether the Vice-President had put pressure on the CIA to accept the Austrian authorities' account of Bieman's assassination. Here, I didn't trouble to make a note; if Hardy couldn't manage his own defense against that charge, nothing I could write would help him, or help Orbis. Otherwise, I was interested only by an appended list of corporation people who'd been told they might be called to testify; besides the obvious ones, Hilde Konwitschny's name appeared. She'd been in the Vienna office, and was brought to the US after the termination of Harness, but aside from translation, and a couple of sojourns in Zagreb to act as an interpreter, what she might have to tell was obscure, and someone (Frank Lupin?), assessing the relative importance of prospective witnesses, had awarded Hilde a firm zero. Whether that was just, whether there was any reason for me to be giving more attention to her strange hints, was not to be part of the record; the Senate committee suspended hearings for the off-year elections, and had not reconvened. Never having issued a final report or heard a terminal gavel, it still possessed, I supposed, a wraithlike theoretical existence, but to Worth, noting the reelection defeat of a senator who'd been the committee's heaviest hitter, Laxitter wrote, "I don't think we'll be sending any more pilgrims to Capitol Hill," and so far he was right.

A curious irony to discover (returning to the Overview file) one of Rockforth Freer's most extravagant lines of argument had turned out to be true: when assailing the Yugoslav government's figures on casualties caused by radiation from the Harness Initiative, he'd written privately about a badly underfinanced Yugoslav nuclear power project which had ill-advisedly tried to convert some dubious lab experiments into a practical fusion generator. The venture, situated not many miles from the Orbis site at Jastrebarsko, had, in Freer's words, furtively wound down shortly after the start of Harness, and Freer's contention was that "its rumored sloppiness and five-and-dime shielding" had resulted in many cases of overexposure to radiation, which the government had camouflaged by passing them off as Harness casualties. This story, as Laxitter confessed, had been taken as another example of Freer's fanatical overkill in defending the Harness Initiative.

Then, when Croatia broke away from Belgrade, among many government documents brought to light was one which strongly suggested Freer had it right, after all; a translation was given in the Overview file, and a most authentic-looking reproduction of the murky original in DOCFILE. The callous gist was that since the power project workers were now unemployed, as many as possible of the suspected cases of radiation poisoning should be placed with "the Americans" at Jastrebarsko, who'd asked for recruits; in that way it would become impossible to place the blame for any deaths or other ill-effects on home-grown radiation. An accompanying note by the translator (at a guess, Hilde Konwitschny) pointed out the new Croatian government would have been eager to see the document published as an example of their habitual exploitation by Belgrade, management of the project being Serbian, workers virtually all Croats or Slovenes.

This seemed important to me, and I worked hard to put the essence of the story into the clear and simple terms of my instructions. It had never been used in defending Harness, since the official Yugoslav document had surfaced only after the Senate investigation had closed up shop, and there was a memo appended in which Laxitter concurred with Frank Lupin's opinion that "Orbis shouldn't be the one to bring this forward now; it's here if we need it." The expectation, clearly, was that all these old charges would have to be dealt with again when the Chile project, Stirrup, was proclaimed a success.

That, as I already knew, was imminent. The STIRRUP file was where I had to search for an answer to the other main

safety question, since on that issue, residual radiation, all the
Overview file had to offer was assertion on one side, denial on
the other. As to the site, resolution ought to be fairly simple,
since either the radiation was there or wasn't, although I could
see merit in the Orbis argument that any Yugoslav government
findings had to be regarded skeptically, as arguably part of the
attempt to conceal their own disaster. As to the chances of
hazardous levels of radiation persisting in foodstuffs, the
subject in which, naturally, the general public had evinced
most interest, Worth had asked Dionne Theobald for an
opinion, and she'd replied that while "improbable," it couldn't
be completely ruled out without extensive testing with actual
samples of the cereals and other crops, as also the animals, or
their meat, none of which was now possible. In a public
statement, for which my own thalamic file readily supplied the
soothing tones, she'd said that, in the first place, we had to
decide what we meant by radiation; every being on earth was
exposed to many different kinds of radiation every day, and
had been throughout time; not all radiation, obviously, was
harmful, some positively beneficial; ridiculous to suppose any
legitimate corporation, subject to stringent regulation by
government agencies such as FDA and the Department of
Agriculture, would, even without such outside standards,
knowingly expose the public to dangerous levels of radiation
from food. As she must have known, the kind of sampling she
specified had gone on throughout the Harness process, but the
reassuring results recorded (*see* DOCFILE) had been challenged
more than once, both as carelessly performed with inadequate
controls, and with darker imputations of deliberate faking.

  These weren't frivolous concerns, and for the first time
I left the insulated set of mind I'd consciously adopted, that of
doing a job as well as could be, and weighed the inexorability
of rent and phone-bills alongside the possibility Hilde
Konwitschny might be right, and my efforts assisting the
triumph of what we'd have to call evil. But to me, the best
argument on the side of Orbis was Laxitter's inflexibility,

about the future rather than the past. In a long letter to
Gerhardt Fiori, chosen to head the project in Chile, he wrote
that knowing Emil Bieman's unimpeachable probity, he was
inclined to accept the published results on radiation
monitoring at Jastrebarsko. As Fiori could see for himself,
while there were some unacceptably high readings in early
stages of Harness, the record showed a steady diminution to
well within acceptable guidelines, and any suggestion there
had been tampering with the figures to conceal persistent
dangerous levels of residual radiation Laxitter wrote could be
ascribed either to alarmism, or to outright malice.

However, he continued, the specter had been raised,
and since the question could not now be resolved with
certainty, the only recourse was to make Stirrup into a model
project; if there was any fault in the monitoring of every aspect
of safety, it must be on the side of excessive zeal, not only for
the sake of Orbis, but in the larger context of human life.

As surely wasn't true of many of the documents I'd read
with astonishment, the higher flights of this one had surely
been intended for public consumption, and I wasn't surprised
to find an edited version had been published in two languages,
in a well-known business weekly, and in Santiago's leading
newspaper, the latter in a box on the editorial page. Still, I
was captured by the unpublished admission that things had
gone badly at the start, and could with a near-clear conscience
construct a pithy rebuttal to any question on this point,
emphasizing whatever doubts had been raised as to Harness,
they would be more than answered when the Stirrup results
became generally available for scrutiny.

Because as the file made clear, Stirrup, learning from
the Yugoslav experience, had so far been an unconditional
vindication of Emil Bieman's faith in the future of radiation-
enhanced agriculture. Gerhardt Fiori emerged as precisely the
man for the job, not an apocalyptic prophet like Bieman, but a
painstaking empiricist whose passion was for testing and

retesting hypotheses, reducing emission-level of the magic pods to the threshold of ineffectuality, and then having them stepped up in micro-increments till he found the best possible balance between effect and safety. His endlessly-diagramed experiments with optimal placement also contributed by permitting a forty percent reduction in the number of pods to the hectare: all this and much more I read avidly as if riding an exhilarating novel to an inevitable happy ending; I was smothered by apprehension when Fiori's attempt at double-cropping above five hundred meters was struck by early frost, filled with joy when the on-shore breeze came in the nick of time to save embattled sugar-beets — yet none of this was all that germane to my own endeavors. Sunday was growing brighter outside my window, and I still hadn't found swift, punchy answers to anticipated questions about ground-water contamination, soil depletion, or "impact on traditional third-world agricultural practices," which I gathered meant, could those yellow and brown people learn how to use selective radiation safely and effectively? In fact, I doubted the attempt to teach them would ever be made, on reflection foresaw the process once more swelling tatty cities, as cost-efficient, ordered, commercial production displaced the subsistence scrabbling of many peasants. Some heartbreaks, losses, unqueried folkways gone for ever, but, sentimental aesthetics shelved, surely more than a fair exchange, if the hungry could be fed, the starving saved.

  I also had still to address the chance of renewed innuendo about some of the payments Orbis made, loosely designated *development* or *promotion*, not only in Yugoslavia and Chile but the District of Columbia. Following Hurd Laxitter's hint, I might visit the library for short-order research into corporate lobbying; how much, for instance, a manufacturer would admit spending to persuade the Pentagon of the excellence and indispensability of a particular tank or missile, and what caused Saudi Arabia or Taiwan to be so fervent to acquire one particular aircraft over any other.

Before that, I wanted the end of the Stirrup story; the file broke off a few months back, in the heart of the southern winter. There was listed a further file, named CHILE.UPDATE, but when I tried to see it, I was peremptorily barred, with the succinct message: ACCESS DENIED: £HARNESS: CHILE.UPDATE: RENEW AUTHORIZATION OR STRIKE ANY KEY TO CONTINUE. Frustrated by this cool last-minute rebuff after a night of warm, unquestioning compliance, I tried twice more with the same result. Fena had told me to call her at home any time if I ran into problems, but any time probably didn't include six-thirty on a Sunday morning. I returned the program chastely to its own bed, turned myself off, and had a nap.

3.

Monday morning on the way to turn in my Candidate's Primer, I was waylaid by Hilde Konwitschny. That's how it seemed, though it's hard to see how she could have arranged it; she wouldn't have spent much loitering time in the short corridor by the two one-stop elevators under the glassy gaze of the closed-circuit camera. Equipped now with my own key-cards, on grunt-and-wave terms with the security man, perhaps it was fortuitous I arrived close enough on her heels to catch her there, but in support of the planned encounter theory it's notable, and a notable lapse in Special Projects' vigilance, that the only place to be sure of not being watched, once the outer ramparts had been challenged, was during that brief shuttle between ten and eleven.

Hilde, clearly, was by no means certain we were free of audio surveillance, waiting for doors to close and slight ascending hum to begin before saying in a very low voice, "They let you see their *Märchen*?"

Even I knew that much German, and she surely knew the English, fairy-tale; she must have wished to evoke grimmer fantasy. Still feeling rather superior after my weekend with company secrets, but willing to respect her cloak-and-dagger mode, I muttered back, "It's very confidential."

Her upper lip did what is melodramatically described as *curling*, and if she hadn't been so bent on defeating any eavesdrop, I truly believe she would have exclaimed, "Hah!" As was, with as much irony as her tiny volume-level could convey, she said, "Let me guess — they gave you a very secret code-name. DIRTYSPY, would it be?" — and the whine ceased, the doors opened, and she left me standing, sortying to exchange cheerful complaints about the weekend weather with the young receptionist, already assessing her fingernails and sighing for coffee.

The next evening's television appearance by both presidential candidates wasn't one of the official misnamed debates, but a still odder campaign event, carried locally only by PBS, simultaneous "town meetings" with Dwayne Hardy in Iowa and Orford Lomax in Ohio, taking turns with questions from journalists and from assembled citizenry. Except electronically, there was no attempt to connect the separate proceedings; a question about wheat sales by a journalist in Columbus could be (and was) followed by one on campaign financing from a farmer in Des Moines, and except when each candidate departed from strict attention to a mooted issue to take a gratuitous stab at the other, nothing to suggest *mano a mano* engagement.

I didn't have long to wait. Hardy, whose initial manner often suggested a man less than entirely confident in his choice of deodorants or intimate apparel, had opened with perhaps an RBI single, off a batting-practice pitch from a friendly Hawkeye: did he think experience should be a factor in choosing a President? while Governor Lomax had to do his best to foul off a nasty inside fastball: how could he hope to move toward a balanced federal budget, when his own state was running record deficits? More at his ease, therefore, than might otherwise have been the case, Hardy faced William Elderbush, notorious administration-basher from the *St. Louis Post-Dispatch*, who asked: "Mr. Vice-President, some commentators have questioned your judgment, in, for example, your uncritical support of Orbis International with their scandal-racked Harness Initiative, the agricultural experiment in Yugoslavia. Would you care to comment?"

"Well, Bill," Hardy replied. "I don't know exactly what *scandal-racked* means, here. You had this highly successful experiment, and then, unfortunately, its director was targeted by terrorists, I don't know if you see that as some kind of scandal. And then there were a number of totally unsubstantiated charges about the results of this project, and at the time I said these things would have to be gone into more fully, and since then there's been, as I understand it, this second, um, project in Chile, and that has tended to vindicate, ah — not all the results are in, but I'm told the results are looking very, very good, and of course that will be gone into very fully."

Unlike *hoi-polloi*, journalists were allowed a follow-up. "There were questions at that time," it came, "about the propriety of your support, as Vice-President, being also an important stockholder in Orbis."

Hardy gave his best regular-guy chuckle. "Bill, if you say I own Orbis stock, you know more than I do. As you are aware, all my holdings are in a blind trust, and, of course, I have no control or even knowledge of what transactions may take place with regard to that. At one time, I may — as you know, Orbis is a very extensive corporation, an important American employer — in all their various phases, they provide jobs for, I think it's in the neighborhood of half a million Americans, and that would mean it provides the livelihood for something like two million men, women and children nationwide, and I think I read somewhere that the stockholders — that with pension plan investments and unit trusts and that kind of thing, along with your ordinary individual who's in the market, that something like eighteen million Americans own a part of Orbis, I think that's the correct figure. So you get — so, if I did have some Orbis stock, I guess I'd be in pretty good company, and I want to say, as far as supporting the Harness thing, I'm in good company there, too, because I think you'll find for example the Speaker of the House and the majority and minority leaders in the Senate are on record as believing

this very promising, very far-reaching research should be
encouraged, and should continue, as it has, and we're watching
the results with great interest." Here, the desk-light flashed,
and the ninety-second chime sounded; the Vice-President
scrambled for a finish, a pat bit of waffle about a partnership
between government and industry working to benefit all the
people.

To say perception is conditioned by preconception is
hardly news, but a few minutes after the hour-long event had
meandered to inconclusion I was genuinely astonished when
my phone rang, and the enthusiasm of Frank Lupin in Des
Moines gushed like a shaken magnum of domestic
champagne; I'd done, he said often, a great job.
Nothing of Dwayne Hardy's answers had more than
remotely reminded me of any words I'd written, but Lupin was
persuaded my emphasis on the bipartisan nature of support for
Harness-Stirrup, and on the notion any lingering doubts about
the former would be utterly dispelled by success of the latter,
had carried the day. The gap between us was in my inability to
make an assessment free from the question of how well (or
poorly) Hardy had performed, to Lupin, and properly, a
complete irrelevancy; enough Orbis had been defended
without becoming identified with Hardy's success or failure.
"Did you notice that bastard Battaglia in the Lomax
entourage?"
"Battaglia?" I said, and then assembly occurred; as
cameras panned the post-meeting melee, I'd recognized but
failed for that moment to find a name for the big, dark man
among the Lomax group, strong face with a pleasant ugliness.
John Battaglia, who, as a senator, had achieved passing media
fame by insistence on proper pronunciation of his name; one
of the news programs had put together a montage from
perhaps a year of public utterance, shirtsleeved at campaign
rallies, serious on the floor of the Senate, lighthearted at a

formal dinner, friendly as a guest on *Face the Press*, saying
over and again the same five words: "Please. Not B'*tag*-lee-
uh, it's Ba-*tahl*-ya." By the time the joke wore thin he'd
established the phonetic value of Italian *gl* (even Frank Lupin
got it right) but he failed to be elected for a second term — I
don't intend to suggest direct connection between the two. In
his freshman (and so far sole) term he'd been abnormally
active; representing a state where hunting was not only a
common diversion but a major tourist industry he'd co-
sponsored a bill (unsuccessful) to ban assault-rifles saying he
couldn't see where the sport was in turning machine-guns on
deer, and why didn't we use bazookas, or recoilless rifles? If
known, I'd forgotten till reminded by Lupin he was also on that
committee which investigated the project in Yugoslavia, and
caused such a frenzy of internal Orbis memos. Though most
junior of all on the committee, Battaglia had been its most
outspoken and persistent member, till defeat in the election
took him out of the lineup.

　　"That's the son-of-a-bitch," Lupin said. "He's the one
who's making all this trouble for us. Who do you think has
been coaching Lomax to make a campaign-issue out of the
Harness thing? And that asshole from the *Post-Dispatch* used
to write speeches for Battaglia."

　　Elderbush, the orifice alluded to, was among brighter
members of the press corps, and what I knew about Battaglia,
with due allowance for his choice of professions, I had
admired. That thought did more than any of Hilde
Konwitschny's melodramatics to make me wonder whether I
might not be on the wrong side; a wrong side, however, which
was paying handsomely for my services.

　　"The word is, he wants to be Lomax's Secretary of the
Interior," trying and failing to make it sound in some way like
a corrupt conspiracy serving ignoble ambition. Though I
couldn't know it, that was the last time I was to have the
luxury of ironic observation from a point I conceived as
somewhere outside (and slightly above) the playing field

where committed participants sweated real sweat and banged real bruises.

Before I could take more than a step in the direction of coffeemaking, the door-buzzer rasped, and it was Paula. Merely buzzing her in was demonstratively inadequate (no, Ms. Editor, not *demonstrably*, I know what I'm saying); spurning the elderly, arthritic elevator I went bounding down six flights, three floorsworth of stairs, so she'd barely addressed the call-button, a brass dome like the flush in an antique public facility, when I appeared on her flank.

I've vowed to keep this account on track, saying the minimum about the purely personal, but I have to be indulged in an evening prematurely cool, Paula in bulky blue-black pea-jacket, jeans, her hair uncovered and coppery, the huge digression of my joy at seeing in her pale, gravid face after eleven eternal days that nothing had changed — and way below that, like some inner organ snagged on an inadequately-hammered nail-head, the fretful misery of knowing, nothing had changed.

We kissed, but events themselves were already editing, stripping us down to essential elements in someone else's story, no time for luxuriating growth of complex personal interaction. Paula had come not for a fresh look at us, but because asked to by Hilde Konwitschny, who'd called her less than half an hour ago — *asked* is decidedly too weak; *implored* is a better match for Paula's account. An elevator, somber, torpid and clanking, how different from the smooth, bright Special Projects one, was again my venue for exposure to overheated enigma.

"She's got my number," mystified. "I was on the phone with the Lupin for ten minutes, but — ?"

"She said she couldn't call you. She was calling from a payphone out on the street someplace; I could hear traffic."

Standing only just inside my apartment, hands deep in the pockets of the jacket she declined to let me take, Paula said Hilde was obviously extremely upset, had apologized repeatedly for intruding on her, and wanted me to meet her at Papageno's, a small and celebratedly obscure little Austrian café on the West Side.

"Now?" My own owlish habits did not create oblivion to societal norms; it was well past ten.

"You have to go. She said it was *absolutely imperative*, and there was no one else she could trust." Resisting her casting as faceless messenger, Paula contrived to make this, additionally, a remote hint of a question about what might be between me and Hilde. Nothing, my love, but what addiction to John le Carré might wreak.

Doubly instructed, I reached decision. "Would you like some coffee, *mit Schlag*?"

"Hilde said you must come alone. She also said, don't drive, take the bus, but get off a couple of stops away, and — "

"Oh, God." Hilde's apartment, though more northerly, was about as far from the Papageno neighborhood as mine, but as surely as if I'd been the imagined follower I knew she'd ridden the bus in an irrelevant direction and dismounted in some nowhere to make her call, before approaching our rendezvous crabwise, with a thirty-second pause in a darkened doorway to be sure she'd lost any shadow.

Excessive; to go at all at this hour was my limit of indulgence for craziness. Paula herself, because easier than disentombing her car from underground parking, had used the bus, a single direct route, that came within a block of linking our dwellings, and when I learned that, I became non-negotiably decisive; I would drive, reluctantly restoring Paula to her place (adequate detour for shaking off spooks), before heading for the West Side rendezvous.

In the car Paula looked straight ahead, hands together on lap. After two or three hours (it was a ten-minute drive) I ventured, "How have you been?" Instead, she told me about withdrawing from the group show at her gallery in a dispute over billing, primacy in wallspace, or incompatibility among styles, maybe all three. Not till we were in front of her building and I turned to kiss her did she say, "I'm going back to Westerlake."

Telling her she wasn't, asking why and when, expressing tragic opposition to the move, wondering why she'd never so much as hinted the possibility, all those together, made my syntax for the next minute too surreal for accurate reportage. Westerlake, a small tree-hatched town in a lactiferous neighbor state excessively pocked with glacier-scooped pools of every size, is host to the art-school Paula attended, melancholy site also of the doomed duel against wife, two boys and domestic status quo of her drawing instructor.

It sounded not quite irrevocable, though she said she could teach commercial art and graphic design there, and had picked out a wooden place to live on a hushed, lawned street. Overcome by urgency of the need for further debate I reached across to put a hand on Paula's arm, as she prepared to leave the car. "You have to see Hilde," slipping away. "We can talk later. Call me."

With Paula's news to numb my faculties I made a final angry concession to Hilde's terrors by parking on a poorly-lighted residential street several blocks away from my destination; I was unsure then how this was supposed to help, and now, after some learning-experience, I'd say the last thing to offer your average Joe Assassin is your extended ramble on your deserted street with just light enough for marksmanship and small chance of other strollers to observe or to unknowingly interpose their bodies in the line of fire.

Papageno's, or, you'll see what I mean, *PA, PA, GENO*'s, was, however, a shrewd choice for the meeting; its site used to be three tiny contiguous shops, each with its own back stockroom, and most of the interior walls, given connecting archways, are still in place, so it's impossible in a quick scan to see who's there. I found Hilde by the back wall of the back room in the middle *PA*, nibbling macaroons with a cup of coffee, *ohne Schlag*, getting cold. An elegant Continental lady, as Paula had maintained from the first, but the wild hope her fears had evaporated, and she'd smile and recommend the *Linzertorte*, was gone in the instant it took her to half-stand, recognizing me, and pull me down into the chair beside her, as if once seated I'd be cloaked in impenetrable anonymity. In a rushed, breathless voice she said, good of me to come, apologized for demanding it, apologized to absent Paula, hoping she'd be understanding, and asked if I hadn't seen the Vice-President on television.

I answered, "What did you think of it?" perhaps trying for a casting vote between my opinion and Frank Lupin's.

"It's terrible, terrible. Nothing was said about the radiation. It's like being the last sane person."

Here, we were interrupted. A young, non-Austrian waitress wearing a short red dirndl, costume admired for its peasant simplicity, in fact the most erotic outfit ever to proceed from the tormented mind of man, asked what I wanted, and I ordered coffee for myself, more for Hilde.

"I don't blame you," resuming when she felt safe to. "How could you know? I suppose you think there was a badly-run Yugoslav nuclear fusion experiment."

I replied there was evidence, and that I'd seen both document and its translation.

"Yes," Hilde agreed. "Freer invented it, and then Laxitter provided the documentation; I think, Laxitter. Well, it certainly was never produced in Belgrade."

"How do you know?" My tone said she couldn't, and she gave me that dark look experts use to make sure they'll never be asked such a question again.

"The so-called government document cannot be the original; it's a translation from English, not the other way about."

"Did you do it? — " likeliest explanation for such certainty, which produced instead a brief lecture on language. The putative original, she said, was in her opinion written by a highly-literate Serb, long resident in the United States or Canada, whose translation retained some North American anglicisms, and who had "failed to keep up with the improvements in Serbo-Croatian since Tito decreed it was a real language."

Suddenly finding I was believing every word, I asked when she'd seen the document. Special Projects, she said, had asked her to look at it, and when she told Worth it was an apparent forgery, he'd said, never mind, comment on it as if it were an authentic Yugoslav government document. "It was like a game, so I wrote what I did about Serbian exploitation of the Croats. But I think they never dared to make it public."

In the file, Frank Lupin had suggested other reasons for shelving this piece of evidence, but no Yugoslav-made radiation would mean the Harness Initiative alone would be responsible for those added cases of leukemia, birth defects, sterility.

"Emil knew — " coming to the heart of her darkness Hilde became if possible more clandestine, eyes going constantly in search of dangers. Her version was absolutely irreconcilable with what I'd seen in the file, early setbacks, a turning-point, new encouragement mounting to eventual triumph. "Emil Bieman, you know. He couldn't face it, right at the end, when he had begun so full of hope. It broke his heart, but he would have made them stop, and then, that bitch who made out she was telling just what Emil meant to say, if he had lived. She owed everything to the man, her career, everything."

The Harness cast was too limited to allow for many wrong guesses as to the bitch. "Was Vera Sobieska Bieman's mistress?" I asked, having assumed it, but not confident Hilde had been where she could know.

She laughed. "No typist, no lab assistant if she was young and petite, was ever safe from Vera Sobieska. No, she was not Emil Bieman's mistress. I was. There." She spread her hands flat on the table, as if abruptly more at ease. "You are the first I have ever told that."

Our coffee came, and proof of the mind's infinite triviality; caught by a story like none my life had ever contained or ever could, there were still some unoccupied units of attention for the dirndled girl, who had a lissome waist and lovely young knees.

The affair with Bieman had to be an absolute secret, the more so, Hilde wickedly said, because Emil's wife, now widow, was a very unsophisticated girl, muddled enough between monogamous ideals and real life to make a perfect American; the lovers had been covertly domestic together when he came to Vienna, had snatched more fleeting encounters when she went down to Zagreb or elsewhere her linguistic skills were needed, and had achieved a handful of extended weekends, twice in Dubrovnik, once at the Salzburg Festival, once more in London, where he had a conference, Hilde an aunt.

"No one in Orbis ever knew. True, they weren't so good, then, at finding things out. That was before they had such a large secret to hide — before Hurd Laxitter came over. Did you know he was twelve years with CIA?"

"How do you know?" In the time-space of three syllables, all my doubts returned. One tries not to be a snob, but credence is tied to taste, and, as a plot-element, CIA only slightly less vulgar than UFO.

"Emil knew him then, it's when they met, about 1970, when there was a Cold War. Laxitter got Emil out of East Germany. He hadn't seen him for years, but then it was Laxitter who brought Emil to Orbis, ORH, as it then was, Laxitter who recommended Emil for Zagreb, and who, in the end, had him killed."

The voice made a sharp turn into bitterness for the last, and I took it to be a manner of speaking, or for Hilde a rare lapse in idiom; she must mean Laxitter's assignment *got* Bieman killed.

"And then, Laxitter came and bought everybody — he bought Vera, who was easy to buy, though she knew almost all Emil did about the dangers of Harness; he bought silly Hanna Bieman and their son, not entirely with money. She quite enjoyed being told she was widow to a great man, like Constanze Mozart. As for me, I didn't have to be bought; no one knew what I knew."

"But you kept silent."

"I wanted to stay alive."

Here, recognizing it hadn't been a mistake in idiom before, I was all at once physically uncomfortable, shifting in my seat as if at an itch in the lumbar region. Emil Bieman, I reminded watchful Hilde, had been killed by Palestinians, because of his Zionist fervor.

Strangely, neither Hilde's fearfulness, nor the genuine persisting sorrow of her loss, was incompatible with a certain whimsicality, as if it amused her to toy with an innocent (me). She allowed Emil had indeed been deeply interested in the future of Israel. "Of all who reprinted the story about the Zionist organization he helped start," she said. "Only one, a little radical newspaper in Essen, bothered to do any checking. The group was called ANTEIL, that's an acronym, but also in German it means *share, portion*. Emil's conviction was, the future of Israel depends on negotiation and compromise with the Palestinians. His proposal for a West Bank test site was part of that belief; he wanted it to be a joint venture, a proof cooperation was possible. The question of sovereignty would somehow solve itself; outside agronomy, he was not a practical man."

If true, as I remarked, this didn't in itself rule out assassination by Palestinian — or Israeli — extremists, although the former were more likely to be angered by *Arab* soft-liners. The one certainty was that Bieman's death had been remarkably timely if Orbis did have disasters to hide.

Hilde said, "Without doubt, it was Orbis who had Emil killed — who but? Laxitter was who ordered it — do you know who *Azraël* is?"

"The Death-Angel?" I ventured. "*For the angel of death spread his wings on the blast —* " My father, who thinks poetry pretty much came to an end with Donne and Webster, once called Byron a `tin-eared doggerel tabloid journalist,' but would still have been proud of me for digging out that quotation.

"Exactly. But *Azraël* is also code-name for a person, a professional killer. The name was in a document I was given in among others to translate into German, but which was snatched away from me when they realized what was in it. It was in Vienna: *Azraël knows how to play the Palestinian card.* Laxitter wrote that, just two days before Emil was killed. This may be a contract person he had used when he was with the CIA."

"You don't know his real name?" almost idly, while my major circuits struggled to process unfamiliar feelings together with new facts, if that's what they were.

"No. He may be Dutch, there was a reference to Amsterdam."

Hilde's bleak vision included no hope of belated justice; CIA, she claimed, either knew or easily could have known who planted the car-bomb, but wouldn't want *Azraël* caught, in case he might talk about jobs he'd done for them in the past. Even imaginable (to her) that a phone-call from

Laxitter to some former associate at CIA would be enough to have them blandly concur in the findings of the Austrian police.

Then what did she want? was a reasonable question, but I put it badly, asking, "Why are you talking to me, now?"

The answer was, she trusted me. When they'd first brought her over from Europe, there'd been another so-called freelancer, planted by the corporation, she was convinced, to be sure she didn't know or guess truth about happenings in either Zagreb or Vienna. He'd gotten nothing out of Hilde beyond damp laments about the wickedness of terrorism and how much she had admired Dr. Bieman, but she'd known right away I was honest.

Flattering, but not what I wanted; how could she imagine I could be of any use? If she believed all she told me, if she wanted, as she said, to put a stop to radiation-enhanced agriculture, she should go to the authorities. I couldn't help adding that dangerous levels of radiation in food, or associated with its production, would certainly be detected before the system was authorized for general use.

"Ah, the authorities," she quoted, and the haunted eyes acquired an intimidating contempt. "Who are they? Tonight, we saw how the Vice-President can be manipulated by our wonderful employer of half a million Americans."

"The administration is not the government."

She half-bowed to me. "We decadent Middle Europeans are always forgetting that. Washington, London aren't Vienna or Budapest, police cannot be bribed, judges are above politics, and government agencies are models of independence; it's not possible a large and powerful corporation has ever been able to cause the FDA, or the Department of Agriculture, or of the Environment to gaze the other way, mm?"

"The press," after a vexed mental attempt to find a refutation for her premise.

"One would still wish to continue living. You think I
have read too many thrillers, fancying my phone, yes, and your
phone might be bugged, asking you to meet me here — and
presently I shall leave, and you'll stay, for at least half an hour,
and have more coffee and flirt with the delightful waitress.
Am I being watched? Who can tell. If I can walk into the
newspaper offices tomorrow morning, and on Thursday still be
alive, then I am as paranoiac as you think I am."

Without answering her uncomfortable charge, I
suggested she could set up a secret meeting, like this one, with
an investigative reporter hungry for a story — with the bloke
from the *St. Louis Post-Dispatch* who'd asked Hardy the
Harness questions tonight.

"If I had some evidence, perhaps. Right now, I can
prove nothing that I say."

As one who'd demonstrably worked for Orbis handling
confidential communications, she might, I thought, create
enough doubt that the whole question of residual radiation
would have to be gone into again, whether or not her
allegations about Bieman's death ever came to anything.
Admittedly, if she truly believed in the danger to herself, the
outside chance of her unsupported word being convincing
enough to a journalist that he *might* risk writing a piece that
with luck would force an investigation was a poor prize against
the risk of death.

She said, "The proof exists. It's in the files."

"I've gone through the whole file."

"You've gone through their window-display. I, too, am
permitted to see that file. There are other files. I don't know
how to get into them, but they are there. If they could be
copied — "

"Any copy could be a fake."

"No, because whoever copied them could also tell a
reporter or an investigator how to get into the system. They
could be verified."

"Such files, if they existed," dropping with distressing ease into a manner familiar from all sorts of deplorable literature. "They would be protected, and at the smallest sign of tampering, they'd — " my command of the jargon failed. "Suddenly, the access code wouldn't work any more," I finished.

"Oh, yes. This would have to be the only perfect crime — a robbery where nothing appears to be missing," she agreed, or rather, challenged.

I declined to make anything approaching a commitment; still a well-paid Orbis minion, I couldn't change sides on the basis of nebulosities like the self-evident sincerity of Hilde's affection for Emil Bieman, or the possibility of the vaunted partnership between government and industry being a conspiracy to sell lethal doses of radiation to a trusting world. If, I told Hilde, if I was given another legitimate reason for getting into the Special Projects system, I might, that was all I could promise, might have a quick peek to see if there was stuff I'd missed. On one hand there was Hilde, patting her lips with a folded paper napkin, nothing like a loony, and on the other knowledge that just for listening, just for letting myself be hauled into this alternative universe of clandestine cliché, I would by bedtime feel like a complete ass.

The waitress's name was Karen, a sophomore, creative writing, and I was an enigmatic but influential person in publishing, but only till midnight. I don't think I left any shed footwear behind, but I did have a folded customer check, on the back of which Karen, at her own insistence, had written her address and phone number. They've been of no use to me.

4.

     With panic-striking promptness, by week's end opportunity came to test my limited vow; Frank Lupin, fresh from the campaign trail where he'd acquired a new, squarer-jawed, state-of-the art style, came to say the sole microscopic reservation he had about my crib sheet for Hardy, which might still be needed again, was that it could have given more detail on the spectacular results now in on the Chile project. I replied I'd wanted that too, but the files had refused me entry to the Update chapter, whereupon he scuttled off to find Fena, who not much later visited me (I was back in my partitioned pseudo-office) to explain. Raw material for the Harness File, she said, was entered as is in a holding file with a separate password to protect it, until it could be proofread for typos, repeated words and like that, documents in, like, Spanish given translations, and the cleaned-up result transferred into the main file. In this case the password entry had erroneously been copied with the material, but she'd now knocked off the superfluous protection, and I could work with the file anytime I wanted.

     Though improved by Fena's no-nonsense delivery, this was an excess of explanation, trying too hard to reassure me there was only one real file, and I'd seen it. But it would be disingenuous to pretend — as at the time I pretended to pretend — that any part of my perception was left unchanged by the meeting with Hilde; now I was downtown in Paranoia City, but Hilde was denizen, not source, of the darkness; now I was watchful, and like Iago-stung Othello could find confirmations in trifles light as air — except the glances I read between Worth and Lupin, Lupin and Keller only contributed to doubt, leaving all my appraisals uncomfortable as they were inconclusive.

Fena offered to make a terminal available, but with Paul Merriam on hand and a sheaf of illustrations for me to choose among, I had an excellent excuse for saying I'd work at home again. I was becoming apprehensive my distrust had achieved independent life and was scattering its spores, but narrowest vigilance could detect no sign of suspicion in Fena, as she nodded agreement, and told me to use the same number as before to dial in on.

Twice that week, Paula and I had met and debated, met and tautly declined to weep. She was adamant everything to do with me had made only minor contribution to her decision to leave the city, which wasn't flattering but can't be gracefully refuted, therefore leaving me only a precarious isthmus of unshifting ground to stand on while trying hopelessly to change her mind. At last, nothing I did or omitted (this is for me a necessary belief) could have made a difference. If I have a regret — God help us, I have whole bundles of them; one, I mean to say, on this particular point — it's about her phone-call Saturday morning, the car that, all the while telling her not to go, I'd helped stuff with odd unshipped belongings, now pointed inexorably in the direction of Westerlake. Though she'd promised to call I didn't expect her start to be so early, and I really shouldn't have let Judy answer the phone. Too late now, and there was never a time when I could have been convincing with the truth, that if Judy, as Paula graphically envisioned, had only to roll over and pick up the bedside phone, I would never have let her do so. Technically, it could be argued, Paula had disqualified herself from the right to assurances, but whenever life decides to go for its misunderstandings to the vulgar level of farce or mawkish repertoire of daytime television, I become paralyzed with misplaced good taste, an unlovable fastidiousness that would rather let the worst be thought of me than descend, however true, to the ridiculous or clichéd protestations of either genre.

That's in general; in this instance there were added and overwhelming elements to excuse my inattention.

The chaste journey into dawn with Judy began at my remark, as I held the front door for her to sidestep through, hugging groceries, that it had gone well, thank you, with her mobile disk, but I'd had some long waits while the screen filled, particularly when it came to diagrams, or to facsimile documents. As computer-folk do, even the nicest, she indicated complete lack of surprise; plainly I was the only person left in the developed world who didn't know a high-speed modem was recommended for that sort of information; I was deficient, I learned, in *bauds*, which, startled, I asked her to spell. If I had to work with that file again, she added, I could borrow her newest modem, the eight-legged Sleipnir of modems, swiftest of its race. Fate, with its structural genius, had sent superfluous Michael off on an overnight mission to photograph a Saturday suburban wedding.

Impatient to test new toys (though I, to be sure, had motives that ran deeper) we declined to make hunger a distraction, munching handfuls torn from a bakery loaf, bits of cheese and near-meat out of my refrigerator, attending to the computer, bobbing as to a tribal shrine. At first, protectively, I continued to exclude Judy from content, doing my best to pick her brains by abstract hypothesis; *if* I'd been able to see only portions of a file, how would existence of more be indicated in what I could see? Naturally, her answer was, in effect, show me, and having excuse and authorization to do so, I dialed in, asked for HARNESS, logged on as DIRTYSPY, and said, "You're not kidding, high-speed," as the opening menu flashed onto the screen. I see now, as absorption prevented me from seeing then, the opening passes in a remote duel between Judy and Fena, electronic thrust and parry, with information as prize.

After earnest jiggling, inevitably exposing her to some text, in which she showed no interest, Judy proclaimed this wasn't a file at all, more like one of those promotional displays for new software, superficially disguised to simulate a real program. Echoes of Hilde, who'd called it a window-display; trying not to be emotional I asked Judy how she knew, and got back a barrage of rhetorical questions about functions, which I think can be fairly summarized, *If this is the whole thing, where's the stuff that makes it run?*

No answer, but observant Judy noticed, or rather perceived the possible importance of a detail I'd dismissed as negligible; while as Fena had promised the Update file was now retrievable, there remained an anomaly about the title line, which still read: £HARNESS:CHILE.UPDATE.

"What's this thing?" Judy said. "All the others just say HARNESS."

"Pounds."

"Uh uh, pounds is that tic-tac-toe thing."

"No, pounds, money. It's the symbol for British pounds."

I'd told her Fena's tale, and she'd scoffed at the existence of a mythic holding file. Now she conjectured £HARNESS might be the real name for the program, inadvertently left on. Growing excited, I asked if that meant I could log off, redial, and ask for £HARNESS, with any hope of getting it.

"Could be," Judy said. We were side by side, both leaning over the back of my empty chair. "Only it's going to ask who you are. Obviously, the DIRTYSPY code name would only be for access to the phony file."

The phony file. That, so soon, had become established fact.

"Have you got some other names we could try?"

"*Gandalf,*" I said, momentarily certain, but when back to where the screen asked what I wanted, I froze, hunted, and despaired.

"What's wrong?" Judy said.

"I don't have the pounds sign on my keyboard."

A laugh. Despite not having known what it stood for, she leaned in, and with a rapid rattle of keys formulated it from memory. "Bingo," she said, as, after a portentous pause, the request for a name appeared. Though tense, I must have felt that, like a dangerous dog, the machine would sense lack of confidence, and I repeated what had to be, *had* to be Fena's code-name.

"How do you spell it?" and then again, "Bingo." Maybe for Judy, but all I could see, instead of the informative menu I'd hoped for, was what's called a prompt, FILE>. Unperturbed, having confirmed with me Gandalf had been programmer, Judy entered DIR. At once, ENTER PASSWORD appeared. "Ouch," Judy said. (*Blades slither, hilts lock, unknowing Fena sneers, `Not good enough, stripling!'*)

My turn again, and I remembered Fena boasting the files were as hard to enter as the Mines of Moria. "Try *edro*."

"What?"

"*Edro*." I spelled it. "It's Elvish for *open*."

"Elvish."

"Gandalf says it when he's trying to get into Khazad-dûm." Unsuccessfully on that try, I didn't say.

"Oh, well, then," parodying renewed faith. She entered it, and obediently a menu of available files appeared.

By now our aptitudes were assigned; I didn't argue when she told me I'd like to look at the listing of authorized users, and she made no comment when, at a new demand for a password, I with absurd assurance gave her *Mellon*, telling her it was Elvish for *friend*. "Two ells," I emphasized.

"Oh, wow," Judy said when it worked. The file which unrolled listed Orbis people, known and unfamiliar, their code names, and what Judy informed me was the level of their rights in use of the £HARNESS program. Thus, both Mark Worth, code-name *Bullion*, and Frank Lupin, *Spinner*, were Level A, All Rights.

"Your Gandalf is a very funny lady. She lists herself as Level 0, Supervise Only, but this is her file. She can borrow anybody's rights — what's to stop her logging on using this Laxitter's code?" Hurd Laxitter was *Sparkplug*, and unique in being Unrestricted, however that might differ from All Rights.

"Here's you, right at the bottom," Judy pointed out, and so I was. It might be mentioned here I've never properly known my middle name; my mother always maintained it was Keith, after her uncle, a respectable composer, while Dad counter-insisted Kaline, for the best all-round ballplayer he ever saw. Either way, I've had no reason to be ashamed of that *K*, but it does make my initials AKA, which can cause lifted eyebrows in law-enforcement circles, and sufficiently explained my allotted alias, *Alias*. My rights were defined as [X], Read Only, the same as for Hilde Konwitschny just above me, coded *Rosetta*, presumably an allusion to her linguistic usefulness. At our same lowly level was Dionne Theobald, whose code-name, *Affirm* could be either a long-legged reference to the racehorse, or, more snidely, to the hiring guidelines that brought a black woman into Special Projects. The [*DS*] appended to all three names must indicate our sharing of the DIRTYSPY designation.

Repeating the self-evident, I asked Judy if this didn't mean I too could borrow a high-level entry code, and break into the £HARNESS file.

"Go right to the top," she advised. "Then you'll be sure you're seeing everything."

Having the code-names was all very well, but I was worried about non-Tolkienian passwords once in. "If we make a mistake, it's recorded as an unauthorized entry, with my telephone number."

Judy shook her head. "I think you'd have to be allowed one free error. Anybody's fingers can screw up. You get it wrong again, the system will shut down, most likely. But anyway — " hitting keys, she returned us to the former menu. "All entries get recorded, authorized or not. Usually. Yes, see, this file here called *Log*."

Incredible, I know, but blithely striding in as GANDALF it hadn't occurred to me I'd leave behind such lumbering footprints; at the most casual glance Fena would know she hadn't been working with the file at this time, and it was she who'd said the originating phone-number would also be captured. (*`Not yet,' she mocked, hurt but still dangerous.*)

Calm Judy said she might be able to fix up the log to cover my tracks, if she could get in, but when she asked for an Elvish word for *log* my so-far infallible prescience failed, and the question had to be deferred for some later, when my powers were renewed.

For entering the main program, her thought that I should use the highest available authority was based on experience with the Board of Ed's system, where she'd found the bigger the wig, the less its wearer wanted to bother about cumbersome security when working with the computer, so a third-grader's score on a math quiz became a better-guarded secret than a supervisor's salary, or charges of indecent exposure against a school principal.

In this instance there was another advantage in choosing the top rank; whereas, with either Worth or Lupin whom she saw every day, Fena might quite casually ask what he was doing, messing about with the files late Saturday night, it was unlikely she or anyone would venture the same question of Laxitter when he paid one of his state visits.

"Here goes," Judy, having returned to the NAME prompt without logging off. She entered SPARKPLUG, shrivelling my soul as she did by remarking laconically, "There'll be a personal password to get in, and after that you're home free."

A personal password! I possessed no such key to Laxitter's soul as Fena's mania for Tolkien, and as ENTER PASSWORD came up, Judy perfected my despair by mentioning it might be changed every week or month.

"Maybe he chooses his own, so even Gandalf can't get in unless he wants her to." Nevertheless, she was regarding me with the alert expectancy of a puppy imploring just one more treat, and the best I could suggest for the alleged former CIA man was *Company*.

While at those odds, the response, ACCESS DENIED: RE-ENTER PASSWORD OR SELECT PATH, was hardly a surprise, it was distressing to damage Judy's faith in my hoard of lore. "You got another one? Or you want me to try defeating the security?"

"Can you do that?"

"If they haven't done anything screwy."

Here began the deadliest and, for me, least reportable phase of the duel. (*Swords useless in these narrow confines, stilettos clamped in their teeth, they stalked each other in silence through the twisting subterranean labyrinth.*) "This is going to take some time," Judy said, and I watched, trying to appear intelligent, while she contrived to fill the screen with unmeaning symbols, issued obscure commands, ran a hand back through her dense, tight-curled hair. "Oh, *I* see what they're doing," yielded to, "Oh, crap," and another assault on the keyboard, renewed rapid scrolling, hiss of breath through Judy's teeth. More than once she pointed, and said, "You see?" then rendering an incomprehensible elucidation of arcane on-screen skeins of characters; at length, tiring of my own poker-faced, hypocritical grunts and sage nods, I went and made coffee.

"I got it now," Judy said when I came back, but many more screensful flashed, and the milk risen to surface on her half-drunk coffee was settling into cold streaks before her next, "*Aha.*" Tensed to pounce, two fingers hovering over the *Enter* key, she proclaimed, "This is it. If they didn't put a watchdog on the back door. Either I'm in, or the system will shut down."

She struck, and never has Catholic church-hall or Florida gerontorium resounded to a more heartfelt *Bingo!* than hers, as a long list of chapters came on screen.

"This is *Sparkplug*'s own file," Judy said, after we'd hugged, then, "Jesus," as she saw its dimensions. "This is going to take you hours just to go through. You better copy it and work from disk."

"Can I copy it, all in one go?"

"You're *Sparkplug*. You can do any damn thing you want." She entered the needed command, and was pleased to note, as predicted, no further passwords were needed for individual files. Even for her fleet cheetah among modems, copying was a lengthy job, ample time for making fresh coffee, and when it was complete she advised me to make sure now, before we quit the remote program, that I could retrieve more than just the directory from the mobile disk.

Embarrassed to exclude Judy after all the expertise, I cleared my throat uncomfortably. Pleasant working with her, but still with the idea of shielding her from what might be unsafe knowledge, I wanted her to go away before I put information of substance on-screen.

Her alert eyes translated me sidelong, and I was relieved at the same time as shamed by her understanding. "I better stick around, in case you need me. Find me a book to read, and I'll be fine — hey, you have the Tolkien thing? If you show me the part where you got the Elvish stuff, maybe I'll find something we can use when we want to get into the log."

I dug out a tattered paperback *Fellowship of the Ring*, found the chapter, nodded inattentively when she said she'd started the book once, but couldn't get into it, and went back to where the computer still waited on the brink. When I'd dismissed the Special Projects connection, no place seemed better to start than another; I selected the file called HAR.1, and began my education.

Take the worst you can dream I could imagine as a result of Hilde's unsubstantiated and (except for murder) rather unspecific impeachments; reality was, still is far worse, and where factually no worse, made infinitely so by the pervasive malodor of callous complacency. From the first I was repelled, and it's proper to confess, as I couldn't have then, that revulsion was made more violent by the stir, somewhere deep beyond the everyday plumbline, of a nasty, unwanted little admiration, God help us, for the deadly, uncaring efficiency of it all. Maybe slumbering in all of us is the savage desire to be free from restraints of fellowship, responsibility, compassion, for the infantine clarity of despotic selfishness, perfect greed. This was a bold, knowing world, where arrogant ends sanctified corrupt means; tell me you've never envied such bland absolution of conscience.

Hurd Laxitter was a methodical man, and his records were meticulously complete, once you mastered the sometimes overlapping, sometimes complementary tiers of his system, which demanded a lot of dodging back and forth between files. Each year of the entire Harness-Stirrup process was indicated by an Arabic number, months within each year by Roman numerals, so that when, following in the main file the most coherent continuous account, I came in November of the second year to a translated report dealing with Yugoslav concerns over dangerously high levels of radiation, I could turn to a facsimile of the original together with accompanying statistics in section 2.XI of the file named DOC, and to Rockforth Freer's consequent instructions, always about concealment, in the corresponding section of the CORR file. Finally, in a file called LX.PERS, I found confidential memos, written records of conversations, comments and opinions by all the principals involved, policy discussions, including Laxitter's astonishingly candid notes, apparently for his own use, presence of which surely confirmed Judy's conjecture Laxitter must set his own private password over this material;

I was certain he didn't want anyone else ransacking these revelations of his space-age ceramic soul.

I could easily be angry over how comprehensively I'd let myself be taken in by the pseudo-file, so eager to find respectable reasons for taking the money. Yet that was a crafty piece of window-dressing, draped with enough seeming-indiscretion to give it a confidential texture, and heavily dependent on selective truth to construct its lies. The terminal feud between Freer and Laxitter, for example, was true, but not the conveyed impression Laxitter's part in the Harness Initiative began only when, exasperated by Freer's attempts to paste press-releases over its fissures, he'd seized the reins, ordering everyone to come clean, opening a new era of happy *glasnost*. On the contrary, it had been Laxitter's project from the start, and the break had been caused solely by Freer's impulsive addiction to independent action, his clumsy denials, which Laxitter complained simply drew attention to questions when, with subtler methods, in a pet phrase of his, they could have been "diluted down" to non-existence.

These, as the upwardly mobile Scot could have said, might rather the multitudinous seas contaminate; the Jastrebarsko venture had been, not site of pesky, soluable and at last mainly solved problems as portrayed in the pseudo-file, but far nearer total disaster, kept from full revelation only by immense and expensive Orbis effort, joined to circumstances which Laxitter called "fortuitous," disintegration of the Yugoslav federation, with its ensuing war and confusion.

To do him maximum allowable justice, he was genuine in his conviction most of the "undesirables" could be brought within acceptable guidelines, which he saw initially as the principal purpose of Stirrup, the Chilean successor to Harness. This was leitmotivic in all his instructions and suggestions to its director, Gerhardt Fiori, easily recognizable under his code-name, *Bouquet*. Yes, but at the same time Laxitter's idea of acceptability was clearly concerned far less with real safety than with sales, which in turn was bound up with permissible limits of collusion with government agencies. The private file included a model exhibit for this thesis, an unofficial letter to Laxitter from a very high appointee, marked *Private and Confidential*, yet still written in that evasive bureaucratic prose, mastic on the page, mist in the mind, which with some effort I could translate into two simple sentences: *Fine, we'll go along with you as far as we can, but don't push it. We can't go on saying "contradictory and inconclusive" if people are dropping dead in the streets.*

The last phrase actually comes from a letter of Laxitter's, reprimanding Emil Bieman for "making it sound like we're littering the streets of Zagreb with corpses." For Bieman, code-named *Stinger*, a pun on his name, the Harness experience was other than an increasingly fractious exercise in public relations, and quite opposite to the happy-ending fiction of the pseudo-file; beginning as a zealot for the selective radiation he'd pioneered, he made a long journey through doubts into alarm, and eventually, I adduced, to torment, wrenched between loyalty to both Orbis and his own former self, and to scientific integrity, fears for the world, that propelled him to his defection — and death.

As his confidential memos to Freer showed, Bieman wasn't a willing accomplice in concealment, yet for a long time, because he wanted Harness to work, he acquiesced in publication of reports which omitted or airily minimized the concerns haunting his private communications. No matter how they tinkered with the pods, any level of radiation that made a measurable difference to plant growth also resulted in sickness for workers, and in contaminated harvests. Among workers by the end of the third year, the mounting incidence of sterility, the abundant crop of birth-defects, were unignorable, though Bieman continued to hope, Freer flatly to assert most of this was traceable to the early days, when admittedly emission level of the magic pods was excessive. Soon, however, it was shown residual radiation had contaminated not only soil but ground water as well, and nearby farm families and villagers who'd had nothing directly to do with Harness were beginning to show the same statistically inexcusable increase in leukemia and other cancers; "they've started to call the region adjacent to Jastrebarsko *Little Chernobyl*," Bieman dejectedly wrote.

There were, by the way, other disappointments not immediately connected to the embarrassing side-effects of radiation; by the fourth growing-season, as tabulated in Vera Sobieska's careful and carefully suppressed analyses, food produced was showing "significant" shortfalls in many essential nutrients, and this Bieman associated with the altogether unanticipated depletion of the soil. He protested wistfully that his equations and the Long Island model trial had led him to predict just the opposite, but the final Harness growing-season was saved only by massive surreptitious introduction of organic fertilisers, which reached the site in a covert operation worthy of arms for the ransom of hostages, shipped to Milan by a German subsidiary of Orbis, trucked to near Trieste by a private contractor, then shuttled into Jastrebarsko using big helicopters conveniently leasable from the US military, and flown in from a base in Turkey. Since the fertiliser was identified on the manifest as "Seed" and "Building Supplies," success of the operation raised serious questions about the olfactory equipment of so many oblivious participants, but left me in no doubt about Laxitter's CIA past.

So far, indeed, though with infinitely more unpleasant detail, everything Hilde had told me had been confirmed; I could picture Emil Bieman as his anguish deepened, unable to talk to his silly wife, or, by now, trust the formidable Sobieska, confiding his worst fears to Hilde in dappled darkness of a borrowed bedding, or walking with her between walls and water in lovely Dubrovnik, then marked only by the softer scars of lapping time. One secret I don't find he told even

Hilde; when, in the dispute over the final Harness report, he at last decided he must break with Orbis, he knew he had cancer of the liver.

Diagnosed by a Vienna doctor, whose records, whether by stealth or bribery, had been acquired by *Ilium*, a Trojan incognito I later decided must belong to the obscure Helena Smitt. Laxitter, typically, assigned the illness a central role in Bieman's revolt, as if the carcinogenic potential of his work could be important only to one who'd contracted the disease himself, not a conclusion to be reached by an independent reader of his urgent memos, or pained letter of resignation.

The original was in dignified, correct English, so that I wondered whether he'd had a hand from Hilde, although Bieman had spent several years in Canada and the US. He asked Orbis, as personified by Laxitter, if the Yugoslav results were disappointing to him, how they afflicted one who had given years of his life, his whole reputation to the principles behind the Harness Initiative. Still unwilling to concede there was no future in agriculture for selective radiation, he suggested the Harness experience indicated its safe, practical application required many more years, perhaps decades of testing and refinement. No law of nature, he wrote, said scientifically sound research could always accommodate itself to demands of profitability. Obvious to him Orbis wasn't willing to admit the magnitude of the problems, much less set about solving them, and he, Emil Bieman, was unwilling to have his name associated with published results which, where not falsified, were deliberately skewed so as to mislead. "*My hope*," he concluded, "*is that my resignation shall bring Orbis to the realization that the Harness principle cannot proceed in its present state. More than profits or prestige are risked here, wide areas of the inhabitable world, the health and lives of many thousands or millions of persons, living and not yet born.*"

That, I mean, is how and where he should have concluded, but suddenly inflated by that blowhard devil of naiveté that persuades the powerless to issue ultimatums, he found it good to add he would for the time being treat the terms of his resignation as confidential, but would in conscience feel obliged to make them public unless Orbis gave unmistakable indications it meant to make Harness safe, regardless of time or cost, before letting the system loose on the world.

In this, unfailing sagacity of retrospect can say, he managed to have the worst of all worlds; if he wanted to go on living (for as long as the liver let him) he should have vowed confidentiality would be eternal, and allowed Orbis to ascribe his resignation to ill-health, fatigue, a whim. If he was intent on influencing the future of his Frankensteinian offspring, he should have sent copies of his resignation without delay to every major newspaper and news agency in the world, and simultaneously given the televised news conference he later, too late, determined on. In fact, that would also have been a better way of achieving object (*a*), since with all his beans irretrievably spilled, there would have been no point to having him killed.

And that's what Laxitter did. Whether he needed authorization, who else at Orbis approved or as much as knew about the transaction, I couldn't tell, but that it was just as Hilde said, and Laxitter its executive director, were beyond sane doubt. His first recorded move was to get in touch with *Azraël* through an accommodation address in Suriname, and he showed extraordinary foresight by doing so months before the Bieman resignation, though not before he'd predicted "*Stinger* may abandon ship, he's getting overwrought," a note appended to the Bieman memo where the phrase "Little Chernobyl" first occurred. In Laxitter's frigid repertoire, a completely detailed design for murder could be put in place as a contingency plan, an option to be exercised if conditions warranted.

He had, though, a cordial personal interface with *Azraël*, dating back unspecified years to exploits not recapitulated, small, lethal victories, I don't doubt, in that late global crusade against the malevolent minions and unwitting dupes of the ever-plotting Kremlin. In the LX PERS file there was the scanned facsimile of *Azraël*'s cyphered reply to Laxitter's initial overture, with a plain text transcription. His bonhomie sent slow spiders in procession up my spine:

> My good old friend:
>   Let us see if you still can work with
> the old slide-rule cypher. What pleasure,
> as ever, to hear from you. By all means I
> can make myself available for a job such
> as you describe. The old Amsterdam
> drop is still good, but I'll need fifteen,
> minimum twelve days notice if you
> decide to go to active — I can't fly in a
> straight line, and the set-up takes time,
> you know. For certain, we can blame the
> lovely Pals, if you don't mind maybe
> some collateral grief, as you are aware
> they are not neat workers, and we must be
> sloppy like them.
>   The retainer you propose is okay,
> installment one to Amsterdam before
> May 1, but I may need more orphan cash
> for the components, I won't charge you a
> cent more than they cost me, you can
> believe. I would ask for a bigger
> completion bonus, but demand for quality
> work has dropped off, just your good
> luck. Between old friends, you might

hear in the grapevine I'm not as good
since the small trouble in Pretoria, but
you know I never bullshit you. I have to
be a straight northpaw now, no more two-
hand ping-pong, but last week I got 94
using one of those lousy Romanian
Beretta knock-offs, you have to
compensate for expansion after about five
rounds. We have to get together and
natter about old times. You ever get
south of Key West? I got five cases of
1978 Pichon-Longueville Comtesse here,
and nobody to drink it with.

Laxitter, hardly man, friendship notwithstanding, to
take *Azraël* on faith, had succinctly commented "*check
condition.*" He'd evidently called another friend in what's
cozily called the intelligence community, and later arranged a
meeting in Brussels between *Azraël* and an agent, trusted but
untraceable to Orbis, to satisfy himself he'd picked the right
man.

As demonstrably he had; the bomb went off in the
Schottenring; Bieman's remains had to be identified through
dental records and a childhood fracture of the right humerus,
and for irrelevant Viennese the "collateral grief" by chance
amounted only to some minor wounds from glass and metal
fragments. At this point I came across the phrase recalled by
Hilde about "playing the Palestinian card," and now knew it
entailed far more and subtler things than a phone-call claiming
the kill; *Azraël* exactly followed the MO of Teheran-trained
Moslem maniacs, down to the components of the bomb and its
detonator, while he or Laxitter had somehow contrived, a
couple of weeks earlier, to plant a story in a grubby little
radical Beirut newspaper, denouncing Bieman as a leading
agent of Imperialist-Zionist expansionism.

That, as far as the files were concerned, was pretty much *Azraël*'s curtain-call, and the stage now belonged to Laxitter, who, in a manner not too much different from the pseudo-file account, soon shoved impetuous Freer into the wings. In Vienna, code-names assigned to his supporting players were expressions of cynical contempt; "he bought everybody," Hilde had said, and she was here: "We don't know what *Rosetta* might have picked up," Laxitter wrote. "Let's emigrate her to Special Projects where she can be monitored." At this point, Vera Sobieska became *Pivot*, tribute, I supposed, to the frictionless ease of her volte-face; she was later responsible, apparently, for creating the fictional Bieman memos for the pseudo-file, to show his doubts and misgivings gradually yielding to irresistible success (she was now in Chile, assisting Fiori, while reporting independently to Laxitter). Only their presence at the Vienna news-conference, subsequent talk-show and interview appearances in London and the US, enabled me to identify two very minor figures as Hanna, Bieman's widow, and Chaim, his ten-year-old son; Laxitter noted: "*Cheerleader* and *Mascot* played very well with the press. We can use them again in DC."

I'd been fascinated, horrified, sickened, filled with a massy, immobilizing despair at the rumbling advance of plain evil, but here for the first time I became really angry, excoriating, along with Laxitter, the dim, sentimental Arthur Ames, who, caught by the fictionalized version, had felt tears surge up on reading the utterly spurious text, "what can we do for his wife and son?"

A sound must have escaped me, a snarl, no, I don't snarl, an explosive hiss through clenched teeth, perhaps an actual sotto-voce expletive. Judy, curled in an armchair, said, "What's the matter?" Putting down the book, prone (I noted that having started at about the three-quarter point she was now nearing the end), she came, and from behind, elbows akimbo, pressed at my shoulders, like a pectoral exercise, but,

as an articulate expression of friendly concern, miraculously
well-timed.

"Don't look," I babbled, trying to conceal the pitiless
screen with one fatuous hand. "It's dangerous." Judy said
okay, but her grin didn't believe it, and neither did I, not
enough, not yet. Oh, I'd absorbed as a datum that there was a
universe of perilous banality, where murder might be a sub-
entry under promotional expenses; intellectually I could
recognize that people willing for profit to produce the global
effects prophesied in Bieman's letter of resignation would
hardly be racked with remorse over removal of any human
obstacle — I knew these were facts, but hadn't yet accepted
that imaginatively. When I was small, the White House,
which I'd been told about, seen pictures of, wasn't as real for
me as Toad Hall, which I'd learned to envision (I'm not sure
that's not still true).

At that very time came to me the thought that Orbis
was less dangerous for occasional acts of overt lawlessness
than for its persistent, looming presence within what we
accepted as civilized life. That not-very-effective young
crook, Bill Fasstin, came back to my mind — oh, I had no
reason to doubt he was really tapping the till, but the mere
assertion, coming from an institution like Orbis, from a
respected figure like Laxitter, had been enough to deputize a
whole society, from the bank just down the street to the
Allenbys and Alleyns of Scotland Yard. How could the word
of ORBIS be doubted? They brought us ballet and opera on
TV, and showed us beautifully made, not-for-profit little films
about programs to lovingly feed the superbly-shampooed
elderly, to prime the creaking pump of public education in a
back-lighted atmosphere of infinite, understanding patience;
generous yet grateful Orbis execs handed out humungous
checks at the end of tennis tournaments; there was a choral
anthem associating the Orbis name with *Brüderkeit* and the
quest for truth, never-ending, enlightened striving for
excellence. The Vice-President spoke well of the corporation.

Within Orbis, the attitude was, near enough, if he doesn't, we'll get another Vice-President — or senator, Secretary of Commerce, head for the FBI. Political operations in support of radiation-enhanced agriculture were closely coordinated, often merged, with publicity and public relations, all beginning well before the Jastrebarsko site was chosen. But only after shutdown of the Harness Initiative, with the decision to ration out news about Stirrup and merely keep Chile in the lower left-hand corner of public consciousness, together with the need to defend the late Yugoslav enterprise against undead allegation and Hydra-tongued rumor, did these come to dominate Laxitter's thoughts, as reflected in the files. Construction of the spurious Yugoslav government document discussing the entirely fictional fusion experiment, was part of that defense, and I discovered the textual author was an accurate match for Hilde's deductions, an evidently ancient Dr. Radic, resident in the US since before I was born, retired from a professorship in Slavic languages at Northwestern, a ferocious anti-Communist, who, back in the palmy days of Assured Mutual Annihilation, had been a regular supplier for CIA of such manufactured scraps of documentary evidence, whether of crime, repression or bungling. From his somewhat dotty reply to Laxitter's renewal of acquaintance, as well as Laxitter's own notes, plainly Dr. Radic regarded his whole-cloth inventions not as lies, but as licensed *dramatizations* of what must be abstractly true of any Communist state. Outside the text of a stump speech, I'd never expected to come across the words "our great Free-Enterprise System," written in absolute, appalling sincerity.

While, as I say, it was more frightening than murder to see how the power and prestige of Orbis could make its appetite for profits come to seem identical with the aspirations of an entire society, the political sections, paradoxically, often made the lightest reading, Laxitter's habitual mordant

pragmatism taking its place in a hallowed tradition of
contempt for elected and appointed officials, an authentic,
ketchup-ready slab of Americana; little but amusement, for
instance, in finding the garrulous minority and beacon-nosed
majority leaders of the Senate encoded as the mythic firm of
Gush and Lush, Inc.

The Vice-President, who appeared often, was *Ollie*,
referring not to a notorious lieutenant-colonel, as I first
thought, but to a namesake comedian, though Dwayne Hardy
isn't fat. That sobriquet may have been current outside the
confines of the files; his eastern patrician wife is Eve Stannard
Forrest Hardy, and Laxitter's records of social occasions set up
to promote Stirrup or defend Harness several times included
"had Stan and Ollie to dinner." Though these events, in
darkest Westchester, were carefully kept from the press, Hardy
may have thought he had a genuine friendship, but then he
wasn't privy to Laxitter's private musings or confidential
memos to Frank Lupin. One, for example, reprimanding
Lupin for assuming a broad hint would be enough for Hardy:
"*You know* Ollie *has to have things spelled out, slowly. He
thinks of Stephen Sondheim as an intellectual.*" Still, when the
chilly threat of the Senate investigation was cooling the clay of
Hardy's feet, his brother-in-law, conservator of his blind trust,
was suddenly able to pull off one of the great trading coups,
purchasing from Laxitter's own holdings 3,000 shares of
Orbisco Preferred at par value of $20; the market price of the
security had slipped a little on rumblings from the Senate, but
from a low of 74 it soon returned to its normal range, between
90 and 110.

Educative to find that bribery — to use a term, evoke a
process, far cruder than any in Laxitter's files — was a great
deal like hypnosis, or like what, in unprovable and eventually
meaningless reassurance, used to be said about hypnosis: few
elected or appointed officials would do when bribed what they
couldn't find a plausible reason for on its own apparent merits.
Some were easy to persuade that campaign contributions,

windfall stock options, complementary goods and services, played no part in changing their convictions, while others, more honest in some improbable sense of the word, said, in effect, "Look, you have to find me an angle that's gonna play with the public."

A specialty of Frank Lupin's. Public outrage, he declaimed in a memo shortly after joining the Special Projects team, could be made to work *for* the Harness situation, take for example the jobs issue. The elderly chairman of the Senate committee, from an industrial state, depended heavily for his repeated reelection on union support, and with worker safety a currently hot issue he was at first hesitant about accepting a generous Orbis contribution to his celebrated Voter Education Fund. Lupin's elegantly rococo argument went: if there were dangers in the Harness principle, and they'd been grotesquely overstated, they certainly weren't in the *manufacturing* phase, if we didn't do it the Japs would, so where was the sense in losing more American jobs to those compulsively overproductive little architects of Pearl Harbor, reliable high-mileage cars and all other conscienceless Asiatic treacheries? The senator took the money, and at the next session of the committee didn't allow to be read into the record the affidavit of a terminally-ill Croat who'd worked at Jastrebarsko, as merely anecdotal and lacking all scientific foundation.

Lupin, who was an observer at that sitting, reported the genuine anger of *Waterloo*, the very junior senator who'd obtained the affidavit. He was already under suspicion; five years before, in his senatorial campaign, as two years before that, when first elected to the House, he'd refused to accept money from Orchem International (an ORBIS company) which had its huge chemicals factory in his state. As a leading manufacturer of smokeless powder, he believed they might hope to affect his as-yet undecided views on gun control. Not hard to recognize *Waterloo* as strongly opinionated John Battaglia (ba-*tahl*-ya).

Few get the chance to play Napoleon and Wellington both at once, yet *Waterloo* was Laxitter's most frustrating defeat, and then his greatest victory. The guy couldn't be bought or threated off, Lupin complained, and Worth chimed in with intelligence that *Waterloo*, having dispatched an aide who got as far as Zagreb, was planning his own fact-finding trip to Croatia in the new session. "He's definitely into the messiah syndrome," Lupin assessed, and in a stunning double mix of images, "Like some big boy scout. He sinks his teeth in and just won't let go." Apprehension about what he might uncover persisted until the Senate adjourned for the off-year election, and then Laxitter let loose the hounds of hell in the form of funds, PACs and negative commercials produced by Special Projects, all with the object of denying Battaglia reelection. The state's pro-gun forces happily found themselves with cash enough to make Battaglia's stand on assault-rifles an obsessive issue, and when Laxitter referred to a poll showing that despite it all, nearly two-thirds of the electorate supported some form of gun-control, the head of the state chapter of the NRA wrote, "Not to worry. Half of that 64% don't vote. ALL our people are going to vote." There were, besides, plenty of other reasons not to return Battaglia; on their domestic screens voters could see pithy thirty-second dramas in which farms were foreclosed and crime raged in the streets while their junior senator cared only about how his name was pronounced; his admission he'd tried smoking grass in youth was associated with an unfortunate picture in which, having just accepted an obligatory sample of some ethnic culinary surprise, a fiery test of manhood, he'd been caught with mouth open and heavy eyelids half-lowered. "We should be able to find a sex situation we can exploit," Lupin suggested, and on cue there appeared a lady who, a score of years ago, had been date-raped by the senator-to-be, and whose lethargic sense of justice had at last impelled her to speak out. In the circumstances, outspent, moreover, in a disclosed eight-to-one ratio, Battaglia's capture of more than

49% of the vote was a stirring tribute to his resilience, but not enough to bring the Harness Committee back to life.

In his new role as a strategist in the Presidential campaign of Orford Lomax, he remained a preoccupation, and his unpurchasability an enigma for the Special Projects team. That he was so bizarre an exception to their rules rubbed in the lesson: where internal ethics have ceased to exist, aroused public opinion is the only force to impose them from without.

Laxitter knew that barring a few more *Waterloo*s, all he had to fear was a sustained assault from the press, equipped with the heavy artillery of scandalous revelation. The painstakingly constructed pseudo-file, which had puzzled me as far too elaborate and costly to have been designed merely to gull the likes of Hilde, Dionne Theobald and me, now revealed itself as a major weapon in Laxitter's preemptive tactics. So was *Ilium*, elusive Helena Smitt, at last recognized as a classic from at least the novelist's version of Laxitter's past; she was the double, treble agent, the mole in defector's clothing. Beginning as Rockforth Freer's ostensible emissary, all the while supplying Laxitter with information about her boss's activities and opinions, she'd apparently been fired by Freer when drifting in the direction of sympathy with Emil Bieman's perilous jeremiads. In fact, she had never ceased to work for Orbis, and as I sat reading her history was still receiving a monthly payment, disguised as the payoff from a matured annuity policy; Orbis had a controlling interest in a major underwriter of insurance, and Laxitter a seat on its board.

At the time of the Senate investigation, armored in the virtue of her dismissal, *Ilium* emerged, ostentatiously surreptitious, and carried to selected members of the press a nervous tale about the Orbis coverup responsible for the termination of her career. One in particular, a celebrated investigative journalist in DC, disguised in the file, though hardly impenetrably, as *Shallow Throat*, who'd already printed one story on the Harness issue, a kind of general reconnaissance threatening more detailed exposures to come; *Ilium* fed him the DIRTYSPY access code to the Special Projects computer.

I'm not the observer to suggest a much-prized representative of the Fourth Estate would make (probably illegal) use of such a tip, nor that any muck-raker worth his dibble could ever fail to; all I know is what I found in the files, where Laxitter wrote, "*Shallow Throat* has swallowed the bait." The professional who did pry open the HARNESS file (no £) would find, as I did, convincing likeness of a confidential record, a few points that, published, would embarrass Orbis, though at the same time acquitting them of rumored things far worse — in sum, a handful of very small potatoes, in not enough dirt to make a respectable mud-pie. Reason enough, perhaps, to abandon the story, as *Shallow Throat* did, and fill in with the colonel-studded standby, Pentagon waste and mismanagement.

Nor was that considerable coup the end of *Ilium*'s services to Laxitter. With a recommendation, it appeared, from *Waterloo*, who, working as hard for his merit badges as messianic pit-bull ever has, was still determined to make an election issue out of collusion between Orbis and the Administration, she'd been taken into the Lomax campaign team, and at well above the envelope-licking level, near enough to inner counsels to be able to feed Frank Lupin advance notice of troubles to come. Her inside tip had created the urgent need for a Hardy position paper, and indirectly brought me to where I was now.

In giving the job to me instead of letting Frank Lupin do it himself, there was, after all, a logic, given Lupin's assessment of me (as concurred-in by Laxitter), an articulate idiot savant, a gullible in the land of giants, turning a neat phrase as a spider spins an elegant web, because I couldn't help it. My edge was my ignorance; knowing exactly as much as any invitational dirtyspy assisted by *Ilium* to break and enter, nothing more, *Alias* wouldn't inadvertently give secrets away, as Lupin or Worth might, by anticipating a question that couldn't be asked. Since my answers, as fed to Hardy, would be an exact match for information the enemy already possessed, they would have the same discouraging effect as if they represented what really happened — like historians working separately from the same circumscribed sources, convinced their necessarily identical conclusions must establish more than that both can read. "*Disinformation*," Laxitter had written to Lupin just a few days ago, recalling, I'll bet, a rubric from his glory days, "*gains credibility through adding generations, especially by word-of-mouth.*" And I had performed exactly as prescribed, taking pride in how my mind had opened to let in all that judicious garbage.

Framed by the window the grey was lightening, and I was simultaneously aware many hours had passed, and several cups of coffee hadn't. Judy was dozing, long-lashed, with *Fellowship of the Ring* spreadeagled to her body.

In the bathroom I had the not-uncommon auditory delusion that the phone and I had begun ringing at exactly the same moment. It's the resonance. I emerged, enormously relieved, and discovered the ringing and I had also ceased simultaneously, not in proof of the hallucination theory, but because Judy had roused just enough to sleepily pick up my phone. Having missed the opening salutation, which must have carried blurred languor enough to proclaim whatever horizontal things the caller wished to imagine, I was in time to hear Judy switch to genuinely pleased recognition, with a bright, "Oh, hi."

"Just helping out," she said. "I didn't realize it was so late. So early, I guess. Time flies when you're having fun. I hear you're leaving us — " the point at which I became certain who'd called.

Also end of the Feydeau dialogue, as a discussion followed about Westerlake, teaching, the relative merits of big city and small town. After not as long as it seemed, Judy said, yes, I was right here, and wished Paula good luck, hoping she'd see her again.

Dazed from my undernight journey through the reeking pits I was having difficulty realigning myself to a more habitual illusion, a world where goodwill might exist. Paula's opening was added confusion, darker half of her longfather genes coming uppermost: "I see you don't plan to be lonely," with some notion of ironic humor, but her voice was so steely, her throat so taut she was only a membranous inhibition away from one of those Celtic termagants who make you wonder if Erin took its name from the Furies.

"I've been working," hearing in her silence more and less than was comfortable, hurried away from my recent past to her immediate future. We discussed, if I remember, curtains and carpets, and how promptly she'd have a viable phone. When it came to when next I'd see her she remarked, carefully restricting it to a simple statement, that quite soon she'd be approaching a whole galaxy of tasks demanding hammer and heft, and settled I'd visit her in just a week's time. How I would face the coming week, swollen with unwanted knowledge and cheek by jowl with the criminals, was gnawing softly at me all the time, and our farewells, Paula's and mine, had the dismissible quality of an interruption, behind which and the disconnecting click a regretful emptiness came seeping in.

Judy said she'd make more coffee, but for that once she wasn't quite straightforward; there was the faintest theatricality in how, just about to vanish into the kitchen, she wheeled, tapped on the shoulder by a random fancy. If so, I understand her purpose, to transform into a crazy afterthought what might otherwise be too dangerously conceivable: "I hope Paula didn't think you and I were — *involved*."

Yet her candid eyes were careful to make a distinction important to my self-esteem; it was Paula's assumption that would be bizarre, not the idea itself. As I made sounds whose dismissiveness tried to take in, all at once, *of course not* and *who cares?* and *what can I do about it if she did?*, one of those sentimental surges in my bawd rate that may come with great fatigue flooded me with the wish Paula had been right. Here, I perceived, was genuine possibility of a state more often hoped than realized; Judy and I could go to bed as friends, and (more crucially) resume the vertical with friendship intact, neither marred, nor abraded into need.

Not making coffee, she'd come two steps back. "I never understood all that," meaning, I think, sexual exclusivity as yardstick of devotion. With what now I remember as excruciating coyness, I told her when we were finished she was more than welcome to sack out here.

"Oh, hey," Judy, without snapping her fingers, or responding to my offer. "I found a log."

She stooped to retrieve *Fellowship of the Ring* from where her sudden rousing at the phone-call had deposited it. Once reminded, I recalled the episode; it occurs when the Fellowship, diminished by Balrog-attrition to eight, is journeying by boat on the Great River, trailed by what Samwise first takes for a log, till he notices it's "a log with eyes."

"*Gollum.*" I knew it had to be the password for the LOG file.

To dial in again with that hope was a little like a burglar forcing yet another lock to steal back the incriminating evidence — a monogrammed hankie, perhaps — he left behind last time. When *Gollum* did work in jimmying the log, however, we found neither that nor any other entry using the *Gandalf* authorization was recorded, probably, Judy said, because Fena didn't want the log cluttered with the many meaningless occasions when she went in for a little quiet housekeeping, or refining of the program. Moderate rejoicing, but there was still lengthy access by *Sparkplug* to be explained, and it was chilling to see the entry, with my telephone number appended, noticeable at the most cursory glance as identical with the one above for the legitimate DIRTYSPY dial-in. Judy started to ask what was the worst that could happen to me, but seeing how earnest I was did some more ransacking, borrowing, as I understood, Fena's housekeeping paraphernalia, till she announced she could replace the phone-number with one of my choice. I'd heard Laxitter was in New York, so chose one with a Westchester County area code which he'd used several times in the past: I conjured a discreetly-lighted study, carpeted and panelled, Laxitter in a brocade smoking-jacket, armagnac at his elbow, smiling quietly as he imported a fresh batch of his venom into the file. By that time lightheaded fantasy was more gratifying than nightmare sense. What miserably plagued me, before suppressing it with a resumption of the really non-existent debate about Judy's sleeping-arrangements, was the care I'd invested in my glossy, ghastly booklet, *Century Without Hunger*, ardent preparation of the Hardy position-paper, the fact that before the weekend was out I had to return to that eager embracing of lethal fraud if I was going to give Lupin his update of the Chilean success-story, where I now knew that patient pilgrim, Gerhardt Fiori, to be a self-deceiving collaborator in deception. I thought, as one does, of quitting, telling them to keep their contaminated money, and was forced to astonished recognition I couldn't, not without arousing some question, which might lead to Fena asking Laxitter about his use, so near to my own, of the files, and from there to sufficient suspicion of what I knew that, unimportant as I was and unbelievable as it stubbornly tried to be, I might end up dead.

6

No recent poverty or present fear of penury accounted for my fixed idea of taking the bus home from the railhead, but only the carefully wasteless habits of a long-standing freelancer; the multiple advantages of a cab only occurred to me when, immediately outside the depot, a cheerful black driver offered his services. I gave him my home as ultimate destination, but said we would first "swing by" Hilde's address, letting him work out to his own satisfaction what that meant; I knew only I had to go there. Whether, with the place quite possibly being watched by a practised and efficient killer, I would dare run into the building and, if she was there, whisk Hilde away, was still to be demonstrated, and I wasn't unaware *Azraël* might already be inside; if I was still undetected as Hilde's ally, that would be over at the moment I came face to face with van Muer. I wondered for a block or two if I could make use of the Special Projects meeting in a fantastic bluff, convince him I was there as a personal courier from Laxitter, sent to say the plan had been scrubbed; my mind, obviously, was luxuriating into the surreal under stimulus of excessive conjecture; van Muer only came out *Azraël* if Hilde's acquaintance was Helena Smitt, and that was no more than a supportable theory — and still what wouldn't shrink to mere speculation was that unknown hand, the damaged left? picking up Hilde's phone, the intact right silently disconnecting, a figure standing impassive by the phone as it rang again, and rang.

Hilde's street had old trees, planes and silver maples, by night more deep, fat shadows than I was comfortable with. Her building, seen for my only time, was stone, picture-palace baroque set back from the street, with gingerbread-arched access to a small forecourt. As we halted in front I saw orange-yellow police tapes, down now but once across the entranceway, and their repeated message, CRIME SCENE, was echoed in a poster attached to a pillar of the archway, which had, handwritten, a telephone number for hearing tips, and the assurance all calls would be treated as confidential. I could see only one policeman, standing sentinel between archway and lighted entrance to the building itself, and deduced it must be some time since the advertised crime.

"You picking somebody up, or what?" my driver asked.

Would I get out? Though with a sour taste of sickness in my mouth I had no doubt what the crime was, I had a stupid urge to confirm my certainty, knowing nothing could be more dangerous than to be spotted here. I glanced back, and streetlights and shadows were a baffling complexity where whole nightmares could be.

"She said she'd be in front," I invented for the restless driver.

My hand was on the doorhandle when the policeman came forward; it may be that cars stopped in front of Crime Scenes made cops nervous, but I'd also read in the newspaper that telling waiting cabs to circle the block was our city's newest remedy for sclerotic residential streets. As he bent to speak to the driver I asked, "What happened here?"

Chestnut, moustached, world-weary at, tops, twenty-eight, he shrugged at me. "Woman got herself killed, I guess. Some old Polish lady, I guess. Guy broke in and was robbing her."

"What time?"

The inveterate guesser took a harder look at me, as if I might be garnering information for construction of an alibi. "I have a friend who lives here," knowing bitterly, though Hilde was neither Slavic nor aged, it should be *lived*.

"What floor's she on?"

"First." I had no idea where Hilde's apartment was, except it wasn't there; she'd once said she'd have a cat if only she lived at ground level.

The cop guessed the *incident* had been on two, as also
that my friend had been or would be questioned about whether
she'd seen or heard anything. He was unclear about the time
of the murder but the police had been summoned around three
this afternoon, he guessed.

Forty minutes before that a hand had picked up Hilde's
phone. "She said she'd take the bus if she didn't see me," I told
the driver, before question could emerge about my friend's
name, or exact location of her apartment.

After the long time it took me to put the key in my own
friendly door and turn it, I thrust the door fully open without
entering; I wasn't going to let sophistication embarrass me out
of precautions that happened to be hackneyed. Beyond the
threshold was utter dark, and I told myself firmly if there was
an enemy waiting in ambush, once past being silhouetted
against lighted doorway I'd have home field advantage,
knowing where all the obstructions were; I couldn't and can't
say how that would protect me against a lurker who had only
to turn on a light, and who could score in the nineties using a
bad Balkan imitation Beretta, which he'd no doubt left behind
in favor of the real thing.

Once I'd been in every room and found nothing
changed, once I'd made sure all windows were secure, my best
notion for a desirable course of action would have been to sit
on my bed and whimper, but I substituted the thought that
more than eight hours having elapsed since my last, not-very-
substantial food, the complex of elusive feelings in my
abdomen must logically include hunger. There was cheese in
the refrigerator, I had staling bread, and while considering
making coffee decided that this, if ever, was the occasion for a
large amount of scotch. Not much later I was panicked by
sour spasms, and, as I reached the necessary bathroom, by

seismic heavings far more prolonged and much higher on the Richter scale than was necessary for their basic function of starting all I'd ingested on its journey back into the ecosystem, cutting out the intestinal middleman. I'd say it felt like death, but one hopes that death, when it comes, will be kinder.

Face washed, mouth rerinsed, I entertained the shocking wish that I could have cold-shouldered my own cleverness and remained in assumed oblivion in Westerlake; in this there was some of that same process that keeps the twinge-warned from seeking competent medical care, the primitive idea evils not diagnosed need not exist. I turned away from that, and agreed my real need was to talk to someone. While running despondently through a short list of friends, I stunned on the television with my handy phaser, and was surprised by ten o'clock, and news on non-network channels.

Our city has an average of about sixteen homicides every week, with the rate peaking between Friday evening and the grey hours of Monday morning; if you include the entire catchment-area of our TV stations, saloon knivings and drug wars in the grimy eastern outliers, more complicated crime, passionate or calculating, to the suburban north and west, most weekends would offer the media choice of at least a dozen killings with which to sell beer, bras, and remedies for baldness. The majority, however, pass unmentioned, and there's no middle ground between complete exclusion and appearance in the lurid teaser slot, charged with the task of keeping the viewer aroused yet docile through the following three eternal minutes of commercials. For stardom, a middle-class mise-en-scène is necessary but not sufficient; a featured murder requires a prominent or attractive victim, elements of sex, greed, close families ties, or the other powerful factor that (added to a slow news day) won Hilde's murder the coveted leadoff position; recognition, the luxurious horror of *it might have been me*, a variety of that same delicious autophobism that sends high-school ogle-and-cleave epics into many

money-spinning sequels, but which, I can attest, loses all
delight when *I could be next* becomes a dry statement of fact.

Hilde's murder as reported, I should say; what jargon
calls target consumers might have found it hard to imagine
themselves targets of an experienced international killer, but
just as the cop outside her building had said, the official view
was Hilde had been unlucky enough to interrupt a burglar,
who had panicked and fled, but not before inflicting multiple
gunshot wounds, of which the first, as a tiny crumb of comfort
for me, was said to have been instantly fatal. I assumed
Azraël, having achieved his primary objective with the first
accurate shot to the forehead, had added subsequent wilder
tries the better to simulate an unskilled gunman who happened
to get lucky. There is, as you say, an irrational unpleasantness
in the picture of a man engaged in such a task, methodically
putting marginal wounds in a body already dead. Time of
death was put as early as two a.m., meaning there was nothing
I could have done to prevent it, nothing except recognizing at
once the possibility Hilde's chance-met old acquaintance might
be Helena Smitt, that African distributor van Muer could be
Azraël, and then finding a means to communicate a warning to
Hilde.

Who, then, had picked up the phone a full twelve hours
after the shooting, and why? The caretaker for the building
had won himself a half-minute niche in the pantheon of
inarticulate heroes at about two-thirty in the afternoon; Hilde's
bathroom sink had been stopped up by soaking hosiery, water
very slightly running, and when the tenant on the first floor
complained about seepage, the caretaker, after trying to get
Hilde on the phone, and "pounden an pounden" at her door,
had at last done what we never like to do unless we have to (a
strange mating of choice with necessity), and used his pass-

key. Well, right away he knew something had to be wrong,
the place was such a mess.

In fact, accounting for the police theory of panic and
flight after the shooting, the ransacking was less than
thorough, but some jewelry was thought to have been taken.
Documents, I suspected, had been more to the taste of this
burglar — but here began my perception of an Orbis team
separate from specialist van Muer, a second visit had evidently
occurred, twelve hours after the killing, to search, as Laxitter
would assuredly wish, for hard evidence Hilde might have
possessed, to account for her attempted overtures to the press.
While still unable to accept in my heart the Hilde who'd
advised me not to marry Paula was dead, I fretted over the
envelope I'd passed her on that occasion, the three abstracts
from Laxitter's confidential file. I didn't know what computer
hardware Hilde had possessed at home, whether she'd had
equipment approaching the capability to penetrate and capture
the files; my printer was a very common model, and the pages
could hardly be traceable to me, unless, and this wasn't
impossible, Laxitter had a friend at the FBI, who could lift
fingerprints from the paper, and match them to mine,
somewhere in their records. The number of times I'd been
fingerprinted was very small, and so far as I recalled had never
directly involved the Bureau, but I had a vague idea they
culled other federal, state and perhaps private collections to
add to their colossal files.

Other than that, which would take time, I couldn't think
of a trail leading from Hilde to me, but by far the best way of
finding out would be if I could have another look at Laxitter's
private musings, assuming he'd been keeping them up to date;
I had no idea where he was now, or where he'd been this past
week. For that I needed Judy.

Phone in hand, I came very near dialing her number,
the one piece of information which, if I was already suspect
enough for my phone to be tapped, I mustn't give away.
Putting a shirt on, I went up and rang her doorbell instead. I

dreaded having to finesse Judy away from intolerable Michael, in whose embraces, considering the hour, she might already be finding adequate gratification, and felt I'd had for one weekend more than enough demonstration that *fine women eat a crazy salad with their meat, by which the horn of plenty is undone* (Yeats is a gassoon my father comes very near pardoning for being born two-and-a-half centuries later than the end of poetry), but the door was opened after an interval by sweatshirted Vickie, the roommate, somewhat taller than very small Judy, with a tendency to a plumpness of face, in contrast with the lean body, but, added to her habitual smile and small, tentative voice, helping to create an impression of childlike inexperience. Not an accurate one, to judge by the tales of near-lurid adventure her roommate merrily recounted; that I should try my luck with Vickie had been playful and familiar advice of Judy's, vibrating, perhaps, with every kind of vicarious, voyeuristic, even bisexual resonance, but hardly real enough to make that much of; while Hilde's characterization of me as a collector might touch on truth, I've never been so for its own sake, an indiscriminate accumulator, bent on running up the most impressive total. That would have been chief reason for attempting Vickie, discounting the undeniable erotic nimbus that always surrounds the notion of *roommate*, like *twin sister*, an intriguing union of reassuringly familiar with the challenging new. I'm not saying Vickie was unattractive, or that we disliked each other. As a sometime dancer, sight of her splendid, entire legs was among the pleasures of summer.

Born in New Jersey, she spent what were for her speech some catastrophically formative years on the west coast, where, south of the 35th parallel, the declarative statement appears all-but extinct, replaced in social interchange by unanswerable queries, as the hearer is asked to approve what he has no knowledge of, every phrase ending on an interrogative inflexion, *'nkay?* Vickie ushered me in, asking for my approval of the proposition that Judy wasn't home, but should be soon. She'd driven Michael to the airport, 'nkay? I was also questioned about Santa Fe, and Michael's visit there. He owned some property in New Mexico, 'nkay? Or, like, family, 'nkay? Anyway, was it all right with me that he'd gone to raise some money in preparation for the next Latin American expedition?

Growing more intimate in her interrogation, Vickie enquired whether she hadn't been about ready to tell Judy she'd have to find another place to live; she didn't like Michael, and, "I don't appreciate, like, having my coffee in the morning, you know, with him prancing around here in his underwear, 'nkay? 'nkay?" The redoubling there looks odd written down, but was clear enough in speech; I in my turn was being asked to supply positive feedback for what Vickie had meaninglessly asked Judy to endorse.

In this one instance I actually was expected to comment on, oh, Michael's exhibitionism, his repulsiveness, the conflict between that and old friendship, but before I could Vickie trumped her own ace, with the bitter but still questioning assertion that she was still fond of Judy, and owed her perverse admiration for keeping her word; "Like, she promised him she would go on this trip with him, and she'll go, 'nkay? That's totally the way she is — " and then the big bang: "Of course, it would be different if somebody like you wanted to marry her." Astounding; very absence of habitual query made all the plainer that a genuine hypothesis was being mooted, one which would have been baffling in three or four different ways, if I'd had attention to spare for fresh puzzles. In the resultant uneasy silence Judy arrived, smiled, and with one swift look, asked me, "Hey, what's the matter?"

Because, Judy said, a new layer of security had been added since last week, it was well past midnight before I was able to open Laxitter's personal file, and know my guesses had been right, though he hadn't found time to bring his records

fully up to date, entering no more than skeletal indications of
where transcripts and documents were to go. Thus, last
Monday, when my worst fear was that my snooping would be
discovered, Laxitter was recording `*Phonecall, secureline,
Ilium: met* Rosetta. R. *wants meeting with* Pangloss: *Harness.
Find out what she has*.

Thirty-six hours later in a second conversation with
Ilium, Laxitter had obviously decided Hilde must have more
than hearsay to offer, and his next entry recorded a Telex,
encoded, to *Azraël* in Paramaribo. Of this I could understand
nothing except `*Lisbon Option, action now*,' which was surely
a signal left over from the old le Carré days. Subsequent
entries for Wednesday and Thursday noted `*instructions to
Azraël, Dall-FW*,' and `*v.M., Milw., Delta, Hertz*,' which gave
the route taken by van Muer, driving the final leg from
Wisconsin. There, Laxitter's entries ended, with a rhetorical
fragment, not reassuring for me: `Rosetta *alone, or... ?*'

Once again, Judy asked, "What's the matter?" and now,
since to recruit her without telling for what might unfairly
endanger her more than the information I'd so far withheld, I
had to give an outline, beginning, and oh, how stupidly
fictional it sounded, at the wrong end, the murder of Hilde to
protect a corporate secret.

"You're *k —* ," she said, start of a pure verbal reflex
she recognized as inappropriate in mid-utterance. The
incredulity, otherwise expressed, remained valid, but once
convinced I was serious her urging I should give this same tale
to the police, wasn't a new idea; I'd begun arguing it out in my
head well before finding confirmation for my miserable belief
van Muer was *Azraël*, beginning, it was now twelve hours ago,
when Hilde's phone was picked up but not answered. I'd
thought then about making an anonymous call, had no reason
to suppose the police would act on such vague inklings as I
could convey. Now that I had more to offer, my doubts, told
to Judy, had a different focus: knowing the influence Orbis in

general and Laxitter in particular could wield in this city, I was far from confident I could come forward with my story and live. An anonymous call, using a payphone to defeat caller identification, to say I was mailing evidence of Laxitter's part in the murder, would be automatically recorded, and I couldn't be sure the tape would never get into Laxitter's hands; I was aware his social circle included the commissioner and other chieftains of law enforcement, and suspected first result of an accusation naming him would be a discreet phone-call, just between friends; corruption at those orbital levels is more subtle and pervasive than overt bribery. Or if, as Judy's unendorsing gaze suggested, that was imagining too much, I still had no confidence in the ability of the police to keep my name out of the papers, nor, with *Azraël* in the game, to protect me once exposed. Perhaps only the famous Witness Protection Program, with a complete change of identity, a new life as a Welsh shepherd or Australian shearer could do that, but that was FBI, and I had yet more reason to suspect Laxitter's influence reached into those counsels.

Watching Judy's perplexed face as I worked through this tangle of fears, I was reminded of my own disbelief in Hilde's scorn when I told her she should go to "the authorities" with her suspicions. Not so much to concede her point as to avoid debate I'd made the alternative suggestion, go to the press, but now I knew both that officialdom was a minefield of Orbis influence far beyond Hilde's suspicions, and that any approach to the information-mongers required great care; of our city's two major newspapers, at the time of the Senate hearings, Laxitter had characterized one as `*a good friend*,' and the other as `*can be intimidated*.' With television, the bullying process had been openly demonstrated in a case quite apart from Harness: when a popular new magazine show, specializing in exposé, planned to do a piece last December impugning the safety of various appliances produced by Servelec (an ORBIS company), the parent corporation had advised the network president Orbis participation in all news

and sports programs (including co-sponsorship with the
network of PGA events) would have to be "rethought," unless
an opportunity was provided for a Servelec representative to
address the charges. This meant, in effect, following the
magazine piece with dazzling Dionne Theobald and a stooge
in a tan lab coat doing a five-minute free commercial for the
Servelec coffeemaker and microwave oven, with no
opportunity for cross-examination or rebuttal. All this was
revealed in the newspapers, mainly tucked away on pages
devoted to interviews with sitcom stars and What's Worth
Watching columns, and the consensus seemed to call it a
faintly disturbing but not indefensible, perhaps in some sense
admirable use of "corporate clout."

Even if I chose a newspaper not falling into either of
Laxitter's approving categories — the *St. Louis Post-Dispatch*,
for instance, or *New York Times* — it wasn't just a matter of
walking in the front door, like Robert Redford at the end of
that *Condor* thing. I ardently envied the stumbling fictional
innocents who find themselves caught up in unimaginable
machinations of vast international powers, governmental,
commercial, a sinister alliance between the two, envied how,
very often overnight, they became not only wondrously
resourceful, with hair-trigger reflexes, an intuitive grasp of
technology, and a handy new strain of ruthlessness, but also
mysteriously sophisticated, knowing, hip. All at once the
newborn babe knows the rules, and can negotiate, bluff,
recognize for certain a winning hand, and, better, be confident
his enemy does, too. With me, it was otherwise; I believed my
copy of the personal files, once made public, would be more
than enough to sink Harness-Stirrup, cripple Orbis, and foster
a whole clutch of criminal indictments against Laxitter and the
other principal plotters, and that the supporting testimony I
could offer would be redundant. In logic it followed there
would then be no advantage to killing me, but I wasn't nearly
so assured that could be made clear to *Azraël*, face to face. and

suspected I might be dead before I'd finished. Besides, where murder had so far been accomplished with impunity, and cost Orbis far less than a fifteen-second disposable razor spot on the Superbowl broadcast, why desist on the grounds it might not achieve anything? Every ad, every poster, glass, menu, awning, wall-plaque, every tee-shirt, billboard, neon sign, mirror and ashtray exhorting us in every language known to humankind to Drink, Trink, Bebe, Buvez the best-known of all sweet, fizzy, red-brown beverages, cost money, and somewhere among all of them must be several that had no additional effect whatever, but who in Atlanta knew which ones, or would attempt to save money trying to guess? With those folks, as with Orbis, success came from doing more of what you'd been doing, but what Orbis had been doing was killing people who threatened the profitability of radiation-enhanced agriculture, which itself promised so many deaths that to espouse it at all was incompatible with the possession of scruples. No, there wasn't any assured safety for me just across the threshold of talking to the press; what I would need before coming forward was a guarantee of protection, concealment if possible, and that meant putting out exactly the kind of feelers that had cost Hilde her life. The one person I would unhesitatingly trust was former-senator John Battaglia, but in that "former" was warning of his relative powerlessness, and in his camp dangerous Helena Smitt was still lurking — I recognized for the first time the reference to Troy in her code-name, *Ilium*, was a double one, to her name, yes, but also to the innocent-looking large wheeled toy the bored Trojans brought within their inviolate ramparts.

We continued desultorily to discuss options while we tidied up, capturing the newest Laxitter entries on Judy's mobile disk, before logging off so Judy could go back in as *Gandalf* and disguise my invasion as one of Laxitter's own; when she asked I couldn't say where he might be, but told her to use the last number he'd dialed in from. One definite decision was made; tomorrow I'd rent a car, both to let me

move around the city without making a display of myself at
bus-stops, and so I could drive back down to Westerlake and
reclaim my own car; I already had a vague notion of making a
dash for some other city carrying the evidence. After Judy
logged off again, we recopied the new material onto the sixth
of my floppies, which I didn't refile among my work. In the
clear light of actual danger I'd decided *The Purloined Letter*,
like Chesterton's tale about the verbally invisible murderer, is
a preposterous literary effect unconnected with plausibility; in
real life, just as that doorman would say, "nobody, that is,
except the postman," so anyone, however daft it seemed,
would look through that bloody letter-rack; how many times,
hunting errant keys, had I gone back over and again to the
pocket where they ought to be and obviously weren't? I took
the six £HARNESS disks, and hid them under towels in my
drawer.

While there in the bedroom I'd intended to have a
discreet sniff at the sheets on my bed to see whether they
might prove an embarrassment, but before I could Judy
followed me, and in a short time we were making love very
nicely. There wasn't noticeably any of that wartime, edge-of-
the-world intensity I'd read about so often, though I was never
unconscious of peril, and the simultaneous conflicting ideas
that I was blessed to be with a friend, and was self-indulgently
putting Judy into unnecessary danger. After a time we were
both very hungry, and I found some eggs to scramble, still
rebarbatively debating available courses of action, while I kept
constant vigilance for sounds of surrepetitious entry.

Necessary to caution Judy once again, but with
maximum earnestness, that from here on it would be much too
dangerous to associate with me, and there could be no reason
for her to telephone me or me her. Judy objected, "But I have
to know what's happening," and touched my face with her
fingertips.

Standing firm, though I knew this was going to condemn me to frightful solitude, I promised to push a note under her door when I'd decided on some course of action, and said she could do the same if there was news to tell me: we could set up a meeting, so long as we stayed off the phone, and didn't advertise a connection that brought her into the list of possible targets. I could imagine an innocent-seeming or official-seeming enemy going door-to-door on my floor, asking whether I had any particular friends in the building: in visiting her apartment earlier I'd used the heavy-doored stairs, invariably empty above the second floor, and it would be best if no one saw her get on or off the elevator at this floor, or could associate me with hers. This, then, a grey hour when encounters in hallways would be rare, was a good time for her to scuttle home, taking the mobile disk with her.

"You're trying to get rid of me," then, "Just kidding." Entendered by fatigue and companionship, the pleasing recollection of pleasure, by the hypothesis of shared danger, conspiratorial reality of shared secrets, agreement on the wisdom of her immediate departure led us back to bed to celebrate the ardor of our unanimity, and some time later to fall asleep.

My telephone rang. The start of waking and an immediate stab of guilt were quickly trumped; standing naked next to the bed I almost physically jumped, when Fena spoke. "Ames? Hope I didn't wake you." The time, I saw, was nine-eighteen; she herself hadn't been up long, her voice with the shallow-breathed, old-accordion quality of the heavy smoker who hasn't yet managed to induce the magma-lifting morning paroxysm. "I thought you would be in Westerlake. I called you there," she went on, in necessarily short phrases. "Had to get the number from information. Paula said you came back. Did you hear about Hilde?"

Everything now might be a trap, and the enemy had penetrated as deep as here, where Judy was waking with a grimace, in a childlike gesture putting the back of a bent wrist to one eye, squinting from the other. I hoped Paula hadn't given Fena a reason for my early return; let her think it another of the fallings-out all Special Projects could hardly have been unaware of when we were both working there. "It's terrible," I said. "I saw on the news, I couldn't believe it."

"Fucking *burglar*," Fena said, with unwise vehemence, and blocked her phone with a hand to mute the consequent coughing. When she came back it was to make some crude racist comments which I omit; they would have been unsupported conjecture if the official account of Hilde's murder had been factual, and in existing circumstances were superfluous poisoned icing on a very nasty cake. I couldn't tell how much Fena knew about the real story; with her ready access to any file it would be strange if she didn't know how Bieman had died, but the cryptic entries to do with Hilde's elimination were very recent, and it's possible at this time she was unaware the death connected with ruthless corporate concealment of truth about the Harness project. As was, we exchanged conventionalities about Hilde, on her side conceivably sincere, on mine, guarded, carefully no more than our slight contacts within the castle keep at Special Projects would warrant.

"The reason I wanted to be sure to get a hold of you, is, Laxitter called from L.A. He was real upset."

"I can imagine," I said, with nothing of my face in my voice. "They went back quite a few years, didn't they?"

"Vienna, yeah. So, this is it, he set up a memorial service at St. John's Episcopal, Monday, ten a.m., and he wanted me to be sure everybody knew about it. We won't open up at Special Projects till the afternoon, so maybe you'd like to be there."

"Thankyou," I said. Mature Hilde had no apparent religion; likely enough, she'd been baptized a Roman Catholic, but for business executives as for politicians Episcopal rites are roast beef in the possible range of spiritual menus, traditional, satisfying, giving no offence. In answer to my tentative query, Fena said Laxitter was planning on coming in for the memorial. We concluded with further noises accepted as indicating loss, Fena having several more calls yet to make, though she was not likely to create again such a surge of terror as she'd brought me.

Judy had a lidded, lingering languor, but I callously insisted on her full waking, to demand the location of the phone-number she'd inserted for Laxitter in place of mine last night.

"I don't know. Area code two-oh-two."

District of Columbia. "We have to go in and change it again. He was in Los Angeles." But when we at last got into the log again, there was among all the numbers Laxitter had used over two years not one with 213 prefix. On the point of making one up, I noticed a 714 number, and with phone book confirmed that was Orange County, near enough to count as L.A. for New York Fena. That small, maybe meaningless bit of tidying-up ought to have produced some satisfaction, and might have except that when we'd tried to dial in, the number had been busy, but no new use of the files had appeared in the log. That meant, as Judy said, either that we'd just happened to coincide with somebody dialing a wrong number, or, far more explicably, that immediately after talking with me, *Gandalf* had found a reason to look at the files — or at this same log. It might be, as Judy in charity to me suggested, that Fena had lost a phone number, and knew she could find it recorded in the log, but that could still mean she'd noticed the impossible D.C. area code for Laxitter's most recent entry; its replacement not only came too late, but would, when detected, inevitably remind Fena she'd mentioned Laxitter's whereabouts to me. Besides, to my eye, not far above that entry, the consecutive ones, my legitimate one for the pseudo-file, and the two-hour session fathered on *Sparkplug* burned like a

beacon: Fena had only to ask Laxitter whether he'd really been
sitting up late that night in Westchester, working with the files.

That lax, indecisive Sunday, lingering Judy repeatedly
upbraiding herself with the reminder Michael would call from
Santa Fe, me loth to insist she leave, was the last chance I
might have had to outrun a hunt not yet begun in earnest. If I'd
gone and rented a car, driven to one of the cities possessing a
newspaper of national repute not easily cowed by ORBIS clout,
delivered the evidence and found somewhere safe to await
developments, it's possible I would have won the game
outright. Only the opposition of competing fears kept me in
limbo: it was nothing like fact I was as much as suspected as
Hilde's accomplice, and then my notable non-appearance at the
memorial service could be the beginning of the process I was
running from. Contrariwise, there might already be a deputy
assigned to follow me; knowing little about work-patterns of
odd-job assassins, I thought it logical *Azraël* himself would
have left town in his rental car as soon as his assignment was
achieved, but a follower, unremarked by me, could put him in
position at my crawling back in a few hours. Or, if not that,
the last part of my program made me anxiously immobile;
there was no telling for how long I would have to stay out of
sight, when, if ever, I could return to work I knew, my books,
recordings, stranded car, the only life I'd had. I was afraid of
staying where I was, but the fears weren't yet enough to drive
me to others I knew not of. In general it must be hard to
recognize the peremptory moment when life itself takes
precedence over lifestyle and its possessions: earthquakes,
hurricanes, fires, floods of water or consuming lava would
claim fewer victims if the mind had an alarm-bell that went off
when that instant arrived, a time when well-loved hillside
home, hopelessly hemmed-in Jaguar, the precious box of
mementoes, even the undisputed Cézanne, must be abandoned
for the sake of preserving that consciousness within which

they earned existence. Wanting to hedge our bets was what made cowards of us all.

St. John's is, on the whole, a successful example of what you could call Downtown Late Gothic, cast concrete masquerading as massive fourteenth century limestone blocks, its situation, dwarfed by the effortless ascent of office space, providing an unintended sardonicism on the feeble upward grope of merely spiritual perpendicularity, compared to the heaven-plundering reach of commerce triumphant.

Considering Laxitter's connections and Lupin's restless opportunism, naive of me to be surprised at finding press both outside and in; three full-strength television crews, several newspaper reporters and an equal number of photographers waylaid the celebrants. Unerringly, they dismissed me at a half-glance as of no importance, but as they swarmed around Worth and a few minutes later around spectacled, chauffeured Laxitter in a dark English suit that, in the manner of a Bentley, asserted by reticence, I had a wild urge to become an instant star by loudly denouncing Orbis, screaming, if necessary, truth about the murder which had brought together all these collectors of followup and color. Was it so irrational? I could hardly be stopped, and while I had no evidence for immediate show, the promise of it would surely get some attention, and how could Laxitter hope to get away with having me silenced after such a public accusation? especially when the fortuitous death of Bieman in similar circumstances was remembered — but then it occurred to me a putative Presidential assassin had been shot dead in sight of millions, and for a quarter-century anyone who remarked the fact that death terminates speech was a certified idiot (my father said, strange mathematics, where one *plus* a thousand *equals* one was orthodoxy. while one and one is two was paranoia). Encouraged by such an example, a desperate Laxitter might believe if I were killed on my way home, and the evidence I was going there to retrieve was never found, the sequence, threat of exposure, death, death, denunciation, death, could still be palmed off as an unconnected series of events, in which only a conspiracy-hooked loony would perceive a pattern. From where I was teetering, that it might be a miscalculation on Laxitter's part was less than encouraging; I'd still be dead.

So, instead, I stood inside the vestibule, nodding to those I knew, taking note of those I didn't, and shortly found Fena Keller next to me. She'd been loitering outside, and might have decided the move would outwit her urge to smoke; her hand kept going to the clasp of the small black bag she carried. I'd almost failed to recognize her; it had never occurred to me to wonder what nationalities might lurk behind the drab, style-flouting tailored dresses and defiant jawline; Brooklyn on both sides had been enough ethnology for me. Now, *mamma* was in the ascendant; Fena was smaller and darker, with black patent pumps, dark stockings, a charcoal two-piece with a faint pinstripe, a black mantilla; to say she wasn't clutching a rosary is to be struck by its absence. I can't say whether she normally wore lipstick, which probably means she used a sparing spread of some unstartling shade, but today the mouth was a burning garnet hue, and she'd also put on some bruise-colored eye-shadow, not in any token of allure, but because she was going visiting. The little, Punch-faced priest in sunstilled Sicily to whom this devotional Fena would be instantly recognizable might think her overdressed for her slender chances of encountering God in a church whose origins went back to nothing more ancient or reputable than Enrico Otto, that Brittanic heresiarch.

Occasionally smiling and raising a hand, Fena pointed out the biggies, some from floors more accessible than our eleventh at the Javelin Building, others from the suburban ORBIS/Orbiscard HQ, which I'd visited back in spring so as to have lunch with larcenous Bill Fasstin in their genteel executive dining-room. She found a proprietary pride in the size of turnout for Hilde, the distance travelled by some of its components, reaching a climax upon entry of a large, big-headed, starkly bald man, thick-lipped and jowly.

"Makomaski. I dint know he was even back in the country." The man bowed slightly at Fena, a courtesy which impeded and brushed aside his small wife, a blonde china-doll left too long in the shop-window.

"You know who he is?" Fena questioned, or challenged.

"He wrapped up the Harness thing in Yugoslavia, didn't he, after Bieman was killed?" taking pride in controlling an impulse to smile. In the file I wasn't supposed to have read, Makomaski was given the code-name *Lightbulb*, which I'd thought was a reference to a well-worn Polish joke. Perhaps, but there was also an available *polish* joke in that incandescent globe of naked head, where a stamped circle showing wattage rating would not have appeared out of place.

Taken by Mark Worth to lunch with Fena, Dionne Theobald (flamboyant still in funereal togs), sniffling receptionist Jodi and one Perry Danton from ORBEX, who dolefully represented himself as Hilde's most intimate confidant, though I'd never heard him mentioned, I had little choice but to return with them to the Javelin Building, where it was well along in the afternoon before I was struck simultaneously by hot shame and a new chill of terror. I'd been congratulating myself on not giving away I knew Makomaski's code-name, but that must mean I shouldn't've known the real name, either: hard to keep separate in my mind what specific things were found in the pseudo-file, what in the truly secret records, but on application of a process too feverish to be called reflection I became sure Makomaski didn't appear at all in the only file I was authorized to see — not, I think, because there was any secret about his supervision of the shutdown at Jastrebarsko, but because the story-line was kept cleaner by making Bieman's death and the Sobieska-

Laxitter press-conference the end of the Yugoslav episode.
Mine was an irretrievable mistake, but thinking back I couldn't
believe Fena had been setting a trap when she asked if I knew
the name, nor that she could say infallibly what information
was in which file; it wasn't as if I'd blurted *Azraël*, or Dr.
Radic, or the diselection of John Battaglia, things she'd know
instantly were close-kept secrets. Inevitably, it would occur to
her, possibly at some time when she was checking the files for
something else, and that might happen tomorrow, next month,
a year from now. Survival suggested I act on the lowest
estimate, and checking out early, I went to do what I'd resolved
to and been kept from yesterday by my Elsinorean paralysis,
rented a car. With nowhere convenient to Westerlake for
turning it in, I made it an out-and-home rental; I'd have to
drive down, see to the remobilizing of my own car, drive back
to turn in the rental, then take the train back to collect my car,
but, remembering Fena's gleeful tracking of fugitive Bill
Fasstin, I had a vague notion such illogical, vehicle-switching
movements might make me the harder to trace. On the same
memory, and the chance a time might come when my credit
cards, after faithfully betraying my every step, would abruptly
become unusable, I'd already gone to the bank and withdrawn
a thousand dollars in cash. "You ought to buy traveller's
checks," the teller had chidingly advised, and that reminded
me I already had them, several thousand dollarsworth,
ceremonially issued to me when I'd done the brochure and
other pieces for the ORBISCARD free checks in spring; "Why
not?" Bill Fasstin had said. "They won't cost you a thing, so
long as you don't use them." Since they were negotiable with
little, out-of-the-way retailers of goods and services not
plugged in to the normal credit-card network, they had the
additional advantage of being virtually impossible to block
from use — the unforeseen disadvantage, it had been, from the
standpoint of ORBIS/Orbiscard, who'd belatedly recognized this
meant they could be offered only to Class A cardholders, those

with an irreproachable record of faithful payment and peaceful domicile within their limits of credit. For me, their possession gave a pleasant sensation of security, and that, if not a separate rule, should provide a general admonition for my conspirators' handbook: don't get smug on any subject, ever; all locks can be picked, all codes broken, insurance policies cancelled; every silver lining has its cloud.

Not having my key-card with me for the basement parking garage, I left the rented car in a favorite quiet spot, more than a fourteen-block drive but only a two-minute walk from my front entrance. I should note my one-way street ended in a T with a stop-sign two-thirds of a block east of the apartment building; the cross-street, one-way north, was lined on the opposite side with small shops and miscellaneous insurance offices, cinder-block clinics and pet hospitals (for example), behind which, in a shabby cutting where ailanthus and ragweed tangled with discarded baby-strollers, tires, beer-cans and bed-springs, ran a double railroad line, not officially abandoned but as far as I could tell and rust-dulled tracks confirmed, altogether disused. Of streets parallel with mine only about one in eight had been provided with a bridge across this obstacle, and on the farther side all others were short dead-ends behind a barrier of dilapidated cement wall crowned with chainlink fencing, more recently wreathed and overtopped with loops of razor-wire. Just a brief zag away from where my street debouched, however, murky access inconspicuous between dairy store and the prosthetics-shop, was a narrow iron-and-concrete footbridge across the railroad, a suspended tunnel, now the high girder sides had been roofed over with arching steel mesh, so that vandalistic juveniles couldn't pitch debris down onto non-existent trains. This, amid a thin copse of more ailanthus, the urban tree-of-hell, and scraggled privet, in summer, coarse grass wherein litter and dog deposits competed for available space, connected with the sidewalk of the brief, blind street, unfrequented except by its residents, where I often parked. During my formative years, such features as here described would have placed me in the heart of a slum, but cities are broken now with no one to fix them, and except for the wealthy all urbanites inhabit precarious islands in oceans of shabby.

Emerging on foot from my crossing of the tracks, veering right past the corner window where a stark monolith of pale-puce artificial leg stood permanently among unthinkable stainless-steel and rubber contraptions, I had to wait for traffic, which gave me time to observe that standing almost opposite my building entrance was a BMW, not black but midnight blue. If I hadn't been thinking today about my visit to ORBIS/Orbiscard I might not have noticed, but there in the ample suburban lot last spring I'd parked my car near a row of four or five identical dark blue BMW's, not marked with the ORBIS logo, not large enough to be chauffeur-driven limousines, but obviously part or all of a company fleet; when I asked, Bill Fasstin had told me they were available to executives on a closely-monitored basis, strictly for business, seldom overnight.

One step too many in the direction of my entrance, I retreated inside the launderette opposite the end of my street, less Dantean than some. I'd made occasional use of it beginning the summer before last, when the laundry-room in my building had begun to depress me, or because the large-capacity machines were better here, or for any reason you like, except my noticing it was frequented by a whole bevy of young nursing-students from the building next to mine. Had ensued some stimulating encounters at the frontiers of medicine, originating in diverting episodes while airy and forbidden things sported, dolphinlike, in the dryers. Last winter, Corey, a bearded and gamey man of fifty or so used to warm himself there till the owner came or the police were called; not a helpless drunk, though he made regular use of the warming effect of cheap fortified wines in flat bottles, he was

when waking amazingly articulate, not with the orotund,
habitually malapropic eloquence of the standard saloon oracle
or philosopher-bum, but with a quiet precision of language far
more impressive and, in view of his inexplicable insolvency,
sad. The owner-manager of the laundry asserted territoriality
by taping up hand-lettered instructions and warnings of all
kinds, and one cold morning Corey, holding me with his
glittering if redrimmed eye, said, "Education, according to our
folklore, is the golden key, but we don't really want it, do we?
This man can come and put me and all my learning out into
the street — " and he indicated the newest cardboard message,
taped to the window: *CHAGE MACHINE FOR CUTSOMER'S
CONVIENCE ONELY NO CHAGNE FOR TELEPHON OR
BUS'S.* The signmaker must have bought apostrophes in a job
lot; elsewhere one was exhorted not to "put to manny clothe's
in dryer's," or use the smaller machines for either "blankit's or
bedspred's." Till now I'd only ever used the money machine to
obtain licit chage for appeasing the alarming appetites of the
washers and dryers, but now I turned several dollar bills into
contraband chagne, while keeping an eye on my building.
Very shortly two men came from somewhere beyond, and got
into the car, which promptly drove off. I could recognize
neither of the faces.

　　Nothing was proven, either way; there must be
midnight blue BMW's in the world other than those used by
Orbis, but equally true the men I'd seen could have gone out of
my building across the garage stairhead into the back alley,
and cut back through to the street farther down so as not to be
seen leaving. Sense would say they hadn't come here to kill
me, not in a car so identifiable, but I remained unwilling to
trust that an enemy would observe the rules my logic adduced,
and I lingered for several eventless minutes before nerving
myself to start for the building.

　　Nothing was unusual about the lobby, though I'd never
noticed before how conveniently the square pillars on either
side of the elevator would conceal waylayers, nor had I ever

cringed when the elevator creaked to a stop, and blind, I had to
pull open the outer slab of brown-painted metal before sliding
back the diamond-barred cage-door. Again, when we labored
to a stop on my floor, I was reluctant to emerge, and jumped as
the outer door opened by itself. Ben Fielding, my next-
apartment neighbor, taking his small, white, ratlike dog for an
airing. He was in private security, and I wished I could avail
myself of one of the sullen blued revolvers he sometimes
carried with him in a tackle-box on his way to target-practice.
"Hi," he said, as I stepped out and held back the cage-door for
him. "I thought you was home."

That supposition, which must have a basis in noises
heard, made it all the more an act of naked courage to unlock
my own door. Once again, I threw the door inward, but this
time there was still light, and I saw immediately I'd had
visitors; never at my most singleminded when working to a
tight deadline had I ever left the floor so bestrewn with paper,
clothing, scattered books.

Unreasonably but thoroughly persuaded that whoever
had made this mess was no longer here, I came in closing the
door behind me, and the more I could see, the worse the
wreckage. Not vandalism, but a rapid and ruthless search had
been responsible, and in my work-area I saw despairingly the
computer had been wrecked, screen smashed, hard drive
removed, leaving a gaping slot. All the floppies had been
removed from my work-files; I wished the abstractors joy of
going through half a hundred boring jobs, though my personal
correspondence was there, too, and might entertain them more.
Going to my bedroom, I knew at once the hidden disks had
been found; all the drawers had been pulled out and emptied,
and when I scrambled through the heap of towels there were
no £HARNESS floppies there. Numbed, I went to the kitchen,
which was comparatively undevastated, and with Hilde
perhaps coming to mind, made myself tea, nothing exotic, a

house-brand tea-bag, from which, as always, I clipped the tag so the bag could be completely immersed and smartly stirred.

I had no idea how the visitors had entered, though the absence of signs at door or improbable windows strongly suggested people who carried great bunches of keys with them, or else an expert job of lock-picking. But this on the whole was crude stuff, not *Azraël*, unless *Azraël* masquerading as an amateur, as when he introduced deliberate untidiness into the murder of Bieman. That wouldn't hold up; he was a killer, not burglar, and there was no good reason for putting me on my guard — that was the salient thought in my head, and a sinister one, that whoever had come here hadn't minded letting me know I was suspected — well beyond suspected, already a known enemy. Surely too soon a reaction to my mistake this morning about Makomaski; was it that unwarned Paula, when Fena called her, had been too informative about my precipitate departure from Westerlake? or there might be a betrayal I couldn't know about, like being spotted at Papageno's deep in intrigue with Hilde. Whatever it was had caused Laxitter to act in haste that superseded all other considerations; further, the searchers appeared to have been fairly certain they would find what they were looking for. Then again, if they hadn't, and had satisfied themselves there was nothing to find, that would have meant I wasn't the danger they'd feared, hence I wouldn't know who to blame for the break-in, but lack of attempt to conceal the entry-and-ransack indicated I was seen as an urgent problem, but one which could be contained. Obviously impossible for them to know what they'd find was all the evidence I possessed; that was merely to confirm Laxitter's suspicions, and with that now accomplished the containment process had to be more comprehensive, more final; after providing me with such a clear warning, no matter how lightly they regarded my capabilities, they couldn't let much time elapse before finishing the job. With Hilde I'd concluded that search, using available, non-lethal resources, everyday Orbis thugs, had followed twelve hours after the contracted killing, but about Hilde, Laxitter had been certain; with me it looked as if the process was inverted; a quick check of the stolen disks, surely beginning with the ones I'd troubled to hide, would confirm how much I knew. Conceivably, a resummoned *Azraël* was already on his way.

It was that *sauve qui peut* time, now: incandescent porridge was rolling down the hillside, and it occurred to me, arguably I was still alive (so far) only because of the difficulties there'd be with two break-in murders within three days, employment at Orbis Special Projects a curious common factor between victims. Based on that need to avoid reduplication, unlikely I'd be killed (or my body left to be discovered) here, but if the greatest danger was waiting outside, that only meant I had to get clear away, not that I should sit and hope they'd grow tired of waiting; when that happened they wouldn't just leave. By acting now, also, there was a good chance *they* would consist only of Orbis staff people, more outwittable, as I hoped, than the deadly freelancer.

First I had to see Judy, and obtain fresh copies of the Laxitter files; if I was going into indefinite exile it shouldn't be entirely meaningless; nothing I did now could increase my long-term danger. With very little settled in my mind as to what and how long I was packing for, I stuffed clothes and some of my camping stuff into backpack and duffel-bag, and looked with a wistful bitterness at precious friends, some now scattered on the floor; original LP editions of the Beecham *Bohème*, the Solti *Götterdämmerung*, Furtwängler's Bayreuth Beethoven *Ninth*, some well-loved, well-thumbed if less irreplaceable books; I rammed a few paperbacks into margins of the duffel-bag, and wondered if there might not be a way quite soon to have an acquaintance unconnected with the Orbis business come here to secure the chiefest treasures.

Though my first sight of the wreck of my apartment
now felt like hours ago, and it must be days or weeks since I
was introduced to my rental car, the time was only a little after
five; Judy's work-day ended early, but I had no secure way of
finding whether she was at home before I went up there and
rang her bell. Slinging the pack over one shoulder and
hoisting the duffel, I moved for the door, and a surreptitious,
rhythmic shuffling sound difficult to locate stopped me dead.
It came again, and then there was silence, so I could hear
beneath my feet the clatter and screech of a contingent from
the two dozen or so small children who lived one floor down,
and went berserk in carefully-scheduled relays so as to
maintain a consistent frenzy. Cautiously rounding a corner, I
saw near the middle of the base of the door a narrow white
margin, downed bags, approached quietly, and stooped to pick
up the note: *What's new? This is killing me. I'll be home —
J., Monday, 5.15.*

Between two terrors, I was marginally more frightened
by the idea of what might lurk in or barge into confining
elevator than by the stairwell, eerily lighted in long slants from
a wall-bracket on each level. I crept up, always listening,
finding new and sinister interpretations for every unexplained
but hitherto dismissible sound: Judy's floor was the top, and
beyond there the stair made a last turn and completed the short
remaining climb to a barred door for the roof, placarded with a
warning, reminiscent in its threatened penalties of those dire
tags found on mattresses and upholstered furniture, the
substance being that the least approach, maybe too intense a
glance, would set off alarms, precipitate consequences beyond
foretelling. One night in the greasy heart of each unendurable
summer, some sweating resident was sure to attempt,
nevertheless, to attain open air beyond that door, and the
modest-sized building would resound with wails, hoots and
chimes suggesting a mass escape from some sadistic *Stalag*,
but at this time of year, no one was going to venture that high.
Not wanting to revisit my apartment, nor to have roommate

Vickie ask questions that would draw her into the circle of conspiracy, I deposited my baggage out of sight around the corner on that last flight of steps, before emerging to tap at Judy's door. Repellent how soon the simplest everyday acts had become heroic; how naked I felt in the familiar quiet hallway with its ivory walls, paint slobbered thickly on, its asphalt-tiled floor with black skid-scars of many movings, and yet how I cringed back when the peephole flickered, and the door jolted open.

Distressing, too, was the warmth of concern in Judy's brown eyes. "Thank God, I been going nuts." We hugged very tight and the simplicity of self-preservation was riskily cluttered with emotions, both distressing and gratifying, alike irrelevant and dangerous.

7

Judy's second use of, "Hey, that's ridiculous" made me realize I had no further desire, beyond necessary recovery of my stranded car, to visit Westerlake, and if I was going to have to endure exile from everything I knew, Paula wouldn't be the woman I'd miss. When she'd said the same, it was a complaint and an accusation, not so much of incongruity, as of my duplicity in dealing with her. With Judy, while it included a faint remonstrance against the possibility I was exaggerating the powers of my adversaries, the phrase was a sharing, a recognition of time out of joint and the unfairness that I'd been endowed with the lone risky chance of putting it right, not for the sake of truth and justice, but because it looked like the one way I could survive.

Specifically, the question was whether, if I called the police, there was the smallest chance of impressing them with the startling coincidence of break-ins, one including a homicide, separated by no more than sixty hours, at the apartments of two people who worked for the same small Orbis unit. The difficulty was I hadn't been murdered; the assenting, inattentive grunts of patrolmen over the dishevelled scene of another two-bit robbery, the patient, head-tilted hearing of the connective theory, the soothing promise I'd be hearing in a day or two from the Something Crime Unit, but in the meantime, once again, could I give them a list of what was missing? *VICTIM ASKED FOR POLICE PROTECTION* was an indignant, futile headline I'd seen before, and that was what Lupin would call best-case scenario; there were far more sinister possibilities involving either impersonation of officers, or outright police collusion with Orbis.

Like Hilde's first allusion to CIA, this sounded to me like part of a not-very-plausible suspense novel, and when I began listing facts to justify my fears, my own stubborn skepticism was as much at issue as any I might detect in Judy's unwavering gaze: factual, I said, Orbis effectively owned a large number of legislators and civil officials, they had unquestioned influence with law enforcement agencies both local and national, even international, and their resources were practically limitless. If I succeeded in eluding them here, they could add to their own hunting pack the whole of outraged society, by accusing me of some such crime as Bill Fasstin's, for which needed proof could easily be faked.

"But if you were arrested, you'd have your evidence to show why they were out to get you."

"The first thing," I said. "Is that Orbis — Laxitter — would be informed, and that means *Azraël* is going to know exactly where I am."

"How would they dare do anything? It would be completely obvious it had to be Orbis."

"Obvious. I'm sure they'd *prefer* to get rid of me in some way that would pass unnoticed as an accident, or, like with Hilde, random crime, but if they're desperate enough, if it's the only way to save the Harness-Stirrup thing, they'll take a chance on obvious, and then work out what comes next. Quite possibly they could get the police or the FBI to turn my file copies over to them as stolen property — or that would be the cover story, if Laxitter has strings he can pull."

Here was where Judy said for perhaps the third time it was ridiculous, meaning now, horrible and unthinkable that innocent I should be handcuffed to this sinisterly ticking valise.

"What are you going to *do*? There has to be somebody on your side."

Oh, true: if we could hold an informed plebiscite those on my side would be an overwhelming majority, but that would also have been so for Emil Bieman; the real point was not approval but power, resources to checkmate the ruthless few and, as before, the only possible answer seemed to be the

press. In the past I'd been dutifully impassioned about the
importance of a free press, less so when front pages were al
bismotered with the matings of those one would least like to
see reproduce themselves, or when wispy threads of
unsupported allegation were twisted and knotted into a
lyncher's noose; now I recognized with peculiarly poignant
force that an independent press really was our last hope. In a
land or world where, so vast were the profits from poisoning,
whether the toxins were poked in our veins, puffed into the air
we breathed or dribbled into soil and water, the poisoners
could easily outbid the public for faithful service, corruption
became the norm, and for most of our designated guardians the
risk of getting caught became the nearest functional approach
to integrity. The sole restraint on the rule of bullydom, then,
was the bullies' anomalous need to appear virtuous; a recurring
theme in Laxitter's files; there was no limit to the laws that
could be bent, lawgivers who could be squared or cowed, so
long as the truth didn't come out, and you could go on
convincing most people whatever had to be done was done for
the greater good, for law and order and general prosperity, full
employment and affordable stuff. Where opinions were made,
not born, the only force to be feared was the press in one of its
convulsions of outrage.

     Very properly, Judy's eyebrows rose, and I hastened to
correct the impression I was taking the press at its own self-
caressing evaluation; effects didn't sanctify motives, and if
fame, Pulitzers and three-book contracts were to be won by
concealing injustice and adulating destructive greed, that's
what journalists would do. Just for money, in effect what
practically all of them did do, every day, except for those rare
times when the bandwagon of righteousness was rolling, and
they didn't want to be left standing on the street.

     "Like sucking mud in a desert," I said. "It may be your
only hope of staying alive, but you wouldn't do it if you had
the choice." Dangerous now to as much as imagine a world
which ran with fresh streams of pure virtue. My task and my

hope were to convince a newspaper outside the Orbis orbit I could produce and substantiate the exposé of the decade, complete with at least two murders, countless briberies, and conspiracy at all levels of government and industry, not to mention the truth all skullduggery had been designed to conceal, the terrible hazards of radiation-enhanced agriculture — and all this while preserving my complete anonymity. "If I can get away from here, I'll drive to St. Louis." It had to be kept in mind that Hilde's supposed connection with the *Post-Dispatch*, the comings and goings of their Bill Elderbush, were altogether fictional, but St. Louis remained by far the closest city where I was certain, on evidence of the Presidential non-debate, that the major newspaper wasn't under the Orbis thumb.

   I'd had an idea of trying to quit the building unobserved at perhaps three A.M. Judy made more sense, pointing out that if there were watchers, the worst possible time to make my move was at an hour so still the stealthy movements of a small grey cat would be conspicuous. She normally set out for her school at eight-thirty, but on occasions when she had some rotating duty that required her to be earlier, she would leave the building at between eight-ten and eight-fifteen, when, she said, activity was at maximum, residents going to the basement for their cars, others making for the bus stop; a secretarial type (whose name, Lynn, I could supply) regularly picked up in front by her apparent and evidently adultery-minded boss, and a lady librarian who waited by the entrance for the cab she'd summoned; in all this there was some chance of confusion or distraction.
   Vickie wasn't expected till late, and if I was to be spending the night it became a good idea to retrieve my baggage from the stairhead, which I accomplished in a quick raid, Judy standing inside an apartment door pulled to, so I could slip back in. Everything was quiet, and seeing the

warnings about the alarm again I speculated that setting off those chimes and howls at the moment of my departure might provide a further diversion; more than guessable those who had rifled my apartment had looked over the building thoroughly, and taken note of the access to the roof; ours was virtually contiguous with neighboring buildings of equal height, and the flat rooftops would occur to any fleer as a possible escape. Outraged Judy wanted to know how unauthorized people could go walking around a vauntedly secure building, and I reminded her, for example, of the mysterious threshold appearances of self-anointed experts on the afterlife with their alarmist leaflets; no one would ever challenge the wanderings of an intruder reassuringly dressed, as in suit and tie, or, better still, clean uniform overalls with a neat logo on the pocket.

"Yah," Judy said, possibly in recognition my loquacity was a kind of numb verbal fidgeting, not product of deep thought, but a defense against it. "So what can I do?"

Quite a lot, so it appeared. We copied a new set of floppies from the mobile disk, and then, thinking about how I might have to negotiate with a journalist from, quite literally, Missouri, I spent more than an hour choosing some of the more revelatory passages for a composite disk which I could turn over as a sample for examination. Though she no longer qualified as an innocent, much of this first-hand material was new to Judy, and our work on what I named *Laxitter's Greatest Hits* was accompanied by her wordless but eloquent noises of abhorrence; when we'd finished she summed up her feelings in an unexpected phrase: "I wish I wasn't going away." Michael would be back from Santa Fe midweek, and they'd set out for southern lands about a week from then; Judy expected to be gone for several months, maybe up to a year.

"That's great."

"I'm glad somebody thinks so." She didn't sound glad. "Everybody else says I must be crazy."

"So do I," was my hasty amendment, not wanting to appear to be breaking ranks in the anti-Michael front. "The good part is you'll be safer away from here. There's a chance sooner or later they'll find out about you working with me."

"How?"

"Paula," after some thought. "I can't call and tell her not to mention your name, not without giving her much too much information. I don't want to use your name on the phone to anybody."

"The bad part — " she put a hand flat against my chest. "Is, I won't know what's happening with you."

"You'll know as much as you could if you were still here. If I can get a newspaper to run with the story, there'll be indictments right away. Once the evidence gets to a grand jury, I'll be as safe as I can ever be."

"If not?"

I made the *que peut-on dire?* mouth (Eisenhower receiving news of MacArthur's dismissal by Truman). "I won't be able to see anybody I know, or write, or phone, or be anywhere they could expect me to be. I have to stay alive till there's somebody who'll listen to me. It may take a new Administration." After the pause, Vice-President Hardy's edge in the polls had resumed its shrinkage: there was no indication of a great surge of support going to Orford Lomax, for whom *reasonably adequate* was about the limit of enthusiasm, but I had an idea a Lomax who chose John Battaglia for his Secretary of the Interior might provide a healthier climate for my revelations.

A final time, Judy said it was ridiculous, and this time (not to crack the wind o' the poor phrase) meant somewhere between exasperating and tragic. While we were holding on to each other in a fierce, hopeless assertion of transcending reality Vickie arrived. Possibly she believed me to be acting on her lumbering but bizarre hint about asking Judy to marry me; aside from enquiring whether there was yoghurt in the refrigerator, and allowing, in reply to Judy's question, that her newest and reportedly richest boyfriend was "Nothing to not write home about," she vanished as soon as possible into her own end of the apartment, but not without the unconsciously chilling remark that somebody must be having, like, a party or something; there were unusual numbers of Vickie-eyeing guys hanging around the entrance and, like, in parked cars, 'nkay?

Very decidedly, not 'nkay, but Vickie's bedroom possessed the only window from which we could have seen for ourselves activity on the street; kitchen, living-room and Judy's quarters alike faced a dim slot of courtyard clasped between north and south wings of the building.

It would be exultant as well as consoling to report that a large part of remaining night kept apprehension on a tiny bead of flame, while Judy and I reasserted or surpassed the very high standard for lovemaking we had already established. Constantly in fiction nice chaps beset with every kind of anxiety and proximate danger take time out to give unperturbed and lavish satisfaction to chance-met partners, and while envying their dauntlessness, I can't help thinking they'd be failures as mates in any sense aside from the starkly physical; what alertness to mood, whim or genuine emotional crisis could a woman expect from such dullards whom no cannon stuns? I'm not trying to invert indifferent performance into a paradoxical boast, but at least my difficulty in setting aside worry and the visceral churn of speculation kept me within the circle of humanity. Comforting, still, to be in touch with a friend, and that Judy hadn't the temperamental inclination to complain contributed, in the end, to her having not much reason to.

Before six, after brief, not-very-useful dozing, I got up and showered, and Judy came padding to find me in the kitchen, sorry for myself over instant coffee. Yet when she asked what else she could do, I was ready. Recollecting how Fena had bragged about dogging fugitive Bill Fasstin's

electronic footprints, I asked Judy whether she could access
those same credit-card records.

"A computer guy I know can tell me how. But you
can't delete from that file." She grinned. "He was very
disappointed, but then he realized it wouldn't make any
difference if you could — it's just a register, they don't bill
from that. You'd have to get into individual credit-card
companies' records, and they have much better security than
the State Department, even."

"I don't want to delete. Can you add to the file?"

"That's what it's designed for. It ought to be easy. Oh,
wow, I see what you want."

Saw, and was entranced by the idea: appearance in the
records of charges for plane-tickets, car-rentals, hotel rooms,
all in my name, and apparently occurring in widely-separated
parts of the country and the world, would make real me so
much harder to track: we amused ourselves inventing exotic
but not implausible itineraries for these phantom Arthur
Ameses, but because I was sure there'd be ways of identifying
the source of such faked entries if they kept appearing I made
Judy promise to end the operation after a few days.

The momentary exhilaration of creating adventures
ebbed away. We leaned at each other across the indestructible
surface of the metal-and-composition kitchen table, muttering
desultory phrases in bleak tones. Judy said I should take the
mobile disk, which was built for rough handling, instead of my
floppies, which, with the exception of the highlights disk,
she'd keep. She wondered whether I could use the back
elevator with immediate access to its own alleyway entrance,
and to the basement garage, but I reminded her that roomy
one, built for freight, was kept jealously locked by the building
caretaker, ostensibly for security reasons but more germanely
because he expected to collect bribes from all movers, whether
in or out.

Judy, cocking her head, reported on the basis of sounds I hadn't heard that Vickie was awake. "I'll take her some coffee," she said, having made a large bubbleful of the real stuff.

I heard not words but voices, Vickie's high and enquiring over what should be grateful surprise, Judy's soothing. In a moment she came back. "I hope she doesn't expect that all the time. There's starting to be people out, so I can't tell whether the building's being watched, but there's a black car, I think it's a Mercedes, on the other side of the street up the block a way. It's just barely moving, creeping along."

"If they haven't been back to my apartment, they may not know whether they're watching for me to leave, or waiting for me to come home." My ears were all at once aware the building had wakened; distant and muffled there were the relentless hammering voices of an all-news radio station, high grinding whine of a blender — no, too long, a hair-dryer — someone asserting sovereignty by blowing his nose with a boastful honk, approximately E-natural.

Time wound on, Vickie took possession of the bathroom, I gathered myself for departure. Judy wanted to know how she'd know I made it, meaning my escape from the immediate noose. "I'll be working in the language lab this morning," she pleaded. "I can give you the number — it's a direct line, you could call me there."

"Once," I relented. "I'll call you if I can at eleven; don't say my name, and don't ask where I am. It'll just be a quick call. We hope they don't know you exist, so far, but if they do, I can't say what kind of surveillance they can manage. It's bound to take them some time to set up, no matter what."

"This — " she began, and her telephone rang.

A classic, a hackneyed moment, a stab of fear, tense eye-contact, momentary paralysis, but such conventions-come-true are characterized, defined, by absolute failure of ironic distancing; all vicarious fictional experience fails to provide a protective callus against terrifying reality.

"I better answer it," Judy said, asked me to endorse, as it rang again.

"Yeah?" Her greeting was tentative, then what? resigned; "Oh, hi. Where you calling from?"

Michael, nothing more (or less) sinister, providing me with the perfect opportunity to evade the awkwardness that had been piling its thunderheads over our parting. Shrugging up my pack, I leaned to kiss Judy softly and silently on the temple, murmured at her one available ear, "Thanks for everything," and stooped for the duffel bag, but she thrust up a traffic-cop hand to halt me.

"Listen, I can't talk now, I'm soaking wet," she misinformed Michael. "I just got out of the shower." A pause for his mandatory bit of lascivious badinage, to which, one supposes, some days of very probable celibacy gave a keener edge, and Judy said, while opening her eyes wide at me, "Not really. Yeah, okay. You at the same number? Yeah, okay, about ten minutes. Okay."

Having thus disposed of Michael in less time than it took my heartbeat to return to near-normal after the ring of the phone, she faced me earnestly. "Is this it? When will I see you again?"

"If I knew that — "
"If you can think of anything I can do — "
"Thankyou," I said.
"You take care of yourself."
"You too."

Vickie, limp-haired, swaddled in terrycloth, emerged with an interrogative proclamation about failure of hot water at some crucial moment, recognized she was intruding on another one, and withdrew, muttering about rinsing her hair.

Still possible to avoid perorations unfavorably comparing the importance of our problems with (for example) that of a leguminous knoll in this asymmetrical world; after

my quick peek to see nothing noteworthy in the hallway our
parting adjourned to the elevator door, where the indicator
showed the elevator reaching *B*, and, after a long pause,
torpidly beginning its ascent. Watching, listening, thoroughly
scared and equally miserable, I can't recall a one of the short,
forced things that were said, but do remember one I prevented
Judy from saying; there was nothing we didn't know, and
nothing but pain and annoyance in speaking it.

The elevator thumped to a halt, and before the door
was open there was a peremptory buzz from below,
presumably an impatient commuter. I dumped my baggage in
the corner of the car, and Judy held the door open, ignoring
and frustrating more irascible would-be summonings, both
prolonged and staccato. I made quickly for the stair, but
continued beyond it to the hostage back elevator. As I'd said,
its prisonlike gate was securely padlocked, but sidling my
hand between iron bars I could reach the brass plunger beside
the true doors, and pressing it heard a massive jolt into life,
and ponderous winding of the machinery over my head. Down
on the ground floor, a rococo bronze pointer like a sweep
second-hand for Big Ben was inching around a grimy sunburst
half-dial: I had no means of knowing how many watchers
might be deployed here, but any tactic that spread them out to
cover various possibilities was worth trying.

Briefly in earshot of angry buzzings from would-be
users of the front elevator, I opened the stairwell door, raced
up to the top, unlatched a large gate-hook, put my hand square
in the middle of the last of the deadly warnings, and shoved
open the door to the roof. The explosion of noise was
instantaneous, like achieving a score of 10^{24} or so in a pinball
game the size of Luxembourg. On detached analysis, only
three major dinmaking elements, a whooping siren, a shrill
bell, and a hoarse, beating gong, but the mechanism of the last
added a peculiar whirring thwack to the ensemble, some of
which was electronically amplified, and the curious acoustical
bifurcation between what was lofted into open sky and what

funneled down into the caverns below gave it all an unreal, hysterical quality sufficient to displace intellectual processes altogether. I went leaping down stairs, turned the corner, pulled open the door, and regained the elevator, where all-but continuous buzzings augmented the cacophony. Judy, grimacing, stepped outside, we mouthed goodbyes and kissed. As I allowed the lozenged grille to close, her face was forlorn, but then, bless her, by sheer force of will, she smiled with heroic normality, and raised a hand in merely amiable farewell, released the big brown slab, and, if she followed my fiercest instructions, scurried straight back inside her apartment and locked the door.

Except, perhaps, for the dash for freedom of some lettuce-fed snail determined to cheat its garlic-butter destiny, there can have been no slower-mo attempt at escape than mine in that senile elevator. Since I had pressed all the buttons, we paused on every floor, including the second where, not surprisingly, no one was waiting, but before that the normally sedate descent had been slowed further by need for discussion about the meaning of the alarm, which went wailing on, as it would for two full minutes, resuming after a fifteen-second pause for breath if no one had secured the door by then. Tension between curiosity and impatience was extreme; the rider who, on four, had hesitated, one foot in the elevator, wondering whether he should "stick around in case there's some kinda trouble," became instantly indignant when a client on three did much the same. I knew all the passengers at least by sight, and retired into the blind corner with my bags, doing nothing to discourage debate, merely shrugging and making a long-suffering face as if to demand what in anyone's experience of life would lead to better expectations? When the fifteen-second pause came like an avalanche of silence, secretarial Lynn, all groom and gloss, said most likely just kids fooling around, and diminutive, pleasant library lady was worried only that her cab would depart without her.

We'd reached *G*, and the door was thrust back to reveal, to my partial view, an empty lobby. The crowded box disgorged, except for two with cars to claim, who stayed, savagely pumping at the *B* button; occasionally the elevator expressed an aversion for the lower depths by turning itself around without going there. After the strangled, undulating whimper of a frustrated vampire, the alarm-system began a new two-minute cycle full force, here somewhat damped by distance and masonry. Mr. Leland from the third floor, who worked for the city, tried, eyebrows bristling, to organize an expedition in search of the caretaker, to find out what in God's name was going *on*, but was his own sole recruit. All the more officiously he marched off on his mission.

I attached myself to Lynn with a loud question about progress of the foreign film course she'd just enrolled in when last we'd spoken.

"Oh... " with a fluttering wave of coral-tipped fingers, dismissing it all as a girlish fancy, whole weeks in her past. With her patron probably waiting in his car outside, I knew she wished she could flick me away as readily as *La grande illusion*; nothing is so gloweringly possessive as a balding, married journeyman concerning the sleek, state-of-the-art RV he imagines, however inaccurately, to be his, but I had my own agenda. Not likely any of the presumed besiegers knew me by sight; my baggage would tend to draw attention to me, but not being alone might introduce at least a momentary element of doubt. Not till I'd ushered Lynn through the vestibule and followed close behind into the street did I recognize how stark and graphic my anticipations had been; stomach contracted like an emptied air-bladder, body cringed in fear, almost expectation, of a simple rifle-bullet or burst of automatic fire.

Lynn's ride was aging right outside, and after unlatching the door, because there was traffic he hummocked over into the far seat so as to let her drive. Even at such a time

I didn't fail to enjoy the long flash of slender, dark-nyloned leg, and then glimpsed rightward on the far side of the street Judy's black Mercedes, stopped or barely moving, with two men indistinct in the front seat. Just then, a cab, obstructed to its left, slid past and swung to the curb immediately in front of the Mercedes, giving a beep to attract library-lady.

I made briskly for the corner, hearing a tire-squawk-and-honk exchange with another car as the Mercedes tried to back up and pull out into the stream. The corner building, an older brick apartment block, came straight down to the sidewalk, so that reaching there, a tight turn to the left took me instantly out of sight of my almost-certain follower. Safety lay in the opposite direction, but I took a dozen steps northward, and didn't like a distant assessment of two men who emerged suddenly at the far end of the block and came slowly toward me, parting so as to have the width of sidewalk between them. The one on the outside was holding a hand up near his ear, and I deduced though couldn't discern some sort of miniaturized walkie-talkie. Meanwhile, the Mercedes, making the most perfunctory gesture at the stop-sign, ran through the intersection, and, as it had to, turned left, to an outraged hoot from the closest oncoming car in a parade of rush-hour traffic. I observed with my chin tucked to a hunched right shoulder that a northbound truck halted in the middle lane obliged the Mercedes to take the far right one and as soon as the truck masked me, I wheeled, and sprinted back, crossing my own street directly in front of library-lady's taxi. A new chorus of protesting horns meant the Mercedes had now dared to halt, obstructing the traffic it had so brusquely invaded, but that only helped me, as I darted recklessly between almost-stopped cars and into the narrow way between the window with grisly sentinel leg and the dairy-shop where there was a special on half-gallons of a fluid queerly called `Homo Milk.' At the run on the little footbridge, confident of a long lead, I distinguished the thudding of a car-door amid the squall of horns, and knew I was all right, so long as my rented car was still there, and so long as it started; I'd had the keys in my hand from the moment I sortied from my building.

Maintaining the same level of daring invention as allowed me to induce the shadowing car to make its fatal turn — if its occupants had followed me on foot they would have been hard to lose — I might have thrown my baggage in the back seat and crouched down out of sight inside the car: they were too many seconds behind to see where I'd gone, and could scarcely examine each of the parked cars, even if it occurred to them to do so. At the time, however, I could think only of instant distance; I jabbed key in the ignition and wrenched the wheel over, seeing in my rear-view I'd given two thwarted pursuers on foot a chance to note make and color if perhaps not license-number of the car I was driving.

There was, however, not the slightest risk they could get on my tail right away; in the direction their car was committed to, closest crossing of the railroad tracks was seven blocks to the northward. I turned south at the first corner, then west as soon as I could, and must have not less than a fifteen-block head-start; traffic was considerable but in this direction moving steadily. It was still in my mind I'd drive to Westerlake to switch to my own car, and as soon as possible I picked up the interstate where it ran northward through suburbs. The city was falling away into wider spaces before I began to question my course; dismal to think of my car languishing on Paula's street, eventually to be towed into captivity, perhaps never to be reclaimed, but as I had to keep reminding myself, these really were life and death choices; there were very few guesses the Orbis people could make about where I might head for, and Westerlake was one of them; my object was not to give them sporting chances but to vanish as completely as could be. The first westward exit, therefore, I abandoned the interstate, and when I came to another set of options took a southerly course on a road where traffic was light and I had the comfortable feeling of being unobserved, near-invisible. Somewhere a more modern band of concrete must have taken over long-distance function of this shielded old US route, largely three-lane asphalt, with double divider line dancing from share to share, double solid, solid and broken, broken and solid, the regular progression of speed-limits, down to 45 as farmland under deep-blue autumn sky was interrupted by camping supplies, carpet outlets, a sudden shopping mall, to 35 where a fourth lane appeared, and Rotarians or Kiwanis or both had erected but failed to maintain their insignia and the turn-of-the-century white frame houses were untouched on wide lawns with twisted apple-trees, lilacs, a browned horse-chestnut for shade, a sugar-maple still with some rare roast-beef foliage. A downslope, a curve, and 25 where structures shuffled together, old houses with ugly, durable new pseudo-fieldstone or pseudo-lapstrake siding, middle-aged houses built in datedly modern arcs and planes, younger ones meticulously archaicized, then Lincoln or Washington or State Street, drugstore, shoestore, coffeeshop, fashionless ladies' fashions, a dozen parking-meters, battered red Dodge pickup waiting to make its left turn under the single gibbeted flashing yellow, and so through the mirror into sequence reversed, 35, right lane tapering to oblivion, 45, and out again into the land of Do Not Pass, Pass With Care, Do Not Pass, the occasional flattened squirrel or prairie dog waiting for the animator to zing it back to instant three-dimensioned, adversary-tormenting life.

Coming, just before eleven, to a somewhat more extensive clumping, which could boast a full set of three-position traffic lights, people who came in at least two denominations, steepled stone and square-belfried wood, a furniture emporium occupying the shell of a still-identifiable movie-house, whose winking yellow bulbs would never again simulate a flow of motion around upright oval sign, I stopped at the handiest of three gas stations, and while I was being filled, dipped and wiped, made use of the phone to call the number Judy had given me. She picked up at once, and had become impossibly distant; I felt distressingly like one of those fantasy-tales where the protagonist, meddling where Man was never meant to, is mysteriously, no, *incontinently,* wefted into another dimension, where as through deep water he can still see and hear those he loves, but attempts in vain to touch them... I gave Judy bare, unspecific information which she said was good, with brittle conventionality wished her a good trip, and at the last put in, "I'll miss you." Instantly, like one who's been waiting for the right cue, she said, but lightly, "Love ya." Amusingly (perhaps) we ended in a long, indecisive silence, neither of us wanting to be the one who broke the fragile filament.

The blue-eyed youth who accepted my non-ORBIS credit-card told me with his prairie twang I could get to St. Louis in "three, three-and-a-half hours." Adjusting for the fact that Indianapolis was scarcely more flat distance eastward, and in these parts visions of Memorial Day champagne danced in most such blunt heads, that meant perhaps five.

As forecast, I found the interstate not far from Springfield, and the surge down the long, mitered tributary slotted me into traffic with almost an audible click, like the seatbelt snapping together at the start of a transatlantic or transcontinental flight, and with the same message; whether characterless highway or crammed plane, efficiency strips away experience, converting travel into mere time to be served out, so that barring accidents routes become tentacles of destination, and to begin, except for intervening boredom, is to be there.

With that thought I began wondering how wise it was to go to St. Louis at all; wasn't it as absurd as Westerlake? I'd broken the cordon around my dwelling, effectively vanished; why now go to the one place Hilde had mentioned to the treacherous *Ilium*? What forces Orbis could muster, was an unknown, but if my theory was right and I was now wanted on just such a charge as had allowed the corporation to mobilize distant Scotland Yard against Bill Fasstin, then it might be the police or FBI in St. Louis were already specially alerted, and whether because of collusion or simple ineptitude, I had no confidence in the ability of either to protect me, once having helpfully let Orbis know where I was.

Steadily, every four seconds shortened the tentacle by the length of a football-field. From the first I had intended to make a preparatory phone-call before seeking out headquarters of the *Post-Dispatch*; now I wondered whether, if I found a motel somewhere in the environs of the city, I could induce Bill Elderbush to come to me there; possible, I thought, if I could attain the right conspiratorial tone — odd how the question phrased itself in those terms, as if the chance of not being believed disputed reality; dead Bieman, dead Hilde, hunted Ames were real, *Azraël* was, and Laxitter's shocking files: it was for Elderbush to rise to the occasion, not me.

With half the interstate distance traversed, I'd found it necessary to stop at one of the drear appended oases for coffee and some safe eggs, and half an hour after resuming became aware the same car, a BMW, which had been just after me on the re-entry ramp, was still in that position, varying between about six and ten carlengths behind. From time to time we'd been separated by other vehicles, but when an intervening car tired of my slightly sub-limit pace and hauled out to pass, or when a van found its exit and vanished, the BMW was still there, with its sole visible occupant. He looked like a fairly young man, and was singularly addicted to talking while driving using what must be a cellular phone; whether he made many calls or kept up one long conversation I of course couldn't tell. His car was a silvery color, otherwise identical to the small fleet of BMW's at ORBIS/Orbiscard — but also to hundreds or thousands of others.

When next I came up to a slow-moving truck, I pulled out and passed, but this time instead of sinking back to low fifties I remained experimentally in the middle lane at perhaps 58. For moments it seemed I'd proved nothing except the state of my own nerves, but then the scattering of traffic in my mirror resorted itself, criss-cross, the silver-grey car emerged and steadied behind. Though space between us had stretched to a dozen car-lengths, after more than five minutes at the new speed it grew no greater, and when at last I faded back into the right lane, letting my speed droop into the forties, the BMW declined to overtake, but crept up to where I could see it had Michigan license-plates, perhaps, I thought, from Kalamazoo, near where Fulcrum Inc. (an ORBIS corporation) has its headquarters. St. Louis was ideally situated for the Orbis empire to call on security forces from every point of the compass; it might be the western approaches were being watched by men from Kansorb, the breakfast cereal and petfood outfit in Topeka; from northwest might come a detachment out of Des Moines, home of Orbistran Aerospace, while the south could be covered by a contingent up from Fletcher-Orbis-Pinelands, the wood and paper products giant based near Little Rock — and we mustn't forget ORB, the pharmaceuticals company in St. Louis itself.

Reason told me while Laxitter must have an elite corps of thugs, secrecy if nothing else would limit its numbers; most security forces must be quite ordinary employees with, albeit pragmatically, a general adherence to lawful or only undetectably criminal processes, not people who could be issued with automatic weapons and sent out to do violence; no matter what crimes I was supposed to have committed against ORBIS and the order of things, there was no imminent likelihood the BMW would overhaul me, rum-runner style, windows down and tommy-guns blazing. Yet every turn of my wheels took me nearer danger, if, as I supposed, the driver was in communication with reinforcements, murder waiting at the center.

In my modest rental I had no chance of outrunning the
BMW, not on this flat and featureless highway; I longed for
the serpentine ways of tire-torturing movie chases, where
miscalculation sent villains over the edge and headlong down
scrubby slopes, mysteriously, but promptly and very properly,
bursting into flame. With the nearest mountain a day's drive
away, what was needed, I reasoned, was somewhere with
crowds of cars to bewilder pursuit, and just at that moment a
sign whipping over my head had bare time to inform me of an
impending opportunity for the Tri-State Mall. Speeding up, I
took that exit without signalling, and going rather too fast, but
my follower's reactions were alert enough to keep him behind;
on the sweeping circle of the ramp I looked across to see he
was back with the cellular phone; shirtsleeves, tie, very short
hair, his style was clean-cut timeless, as acceptable for a
supporter in the Presidential campaign of one of the late Mr.
Hoovers as applying for a job with the other, or peddling junk
bonds in the Reagan decade. *Keith*, probably. He kept his
profile firmly pointed at me, as if to glance in my direction
would acknowledge more than he was willing to.

From the interstate crossover, a dreary little stump of
divided highway led to the broad acres of the mall. There may
have been suburbs somewhere beyond, but this cozily specific
routing proclaimed spectacular political boondogglery. For all
that, the place was disappointingly unbusy, with cars huddling
for comfort close to the central barns, leaving great swathes of
empty color-coded lot; Section Blue was left in fallow
altogether.

Speeded-up projection, Keystone-style, was required to
excise absurdity from our sedate chase, slowed to a jogtrot
pace after I turned into the mall's main entrance, following a
remarkably preserved classic station-wagon, and followed at a
decorous interval by the BMW. As we approached the heart
of the mall, and I swung in between parked rows like one in
search of a convenient space, Keith, recognizing how easy it

would be to get entangled with arriving or leaving cars,
declined to be drawn into that arrow-obeying warp, but stayed
on the perimeter, woof, woof, passing slowly in front of the
line of stores, and giving every sign of continuing to hem the
border for as long as necessary. Caution was Keith's style; at
office parties the innuendo he wafted at maidens of the typing-
pool would always leave open the slight, wide-eyed possibility
of misinterpreted innocence.

Reminded by his renewed telephoning it couldn't be
very long before he had reinforcement, I wondered what he'd
do if I were to park, and emerge from my car. Follow on foot,
I hoped, a chance for me to give him the slip and double back.
Just then a woman with the satiated face of a fulfilled spender
slid out of her parking-space just ahead of me, and I rolled up
and backed in, not yet turning off my engine, sitting to watch
Keith. I believe he momentarily lost sight of me, and when he
had me again also found a vantage-point under a stanchion
supporting a cluster of lights, from where he couldn't fail to
see if I started to leave. He was right on the boundary between
Section Red and Section Green, not far from the end of the
row where I was stopped.

Turning off my engine, getting out, and locking up, I
made for the nearest store. I'd decided Keith couldn't be high
enough in Orbis counsels to have authority either to break into
or try to disable my car, nor yet to attempt apprehending me;
such forces might well be on their way, but his brief went only
as far as keeping me in sight. Reaching the sidewalk by the
stores, noticing a mailbox, I remembered to post the check for
my November rent, and saw Keith was out of his car, but
leaning against it, using his telephone with increased
animation.

I wandered into a store, one of those energy-wasters
open across practically the entire front, less spendthrift on a
day like this, moderately warm with no need for either heating
or cooling. An odd mixture of camping and gardening
supplies, barbecue equipment, sports goods and a small

selection of what's called leisure wear, jackets, sweatsuits and humorously-priced gym shoes; I circled a pyramidal island of rakes, stacked boxes of grass-seed and coiled garden hose, and could still glimpse Keith. He hadn't moved, but was no longer trying to perceive where I'd gone; instead with the singleminded intensity of a cat at a mousehole he was watching the row where I'd parked. Obviously his instructions were not to lose sight of my car, and I wished I'd brought my baggage with me; these malls, I knew, always had some sort of bus service, and against strong arguments in favor of abandoning an identified and identifying car there was only the one drawback, a rental bill mounting to the ruinous, but which, if I ever had to pay, I'd pass on to whatever newspaper published my story.

The silly realism of this analysis abruptly made me very angry with Orbis, and specifically with its nearest available manifestation, dutiful Keith. I was standing next to a pseudo-barrel, heaped with what were described on a printed sign as "Imported Hunting Knives," toy weapons in simulated leather scabbards, mass-produced in Hong Kong or Taiwan, and priced well within range of a child's modest allowance; edge on the stamped five-inch blade was merely notional, but point and hardness were adequate to inflict a fatal wound on an exasperating playmate. I bought one, superfluously informing the indifferent cashgirl I thought it would help my small nephew work through his psychotic episodes, then passed through the store to where the other end opened on a midway, with an ineffectually dribbling fountain and some alarming bronze replicas of formless scrap. Following arrowed signs I made my way to Section Red of the parking plain, and across the tops of cars could catch sight of patient Keith indomitably monitoring the wrong direction. As I threaded to where I could come up from directly behind, he was apparently struck by the thought, or perhaps prompted by phone, that I might make a headlong dash back to my car, flout the arrowed indirections, and obtain a clear lead while he was still getting started; he got back into the BMW, and I was now close enough to hear the engine throb into life. Happily, he didn't move, sitting slouched to one side, telephone clamped to his ear, and I altered my approach so as to avoid any chance of being glimpsed in his rearview mirror.

With desperate wrenching I'd ripped the diaphanous but tough stapled plastic bag away from my purchase. Dumping wrapper and papery scabbard in a trash can, I came up on the BMW from left rear, and with a quick, punching motion drove the knife into that tire, surprised by the ease with which it buried itself to the flange of the hilt. Ducking away still undetected, I smiled at a puzzled-looking male shopper seeking his car, craned my neck, and grossly overacted brow-smiting recognition that I'd come to the wrong section.

By a circling route I returned to my car, noting nothing appeared to have happened to the sentinel BMW, confident the knife wouldn't remain stopping up the hole it had made. As I slid from my slot, turned, and came down to the perimeter drive, swinging perhaps ten yards in front of him, we were nearer face-to-face, Keith and I, than ever before. I raised a solemn hand in grim greeting, but he was busier than ever with phone, and his bland face registered no acknowledgement. His right shoulder dropped as he put the car in gear, and then I was trundling toward the stores, watching for him to arrive in my mirror. Came an indecipherable scraping clunk, perhaps a complex interaction involving knife-hilt, the ground, and then underside of the car, and next, the dreaded lolloping noise of a wheel-rim jouncing on an emptied rubber sac; after making my turn I looked back to the satisfactory sight of halted, bewildered Keith opening his wrong-side door, tilting over to not see the damage.

I never discovered the origin of the name, Tri-State Mall. Not many miles away Illinois glowered at Missouri across the unimagined width of the Mississippi, but there was no guessing what third state the mall had in mind. A light rain was beginning as I left it for the remainder of my life.

8

Though it might be an eternal joke for the immortal gods, it was not the farcical aspect of my duel with Keith which was uppermost in my mind as I ignored the interstate and took once again to minor ways. Analytically, his encounter with me was probably pure chance; I couldn't believe Orbis had set up their cordon as far from St. Louis as we'd met; perhaps he'd been on his way to join the defenders when he alertly picked me up. Or, more discouragingly, they were able to patrol major routes anywhere I was likely to be. That they had the resources for it wasn't really the issue, but their willingness to use them, an obvious risk which increased with the numbers involved: if I was being characterized as an embezzler or thief, expenditure, in the attempt to apprehend me, of far more than I could ever have stolen might cause even the loyalest and least questioning Keith to wonder what his corporate masters were up to.

Eventually. In general, while Keith can be good for a laugh, he's no joke; without his neutral acquiescence there can be no extension of individual power, no greed beyond the capacity of a few robbing the few, whereas with Keith to call on there can be conquerors and despots as well as city-builders and givers of law; he takes pride in making himself a useful tool, and has all the moral discrimination of a hammer, adapted with equal equanimity to the hand of a master-craftsman or sot on a murderous rampage. Unlike a hammer, however, he loves approval, and is devoid of any wider field of vision; in this he's like a dog, happy when his master is pleased with him, a friend to gratify the ego, but implacable as an enemy. Orbis could call on whole hunting-packs of Keiths, all over the country and the world.

If a list were compiled for worst-placed motels in America, Happy Haven would surely be in the top ten. I found the establishment in late afternoon, brooding in dingy obscurity on what might well be Mr. Frost's Road Not Taken, and my arrival was greeted with an enthusiasm under which lurked visible astonishment.

The owner-manager was a frayed cougher of indeterminate age, originally from rural Alabama, who divided all time into two eras, the current one, and a lost golden age, when equipment now defunct worked, repainting was accomplished, multiple-unit parties inexplicably checked in at Happy Haven, and there had been plans for an attached restaurant, all "when my good lady was still here." Then, I silently ventured, he wouldn't have been seen daily in the same checked shirt with collar beginning to detach in a hairy fringe of fatigued threads, nor the few brochures on a side-table in the office permitted to mature under a mantle of fawn dust.

He never reminisced about the military, but used an ancient olive-drab bakelite Zippo to light his cigarettes, which he then smoked as if surreptitiously, keeping the burning end pointed back inside a cupped hand. His name was Ned Bates, but he liked to restrict the first name to an initial, *N. Bates*, with a flirtatious glance to see whether you got it, repeated when, opening up and displaying my windowed box of a room, he laid ponderous stress on: "and here's the *shower*." Possibly he hoped he was establishing a wry reputation which would make his motel into a mandatory stop for tourists, but so far they'd failed to flock. He was also trying to negate his unfortunate location with a tactic his late espousèd saint would surely never have sanctioned, an appeal to the concupiscent; his roadside sign, which suffered from deciduous lettering, offered both DULT M VIES and Fantasy Settings. Of the latter there were two, and Ned allowed me a glimpse of the *Romeo and Juliet* room, aptly named, since it struck me as an admirable venue for suicide by poison; the only fantasy it

brought to my mind was Poe's *Masque of the Red Death*,
although in fact there was no true red used in the garish decor,
only raw pink for accessories, ferocious magenta and an
overripe burgundy, the colors in the wallpaper, and
respectively of linen and quilted satin spread on the vast bed,
beside which there was a coin-slot for making it tremble with
passion. That bed, as also the framed mirrors on the wall and
a dried-blood bedside rug, were all what's called heart-shaped,
but I've long maintained our symbol for affection bears no
resemblance to the form of that organ, and more nearly
imitates upturned buttocks, here emphasized by a couple of
taut, pink pillows in the same shape, perched lewdly at the
head of the bed. "The gals love it," Ned alleged. "And the
guys love it because it turns the gals on." Racking my brains, I
could conjure no woman of my acquaintance for whom this
decor, or let's say, this ambiance, to include the faint overall
linger of pine solvent, might be irresistibly aphrodisiac — oh,
Jodi, the Special Projects receptionist, perhaps; I'd seen her
poring over paperback books dealing with cleavage-baring
escapades of Felicity, Tiffany or Hope among Regency rake-
hells, Barbary pirates and Yankee traders (all frilly-shirted, by
the way) — but had to allow I'd love to be here with Judy, so
we could laugh ourselves silly over the depiction, luminous
paint on black velvet, of a very androgynous Montagu
embracing a torpedo-breasted, wasp-waisted Capulet, right
next to the condom-dispensing machine (*For Prevention of
Blood-Feuds Only?*), or the discreet text on the wall behind a
bathroom-fixture: THIS IS A BIDET. IF YOU DON'T KNOW WHAT
IT'S FOR, PLEASE ASK. — it would be fun trying to guess what
creative misuse of the device had led to posting of that notice.
On the grounds of an ever-nearing deadline, I turned aside
Ned's offer of a look at the flatulent-sounding *Gone With the
Wind* room next door ("Tara-ra-boom-de-ay," I muttered
inaudibly), to which, candidly, my dears, I was utterly
indifferent; privilege of this viewing was accorded me when
I'd gone to the office to tell Ned I was staying another night, at

which time I'd felt quaintly obliged to offer an excuse for my presence where so few ever ventured. I was working, I'd said, on the outline for a book, and wished to remove myself from all distractions so as to get it done. Noting I hadn't brought a typewriter, Ned offered me the use of his office one. A generous gesture, but I had nothing to type, and if I had, my fingers, pampered by computers, would have limped painfully trying to depress the girder-mounted keys of the massive black pre-electric Smith-Corona he showed me, on which (I could remember) *Shift* was like levering a car out of a ditch. Declining with thanks, I invented a faithful typist, skilled at interpreting my longhand scrawl, alertly waiting for my return.

Happy Haven was farther south in Illinois than most, with windswept shores of Lake Michigan in mind, can envisage the state going; I was more southerly than Louisville or Lexington, about the latitude of Richmond, Virginia — for comparison's sake, of the Gulf of Tunis, of ancient Carthage. These cartographic musings mirror my living paraphrase of Baudelaire; how large the world had glowed when with Judy I childishly plotted the globe-trottings of hypothetical Arthur K. Ameses, and to the real fugitive, how constricted it became. As I brooded in my vinyl quarters, books and a couple of yellow pads from the duffelbag laid out on the chenille bedspread to reinforce my cover story, one phantom me, having just about made the connecting flight to Los Angeles, was touching down in Honolulu, and would mysteriously check in at the best hotel in Hilo, while another was waiting in Atlanta, and would take a plane to Boston tonight; he might or might not be the same who tomorrow would fly New York to Stockholm, while the one who rented a car in Tampa would apparently drive across the gulf to Brownsville, and last be heard of in a Tampico hotel, at the same time as yet another electronic Ames materialized in Saskatoon and rented a Beechcraft (I'd made Judy laugh with my imitation of Fena: `*The bastard never mentioned he could pilot a fucking* plane.').

All these adventures, as I'd made Judy promise, would be over in five days, but after the bad luck of being spotted by Keith, I hadn't much hope of creating confusion; the only one who might still be plausible was the Arthur Ames who, all invisible, terminated rental of the car I was driving where it began, and kept never more than a couple of hundred miles from home, using suburban hotels, renting everything from Lincolns to Cicadas, and making mysterious purchases around town.

Though they might not for my adversaries, the farthest-flung and most fanciful excursions, no matter what their illogicalities, created for me an insistent reality; just to think of a pseudo-Arthur in some remote place was in some mimetic sense to be there. Wistfulness was part of it, as if distance could bring back my safe, familiar life, although I knew very well the international vastness of ORBIS made Tokyo or Berlin no safer for me than New York or Seattle; in a place where I wasn't perfect in the language I'd only be more conspicuous, and that was yet truer for momentarily tempting spots whose farawayness is unmodified by time and the thunder of jumbo-jets; Palau, for example, or Sikkim, where the arrival for an indefinite stay of a lone American would be widespread gossip in a day; up-country, up-river, there were no more Maugham or Conrad corners to be lost in; in the heart of darkness (as Keats very nearly said) there is light.

Of course I couldn't seek refuge with, and thus endanger, my sister in San Francisco; briefly more tempting, my parents' place of retirement, Virgin Gorda, was equally off-limits, although my father, if asked, might relish the chance for some excitement; he regularly threatened to abandon my mother in what he called Virgin Limbo ("It's like St. Helena, minus the social life"), and go where something might *happen*, if only an occasional vagary of weather. But the enemy would know about those places, and be on watch; whatever I did next had to be unpredictable.

Notably, but at the time unobtrusively, my mind had
moved away from the necessary partnership between safety
and whistle-blowing; the Keith episode had made survival my
overriding concern. In this I recognized my own unworthiness
measured not only against literature but the standard
established by Hilde, who, unlike me, could have kept herself
safe by silence. True, she had personal motives, but when first
trying to make an ally of me, she'd said, *they must be stopped*,
not *Laxitter must be punished*. Now Hilde's death had time to
be more than a warning for me, I could recognize how much
I'd liked her, in circumstances which it's gross understatement
to call unpromising. Ardently, I wanted justice to fall on
Azraël and his bland paymaster; coolly, I riposted that it
wouldn't bring that objective an inch nearer for me to do
something suicidal.

Briefly, the moral wind blew from a new quarter,
bringing a moment of heated righteousness when I almost
made up my mind it was an absolute imperative for humanity
to be saved from the evils of radiation-enhanced agriculture,
which I alone could do. Again, this was chilled by an ignoble
desire to go on living, an almost petulant rejection of
martyrdom in a cause where so many whose job it was had
failed; why should I risk giving up existence where a cabinet-
level functionary wouldn't forgo marginal enhancement of his
already-affluent lifestyle for the sake of a few hundred
thousand painful, unnecessary deaths?

All was clear now; St. Louis had been the right plan in
the wrong city; Bill Elderbush must still be covering the
Orford Lomax campaign, and that would reach its end just the
other side of an extruded weekend from now, with the
election-night vigil at the governor's home in his state capital,
a long day's drive to the northwest of where I was havering.
Staying away from major roads I could find another obscure
motel somewhere on the outskirts, and on Monday, election

eve, discover where Elderbush was staying — if necessary,
call the *Post-Dispatch* in St. Louis and convince them it was
absolutely vital; if they wouldn't tell me his whereabouts, they
could hardly refuse to call him and give him my number. At
the last, if that failed, I'd be where I could try to reach John
Battaglia, without tipping off the lurking *Ilium*, as to whose
covert activities Battaglia should, however belatedly, be
alerted. Before all else, I had to change cars; if a millstone can
be an identity-tag, my present rental was both around my neck.

What I was going to do, and in what sequence, finished
working itself out in my head at about the time the motel's
main light out at roadside, having beckoned virtually in vain to
either traveller or fantasist, switched itself off, leaving only a
couple of forty-watt bulbs to keep vigil over the Happy Haven
sign with a block-cursive orange glow of *VACANCY*, preceded
by the faint, spidery ghost of *NO*, trembling in eternal and
eternally mortified anticipation. Eleven-thirty, and with clarity
came a surge of decisiveness; there was no reason not to start
at once; I'd paid Bates in advance, using ORBIS/Orbiscard
traveller's checks. Swiftly, not to allow fresh doubts a
gestatory moment, I restuffed my duffel, blessing my foresight
in having used the cramped laundry-nook today, and before
one A.M. had crossed the Mississippi, and was soon alone on
roads profoundly dark, sweeping like a rumor through god-
fearing towns where nothing stirred, a police-cruiser quiescent
next to an all-night diner, a white church with a blinding
dazzle of illumination for the message, *CHRIST LOVES THE
SINNER*, and looming from the ensuing blacker darkness, a
less fortunate stag scrapped beside the road.

By the sweeping assessment of the geographer I was on
the southern Great Plains, and there seemed an unwarranted
excess of topography; I wound through what to my obscured
view was very like wooded mountains, where cornerwise signs
with reflective macaroni arrows recommended drastic
reductions in speed; nevertheless, as sky and the splash of my

headlights began to pale I saw I would achieve my goal. The car I was driving had been rented from one of the big national chains, and without going through the risky process of turning it in, I wanted to leave it at another of their branches, so as to avoid the steadily-mounting charges that would result from simply abandoning it at roadside to be found, towed and recovered at some indefinable time. Shadowed as I was by death, this preoccupation with financial matters might appear in retrospect grotesquely bourgeois, but it may be I found an obscure relief in human-sized anxieties to distract me from worse ones I could do little to change — or perhaps I was comforted, if not quite to assert, then to assume a future where unpaid bills and my credit-rating would be exactly what I had to worry about.

At any event, in a moderate-scale metropolis still largely slumbering I found a branch of the right agency, left the car in their lot next to the office, pushed contract and keys through mail-slot, and humping off with my baggage found a breakfast-place evidently catering to those rural folk who already had a half-day's hard labor in by the time they hit town at seven or so; at a table with a clean and actual cloth, I worked my way doggedly through *No. 3*: juice, eggs, sausage, a pancake which completely hid a dinner-plate, toast, cornbread, strawberry jam, a crock of butter like a cardiologist's nightmare, and coffee from a thick cup kept constantly brimming by a waitress so maternal at twenty or so I was glad there were no greens for her to embarrass me into finishing.

Sticky, tautly overstimulated, replete, I found a bus that went in the direction of the not-very-distant northwest outskirts. Some years ago, I'd discovered that motels in such airport-encircling suburbs all had business-cards from independent local agencies, who offered a wide choice of cars at very competitive rates. Just such a rental (irrespective of rate) I wanted now, believing the charge would take longer to show up on the national register, and verification of make, model and color of the car would be far more difficult; it might require my pursuers to come here and visit the agency. Though they might postulate Lomax campaign headquarters as one of my possible goals, not all the Orbis clout could put up roadblocks around the state capital; impossible for them to check out every car with a lone male occupant; all I needed was a headstart long enough to find another obscure haven with a telephone.

No difficulty in knowing when I'd reached the right neighborhood; I got off the bus right outside the *Enola Gay Bar & Grill*, over which drooped a tattered and faded windsock, and found it was next door to the *Lucky Lindy* motel, a compromise, I suspected on meeting the proprietor with his steely eyes, cropped hair and stubbornly labiodental *w*'s, with the desire to call his establishment the *Hermann Goering*. He was, however, especially considering I showed no signs of turning him a profit, *Gemütlichkeit* itself, giving me the name of a nearby rental agency, insisting they'd come over and pick me up, allowing me to use his desk-phone, offering me coffee (declined, my blood-caffeine level being already well over the wriggle limit) while I waited.

An important narrative element may be a that Jason Oates, the puffy young man who did the renting, had a manner ever more common in the tedious world of commerce, performing necessary preliminaries like one on automatic pilot, while his attention, if it existed, was elsewhere entirely; he preferred to let me fill in the name and address spaces on the form, and recited the terms, together with the usual offer of outlandishly-priced collision-insurance, with as much meaning and conviction as if they were the Pledge of Allegiance or the Lord's Prayer; if instead of my (non-ORBIS) credit-card, I'd handed him a graham-cracker, I swear he would have tried inserting it in the imprinting device.

Feeling newly invulnerable in a car different in make, size, color and state of origin to the one my hunters could identify, I made a cheerful stop at the small airport, as serious about looking so far as possible like O'Hare or Heathrow as casual dealing with the mundane business of catching planes; the high proportion of cancellations I noted chalked up behind the desks of unfamiliar, folksy carriers suggested flights here were well-meant recommendations rather than settled plans, while the one relatively major airline, having overseen its 6.50 arrival and (delayed) 7.25 departure, had deserted its post until somewhat nearer its singular evening arrival-departure pair.

On offer at the newsstand were a well-matured *Wall Street Journal* and a Sunday *New York Times* now past its best, a *Christian Science Monitor* beyond all healing. The *Post-Dispatch* hadn't arrived, but there was a scurrilous rag from the westward metropolis, and that early arrival had brought with it one of my two home-town newspapers, the wrong one (Laxitter's `*good friend*'); its front page, as so often, had found another murder it could orchestrate with its lurid screams, but I bought it anyway, thinking that tucked away internally might be some small mention of the charge, embezzlement or whatever, I assumed Orbis had brought against me. To that I added yesterday's *Washington Post*, which had **HARDY SLIPS IN LATEST POLL**, and might bring some coherence to contradictory reports I'd heard on the radio about who now was best bet to win the Presidency.

Back with my fresh car, I slapped the folded newspapers on the front passenger seat, and they flopped open, hometown one on top. One of the twinned pictures on the front page was of me. The big, black headline was ***SEEK WRITER IN TORTURE SLAYING***. and the boxed photograph to the left of *Murder Suspect Arthur Ames* was *Victim Paula Leahy, 28*.

This one, folks, had everything, a beautiful young decedent, gruesome details for the lingering death itself, sexual jealousy and the rancor of rejection as the proposed motive, a secluded street, a tranquil town devastated by sudden violence, all the elements for the not merely regional but nationwide revulsion and relish soon attracted.

It certainly altered my plans. From being wanted, perhaps, for some genteel, low-priority, white-collar misdeed manufactured by Orbis, I'd become a fugitive monster, the risk to me vastly increased; the number of alleged embezzlers annually shot dead while fleeing arrest is negligible, but one accused, however falsely, of a sadistic murder is anybody's target, and every small-town cop with dreams of sudden glory carries at his hip the power to negate all our legal safeguards, shatter that primary jewel of Anglo-Saxon law, the presumption of innocence. As do our garish media; though I didn't know it then, the vulgarest of all tabloid TV shows would soon be further inflaming sentiment against me by mounting a fully-simulated 'reenactment,' with an actor as much as possible like me in sinister low-key lighting, not-quite seen doing, but certainly shown as enjoying the terrible things Paula had suffered. Within a week, all three of the network audience-inciters (White momma, Black momma, and momma's best little boy) did shows which, though with airy offhand disclaimers, took my monstrous guilt for demonstrated, and the usual gang of quasi-academic crypto-feminist gangsters extrapolated that and the supposed motive into another ferocious condemnation of male sexuality at large. If they'd been forced to see what I knew beyond doubt, that the murder had nothing to do with spurned romantic advances or outraged possessiveness, but was, had to be, hardnosed corporate policy as pursued by just such a commercial enterprise as kept their host charlatans on the air, though they might have admitted the error *in this case*, it would have done nothing to disturb their dogma, which, like radiation-enhanced agriculture, was poisonous but profitable.

When I compelled myself to reread the newspaper story with my mind locked on analysis, it became plain that if they had the times right I could prove my innocence. I'd been

connected to the crime chiefly by my disabled car, and by
some helpful hints from a source-authority who wished his
name withheld (just as you say, Walter; we can't let a messy
little murder disrupt your union with that Franco-Teutonic
hybrid you so much dislike), but who knew for a mealy-
mouthed fact Mr. Ames had been `upset' over Ms. Leahy's
return to Westerlake, and was always a very moody and
unpredictable — oh, Jesus, I can't do this. I've been trying to
set down my narrative uncluttered by the emotions of that time
which came near swallowing me, the shock, sadness,
repugnance and suffocating anger, the loss and, yes, the guilt.
An ultimate repudiation of the polygraph, that still, right now,
if I were asked, did I kill Paula, I would answer truthfully, no,
and all the needles would skate jagged and overlapping sierras
across the coiling chart. It's probable a question about Hilde's
death would likewise show me as a liar, and conceivable I'd
also register some remorse for the dead and painfully dying in,
for example, Iraq. Legal innocence is nothing like absolution
for us, the unwise, *who with a thought besmirch blood over all
our soul*, and for the atrocious murder of Paula I have to bear a
more focused blame; it clutched and clutches at my heart like
an alien parasite, unreachable by surgery. For a time, trying to
draw strands of fact from a tangle of sensations, because there
was no logic in Paula's death, I imagined Laxitter had ordered
it with the sole purpose of pinning it on me, but that couldn't
be sustained; such a frame would have been made to fit better
than this. For a few minutes I, no doubt like the police,
wondered about *unnamed informant*, a mean-spirited churl
with an annoying hairline, but while there was a theoretical
scenario where the other woman, threatening to go public, is
silenced by the apprehensive adulterer, not one that worked as
soon as you gave these names and personalities to the cast-list.
Beyond that was the sheer pointlessness of the torture, which
included — Breathe normally, begin again. Strange, but it
would be less hard for me to make peace with what's

irretrievable if it weren't so clear in memory I'd stopped trying to love Paula. Not that I'd betrayed her with Judy, none of that soapy eyewash for forcing unreal tears; it was as if discarding her I'd sanctioned her removal: an Arthur deluding himself he could still have been in love with her would imagine a greater loss, but feel smaller guilt.

In the narrowest sense, where my anger soon was channeled, I knew who her killer was. She'd been bound to a chair, and there were marks of cigarette-burns, as of at least one other technique for producing agony; not being a newspaper building my circulation, I don't give the nasty details, but a form of torture I remembered having been used, according to Amnesty, by South African security forces trying to extract information about black militants.

Van Muer, *Azraël*, to make certainty out of what had never really been in doubt, but while I can't say whether he derived any pleasure from having and exercising absolute sadistic mastery over a beautiful woman (in which he wouldn't be unique), his frigid efficiency meant there had to be some purpose; my car standing under the silver maple outside her quiet house must have convinced him Paula knew my whereabouts, and was stubbornly pretending not to; he couldn't interrogate her without giving himself away, and then death, in his world, would be simply tidying up. In tardy retrospect, obvious her address, one of the very few places they could associate with me, would routinely be checked by someone from Orbis, but I couldn't rationally blame myself for failing to warn Paula; at the time I'd believed the attempt to do so would put her in the danger I was trying to keep her from. For the last-but-one clause, the weighted word is *rationally*. In that obscure ghetto of the brain where dream-ripostes win long-dead debates, and dream-amends are made, fit and altered till they own every perfection except existence, I've phoned her hundreds of times to tell her in the masterful style of adventure fiction not to ask questions, to get out of that house,

go and stay with her parents or a friend, just get out, *now*.
Then. She wouldn't have gone.

Having always found myself resignedly free of
vengefulness, I don't dispute need to expunge my own shame
was part of the sudden voluptuous desire to kill van Muer, to
have him die the slowest, cruellest of deaths. A shock to hear
myself making the words for barbaric methods, and I
recognized it was also a half-deliberate procrastination, a way
of not facing the new reality of being a seriously — had I
known it, hysterically — hunted man, with all the resources of
society looking for me. Knowing me by name: my face is not
strikingly different from many others, fairly symmetrical
features, clean-shaven, without scars or lumps, but it might be
only the wondrous inattentiveness of Jason Oates had
prevented my being recognized when renting the car, and I
couldn't count on the same abstraction anywhere else credit-
card or traveller's checks demanded use of my name.

If there'd been nothing but suspicion of murder, a rap I
could surely beat, the danger cited above, that I'd be mown
down by some tank-town Eliot Ness, *judex, lictor, et exitium*
(who, after all, had *seen* me on the *tee*vee, doing unspeakable
things) would have made it saner to surrender to the nearest
available police, if necessary, as hostage-takers sometimes did,
using the intermediary of print or TV journalists as insurance
against the trigger-happy. But still, among first effects of my
arrest would be to inform my more lethal enemies where I
was; I didn't trust the FBI, was dubious about my hometown
police, and in all my nightmares, whether of carelessness or
collusion, there was the Death-Angel lurking among the
photographers, emerging red with a ruby flame to fire point-
blank. Not van Muer himself, no, no; he'd find some
malleable soul who'd fallen in love with Paula's picture,
persuade him that with all the loopholes and the falderol, the
slick, constitution-exploiting attorneys, with their writs of
Habeas Corpus, the chicken-hearted jurors, all the bizarre

sensitivity to the *rights*, for Christ's sake, of a blatant fiend, he must become the instrument of swift retribution beyond the undoing of legal legerdemain.

Time for a new literary model: I'd never had the resourcefulness of the *Condor* character, while Hannay in *Thirty-Nine Steps* had a sanctuary I lacked, his not-misplaced faith in the ultimate virtue and fairness of his society and those chosen to keep its laws. In *Rogue Male* those forces are still benign, but impotent to protect, and the only difficulty with the solution found by Mr. Household's likeable fugitive is that he can never know when, if ever, it's safe to leave his lair; unlike the hidey-hole itself, his commitment to it is open-ended.

Mine, if I went to earth, would be different: for short-term survival and an opportunity to prove my innocence, my chances would be greatly improved if I could lie low till I was no longer front-page news; against that were the dangers in getting to the hiding-place I had in mind, driving a car that would surely soon be described to every police force in the country. But the eventual safety that could come only from exposure of Orbis, the indictment of Laxitter and other principals, might need a change of administrations; I was by now convinced that so long as Dwayne Hardy was in power, even the evidence I had might not do it, or would triumph only after a bitter political fight, a long press campaign, a public outcry that would persist over all denials, reassurances and clarifications, the impugning of accusers and deification of the accused, the tactics we were by now familiar with from an administration in trouble, where evasions, fractional truths and lies of contemptuous transparency more often than not miraculously prevailed. I couldn't hide myself away for four years; if Hardy succeeded to the Presidency I'd have to take my chances with that process, though I could foresee **Suicide of Key Witness** as an incident in the battle, with the clear implication I'd decided to hang or electrocute myself, or swallow lots of poison, to avoid being discredited, publicly exposed as a forger, maliciously manufacturing the so-called Laxitter Files.

But according to detailed polls in the *Washington Post*, Governor Lomax was now leading or level in a collection of states whose electoral votes were enough to make him President; Hardy was still ahead in more states, and the quirkiness of electoral arithmetic meant that while a four percent overall gain for Lomax would make little difference to the narrowest of victories, an evenly-spread two percent swing to Hardy in those key states would make his win look like a landslide. Yet I didn't foresee a man whose lead had relentlessly declined from forty-two points to statistical nothing coming back in the final weekend, and a Lomax Administration meant the dismantling or at least disruption of Laxitter's web of influence, meant John Battaglia in the cabinet, with the power to pursue his old questions about Harness-Stirrup — the power to protect me. My proposed hermitry would be lonely, boring and uncomfortable, but connected to the outside world by the small radio I had with me, and regardless of how the election went, limited in duration.

First, I knew I must make the tedious and risky drive back the way I'd come; according to the newspaper account Paula's death had occurred late Tuesday to early Wednesday, and my presence that night at the Happy Haven was recorded in the register, but no evidence not under armed guard was safe from tampering, and to secure my alibi I would go back and demand a receipt from Bates, showing exact times of my stay.

Corn was in, pumpkins were starting to swell, foliage had peaked for color and was dwindling in mass, but the sun was hot in a sky like hydrated copper sulfate, like Windex, and where before I'd exulted in the emptiness of these byways, now I felt ostentatiously visible in my metallic-bronze car, a

cockroach on an idle cookie-sheet. In logic I knew every rural
sheriff and township cop wasn't watching obsessively for me;
far too early for them to have a *make* on my fresh car, yet
when I had to pass a slow-moving patrol-car, I didn't dare
glance over as I drew level, neck rigid, right cheek tingling
with the effort to ward off diagnosis. As I drove, bitter regrets
for Paula were overlapped by new fears for Judy, whose trail-
muddling at the computer could now be construed as a serious
felony, assisting a known fugitive. Efforts to identify the
source of the spurious entries would surely be redoubled, and
while confident she would never believe me guilty, I only
hoped the huge publicity given my supposed crime would
rouse the prudent rather than defiant component in Judy's
nature: like me she would be in far less danger from the law
than from the hit-men for whom the law could obligingly
finger her. Near-consolation lurked in knowing she'd be
heading south with Michael as soon as they'd voted, but not
nearly enough, and I resolved to break my own ban, and risk
the call I regretted not making to Paula. In a small town
phones beckoned from a pair of roadside booths, a bar, a gas
station, but I passed them by, and waited instead for a
shopping mall, for the same reason as when tailed by Keith; I
would feel less conspicuous with the car lost among its fellows
rather than standing alone at curbside.

    Finding a feeding-stall phone I dialed Judy's number,
my left fist full of change — no, of *chagne*, still the
launderette legacy. No answer. The only other number I had
was the language lab, and she wouldn't be there today; actually
I didn't know what day would be her last at work; I stood in a
kind of tunnel leading to what euphemism insists are rooms
segregating us by sex for the purpose of resting, and my
feeling of utter impotence translated itself into an ultimate
loneliness, at odds with constant terror each passerby might
point an Emile Zola finger with a cry of, "*C'est lui, le
monstre!*" A covert glance at a newsstand on my way to the
phone had told me my notoriety had crossed the Mississippi

with ***JILTED, HE TORTURES, KILLS GIRLFRIEND***, not
the smallest hint this was at best feckless conjecture.

Needing supplies, I saw a health-food chain was
closing its branch here at the mall, and having what it called a
Case Sale; steeling myself, I went in and purchased a quantity
of raisins, apricots and pecans, a supply of vitamin C in half-
gram tablets, and a case of 24 one-pound packages of toasted
wheat germ. At the supermarket nearby I added two giant-size
boxes of instant dried milk, a number of large bars of milk
chocolate, two hundred teabags, some package soups, a supply
of batteries for radio and lantern, a six-pack of toilet-paper,
and in a liquor-store, a big bottle of scotch. Making this last
purchase, I was stared at by the cashier, dark, with heavy Elvis
Presley lips and eyelids, as she dragged the barred price-label
across the all-seeing asterisk. Her mouth opened, and I tensed
for flight, but then she said I was like this guy who came in all
the time, and for a moment she'd thought I was him. That's
what she thought she thought; I could see a folded newspaper
next to the register, and did not linger to give time for her to
place her recollections more accurately. On my way back to
the car I saw lightweight quart-size polyethylene bottles
outside a housewares store, bought half a dozen, and when I
found a quiet side road where I could stop, transferred the
whiskey to two of them, and filled the others with milk
powder, leaving glass bottle and boxes beside the road. I'd
soon be bored by a diet of wheat germ with milk, and would
yearn for meat, but had food to keep me alive for weeks if
necessary, nothing that needed refrigeration or more than a
few minutes cooking. Since all the food, with my other gear,
would have to be carried about a dozen rough miles, that there
was now no more than a pound or two of packaging for the
whole load was an important point.

All my plans for disappearance were dependent on
being able to find my way back to a wilderness place I'd
happened on just once, and my experience with Happy Haven

was not propitious augury; only at third traversal of the same stretch of highway did I again identify the obscure turnoff, and after negotiating many more curves than could be right, came upon the motel. With what seemed a laughable excess of caution I parked at roadside out of sight of the office. Early evening, and I was hungry, but I left open the question of whether I would revisit the hamburger lean-to where Ned Bates had directed me two days ago, a couple of miles up the meandering road, and then perhaps return here for another night.

Was there some wariness in Bates's greeting? Maybe I was first of his clients ever to return, or he'd been offended by my unwarned midnight departure. For that I'd prepared the explanation that I'd finished my work and decided to get it to the typist as soon as possible, but now (I alleged) my accountant had insisted I obtain a receipt without delay for this eminently deductible expense. I was using too many words to excuse a perfectly reasonable request.

"Oh, sure," after a ruminant pause. "I got the receipt forms in back," and he vanished through the door leading to his own living-quarters. After a moment, on the desk where the ponderous Smith-Corona lived, I saw one of the buttons on the telephone light up, and instantly knew the reason for mine host's unease with me. He must have seen a newspaper: chances were I'd already been a topic of talk, and he might well have called the sheriff or state police, and been told to call back in the unlikely event I returned. That he must now be doing.

Delaying only long enough to lean over the counter and add a small genuine larceny to my large invented crimes, I left quietly, thankful I'd given Bates no glimpse of my latest car; logically he and roused authority would have no reason not to assume I was still driving the former one whose plate numbers were recorded in the stiff-covered, blue-grey and brown, old-fashioned stationery store journal that served Bates for his

register, and was now in my possession; no one was going to
erase or alter that precious memorial. I was glad to note,
equally, Bates thriftily left no empty lines between entries,
which spread across the double page, and while Happy Haven
had scarcely been enjoying a surge of prosperity, there were
three arrivals later than mine, making it hard for me to have
falsified my entry, if intimidation later were to persuade Bates
to change the story. Well, to prove I hadn't faked all the later
guests, it might not be easy to track down the *Mr. and Mrs.
John Smith*, no occupation, Missouri license plates XYZ123,
who were booked into the *Gone With the Wind* experience half
an hour after I'd left last night, but *Gary Pfeiffer, student,* of
Indiana, looked authentic, and above his name, immediately
below mine, was the bold, sprawling signature of the
unimpeachably, uninventably genuine *Orville W. Springle,
Hay Sales*, from Paducah, KY; I remembered seeing his
battered van a couple of units down from the one I occupied.
The journey, round trip, between Happy Haven and
Westerlake, would be not less than eight hundred miles; my
alibi was solid by any measure except the stop-watches and
slide-rules of those once-popular timetable mysteries, which
relied on concealed aircraft, unsuspected roller-skates in the
gladstone-bag, or acrobatic assassin dropping from a bridge
near Watford onto the roof of the 8.05 from Euston — tales
which almost always ended with the blurted *All right! I did it,*
or abrupt suicide of hitherto-imperturbable precisian, saving us
from doubting how the sleuth's intricate exposition might play
in front of a stolid jury: to show a gambit was just possible is a
long way from proving it happened.

  I jerked from near dozing as an angry howl behind
close headlights reprimanded me for straying almost onto the
wrong side of the tracer-bullets which arched without end
from darkness, not quite able to convince myself these
wandering thoughts had been part of the consequent resolve to
find a good attorney as soon as I emerged from hiding. I could

only be somewhere in Arkansas, with forty sleepless hours
behind me, the last twenty-two practically all driving, making
it perilous to keep going on a poor road which squiggled
increasingly as it mounted into what must be the Ozarks.
Wanting to get clear of any hue and cry raised by the Bates
call, I'd crossed two big rivers, two and now three state lines,
before, with needle only a couple of cupfuls above *E*, chancing
a stop for gas and cardboard coffee like liquid lye. Munching
dried fruit, foul of breath and sour of stomach, I'd kept up a
debate which still went on as to whether I dared risk
recognition stopping at first a restaurant and then another
motel, if possible both together. Either that or find a quiet spot
to sleep in my car, but whereas at a motel, though I had to
show my face, I could pay cash and use a false name, if I
slumbered at roadside and an officious policeman checked out
my car, I'd have to produce my driver's license, and that would
mean certain arrest; ***ALERT COP NABS TORTURE FIEND***
— I was starting to make the plausibility of headlines a test of
my actions.

     NEW LEISURE CENTER FOR NOWHERE: having
been for some miles on fairly level plateau, I came to a curve
and a dip, and was looking down into a valley, and where a
road from the north came swooping in there was a sudden flare
of brilliance, an inexplicable implant borrowed piecemeal
from Nashville and Vegas, Cleveland and Miami Beach,
several acres of floodlit concrete set with a giant motel and
`full service' hotel, at least two restaurants and a red-and-white
candystripe ice-cream emporium, a moviehouse containing
eight separate bunkers with their own screens, a Bowl-O-
Mania with 32 Lanes 32, a theatre offering Continuous Live,
Live, Live Country Music, a glazed gift-shop glittering with
ceramic ballerinas, bulldogs, Jesus Christs, Day-Glo shirts,
ten-gallon hats and fringed vests, plaques and plates and
posters, textually divided equally among religion, domestic
sentimentality, outhouse humor and country-western celebrity.
Flanking the paved island as I drove down was an enclosed

dirt-track with lofty light-trees and bleachers, idle now, but often the scene, as proclaimed by a sculpted signboard borrowed from a drive-in movie, of Demolition Derby, other sidesplitting capers involving Big-Wheelers, Tractor Pulls, and Funny Cars, and a Giant Fireworks Display Every Saturday. According to a banner strung over the entranceway, the arena would also accommodate, presumably at a different time, a Big Revival Meeting, with 60-voice Gospel Choir, Baptism, Healing and Laying On of Hands (and an impressive display of fire and brimstone for the recalcitrant?).

And it was busy, this little man-made waste in the vast mountain greenery: traffic had been light on the road I'd taken, and was only slightly heavier on the north-south route, but here the parking lots were three-quarters full, with a higher proportion of pastel-shade vintage Cadillacs than I'd ever imagined, license-plates from Texas, California and Georgia as well as more probable Oklahoma, Kansas and Missouri; the walkways were thronged with predictable groupings, standard families with children from six to fifteen, older couples, knots of prowling youths, their heads set at challenging angles, skeins of adolescent girls, who giggled or bridled at the boys, but drew closer together; rarest were simple pairings, though the full service wing of the hotel-motel offered Honeymoon Suites in letters four feet high, all the *O*'s outline upturned rumps, and I would bet somewhere there was a wedding chapel, for those romantically overcome by all these stimuli. Perhaps I had a fatuous thought so much activity would help me pass unnoticed, but under the remorseless glare of white fluorescence as I entered the *Buckaroo Beef-n' Burger Bar*, I would have felt no more conspicuous dressed in a maharajah's ceremonial costume; I was, for a start, virtually the only male in the place not wearing a satin shirt with contrasted yoke, and might well possess the only feet in shoes rather than tooled leather boots. In uniform, I would still have drawn attention; I glimpsed a pair of apparent truck-drivers at a table, and there were booths peopled with whole squads of youthful buckaroos, but single diners were rare to non-existent. I was somewhat grudgingly allotted a tiny table meant for two up against the window, Westerlake Monster brightly illuminated behind plate-glass for every leisured ambler to examine. Happily, I could see no newspapers among the passers-by, and I doubt the distant northern murder was getting much play on either country-music radio or preach-and-reach TV.

Not content with the stir I'd created so far, I shocked the young waitress by asking if I could have a beer. Cherry-bright, pouty lips in a pallid face, pseudo-rawhide vest over checked shirt, a mass of tinder-dry, colorless hair, but nice enough legs between short, fringed skirt and close-fitting suedoid boots, she instructed me severely that this en-tire complex was *drah*. Chastened, I picked my way through the thicket of adjectives on the menu to order what was foreseeably an ordinary steak sandwich, and noted she like all the waitresses had slung at her back an impractical three-liter hat, like some vestigial organ, or the rudimentary wings of a flightless bird. My having called for alcohol was apparently worth relating to the probable manager, a heavy, leather-faced man who liked to find excuses for touching, patting, making minor adjustments to the costume of what he very likely called *mah gals*. In this case he put his wrists on the waitress's shoulders, looming over her with some earnest talk, then took the check with my order on it, and disappeared through the swinging saloon-doors to the kitchen. At once the waitress, ignoring intervening fingers that beckoned or snapped for her attention, made her way back to me with cup and pot, to ask sweetly whether I'd like my coffee now.

If this was a ruse to keep me docile while the law was summoned, I was simply too weary or hungry (I couldn't tell which came uppermost) to react, and only hoped passively my sandwich would arrive before the deputies. In the event, it did come with exemplary swiftness, medium rare as I'd ordered, and a more succulent piece of meat than I would have expected for the moderate price. Not far behind, the leathery one emerged from the kitchen, and bore down on me with massive determination, halted, beetled, and asked me if everything was all right. Satisfied by my brief yet gracious response, he rumbled off, showing I hadn't been singled out by stopping at tables right and left to ask the same. Yet before he went on a tour of inspection behind the service counter, he took a lowering look back in my direction, as if to be sure I'd observed his progress.

All this was mystery till I'd taken a room at the relentlessly colorful, ferociously sterile motel, signing in as Fletcher Beaumont, and acceding reluctantly to the apologetic (but unconnected) stipulation I'd have to pay for double occupancy; with unusable credit cards and unspendable checks, I was beginning to worry about the steady attrition to my cash. When I entered the second-level room and went without delay to the much-needed bathroom, I saw in the mirror I still had on the cap I often wore while driving, especially when heading east in the morning, west near sunset, and to which, after who-could-guess how long, my senses had become so accustomed that its presence lingered more convincingly after I'd taken it off. Dark blue, like a modified baseball cap with an extruded bill, similar to those seen aboard aircraft-carriers, or their depiction in movies, it had been given to me by Bill Fasstin at ORBIS/Orbiscard, where they were worn by the younger executives. It had, in fact, a neat golden ORBIS logo, front and center.

As part of the checking-in ritual I'd been handed a glossy little gatefold brochure delineating the varied delights of the center, which revealed the *Sleepytime Motel* (with its *Cock-a-Doodle Coffeeshop*) and the *Dixie Monarch Hotel*, together with both the *Buckaroo*, where I'd eaten, and the more formal, Tara-pillared *Plantation House Restaurant*, where the waitresses didn't wear hoop-skirts, and, yes, the *Premiere Octoplex*, were all presented for my pleasure by Leisuremode Division of Transvax (an ORBIS corporation). In rumpled jeans, my casual but obviously city-and-eastern shirt, my ORBIS headgear, the *Buckaroo* had taken me for a spy from corporate headquarters, lamely trying to pass myself off as a good old boy, out to trap them with my request for alcohol; that explained why, though I'd been served carefully selected food and plied with regal service, they'd been so punctilious about giving me only what was due, and at such pains to let me see this was how everyone was treated. They hadn't even dared bribe me with a free dessert.

Dawn was when I made my escape, too early for the *Cock-a-Doodle*, but before stopping for coffee I meant to subdue a few of the many westward miles I still had to cover. Its walks empty, this concrete raft was eerie by aqueous morning light, but scarcely stranger than when fully peopled; as once when, not to be spoilsport, I allowed a couple-and-a-half to persuade me to Las Vegas, and stood, battered by flashing lights and raucous noises, unseduced by dismal pastimes, marvelling others of my species had found lost Eden in what was precisely my idea of hell; as sometimes when bemused by the fierce, unreal debates of daytime television, or gazing at bulk-mail evidence of what otherworldly flotsam could be sold to someone, somewhere — or when we choose our leaders, no matter what their ignorance, banality or servile collusion with polluters, poisoners and thieves, because they're apparently monogamous, and smile nicely at their spouses, I felt here like an alien who's alighted from the galactic bus at the wrong stop, bewildered by difference.

A fitting thought for the first day of November in a year divisible by four. On my car radio the only alternative I could find to lachrymose people called Tammy and Jimmy, Willie and Loretta, Johnnie and the Late-Great Hank, was a Vaseline-voiced Messiah-monger who had the goods on God; daunting to reflect that all those who followed his instructions and sent "*twenty-fifty-a-hundred-dollars, whatever you can spayah*," to have their prayers prioritized, could also vote.

The reason, near start of this narrative, for my outline account of an adventure with a musician I called Antonia, thwarted by the return of her conductor-husband, now becomes apparent; it was on that non-coital western trip, when I made off into the hills by myself, that I'd found my hideaway.

9

What disgust with or terror of other humanity had caused someone to build in a place so inconvenient I couldn't say; not a prospector trying to keep his claim hidden, or at least there were no signs of mining nearby; all the modifications to the rockface or the natural recess had been to accommodate the dwelling, or obtain material for its skilled and economical construction; cut stone and natural fragments had been deftly fitted to each other and to the living rock, so one windowed wall, one long and one short side-section had been enough to complete the cabin, with roof supplied by natural overhang, except for a foot or so of split-stone eave supported on timbers. Because of its sheltered position, deep in a narrow cleft with the crags some hundreds of feet above, its age was difficult to determine; none of the wood, not the stout door, three layers of planks nailed together, vertical sandwiching horizontal, had ever been painted, but creosote had likely been used, and weathering was a long way from devastation. Heavy, wrought-iron strap hinges looked Victorian, but there might well be a small-town hardware within a hundred miles that could still duplicate them from dusty and jumbled stock.

In a letter to my sister after my first discovery of this curious habitation I'd speculated it might have been built by a theologically disputatious Mormon on the lam from adjacent Utah in the *Study in Scarlet* era, a place of refuge from the ruthless enforcers of orthodoxy. That had come to loom as dark unconscious prophecy.

Back in September, wanting to get into back-country, driving what itself was a less-travelled road of small pretensions, I'd been seduced by the tree-hung opening to the rutted, bumpy and poorly-graded lane, which led in the general direction of folded, gracious slopes that asked to be traversed

on foot. I was soon convinced this was no public way, but
access to a ranch or farm. After about three jolting miles,
often flicked at by overhanging branches, I found it was that
no longer: creeping gingerly past where a tumble of loose
earth and rock had narrowed and almost closed the lane, I
looked down a slope to the deep gash of a watercourse, where
the way ended in a fence, a warning sign, and the remnant of a
wrecked wooden trestle-bridge. Beyond that, with most of the
trees removed, there was sparse grazing land for horses or
cattle, although no animals were visible, and the command-
post must lie somewhere beyond where the winding course of
the track's continuation vanished behind a low brown ridge.

By inching down the slope and using every available
centimeter of space by the fence, I'd managed to finesse the car
around, and it was on the return journey, still a couple of miles
from the road, that I just discerned the partly-overgrown slot
which gave access to a concealed bay where gravel or sand
had once been dug. Above the embankment formed by that
long-ago quarrying, the lightly wooded slope was as good a
place as I'd found to begin my wanderings, and I was unlikely
to find a safer anchorage for my car. Best of all, the tilt of
hillside whose flank I was soon climbing pointed in the
direction of craggier country that showed its bones, offering
just the challenge needed to exorcise lingering frustrations
caused by Antonia's poorly-timed marital reconciliation.

My defiant mood may well have played a part in
finding the invisible cabin, since to reach it required, as well as
luck, the ignoring, more than once, of plain visual evidence a
dead end had been reached, first at the head of a dry gully
where a cliff-face above a minor talus yielded an unexpected
opening screened by a precarious clutch of ancient, tormented
pines, again where, after crossing a kinder grassed stretch with
clumps of aspen and alder I'd laboriously mounted a series of
tilted blocks, and that I was looking ahead and upward not to a
minor recess, but to an overlap of rock slabs, was revealed

only by abrupt disappearance of a chipmunk I'd been keeping
an eye on, as he on me. Passing through a narrow opening, I
managed to make a tortuous ascending way, zigzagging among
rocks, reaching an impasse where another clench of toenail-
anchored pines leaned over the sheer fall of a deep cleft too
wide to cross without equipment I didn't have handy.
Beginning an inglorious retreat, I saw at my right what seemed
like (and I afterwards concluded was) a step cut in the bulge of
a great boulder, leading me to another cramped fissure, then to
the astonishment of a simple log bridge across the narrowest
section of the cleft, and, with the rounding of a final corner, to
a widening, containing the ledge where the dwelling had been
fitted and sculpted.

When I first saw the site it was enchantingly immersed
in the soft glow of late sun reflected and diffused by the rocks
above, and I found a notch beyond the cabin where I could
clamber up and look out to see the true mountains, huge at a
distance of forty miles, dark and jagged against brilliant sky,
intervening land a mysterious bowl of grey and chocolate-
brown and violet swells. Below from that side, the lesser rock
I'd mounted fell sheer, nor was the place I was in reachable or
even visible from any vantage-point on the heights directly
above.

Sunset came sooner now, one-seventh of a year nearer
the winter solstice, but though the light was the same glow
when I found my way back, the enchantment was wasted on
my complete exhaustion. Settling on this as my hiding-place,
I'd first spun an elaborate plan to achieve maximum confusion,
where I would drive to the same spot as before, trek in with
most of my supplies and gear, coming back to the car, and
driving to abandon it a thousand miles away, say in Oregon, or
New Orleans. I'd then return by train and bus to the town
nearest here, and do the rest on foot: finding the rental car
would thus give my pursuers no clue to where I'd gone. But

the net gain in mystification was inadequate against the risk of being recognized whenever I made a purchase or sought lodging for the night, and the car, left in a situation hardly to be seen, off a roadlet there was no reason for using, would probably never be found. That's not exactly true; if it were I would have taken up residence there, with cushions to sleep on, and heat available as long as there was gas in the tank; I meant, searchers weren't likely to find it, and if stumbled on by hunters, for example, it might well be ignored — or, if not, there was no trail connecting that place to the cabin, which was inaccessible enough to elude a quite thorough search of the area. Twelve miles in any direction traced out a circle containing nearly three hundred thousand acres.

The final argument for simplification was my late recognition that about fifty pounds weight in food alone added to the rest of my baggage and camping gear, all to be negotiated across rough terrain, would require two trips at least, three traversals of the distance, close to forty miles in all, two thirds of it carrying my maximum load. Distressing calculation told me it would have to be spread over most of three days; while unencumbered I could manage the journey back down to my parking-spot in perhaps five hours, it would be a foolhardy overestimate of my powers to attempt the uphill return, fully laden, within the same allotment of daylight, and uncomfortable, if nothing worse, to be overtaken by darkness in mid-trek.

Just the first leg was too much for me. I began tired, driving the last three-hour slice I'd failed to add to yesterday's score, when I'd hammered out every mile I could, till my neck and shoulders felt like a mass of bruises. One additional drawback of being wanted by the law was to keep me within or very near the speed limit, not excepting those broad straight highways where seventy-five was the going rate; at school long ago I became a model of virtue, not out of priggishness, but because I'd discovered if every kid in class helped cover the blackboard with pitiless assessments of the teacher's character, I would always be the one caught white-handed, and it has remained true that I'm one of the rule-cursed who can commit commonplace infractions only with punity. Under that handicap, more than six hundred miles was an heroic total, and in the end I'd found an old logging road in densely wooded country, and tried to sleep in the car. For the foregoing hour my eyelids had been closing with the persistence of an infant's mouth when the strained spinach choo-choo is on its way, but sleep was out of reach as soon as I'd stopped, and all anxieties came swarming; over and again I went through the routine for finding my way back to that obscure lane, and was still in terror of missing one of the turns, while on a separate track I replayed inconsequential details from the journey just finished, both programs liable to be preempted, as soon as I detected the approach of sleep, by nervousness about my present vulnerability, or by my lower intestine, protesting bitterly about the irregularity and oddity of deliveries from above, to encourage an easement threatening an explosive and disgusting tantrum. I became cold, but to hunt up more clothes or the sleeping-bag meant abandoning the trancelike immobility I'd adopted, hideout for my wily, continuing ambush of sleep, which only just failed, time after time. Incontrovertibly, some dozing did occur, because I woke stiff-necked, chilled, and in a panic caused by the pressure of far more fluid than I'd ingested in three days, a problem compounded by numb ineptitude of fingers and thumbs.

At my best, well-rested after regular exercise, it would still have been an impossible task to traverse the rockier portions of my route carrying what I estimated at sixty pounds of gear, which left most of the food behind, locked in the car. There was nylon rope in my camping bag, and more than once

I had to work my way up carrying only the pack, and then haul the other two bags up, one by one; by this method it took me into the afternoon to reach where I'd been guided before by the disappearance of a chipmunk. Here, I gave up; there was no certainty I remembered the way ahead, and it could be disastrously stupid to carry the full load where false starts and backtracking might occur; I redid the pack so it contained the most essential equipment and a small amount of food, strapped bedroll on top, crammed everything else into the other bags, and cached them in a cleft between rocks, site marked by the ragged pillar of a dead tree. Too winded for hunger, I made myself sit down and eat dried fruit with some cheese I'd bought at the quaint general store attached to the last place I'd stopped for gas. The day had begun cool and dank, so rain wouldn't've surprised me, but was dry now under high overcast, and I was glad of a full canteen.

All my panicky irritation would live again in describing the wrong turns I made, or, worst of all, the right turn I lost faith in and had to reconfirm by retreat, meaning one bruising stretch I covered three times with remaining daylight hours rapidly shrinking, the sun emerging late at the far westward edge of the white ceiling to send elongated shadows back the way I'd come. By then, nothing was familiar, and I was near convincing myself there must be two or more separate log bridges over the long ravine, when at last I sidled past the bulge of mottled rock and had found the cabin again. My fatigue was penetrated by a feeling above relief, more than the pleasure of an end to exertions, and I recognized the hidden dwelling answered a need quite aside from the troubles that had brought me here, the powerful appeal of hermitage, of absolute self-sufficiency and freedom from the demands of human transaction. Not an exclusive yearning, one that could exist in eternal disharmony with a desire for Pickwickian good fellowship and shared warmth, both visions doomed in the end by their romantic unreality; austere solitude could never remain so serene, nor company so infallibly gratifying: as when vacillating between two loves, regal Ariadne and effervescent Zerbinetta, each was most rewarding at the point of maximum satiation or maximum disappointment with the other.

      No chance of going back to reclaim my checked baggage in what was left of today; entering the cabin, I laid out my bedroll, pad and sleeping bag on a low stone shelf or broad step probably intended for just that purpose, occupying the side wall between corner and jutting fireplace, so as to take advantage of both warmth and what light filtered in through the murky windows. From the standpoint of secrecy there'd be small risk in lighting a fire using dry fuel; in a dead calm the slight smoke would rise to emerge, scarcely visible, two or three hundred feet above, while wind coming through the westward gap would diffuse it instantly. But I doubted I'd use the fireplace; there was little fuel to be found nearer than an arduous mile away, I had my small stove for minor cooking, and was banking on the climate following the pattern of the past few winters, whether a sign of global warming or a cyclic phase, with mild weather persisting in these parts well into December; if snow came earlier the temperature shouldn't drop below uncomfortable into the dangerous range.

      When here before I'd had a flashlight with me, but not my multicell lantern, which, besides a primary beam quite up to anti-aircraft standards, and a flashing red beacon for a distress signal, possessed a pair of cool white fluorescent tubes which gave a pleasant radiance, lasting an astonishingly long time before the batteries faltered. By its light I now saw details hardly visible the first time; decorative leaf-carvings on the inside of the door-lintel, which once had known the open-air life as a railroad tie, some big iron hooks overhead in a deep natural niche of the solid-rock rear wall, a harbor for hanging hams or maturing cheese rather than the clothes-closet it suggested. Deeply incised in the large central stone above the fireplace was an inscription,

Z. B.
1893
S.L.C.U.

— which gave me a date, and offered some confirmation of
my guess as to the builder; Zachary, Zachariah, Zebedee,
Zedekiah, Zephaniah, Zophar — all the (mostly awful) male
names I could think of beginning with *Z* came from the bible,
including the (cheat) diminutive, Zeke. The second set of
initials suggested an educational institution, but I couldn't
think of one that fit: Southern Liberal Christian? Southern
Louisiana Catholic? The date was surely too early for a
university to be named after a still-living Mark Twain. Then I
saw it had to stand for Salt Lake City, Utah.

    A long journey, over five hundred miles from here, and
far more by any route he could have taken in those days of
hooves, feet, and iron wheels. Old Zeb must have had the use
of a mule, or, better for this terrain, a strong, sure-footed little
donkey, but he hadn't simply arrived here, exclaimed *This is
the place!* and begun to build — or I couldn't imagine him
wandering about with all the needed components, hardware,
the lintels, the sixteen two-foot square panes of thick glass,
never without flaws and bubbles, by now weathered to
whiteness, though only one had cracked. Nor had he sawn his
own boards; there were no nearby trees of that quality, and the
outer layer of the door was oak, not seen hereabouts. Like me,
he must have believed he had a considerable head start on
whatever pursuit he expected, and felt secure enough to make
sorties in search of materials. What he did for food, beyond
perhaps some hunting or trapping, I couldn't tell, but the site
he chose had one priceless advantage, an unfailing supply of
water: it issued in an icy jet from the rock face under the
recess just beyond the cabin, and since it had been flowing in
September at the end of the arid months, safe to assume it

never dried up; it might freeze, I supposed, but then there'd be snow and ice for the melting.

Here, Z.B. had been at his most inventive; he must have found a way to divert the flow for a time, while he hollowed out the rock where it fell — or rather, widened and deepened a hollow the water had worn for itself. In this way a capacious cistern had been made, and its overflow was a channel which, in effect, gave the cabin indoor plumbing, since it used a terra cotta pipe to pass through the wall, and inside fed a smaller stone tank, from which the overflow in turn was channeled through a dividing-wall to spill on a tilted stone slab directly beneath a latrine, a plank box with a hole cut; its position, bridging a narrow crevice of unknown depth into which water and waste vanished, suggested precariousness, but it was resting both ends on substantial stone with only a foot or so over space, and the box, like the cabin-door, had been made to last. The entire waterworks area was screened and three-quarters closed off from the rest of the cabin by a stone wall jutting from beyond the fireplace, and a line of smaller iron hooks above suggested some sort of curtain had completed the enclosure; climbing up on an unstable pyramid of my baggage I was soon to find the grommets of my tarp would go over the hooks, giving me the same genteel arrangement, and muting the faint tricklings and plashings of the never stilled water.

Hardly accommodation here for a significant selection of wives, but lonely as he must have been my fervent hope was old Zeb or Zadok had found what he sought, and had lived in tranquillity, safe from the agents of outraged conformity — the *Avenging Angels*, Conan Doyle names them, a near-plural for my own *Azraël*, though their god was not his; at worst estimate Z.B's enemies possessed the perverted merit of *having* a conviction.

Just to be free of driving across a landscape filled with dangers, the tense moment-to-moment expectation of being recognized and denounced, was like a victory; stretched out in my sleeping-bag I warned myself against smugness, which had less to do with real achievement than with the pampered sensation of cramped fatigue ebbing from calves and shoulders, the sure approach of deep sleep. I promised to be less irresponsible tomorrow; using only moderate care I could traverse practically the whole distance between here and my car without a chance of being seen, but today, I'd disregarded secrecy entirely. Another rule for my handbook, one easier to formulate than to follow: don't get tired: an oddity of any precaution is that when it works perfectly, it must appear unnecessary: I'd never know, for example, whether I'd been excessively cautious in renting the second car from an out-of-the-way independent agency. With nothing to distinguish between the successful and the superfluous, prudent precautions very soon come to resemble obsolescent ritual, like the sonorous challenge to the keys at the Tower of London, and fatigue can easily cause irritable omission: I'd given myself the angry excuse I had more than enough hassle humping my baggage over rocky terrain, without worrying about being seen. Weariness makes lies in the brain; the truth was that without secrecy, there was no point to the exercise; it might be true I'd outdistanced home-based pursuit, but as the Westerlake Monster the citizenry was my enemy, and this country was sparsely populated, not empty. The ranch where the lane used to lead was obviously peopled, and where my car was left I'd seen a couple of expended 12-gauge cartridges. Weathered to a powdery pink, they must have lain there for more than a year or two, but still remained evidence of inhabitants, a reprimand.

Election night and well into the chill of Wednesday morning, I stayed with the radio drama of a battle for the Presidency made epic by its fluctuating numbers rather than by heroic qualities in the combatants. Regardless of outcome the date meant Judy, whom twice more before leaving civilization I'd been unable to reach by phone, was on the road, southward bound in the elderly VW she'd bestowed on Michael; I could have wished her better company (as I would have wished myself hers), but was cheered to think of her moving away, as she surely was, from danger.

The day had been cooler, and the night, first time I hadn't burrowed early into the depths of my sleeping-bag, became gnawingly cold; before midnight I erected my domed exoskeletal tent, and retreated inside with hot milk and whiskey, knowing in theory the enclosed space was being warmed by my own body-heat, but in the end sitting up, wearing the sleeping-bag like a burnoose, while states four-fifths counted remained too close to call, and I revised my decision on using the fireplace, planning sorties to gather firewood, hoping the chimney, crumbled away at the top, never best example of Z.B's stonework, wasn't blocked.

Through a long broadcast night the expert interpreters struggled to find a trend, a pattern, some logical template to fit facts that refused to behave themselves. A disproportionate share of their high-wire contortions consisted of elaborate, periodically superseded explanations of what was wrong with the last analysis, as the candidates took turns capturing northeastern industrial states, border states, Old South states, farm states; the Women's Issue that won Maryland for Lomax didn't live up to its expectations for Illinois, while the perception of Vice-President Hardy, that friend of industry, as more likely to create new jobs, said to have taken Ohio for him, failed in West Virginia, where unemployment was higher still. Demographics, exit polls, entrails, all methods of augury were failing, and the sole certainty was that while barely half those eligible were voting, results in most states were slow to

arrive, with no one willing to venture whether there'd be
enough suburban and outstate Hardy support to overcome the
modest margins Lomax eked out in the cities.

What we were seeing, as I could have advised the
pundits, was an ultimate expression of the principle by which
the last half-dozen Presidential elections had been decided, the
Balance of Apathy; the lukewarm struggle of familiar and
despised with unknown and distrusted. There was finally
choric agreement *it all came down to California*, but that too
turned out to be an oversimplification; by midnight Pacific
Time while Hardy *virtually* had to have California to win,
Lomax could *mathematically* triumph without it, in the
remotely possible event he swept all widely-separated five of
the large states yet unclaimed, including Pennsylvania and
Florida, where it was three A.M. and they were still counting,
as long as he held on to Georgia, where the margin was small
enough for a recount. In hours when humans normally do
little but die, the dogged struggle went on, and there was an
interminable forty minutes when the California totals stuck
with each candidate at about 46% of what was counted. The
wild card there was an Earth First candidate, who garnered a
protest harvest of quasi-abstaining votes in Sierra Club
suburbs, but being also fluent in Spanish had hit-and-miss
success in one or two hungry neighborhoods where one would
think the future of the spotted owl a very low priority concern.

At twenty minutes to three where I was, the Vice-
President was pronounced winner in Florida and Missouri, and
I despaired; five minutes later Lomax rose from the dead to
capture Texas, and at three, after a fresh flurry of numbers, the
Hardy campaign chief for California acknowledged the state
was lost, evidently unaware that in doing so he was usurping a
prerogative of the national campaign headquarters, in effect
conceding the election itself. I gave the best cheer my chilled
and drowsy condition could raise, and found myself wondering
about Frank Lupin, somewhere the sky must be showing hints

of pale, exclaiming *oh, shit*, no longer bothering to pretend indifference about Hardy's failure. That pretense, and perhaps the reality of not much caring who won, had been possible while the Orbis people knew fresh investigation of the Harness Project could be based only on rumor and unsubstantiated allegation, but now I was on the loose, very possibly with documentary evidence to display, everything was changed, and as much as I longed for, they must fear John Battaglia's appointment to a cabinet post, or as head of any of the several agencies which could withhold approval for radiation-enhanced agriculture.

In all the radio coverage, winding down with both victor and vanquished, said to be `resting' now, promising early-morning statements, I hadn't heard Battaglia's name, and had wished for television, where I might have had a reassuring glimpse of him at Lomax headquarters; not till now had it occurred to me the Orbis conspirators would anticipate an attempt on my part to get in touch with the arch-enemy they'd been unable to persuade, or buy, or intimidate. I'd never supposed election of Orford Lomax would bring about overnight change in my fortunes, and it was clearer than ever I still had to lay low for a time. I couldn't hope to hold out through midwinter till after inauguration, when the Laxitter influence should be at its lowest ebb; but the President-Elect was "expected" to begin naming his first appointments in a week or so, and Battaglia ought to be among them; what would be called the Lomax Transition Team should be positioning itself shortly thereafter, sword ceremonially aimed over cocked left forearm, to give the *coup de grâce* to the lame duck.

Thanksgiving week, if I dared emerge so soon, began to appeal to me; the District of Columbia was immensely distant, but John Battaglia's own state was within a day's drive, and he, like everyone, would surely be home for the holiday. Just where that home was shouldn't be hard to find out. Three weeks; long enough for several subsequent grisly killings to put the Westerlake Monster entirely out of public mind.

Waking late, I was sweating now in the Amazonian microclimate my own heat and moisture had made, but the need for washing soon reinforced my resolve to gather firewood; though I boiled a kettle to modify the chill of spring water in my plastic bucket, the ordeal was enough to provoke in my mind an eloquent polemic against obsessive cleanliness: our folkloric propaganda grotesquely exaggerates or flatly falsifies the relationship between personal cleanliness and health; the question is mainly aesthetic, only five percent hygienic, so long as you eat with clean hands and don't let open wounds get dirty. A whole range of insects and rodents are far more threat to health than a failure to keep clean, and a fugitive in fear for his life ought not to be unduly worried about his smell, unless the bloodhounds are baying. Only by chance I'd found a refuge where my fastidiousness could be indulged — all excellent points, and if, perhaps, I'd ever been part of a hyper-male circle that once or twice a year went off to *the cabin* for alleged hunting and fishing, undoubted swilling, meanwhile, as legend had it, suspending all effete rituals of personal maintenance, I would have been readier for an instant slide from prim to primitive, which I might yet achieve if my exile was to be prolonged into months, a year; but as soon as I was towelled and clothed with my hands coming back to life wrapped around a fresh mug of tea, it was obvious while washing might be uncomfortable, I'd never be comfortable unwashed. The agony of cold-water shaving was a ritual I'd already shown a willingness to forgo.

Using a few crumpled sheets from a yellow pad I tested the fireplace, and the greed with which smoke was sucked up the chimney not only established its usability but at the same time suggested there were places where the weatherproofing of my dwelling could be improved. Lingering questions about visibility of the smoke would cease to nag if, except at

absolute need, I lit a fire only at night: with hardly any trees
closer than a mile of hard toiling it would be donkey's work to
fetch enough wood to keep a fire going more than a few hours
a day. Washing thoroughly last thing at night, I could also
heat the milk for my whiskey, conserving gas for the stove; at
the present rate of consumption my full case of canisters
wouldn't last three weeks. As soon as the usual dreary
breakfast of wheat germ in reborn milk was disposed of, I
went purposefully forth, resolved to get as much firewood as I
could.

My original estimate for the elevation of the cabin may
convey a false picture of loftiness; six thousand feet *above sea
level*, but I was hardly fifty miles from that high, wondrous
spot where, simply by turning around, one can pee alternately
into the Pacific Ocean and Gulf of Mexico, and the lesser
heights I inhabited, too modest to be called a range, too
jumbled and craggy for a ridge, hardly rose three thousand feet
above the considerable altitude of the surrounding terrain.
Insofar as they had a line, they ran to the north and east, where,
perhaps a mile-and-a-half from the cabin, they began tapering
down.

Descending to where Z.B. (I was now fairly sure) had
hacked out his rough step in the great boulder, and working
around to the northward side, I could have picked a way to the
broken crest, and with some scrambling and a few goatlike
leaps followed that down to where, like a fist shaken at the
idea of endings, the crags flung up a final outpost, a separate
pillar, sheer as a cliff on the sides which faced the lowlands,
but from what I thought of as the rear easily scaled by a kind
of bony ramp. But crossing a couple of minor barriers beyond
the stepped boulder made it also possible to attain a kind of
slot, an ancient fault or point of unequal slippage between vast
tilted slabs, on occasion, though rarely, a watercourse, perhaps
in the spring of years with copious snow. By this route, as
near safe from observation as could be, I could reach a place
below the topmost turret of the tower, a pleasant, sheltered

hollow, ringed by trees and toughly grassed. From there the ramp mounted in tumbled blocks like irregular steps, some waist-high, to a spot, still fifty feet below the pinnacle, from where, as I'd discovered back in September, the whole country was spread out for viewing. Unimportant but curiously enjoyable then that cover was provided by a clump of stubborn pines, dwarfed and tormented by their choice of sites into a suggestion of bonsai.

Near noon of a brilliant day I perched behind their screen and kept watch. By night I'd heard coyotes; I didn't think this was bighorn territory, but there would no doubt be some deer; stocked as it was with small rodents owls axiomatically haunted the night; I'd encountered raccoons on my first visit, but now I saw nothing but birds in all the sweep of my survey; humans were what I was checking for. Eastward the land fell in rocky terraces and a final abrupt drop to what must be farmlands along the course of the main road, clearly visible more than ten miles away; using my small binoculars I could catch the infrequent travelling gleam of a car or truck. Beyond that the vista was bounded by a line of dull brown hills, while swinging to my right gave me the view back along the skirts of my own eyrie, tortuous rockscape it occurred to me now was typical cougar habitat, still from this height resisting visual exploration; there was no working out the direction where the lane with my forsaken car might lie, although I surmised that from the summit of the heights at my rear I might be able to glimpse distant pastureland, the ranch beyond the broken bridge.

Swivelling, in the arc from northeast to northwest, I came to the gentler folds of checkered country, patches of deciduous woodland interspersed with grasslands, rocky outcrops, and with pieces of landscape from Mars, red-brown, wrinkled and bare, except for occasional tufts of scrawny weed; here and there like debris trailed by a comet lesser islets of jagged rock thrust up, till to the north the terrain mounted again in rounded slopes, eventually closed off where the big mountains swung eastward, hard and snowcapped spikes astonishingly in unblurred focus at a distance of perhaps eighty miles. That direction, somewhat west of due north, had been my choice in September, rather recklessly, I suppose, with no map, minimal food, only a compass and arrogant conviction that the deep hidden crease before the ground began to rise again was exactly the kind of place to find a town. After the woods gave out I'd wandered frustratingly in a tangle of arroyos, camped, as I found, uncomfortably close to a popular bivouac for rattlesnakes, and at last struck a deeply grooved pair of tire-tracks, which turned into a dirt road and wandered among outlying dwellings and denser woods where logging went on, down into the abrupt obliviousness of a smug little town: it's a peculiarity these settlements, on the edge of wilds as unpeopled, primitive, and in their way as dangerous as any in Africa or Brazil, decline to acknowledge it, preferring to pretend they're set among lands as tamed as Belgium or Connecticut; no caravans come nodding down the street with dates and animal-skins, no native artifacts are spread for sale, or native guides offer their services; there's never an outfitter to supply trade goods, mules, sacks of flour and beans. Instead, I encountered the same octagonal red signs, the same mailboxes, the same Kodak logos stuck to the inside of glass doors, a food market trying earnestly to be super, with specials on cornflakes and styrofoam bread; there were a couple of short streets borrowed from suburbia, lawns, Japanese cut-leaf maples, hedges (*We don't have to grow no steenkin hedges*). Brandsville. No, really, that was its name.

     I was hunting now for something nearer, only now recollected, and soon found again; not far into the woods on that gentle northern slope I'd come to a devastated zone, a couple of acres where all the trees were dead. Why I couldn't tell; experience has taught us to think first of some man-made folly or crime, but it may be this die-off was the result of a wholly natural catastrophe, or normal cyclical process. A victory, at least temporarily, for variety, with a single mature species being replaced by seedlings of four or five, though some were bound to fail when competition intensified; at about three years old there was room for all, dark gymnosperms or paler alder and aspen. More germanely for me, the initial massacre had made easily available a virtually unlimited supply of ready firewood, scarcely a half-mile away, practically all under cover, except for the broad rocky rib that must be crossed after emerging from the hollow and before descending among living trees.

Having cord and a knife with me, I spent some hours breaking dead wood into usable lengths, tying it in bundles, and carrying them up to the hollow behind the watchtower, from where I would relay them to the cabin; the sky was duller now and cloud was edging from the west, making plausible what earlier had been the absurd radio prediction of rain by evening. Wise to get a supply of wood to where it would stay dry, and I kept furiously at my task: deep in recesses where proportion is preserved I must have recognized unreality in the critical importance it had assumed; wood brought indoors would dry out fairly quickly, and at worst I could live without a fire, but I'd been existing on the solely negative stimuli of escape, evasion and concealment, and was bound to fall in love with the first positive project that came along.

The day was becoming humid; I was sweating when I came back up the slope, moved swiftly with my fresh bundles of wood across the one exposed stretch, and jolted down into the hollow. Beside my stock of firewood, a girl was sitting on a stone. Small, slight build, dressed in an olive drab army field jacket and well-worn denims hacked off at an awkward length just below the permanent bulge knees had made, neat brown woolen socks and walking shoes of yellowish leather. How she'd materialized here wasn't as baffling as a desire to defend my own vigilance was trying to pretend: I'd been determined to keep one eye out for things that moved, and had glimpsed nothing except a pair of foxes trotting briskly through sparse brush, but I'd been preoccupied with my task, and there was ample territory for an approach out of sight from where I'd been working in the woods.

No point to retreating; she was looking straight at me with a guardedly friendly face. At first I'd placed her firmly below the age for admissible sexual stir in me, perhaps twelve or thirteen, but as I approached could see that if *tousled* could be used of her short, light hair, it was as past participle rather than adjective, preceded by *professionally*; the cutting skilled enough to shrug off a degree of neglect. Notwithstanding, also, the large eyes in small features, signal for youth not only in humans but with most other mammals, she was — I wasn't sure. Seventeen would be the median for my range of guesses, two years on either side. If I'd still been in that sullen era myself I'd have had a better chance of placing her more precisely: in general, the larger the gap between ages, the harder the sums, or the less it matters: I recalled my mother on the beach in Virgin Gorda upbraiding my father for gazing too ardently at "children," the infants in question being bronzed and breasted in buttock-cleaving rudiments of costume, and my father muttering that at his age he found it hard to tell whether children were fifteen or twenty-five, and could see ample reason not to try. But in this specific instance the arithmetic was complicated by ambiguities inherent in face and posture, where the calm of maturity yet to come overlapped with a past intense earnestness, as in a six-year-old.

"Hi," as I came up and unburdened. "You're working hard." This was other than the I-have-to-say-something convention it echoed, actual observation of an interesting phenomenon. "I was watching you," she testified, "from up in the Crow's Nest."

"I call it the Watchtower." Saying the word aloud brought me a nostalgic stab; it not only felt like but was part of a lost other life when I'd reminded Judy of those insistent,

smarmy doomsayers who often on Saturday morning went
door-to-door in the apartment-building, hawking posthumous
lifestyle-insurance.

"You must be the guy who's camping out up in Zack's
shack. I was up there a couple of days ago — Sunday, but you
weren't around."

Sunday. I'd been making heavy weather of my final
trek from car, overloaded by the inclusion of many odds and
ends — I worked this out as if I'd missed a date for afternoon
tea, while most of me was still reeling; what I'd taken for a
hideaway known only to me was transforming itself into a
popular attraction, perhaps, who knew? with guided tours
twice weekly. I said, "Zack's shack?"

"That's what my father and I always called it. My
father decided he was Zack Brand, Brandsville was named
after him. He was the world's worst prospector. There was
Ornery, his three-legged mule, and Zack staked claims on
pyrites from Cabo San Lucas to Point Barrow. This was his
hideout after he was almost caught trying to tunnel into the
Denver Mint, only he waited till he finished his evening meal,
because — "

"He felt like an after-dinner mint," I guessed.

"Very good — " the girl's approval was joyous; she'd
been using a knowing smirk, presumably derived from the
father, but now came a brilliant smile of her own. Clearly this
game was a treasured memento, and with the instant
supposition her father must be dead, I was careful not to let my
face twitch into the standard grimace demanded by other
peoples' puns. I said: "I recall Zack had a Mexican cook,
named Estreñido, who used to say, `*Bedgies? We ain't got no
bedgies. We don't need to boil no steenkin bedgies,*' — " but
this was a break in style, and either because dad's humor didn't
reach to parodic quotations, or because the Legend of Zack
was canonic, with no room for apocrypha, her smile, like

reducing the heat to blue simmer, sank back to the merely polite.

"Once," she resumed, but *diminuendo*, and her eyes, the color impossible to name, but the emotions so easy to read I was embarrassed to, registered the perception that Zack's moment had passed. "Anyway," she said. "What are you escaping from?"

The barely detectable emphasis here was on *you*, important, if I could work out what it contrasted me to. Did it mean, however improbably, that others before me had used the cabin for a sanctuary, or was it a fellow-fugitive's offer to swap stories?

Choosing shock for policy, I told her I was wanted for murder.

"How many murders?" Either she hadn't heard about the Westerlake killing, or didn't connect me to that well-publicized occurrence.

"Only one, so far. I didn't do it."

"I know that." Quite unperturbed, so I wasn't sure whether she heard this as another game, like Zack Brand. From the first she'd had none of the wariness that defines and accuses our era; it's true there was a small, cheap, bolt-action .22 rifle leaning on the rock beside her, and while she'd shown no inclination to reach for it, the notion of being armed might have contributed to her confidence. But I doubt it; she was, as I found, complicated, but alarmingly straightforward in her responses, and here she'd made an instantaneous decision to trust me on pure intuition.

There was, also, a conspiracy pending; she was suddenly (and atypically) cagey when I asked where she lived. Convenient, here, to move ahead a little, and say here she was Fern, daughter of Matthew Thomas, eminent botanist.

"Polygonaceae," naming his specialty, and looking to see if I knew. As it happens, I did (there is a widely-used high-school botany textbook, with the names of two PhD's on the title page, in fact written by me with the publisher's science editor); they're the plants popularly known as buckwheats, although it's a vast family, not all with edible seeds.

I said, "I would have thought Filicinae — " and she made a face, having heard that before. Her mother, she said, had been an amateur fern-fancier.

Not a mother, it was easy to tell, of whom this Fern was fond, and because (she said quaintly) I have the face of a "just" listener, she soon gave me a selection of reasons, beginning with her parents' estrangement, nine years ago. Mother, Lenore (née Purcell), had moved from book development and foreign sales for a big publishing house to doing much the same things as a freelancer, and had spent increasing amounts of time in Europe, sometimes with her infant daughter in tow, showing ever-diminishing interest in the reunions with Matthew, who was teaching at the same West-Coast university where Lenore had once been his student. Small Fern had not been with her mother on the sojourn which began with the Frankfurt Book Fair and ended near Christmas in a return that was more like a raid, with divorce as its objective, Lenore then being five months pregnant after a six-month absence.

"It would have been better," factually, "if she'd never come back. She was afraid she wouldn't get all her stuff — " which I was to understand as meaning clothes, a car, jewelry, perhaps.

"And me. She didn't *like* me, I was just part of the booty. It was beyond her dreams that my father would fight for custody." But he had, and recognizing her condition would, in more than one sense, cut a poor figure in court, fearful she'd be excluded entirely, Lenore settled for promised visits by her daughter to Berne, where she would be living with her next husband, a Swiss publisher, Miki Frisch — I heard the name as *Mickey*, till Fern, with corroding scorn, gave the spelling. She'd been ecstatic recounting how her father had, contrary to form, dug in his heels, but on the basis of the

unlimited energy which seethed just under Fern's cooled
mantle, calculating the thrust it might develop driving the
passionate singlemindedness of an anxious child, I suspected
that, rather than finding a new resistance to female will, mild
Matt had simply been propelled by what was for a time the
stronger of two.

Fern had indeed spent some parts of summers in
Switzerland, where she disliked a small half-brother and
smaller half-sister, whose names, Rudi and Heidi, God, *Heidi*,
she gave with almost as much disdain as she had for *Miki*, but
her heart had remained where her father was, especially
summers and sometimes Christmas in this country, where,
from a cottage by a whitewater stream in the woods above
Brandsville they'd explored on foot or assisted by a variety of
four-footed and four-wheeled carriers.

"Just the two of you?" probing for at least two pieces
of information.

"Yep. Always." She studied whitening sky. "Didn't
you ought to get some of your squaw wood under cover before
the rain comes? I'll help."

A crux was lurking near. With my survival in mind,
and the possibility of being forced to resume a doomed
nomadism, surely I wasn't unduly self-centered or discourteous
in listening with divided attention to Fern's unexpected baring
of her past, alert for clues about my own future. Observation
told me she'd exult in being sworn to secrecy, might insist we
make cuts at the base of our thumbs (I omit the name palmistry
confers) and high-five to mingle our blood, a stirring but
meaningless flourish if half Brandsville was already discussing
that guy up at Zack's cabin.

"It's getting late," I said.

"Doesn't matter."

"You're a long way from home."

"My little ORV is only a couple of miles down there —
" she pointed approximately northeast. "It's four-wheel drive; I
go all over in it."

"Not after dark, not off-road."

"No," complacently, slinging her small rifle and picking up bundles of firewood. Standing, she appeared a neat exercise in metric conversion, 59 inches (150cm.).

Loading myself, I accepted what I had no remedy for; if my efforts to get rid of her had been half-hearted it was in recognition that unless I first found out who else might know about my being here, I'd have to vacate my refuge before it turned into a snare; the spotlights, rifles, bullhorn ultimata. When, fishing for her age without bluntly asking, I wondered whether she had a driver's license, she tightened the screws further with: "Out here, who cares? Anyway, Sean Gomez is my buddy — the police chief in Brandsville. He likes my bad coffee, it reminds him of his sister. He stops by a couple of times a week, and says, `You got any of that river-mud?' He's going to teach me how to tie flies."

Now we were lugging firewood, with some awkward straits to negotiate, the talk was more spread out than it appears on the page; minutes went before I asked her direct whether Chief Gomez knew Zack's Shack was occupied.

"Uh uh," and then with devastating trust in her own intuition, "Nobody else knows."

Having turned to ask my question, I lay down my burden, and my agonized appeal to the heavens incidentally let me know a fine drizzle had begun. "My God, Fern," noting for the millionth time in my life how the reallest emotions reach out to the most theatrical expression. "If I had really done what they say I did — "

"You'd be dangerous as hell," she interrupted. "And I'd be dumb as a paperweight for what I just said. But you didn't do it."

"As it happens," maintaining altitude. "But — "

"Oh, Jeez, lighten up. There's no fuckin' way you can make this a *learning experience*. In all the rest of my life, how often am I going to be alone on a mountainside with an accused killer?"

Unnerved, as anyone might be, by how rapidly the extremely intelligent person could alternate with the peevish child, I conceded the point. Fern said seriously, "You must be able to prove your innocence. Can I help?"

"Forget you know I'm here." I resumed the march, suddenly turned brisk by thought of the word *evidence*: on Sunday when Fern had come calling in my long absence (and might have been anybody), the motel register that established my alibi was unguarded and not particularly well concealed in the cabin, and so was Judy's mobile disk with the Laxitter files, as both were right now, or had been when I left.

Nothing was physically changed, but everything was; impossible now to restore the cabin to what it had been, a hide outside the edge of human consciousness. To what extent it was known to Brandsville was what I tried to ascertain from Fern, who, after dumping her load of wood, showed no urgency about leaving, but wandered the cabin checking my arrangements, approving of my lantern and the small stove. According to her only half-attentive reply, none of the oldtimers in town had known about the dwelling when her father first happened on it, and after seven or eight years there was no reason for them to remember his enquiries.

She asked what I was using for food, and made the comic-strip retching noise over wheat-germ. "I've got a ton of practically legal venison in the freezer at the cottage. You're not a vegetarian, or anything? I'll bring you some."

"No." Preposterous; patiently, I tried to explain I meant it precisely when I said she should forget I was here; her knowledge was dangerous both for me and for her; she wanted to play Little Red Riding Hood to my granny, while I could see no escape but flight from a situation I was impotent to control. As I told her, if I were really the ruthless Westerlake killer there would be no choice (if I let her live) but to make her my prisoner, but since her disappearance would bring about an intensive hunt within a fairly narrow compass, that would leave my position as untenable as if she were free to blab.

Her childish strain spent a moment relishing the prospect of captivity, before she brought herself into frowning focus, and said, "I'm not going to give you away. Really — " and now at last came the deal that had been hovering ever since she first asked what had brought me here; she offered me the information she too was in hiding, and I became, she said, the first person in these parts, except for *Maretta*, a close and trustable friend, to know her father was dead.

The dying had been a protracted process, ending three weeks ago in Sacramento. Unspecified "family" had managed the obsequies, which Fern's mother had not attended, but from Berne a fiat had come advising Fern she would now be part of the Miki-Rudi-Heidi family, and she was to get on a plane to Switzerland forthwith. Overseen by her late father's elderly cousin, who'd also received instructions from Lenore, Fern had taken a plane to Chicago, where, although all but her hand baggage had made the connecting flight for Zürich, she had not, instead flying back to Kansas City, and making her way here by a variety of means; elision of detail made me suspect they'd included the dread hitchhiking, against which all Ferns are (very properly) so often and luridly warned. Odd that at exactly the same time, for our widely disparate reasons, we'd both been reaching what we hoped was safe haven, exhaustedly dumping our baggage and wishing beds and beverages would make themselves.

Neither in smug Switzerland nor sun-seared Sacramento could authority now know where Fern was. In the summer following the divorce she and her father had begun coming here, and he'd been passionate about preserving its secrecy; their cottage had a phone, but not even his department at the university was given its number; during longer summer stays he went to the lengths of having mail forwarded to a

post-office box in a small city more than a hundred miles away
and in another state, making the drive twice weekly.

"It was *our* place," Fern said.

"Your father never thought about marrying again?"

"Oh God, no." If there was more in my question I
wasn't and am still not aware of it, so can't judge whether Fern
reacted to an unconscious insinuation of mine, or to her own
misgivings, which, as will become clear, certainly existed.
She said, "We were buddies, best friends, there's nothing
strange about that." For the first time, there was a quaver, a
crack in the brisk manner she'd adopted for dealing with the
loss.

"Of course not," quickly papering over by asking what
her plans were, how long she meant to remain in hiding.

"They're not going to make me go to Switzerland and
live with that bitch. Knowing her, she'd try changing my name
to Ferni — " this with exaggerated Continental pronunciation,
Fairr-nee. "When I'm eighteen, I can do what I want."

"How long is that? A year?"

"Nearer two," pugnaciously. "Over a year-and-a-half,
anyway."

She was defying me to tell her it couldn't be done, as
obviously it couldn't; her friend Chief Gomez wouldn't be able
to protect her from questions the non-appearance of her father
would provoke; he, indeed, would be the one to ask them.
There was also a good chance he'd recognize his friend in the
missing person circular there would certainly be. So far she
was telling storekeepers, and others she had to deal with, that
her father was soon going to join her, and it seemed she'd
persuaded Gomez he'd just missed his friend Matt Thomas,
who'd come and gone in the week between the chief's visits,
but would be back.

To avoid giving my bleak prognosis, I asked what she
was doing for money, and there she'd managed quite well;
over two years ago, at a time, it had since become apparent,
when his condition had been diagnosed, her father had

transferred a considerable proportion of his money to her, and she'd made regular cash withdrawals during the six months of his terminal illness: when she boarded plane in Sacramento she'd had unwise amounts of currency wadded about her person, and using fake, or rather borrowed ID, she'd now opened a savings account in the same town where her father used to have his mail sent, and had more than enough (as she reckoned) to cover two years of food, replacement jeans and other expenses; the cottage was legitimately hers outright under her father's will, where (she answered my question before asked) it had not been identified for the curious, but was merely part of unspecified residual property.

"So, you see?" in summation, meaning her case was made; we were natural allies, each with the goods on the other. But we'd only start even if I'd been nothing more than the falsely-accused fugitive from the law she'd been allowed to see, and I reluctantly acknowledged for her safety as well as mine I was going to have to tell her some of the larger story.

"I'll see you on your way," elbowing on my small knapsack, where I'd now put mobile disk and motel register, not again to be left here unattended. I'd decided to go for another load of firewood, before completely sodden. The drizzle was steady, and the sun wouldn't be back today.

"Aren't you going to offer me some tea?"

"No."

She wrinkled up her face in intense consideration. "Do you think it was, between my father and me, incestuous? I know it wasn't o-*vert*ly. Maretta said it was obvious — this was when my father was still alive. She says it's not all that uncommon."

"Universal," lightly. "According to those who read our souls." I'd opened the door, but Fern, though she turned to face me, didn't act on the hint.

"Well, but he was always saying he'd have to spank me, any time I got home late or gave him an argument. He never did it, but he never even threatened to until after I was about thirteen. That's supposed to be terribly sexual, Maretta says. In fact, according to her, a good spanking can be highly enjoyable, if you like somebody." While her tone withheld a personal verdict, there was a small, challenging head-gesture; but that, surely, had been borrowed together with the thought from the surely older, intriguingly corrupt Maretta, and I was certain we needed laws against the making of such high-risk loans to improvident minors. The adroit haircut, so unlike the rest of Fern's uncalculated self, must derive less riskily from the same source.

Decidedly, no comment came from me, and as if I had been the one creating delay, she became brisk, making the ingenious suggestion I take my tent, set it up down below, and fill it with the firewood I couldn't carry back today. "Not in the clearing," to my objections about visibility. "Nobody will see it down in the woods. Nobody comes there, anyway."

"You did." As we covered the now-familiar ground I told in fairly general terms the reasons why my peril, overdrawn to her, couldn't be cured by possession of an alibi for the murder. I'd hesitated so far, not because I thought she wouldn't believe me, but for the opposite reason; as was predictable she leapt at a tale of international corporate conspiracy and corrupted institutions, devouring it voraciously, till I could sober her with the real story behind Paula's ugly death.

"But she didn't even *know* anything. Jesus."

"A lot less than you do." This was callous exploitation, but in a good cause: at last Fern showed symptoms of a salutary fear.

Yet remained unpredictable, saying I should have a gun, and offering to lend one. Not the .22, carried mainly to scare coyotes; once timid but yearly bolder with the growing recognition of their protected standing, they often caucused in packs of ten or a dozen around the outskirts of Brandsville, and could be menacing when encountered by night, but were still cowed by the noise and flash of guns. There were, Fern said, a couple of deer-rifles she never used at the cottage, "or are you anti guns?"

"When they're pointed at people." Though I could never shoot at animals, or rather, bear hitting them, no carnivore has the moral right to condemn hunting, if the target is edible, and is meant to be eaten. Rather surprisingly, to myself as much as others, I'm an excellent shot; in my youth, an uncle, least-acclaimed among my mother's three brothers, owned a sporting-goods store between Ann Arbor and Ypsilanti, with a basement rifle-range, where I spent many hours and boxes of generously-supplied ammunition putting holes with constantly improved predictability in paper targets, and this was nonsense; flattered, is that it? by this girl's trust, I was letting myself be mesmerized into fantasy. We were back at the place where we'd met.

"You're not going to bring me anything," I told the girl. "Or lend me anything, or tell me anything more. You're going to go back to your cottage."

"Aren't you going to set up your tent? I'll help you."

"Or help me. I'm glad we met."

"You don't trust me," darkly sullen.

"I want you to stay alive for a long time. I hope you can work it all out." Not seeing light return, I took the perilous plunge into advice: "What you need is a lawyer. You know, you can petition in court for emancipation."

"Like Dred Scott."

"But a happier outcome, I would think." With good coaching from an attorney to keep the present infant out of sight, Fern stood an excellent chance of impressing a court with her adult competence.

"Can't I come and talk to you some more about it? You know about this stuff."

"Any lawyer knows a lot more than I do."

"I thought we were going to be friends."

For me, a surge of righteous anger sweetened with a sticky dollop of self-pity, as she walked away without a farewell: damn her, if she couldn't see it was because I was a carrier of death that I couldn't have friends; I was at the same time hounded fugitive and self-exiled plague-bearer, and still sick with guilt over Paula; if getting Fern mad at me was the only way of both shedding and sheltering her, so be it.

With her muted colors she didn't have to do much in these conditions to make herself inconspicuous; she emerged just once into my plain sight, smaller in the huge landscape, by weather made doubtful, homogenized to undifferentiated grey. Not the first time the word *lonely* had come to mind, but the definitive instance, and I could have howled my sorrow for the solitude of her life here, with no one to talk to but a seemingly good-hearted but now inevitably threatening cop, and Maretta, her mentor, the kinky hairdresser (conjecture). I had an urge to go galloping down the rocky hillside to catch up and make absolutely sure Fern knew it wasn't out of dislike I'd sent her away, but of course I didn't.

Instead, I erected my tent among dripping trees, stacked it with wood, and carried my maximum load on the day's fourth traversal of the rough route, after which my knees and lower back whimpered I'd done enough for the day. All I'd brought back was inside the cabin, and there was suddenly a strong probability that what I'd taken and was using for a sleeping-shelf must have been where old Zack kept his ready supply of firewood; the main pile would have been stacked on the flat surface next to the cabin on the opposite side to the water-supply, partly protected by the overhang, and I'd do the same when the rain stopped, using my tent-fly to improve the cover.

Late, the warming effect of the fierce little blaze I started, like bright sun on a bitterly cold day, was far more than a thermometer would register, what the eye perceived acting on the mind, and with rain now pattering in earnest, I made blissful entry into the sleeping bag with a rush of concentrated complacency such as may be read in the eyeless grin of a safe and puddled cat, as if warmth and comfort in the midst of foul weather were my own invention, a proud achievement. If dreams came, they remain beyond reach of any statute.

10

Rain, dwindling often but then lashing back in snarling squalls, kept me mainly confined, or prudence did, seeing limited resources there were for getting me dry and warm. The weather supplied the first real test of my self-sufficiency, and scored on a scale of serenity, I failed it. Like every writer who's ever committed himself to delivering thirty thousand words of finished copy by the end of next week, I'd had experience of self-imposed hermitage, but that was a condition I controlled, and urban solitude is inevitably punctuated and ameliorated by necessary sorties to buy milk or a fresh supply of, oh, escargots; when I was here before, there'd been an irreconcilable couple of frustrations to obsess me; now, with time to be passed, I was restless and diffuse, unable to surrender myself to reading or writing, dozing readily when I attempted either, making tea more often than was compatible with concern over my gas-supply, constantly chilled, counting hours till I would permit myself a fire.

Admittedly, this time would have been easier if Fern had never occurred — that shouldn't be read in a sentimental sense; Fern, I mean to say, as representative; while her oddities were diverting to recall, not so much the girl as the idea of company she'd introduced had disturbed my resolve. That's still not complete truth, because things had happened to link our solitudes, twenty miles apart; now there was some of the same perversity detectable in the urban loneliness that has its venerable sufferers hammering for quiet on the walls of each other's cubicles, instead of joining forces to share their macaroni and cheese. More practical fears isolated us, but the division was equally artificial.

I emerged on the third morning into a displaced midsummer day, with haze rising in sun that promised real heat. I decided to go and climb the Watchtower, Crow's Nest

to Fern, and, after a survey of the country at large, continue
down into the trees, and see how my tent had withstood the
weather.

When I had clambered down the stepped boulder and
crossed into the long slot, where fresh darts of sand and
unweathered deposits of small debris were evidence of swift
water having passed this way, I became aware of a machinery
sound, one I could soon identify, a distinctive surging throb,
oddly menacing even when one has nothing to be menaced
about, a helicopter in flight, not close, although within hearing
was too near. Where I was, among rocks, beneath broken
crags, the scattering effect on echoes made direction difficult
to tell, and needing a place where I could command a larger
view without unduly exposing myself, I went on with creeping
caution, till, not far short of the drop into the hollow behind
the Watchtower, I came to where a big bite had been taken out
of the steplike rampart to my right. On my belly, I wormed to
the crumbled edge; the engine noise, sometimes growing faint,
had never ceased, and I soon spotted the aircraft, skimming so
low it was actually below my elevation, miles away to the
south and east, stooping over gullies, vanishing sometimes
behind hills, ending a long eastward sweep near the line of the
distant road, and doubling back. Is it the forward lean that
makes the flight of a helicopter so sinister, reminiscent of a
mosquito? although this was one of the fat-bodied kind, and as
it turned in sun I saw it was a glossy yellow.
  This was dreadful — the fact of the helicopter, not just
its color. My instant megalomaniac assumption was it must be
searching for me: the searching couldn't be doubted, and if no
more than a cowpoke on his high-tech cayuse, seeking a
strayed dogie or ornery maverick, the risks remained.
Furtively, I left my vantage-point, and went slinking back the
way I'd come, freezing when a trick of air-currents or the
complicated echoes made it certain the noise was headed in

my direction. Having the stepped boulder to cross, I waited, crouched at its base, and in the small relevant segment of sky available to my view saw the helicopter, still distant though now at its closest to me, sailing on its westward course, which would take it just about over where I'd left my car. Once shielded by nearby crags, I hastily negotiated the exposed boulder, and in a headlong scuttle covered the rest of the distance back to the cabin.

I was shaken; two centuries of steadily improving aerial surveillance, from fierily soaring Montgolfiers to orbital cameras able to read conditions of sale on an airline ticket from fifty miles up, had still left me altogether unprepared for this abrupt change in the geometry of concealment; most clutter, which is also cover, occurs where we live, on the surface of our planet, and not much can be done to impede the immense unobstructed vista overhead. True, without prior knowledge of its existence there was small chance the cabin would be seen from above: even a very slow-moving aircraft would have only a fraction of a second to glimpse and identify the structure, but I was anxious now about the two signs I'd left to bracket me, car away to the southwest, tent much nearer to the northeast, both placed under trees from which much of the desiccated foliage must have been ripped by more than two days of squalling weather. Again, neither would mean much to a random passerby, but the steady quartering of the helicopter was hardly casual; I was certain it was looking quite specifically for me, at the same time as I was sure no one could have traced me here.

I sat trying to reconcile that pair of opposed ideas, while the drone faded to the threshold of perception, and just when I thought it gone came surging back, once passing very near, noise so great it was impossibly about to land outside my door. It faded away, to the northward so far as I could tell, and for a time, applying a safecracker's fingertips and ear to the dial of my little radio I was able to bring in the station of a distant college town, and heard a Mozart recording in which

Antonia was soloist, not up to her best, I thought, with her
husband as conductor, her long raptures hardly more than
dutiful under his unimaginative baton. A taped *Schöne
Müllerin* from Salzburg was next, but influenced, maybe, by
the Schubertian aesthetic, the frequency began wandering, and
the station soon vanished over the horizon, not to be retrieved.
I let myself be immensely annoyed, aware that behind anger
numbing fear was waiting to seep back in. The paralyzing
question was which fear should be yielded to: let the mere
appearance of the helicopter flush me from cover, with no
hope of finding a comparable hiding-place, and every chance
I'd be captured? or stay where I was, where the advantages of
my fastness could so easily be turned into a trap? In any
conflict where the virtues of doing something and of doing
nothing are in balance, inaction will always win, or appear to,
since its effects are indistinguishable from unresolved debate.

One's apprehensions can be refined to where absence
of what caused fear is as frightening as its presence; in early
afternoon I noted with a start the sound of the helicopter had
ceased minutes ago. The thought it might be only a refuelling
stop for machine and pilot kept me where I was, although I
wanted, if belatedly, to go down and strike my tent, now like a
beacon proclaiming my nearby presence. At the same time,
with radio warning me the unnatural heat couldn't go on, and
precipitous falls in temperature would soon be bustled in my
direction by northwesterly winds, it would be wise to increase
my stock of firewood. Still reluctant to risk being caught in
the open, I read a chapter or two of Wodehouse, and spent an
hour trying to think of at least one opera for every letter of the
alphabet (Z is easier than you'd think; English versions of
Tchaikovsky and Handel titles cover the other awkward
letters), all the time listening for the helicopter to return, all
the more startled by the sound that did come, a gentle tapping
at my door.

Van Muer, *Azraël*, it was instantly clear, had been in all my thoughts, riding the air like lord of the *Nazgûl* (Fena), stalking me with icy competence, left hand jammed out of sight, right curling around an efficient little pistol, of which he was the extension, a mere guidance system, more dangerous, certainly, than most of us, but fitting emblem for a world that let its humanity be defined by the function of tools, with *how?*, not *why?* its arbiter.

A small voice said, "Arthur?"

Fern, altered in ways which, adding sophistication, might have been expected (and meant?) to make her look older, some brush time spent restoring the designed disorder of her hair, sparing color applied to large-eyed face, a big-collared gold shirt under the same drab jacket, tapered jeans, not cheap, in place of the frayed cutoffs, soft boots that trod a fine line between decorative and practical. The net effect was endearing, but in the opposite to the intended sense; modishness can be an assault on or a defense against the world, but Fern's earnest efforts only increased her vulnerability.

There were more reasons than ever for her not being here, but the difficulty of reprimanding a small person with large strange-colored eyes, already filled with contrition, was, I'm sure, in Fern's calculations; she was surely not consciously manipulative, but life with her (as one deduced) often abstracted best-buddy father had inevitably fostered some survival skills. "Don't be mad," face in torment. "I was very careful about not being seen, but I had to come. There's stuff you have to know. I was coming to see you yesterday, but I chickened out — I left something for you up at the Crow's Nest. Hey, you were on TV."

No matter how low one's general assessment of the medium, that's a remark to focus attention. Fern herself was hardly a devotee; she'd become aware only that week there was a program called *Infamous Fugitives* which, with recapitulations, often reenactments, of real-life crimes, profiles

of suspects, and a crusading style, prided itself in having
helped hound down a number of luckless wanderers, and
consistently was listed among the dozen or so most-watched of
offerings. This week, the Westerlake Fiend had been allotted
a generous segment, and Fern, using the flicker to hunt for
improbable reptilians from Madagascar or the Galápagos,
instead encountered a full-screen picture of me, more clean-
shaven, slightly younger, a great deal more reputable in jacket
and tie, and learned I "was reported by some sources" to have
fled the country, the more plausible in that I was "known to
have knowledge of several languages." (Do I hear Hilde
Konwitschny chuckle?)

    As for the account of my crime, "Tendentious
garbage," Fern said, admitting she'd clicked in at the middle of
a piece filled with things I *might have* and *could have* and *had,
conceivably* done, and pseudo-questions beginning *Did Ames
then — ?* "But the Westerlake police chief was interesting.
Interesting, that is, how they tried to edit it to be consistent
with their thesis, when it was obvious he has considerable
reservations." (This is word-for-word; when making a report
Fern readily paid visits to the literary and somewhat stilted
manner of, as it might be, a botany professor and author,
conscious of his eminence.)

    Willing to call my disappearance no worse than
unexplained, the chief, "ironically" named Leahy (TV
routinely labels as irony what real life sees only as mildly
interesting coincidence), no connection with the victim, had
allowed he'd still like to talk to Mr. Ames, with the clear
implication his suspicions were now elsewhere. "The TV
people did this but-we-know-don't-we number, maybe he was
trying to reassure you if you were watching the show, but that's
this — " and she made the parody of a confidential wink, using
an ostentatious forefinger to overindicate it.

    Fern seemed to be saying if the police, without yet
seeing my alibi evidence, no longer believed I was the

murderer, it should be safe for me to come out of hiding. I reminded her, patiently enough, that, ignoring any amateur avengers inflamed by the portrait of me as an Infamous Fugitive, my emergence was likely to be greeted by a highly professional tidier-up.

"Wait, don't get your — don't get in an uproar," Fern interrupted. "That was Thursday. Yesterday afternoon Sean Gomez came by to see if I was okay. He's starting to get pushy about whether I'm *sure* my father knows I'm here all alone."

Was it only my own nasty-mindedness that made me wonder if Brandsville's head policeman harbored thoughts murkier than the turgid coffee he cited as Fern's chief allure? He had, be that as it may, a justification for concern; what kept things cool in a town that size, he said, was everybody knowing everybody; you start getting transients, that changes the deal. A young girl, all by herself, she's just not safe.

Indeed, *mon vieux*, as you say. "Transients?" I queried, exactly as Fern had.

Yes. Mainly in a huge, glittering, many-wheeled motorized domicile too clifflike and costly to be called a camper, now renting resting-space from Tony Arkle, local dealer in building supplies and miscellaneous oddities, from live snakes to alleged Indian jewelry bearing every attribute of urban mass production. The number of denizens the intruding vehicle contained could only be estimated at from four to eight, since, with the one who'd negotiated with Tony, they appeared to be essentially identical, young and slender men in neat business suits, seen going in pairs, wearing neat, powerful ties and polished oxfords, as alien an irruption here as a troupe of New Guinea mud-men might be. Speaking of aliens, one fringe theory for their mysterious presence was they must be "government fellas," keeping tryst with an ambassadorial UFO. The more accepted folk-tale, that they were corporate high-rollers spying out possible sites for anything from hotels, condos and a casino to all of those in connection with a glitzy new ski resort, had, according to Gomez, boiled up the ever-simmering dispute between Developers, who believed new money could give Brandsville a tremendous future, and Traditionalists, afraid that might be true. With my attraction to abstract over actual, I was ready to side with the standpatters, while convinced, as Fern was, this invasion had nothing to do with beautiful people and inflated property-prices; it reeked of Orbis.

Wait, that's not all. Without postulating a connection to the suited ones, except as part of his inventory of unusual strangers in town, Gomez spoke about another visitor, who'd come to see him after ascertaining Brandsville had no public library, an historian of the American West, seeking information particularly on ghost towns, abandoned mines and the like. His insistence there must be examples nearby was eventually irritating to Gomez, Brandsville-born, and not willing to be instructed by a guy who wasn't even American; he guessed he was Australian or some such.

"South African," curiously satisfied that I had in some way felt his proximity, though baffled how van Muer could have tracked me here so soon. No one now living knew about this place, and my mention of it to Paula had been too vague and cursory for him to have learned anything from her to put him nearer than a couple of hundred miles, but then I remembered: when they broke into my apartment, they'd taken the hard disk out of my computer, and all the floppies with my own work and personal correspondence; against all reasonable prediction, Laxitter must have assigned a reader, or, in view of their bulk, a small team, to comb through for clues to my whereabouts. After returning from the September fiasco, I'd made some diary notes to assist with possible letters; none had ever been used for that, and while I couldn't remember exactly what I'd written, such notes were usually sketchiest of memory-joggers — but I had recorded the name of the town in a feeble pun (`not nationally-advertised Brandsville'), and close reading might extract the information I'd camped in an abandoned cabin more than a day's trek from there. Once it was recognized the confusing electronic trail Judy had helped me create was not to be relied on, the generally southwestward course of confirmed sightings — outside St. Louis, Happy Haven motel, the town where I'd changed cars, perhaps by now the leisure center in western Arkansas, or one of my subsequent stops for gas — had apparently been enough to bring both *Azraël* and an Orbis team, whether independently or as backup, to Brandsville.

"That's a long way from finding Zack's shack," airily, not for a moment considering her journey here might have given inestimable aid to a canny observer. I spoke about the helicopter, and to me, whose universe had been filled with its threat, there was shock that she could be so casual; no, she hadn't seen it, though she had heard it, but in this country (as I knew) such sounds could be heard from many miles away.

"The so-called Australian guy asked Sean Gomez whether anybody had a chopper he could rent, and he told him there was usually one on the Preston place. They use it for a limo, and sometimes for roundups, but they loan it out when there's a fire or for a search, and rent it to other ranchers. It's a real ugly yellow. I'm going over there to see what I can find out."

"What are the Prestons?"

"Maretta's family. Everett Preston the Third, that's her father."

The lift of her eyebrows suggested I should recognize the name: a quick subsidiary perception was that Fern's go at stylish dress, to my almost unmixed relief, had nothing to do with impressing me, but must be deference to her mentor, Maretta, not a hairdresser. The Prestons were moneyed, but while Everett III had offices called Preston International in far-off Dallas, the wealth, according to Fern, wasn't attached to any particular identifying enterprise or commodity; he wasn't an oilman or a grain dealer or a manufacturer; to the slight

extent he was a cattle baron it was in the breeding, on his
spacious nearby ranch, of various Brahma-Angus-longhorn
hybrids, said to be mainly a tax writeoff. His wife was Elise,
and there were three Preston offspring; Maretta was one of
non-identical twins, and management of the ranch was now
largely in the hands of their elder brother, Everett IV, whose
absorbing hobby, however, was a nascent winery in Oregon;
while studying botany at Davis as part of his enology course
he'd discovered he and Fern's father were, on the expanded
scale of this empty landscape, summertime neighbors. When
Fern remarked that with the bridge broken on the back way,
she'd have to return almost to Brandsville, I realized my car
was just off what had been an access road to the Preston ranch.

    Very well, but if *Azraël*'s wings were being supplied by
the Prestons, why did Fern want to go there?

    "I was going to talk them into not renting him the
chopper, if they're doing it, to stop."

    "How?" I challenged. *Why* was a question I could
answer; she saw this as a game and had decided to play on my
side.

    "I'll tell Maretta he's only pretending to be interested in
history. I can say I heard a rumor he's really looking for a
good site for a toxic waste dump. They're very anti that," she
added, with a touch of irony.

    "What if you run into him there?"

    "What if? He doesn't know me, there's no reason for
him to connect me to you. Anyway, I'd rather run into him
there than wait for him to visit me at the cottage, like in
Westerlake."

    "Can you stay there?" I was struck suddenly by the
terror of her solitude, and knifelike renewal of my part in
Paula's death.

    "For a while, sure. They know about my father, but so
far only Maretta knows I'm hiding out here." That wasn't
exactly what she'd told me before, but let it go.

She was seated on my bed-shelf abruptly forlorn, and was not enthusiastic when I suggested prominent Everett Preston III might be of help to her, in finding a lawyer, if nothing else. Her wary ambiguity — "he doesn't *hate* me," she said — reflected mine: the Prestons sounded for my comfort too much like the Laxitter milieu; for all I knew they might be personal friends, and would almost surely have friends in common. And for the life of me, quite literally, for my life, I couldn't risk offending the girl by cautioning her not to talk about me. Not until, that is, I'd listened patiently to her countersuggestion the Preston influence might be useful to me, and then, only gently, reminding her it was precisely the money establishment that was threatened by my knowledge.

Still I'd hurt her. "I only thought," wistfully, "Maretta could put you on her TV show, and you could get your story out." I learned Maretta helicoptered into the state capital once a week to tape a half-hour celebrity interview program. "She'd love to have the scoop," Fern said.

Perhaps the Brenda Starr vocabulary stimulated my recollection of a small paragraph in either *Time* or *Newsweek* a year or so back, under the heading *Rocky Mountain Horror Show*, in which the "youthful, trendy host" of just such a program was described, with illustrative examples, as having "plumbed new depths of feckless irrelevancy."

I said, "She wasn't the one who asked Margaret Thatcher how she felt about garter-belts?"

"It was going to be her question," Fern explained evenly. "Like, *if you were ice-cream, what flavor would you be?*, her logo, but it got so much publicity she had to stop using it, people were getting off preemptive responses. She got some good answers at first — like from Jocko Battaglia."

"Jocko?"

"Yes, you know, Senator, was-Senator Battaglia."

His state adjoined this one; he'd known the Prestons before, and had become a family friend since the TV show,

had visited them here at the ranch, "*with* Eugenia Battaglia,"
Fern said firmly, naming the senator's respected wife, but not
dislodging my impression more than an interview had
occurred with Maretta, processes to translate John into Jocko.

Rather brusquely elbowing aside an account of his
solution to the garter-belt question, and at the same time
shuffling away the notion of exposing myself with Maretta —
whose station was an affiliate of the Orbis-controlled network
— I wondered whether the friendship was sufficient to bring
me in contact with Battaglia. Fern, with a puckering of her
mouth, observed he must have less free time now, but that was
least of the difficulties; I was certain he'd find time once he
knew the magnitude of my revelations, but because of
potential for political embarrassment he'd have to know in
advance he was meeting with an infamous fugitive wanted for
a particularly repellent murder, while I would need a promise I
wouldn't be promptly arrested. Grudgingly, I recognized I was
going to have to face some sort of official cleansing process at
some time, but documentation of my alibi was strong enough,
together with existent doubts, for the murder charge to be
dropped without an arrest, and in any event I had to see
recognition of the danger I was in, and guarantees for my
safety, at least till the whole Harness-Stirrup story was made
public, and preferably till after Laxitter and the other
principals were indicted, better still, safely convicted.

Outlining this, and foreseeing the bitter legal and
political wars there would be, I knew with a sudden wave of
certainty there was no happy ending; as Fena Keller would say,
I wasn't Bilbo Baggins, helping to kill the dragon and win the
treasure, going back home for sixty more serene years, but his
less-fortunate nephew, who could only triumph at the cost of
everything he'd known. There would never be a time when I
could resume my life as it had been; retribution would never
be out of the question, nor desire to warn others like me that
whistles weren't blown with impunity. Better perhaps, if, as

the program suggested, I had left the country and sought permanent obscurity.

Fern said, "If Maretta told him it was really, really important, Jocko would talk to you."

"And if you told Maretta it was really, really important?"

"I'd have to tell her more than that."

On a double compound crux, I hesitated. With hunters no farther than twenty-odd miles away, and possibly much nearer, my time here was running out; it would be stupid not to take advantage of this fortuitous means of access to John Battaglia, and still I balked at authorizing Fern to give Maretta what she knew of my story — an absurd reservation, recollected in aftercalm, because short of forcibly detaining her I couldn't prevent Fern from telling anything to anyone.

Her quickness with feeling and motive was diabolical. "Maretta is my best friend," she reproached, before I'd said another word. "You have to trust somebody. I would trust you."

The grammar was conditional, but not the declaration: she *had* trusted me with the secrets she held, but was now bidding beyond that, so it would have been inappropriate for me to point out the disparity between the worst I could doom her to, a year-and-a-half with a family she disliked, and the possible effect on my continued existence of betrayal or indiscretion on Maretta's part. True, too, Fern had trusted me not to be a sadistic killer, which might give her some claim. The debate, such as it was, suspended itself, with the renewed sound of an approaching aircraft.

"Where did you leave your ORV?"

"Not far. A couple of miles."

"It'll be spotted."

"Not where I left it. It's next to like a little cliff, right under some pines." We were both speaking in hushed tones,

but far from coming near enough to overhear us, the drone
resolved itself into nothing more threatening than a passing jet.

What Maretta was to be told was still a riddle; perhaps
she could be persuaded by the same archetypal conflict of
embattled Us *versus* greedy Them that made Fern my ally, but
it must also be enough for John Battaglia to recognize at third
hand his old adversary, radiation-enhanced agriculture, all
without exposing Fern to the dangerous infection of specific
knowledge — or, for that matter, making me potentially
Maretta's hostage.

"You could write him a note for her to give to him — "
Fern cut through the tangle. "Seal it, if you think it's too hot
for *kids* to handle — " and while wincing at the jab, I saluted
her silently for not saying *girls*, or *women*, the tiresome rote
gambit.

Fern turned her wrist to glance at a non-existent watch.
"Maybe I'd better spend the night here and get started at
sunup." Some eyelash business went with this, but I ignored
it, as one does automatically with much smaller girls when
they transmit signals of an allure they can't understand,
imitated from, oh, *daytime drama*, probably.

"Too dangerous," meaning only (I promise) that with
van Muer on the prowl, anywhere was preferable to my
vicinity.

"I feel safe with you." This time there wasn't a chance
of error; she leaned sideways on the bedroll, extending a
looped arm as if to encircle and caress what passed for a
pillow; I felt the leap of familiar greed, and slower rise of rarer
misgivings.

"Feelings can be very misleading. You'd be safer with
a tornado. Come on, I'll see you to your car. Your thing," I
amended.

"I don't know if I can make it back to the road before
dark."

Game and set, though not necessarily match; she was correct in assuming I couldn't in conscience dispute her calculations, though some light would still be lingering two hours from now. She'd already opened up the small pack she'd carried, and was excavating a toothbrush.

With the promised icy winds still swirling, unable to get out of Idaho, the night would be warm, and there was nothing inherently absurd in my intention to let Fern have the bed-shelf while I sat up with a Michael Innes to read after I'd written the proposed note for John Battaglia. Having started a small fire, I made a kind of mid-floor nest for myself, using pack and duffel-bag, and what I was really doing was dressing the set for a peculiar sexual dialogue.

We'd had tea and some cold food, and now she remained sitting on the bed-shelf, jacket off, bright shirt untucked, watching my arrangements with a cat's disconcerting amalgam of intensity and complete indifference.

"You're going to wait till I'm asleep, and ravish me," she theorized cheerfully.

"It's no fun now you guessed."

"I think you ought to know, I'm not a virgin."

"You're not? I am," keeping it bright, while internally dismayed by my own dismay; there was no reason why she should be. Half my life ago, when I was a high-school junior, the assumption (if no more) was that girls without experience were a straitlaced, timid or utterly unappealing minority — and numbers of my male classmates by now had married, reproduced, and, statistics suggest, found it unexpectedly rewarding to transport babysitters as young as Fern, younger. There were a million or so unmarried mothers of her age.

In a billow of gold she left her perch to alight next to me. "Nothing to be afraid of," she said, her incandescent grin spreading, and leaned to kiss me, though chastely enough, on my furring cheek. She was wrong, however, and among many fears, not yet counting law, we could begin with the least dignified, least amenable to treatment by chat, except I was hesitant to explain to this child that the survival-kit hastily assembled at my precipitate departure had necessarily omitted to provide for what at such a time were frivolous contingencies. On reflection, more than possibly in these plaguey times she carried her own supply, which I found at the same time laudably foresighted, and intolerably sad.

Did I ask for confirmation of thoughts on plundered illusion? as I straightened, she followed me up, lunging for a more ardent and artificial kiss, tongue and pelvis thrusting in simulated passion — no, that's unjust; means of expression, their clumsy pretense of expertise, might still have real feelings behind them; the fake part was the whorish design for arousal; whatever Fern wanted from me wasn't the brisk business that technique belonged to.

Taking her face between my palms, I kissed her, defensively rather than tenderly. "Did Maretta teach you that?"

"What?" scarcely pretending not to know. "What's wrong?"

Not at my most articulate, I tried to convey at once the thoughts that our bedding together was inadvisable, but if it did happen (which it wouldn't), it would be for reasons more complex than getting it on and getting laid, with which, however, in other circumstances, there was nothing wrong.

She laughed. "Maretta said, guys all talk about how sensitive and romantic they are, and how much more there is than just sex, but Little Miss Moonlight-Walk-on-the-Beach is gonna lose out every time to a gal who knows ways to bust their nuts."

"Did she?" Such LCD generalizations tend to be self-confirming, by selecting the types and inviting the behavior they describe — like putting up a sign, *ALL YOU CAN EAT, 50 CENTS* to prove it's a greedy world. Besides, leaving male variance out of it, what was true for Maretta wasn't necessarily so, could never be so for Fern: she might achieve some impulsive follies, but wasn't going to become an erotic Metternich.

Not unaware of my lack of enthusiasm, Fern said defensively, "You look at me in a sexual way. Your pupils were like licorice dimes when I talked about enjoying a spanking."

As is my wont, so Paula once told me, when feeling cornered, I became sententious (the words she used were worse). "In my normal life," meaning what it used to be. "Every day, there must be a dozen women I look at in a sexual way. Of those, there might be a dozen every week I think about sexually on the conscious level. That doesn't mean I can go to bed with all of them, or that I would if I could, it only means I'm a male animal with the reproductive urge that drives any organism."

Astonishingly, with what sounded like pure, youthful curiosity, she asked, "When you do decide to go for it, what's different about those women?"

Careful, careful; this innocent proposition contains *Why not me?* "Absence of contraindications," hiding behind pompous jargon, but then recognizing the thought was piercingly true: masses of romantic muddle could be avoided if instead of the exceptional imperative, we regarded attraction as the norm, with more or fewer reasons against acting on it.

"And," I superadded, as Fern made a glum face. "There has to be admiration — it might be superficial, like — "

"A nice rear end."

"Okay, or it can be profound admiration."

"Like with Judy." That was startlingly alert; my mentions of Judy in recounting my escape had been, I thought, quite casual.

She, Fern, wound herself up. "But she's gone to Guatemala with this creep, maybe you'll never see her again — are you going to give up sex for the rest of your life? I don't

expect you to admire me, but what about my
contraindications? Jesus."

Embarrassing to recall, I put my hands on her
shoulders like any condescending jackass. "You don't need to
worry about admiration. I'm not going to forget you if I live a
very long time — no, I mean that. It's better, take my word for
it — "

"No, I won't. You don't have the right."

Again, unexpected. "*Right*? You mean, only women
are allowed to say no, men always have to say yes?"

"Not if you don't want to. Go ahead," she challenged.
"Tell me you wouldn't like to make it with me. Yes you
would, never mind all the bullshit about pistils and stamens
and the reproductive imperative, tell me you haven't wanted to
screw me, since eight seconds after we met. I'm saying, *me*,
not some — sandwich. You don't have the right to decide I
don't know what I'm doing. That's what you're doing."

She was right, but with the wrong conclusions: true, I
was trying to be prudent on both sides of the question, on hers
because she had a flagrant crush on me, and was only a step
from being seriously in love with one who had no means to
honor his side of such a transaction. That may sound arrogant,
but is only observant: we'd met in what to her were
destabilizingly romantic circumstances, and she was
particularly susceptible, deprived of her best-buddy father.
And I could caution her in a dozen different ways that in
mating we would *not* be making love, because I had no place
to put any I made, and she could say, undoubtedly would say,
in effect, *okay, I understand, it's a deal*, but I'd still be taking
unfair advantage of her vulnerability. Those are the rules for
the elder party, and I don't quarrel, although in real life I'm as
bewildered, uncertain and volatile as ever I was at Fern's age,
maybe more so; in country matters, maturity is a socio-legal
fiction.

Oddly, this thesis incubated its own negation: the quick glow of admiration for my own heroic empathy with the child was an element in the warmth that seized me for the woman (*Ay, that antithesis of persons is a most established figure*), which she instantly read. Though I wouldn't swear to exactly eight seconds, she was right, too, about that; I at last admitted the quirky riddle of her ambiguous identity had been from the first a peremptory sexual challenge. Now, after some touching that was like mutual discovery, she said, smiling blurrily, "It's all right. I can take care of myself. All part of the 'mancipation procedure."

The invisible border had been crossed; she was going to be in love, and nothing I did or failed to do would stop it; while I might break her heart I'd scarcely have time to blight her life: the individual objections I continued to raise became more like an astronaut's checklist before *we have ignition*. The law? Not without her testimony, which torture would never wring from her. Pregnancy? There is a calendar that shapes our ends, rough-hew them how we may. Anyway, Fern said, and answered the next and unaskable question, she indeed had in her pack what I'd omitted from mine.

"Anyway — " she permitted brash Maretta one more contribution, "there's plenty of ways we can get it on without doin' *the thang* — " lots of other fun rides at Zackland if roller-coaster was too risky.

There were, there were: not, however, in a seamless modulation from idea to act; Fern's verbal readiness was founded on the misconception, bred by compliant past experience, that by far the larger part of her delight was to be in gladdening me and *saying* she loved it; for this, as we've seen, she was more than eager, and it took patience and some teeth-gritting evasion of easy victories to coax her to readiness for a less bystanderish enjoyment, and into participation so sweetly surprising to her that gratitude became indistinguishable from young appetite, and there was indeed diversion fierce and extended enough to drive into a gnawing

corner of consciousness the camper-load of enemies in
Brandsville, ransacking helicopter, the various bits of
carelessness that had brought finding me into the domain of
the possible. Who cared, then, that when time out was over,
the score would still be the same?

11.

As I learned in one of the calms, Fern's loss of
innocence (of which the sardonic might name me beneficiary)
had occurred the summer before last, some weeks before her
fifteenth birthday, on what she didn't call a double-date; a
concertgoing expedition to Santa Fe, requiring an overnight
stay. Maretta, six years older than Fern, as she was from mid-
April each year to early August, when it shrank back to five,
had been accompanied by a wine-distributing friend of her
brother, Everett IV, and in turn had provided Fern with a
college chum of Graham, her fraternal twin. Maretta, in the
crabbed idiom pertaining to that province of Fern's experience,
contracted *the hots* for her *date*, so Fern had felt obliged to go
along when it was proposed chaste pairings of the two hotel
rooms be counterchanged into couples, and the same
unfocused notion of not making spoilsport noises to wreck
Maretta's easygoing tryst caused her supinely to accede when
Graham's friend (named *Keith*, naturally) slithered across the
gap that separated their twin beds and had as much of his will
with her as several beers and pizza with everything had left
him capable of wreaking. As Fern did, I omit any terror from
this account; she allowed only that the bout did not rank
among life's happier memories. As for the chief legacy:
"Before, Graham always thought of me as that kid his sister
hung out with, but Keith must have told all about Santa Fe,
and after that Graham took a new look at me. We made it a
couple of times since then, no big deal."
For whom that assessment was supposed to be true
remains obscure: if I'd had time, and hope of influence with
Fern, I would have used both for an attempt to persuade her
that in striving to adapt her own vulnerable and still-
delightable nature to the hardedge rubrics of Maretta's

knowing world, she ran risk of contracting a distanced anesthesia more killing than any disappointment such hipness sought to defang. But she wouldn't have believed it at that feeling time, and might have confused me by asking how I could possibly know.

Puzzling to me there'd been no objection to the Santa Fe expedition from her father, but Fern allowed he'd never been good with ages — like my own father, only with opposite effect; whereas I'm fairly sure mine, impassioned teacher of a passionate subject, hadn't always mortified the moist-eyed adoration Ann Arbor kept bringing him, semester after semester, Matt Thomas, judging by available evidence, had maintained a more botanical blood-temperature, and was only dimly conscious Maretta wasn't still the leggy but hipless thirteen-year-old he'd first met, the small girl who lent smaller Fern a Shetland so they could ride together.

"What about her family?"

"Oh, they're *rich*," simply, as if it fully explained indifference to such middle-class preoccupations as statutory rape, contributing to the delinquency, state lines.

Morning was irrepressibly sentimental, a time impossible to sustain, when discomforts themselves were delicious; return from cramped and odd-angled dozing, shuddering chill when I half-swung, half-rolled from bed to get a fire started, then blanketed Fern came to put her bare, cold feet on top of my zorried ones so she could reach up and kiss me with world-embracing tenderness (*eines Freundes Freund zu sein*). "Isn't this *great*?" bright-eyed, and by way of reproach: "Are you always so hard to get to enjoy yourself?"

"Only with cause," a silly answer, but she should talk, and silly time, with more than adequate melodrama tapping its toe in the wings; the need to extend the *divertissements* doomed Fern's dawn start. The chill on water placed near the fire had ample time to disperse, and still after we'd washed and dressed and had breakfast, to enhance which Fern produced from her pack a couple of oranges, there were delays: important, for example, for Fern to tell me about her brief enrollment at an Anglo-American School in Zürich, where the gaunt, long-jawed attending physician sported the incongruously ornamental name of Emmy Frühlingsblume, and was dubbed by the girls Doktor Croak-us.

These were tactics Fabius *Cunctator* would have recognized, and the military mind would also understand our double interpretation of unevent; continued non-return of the helicopter either meant he'd given up (good) or had seen what he sought (very bad).

When girded loins brought us at last to the *by the way* and *that reminds me* phase, loyalty to her friend had Fern make a final shyish attempt to book me on her show: "She would love to do one of those Undisclosed Location numbers, you sitting with the light behind you. And then refusing to reveal her sources and a First Amendment brouhaha — she'd be in heaven."

Once more I reviewed the dangers, for Maretta as well as me, but promised I'd do an exclusive interview with her once instigation of legal action against the enemy made it her *scoop*, not my suicide.

"Oh, that reminds me, on that TV show, they said you were *linked* to another murder."

"Hilde." I'd told her about that death, but her reference to it now had me wondering for a sick, dizzy moment if Fern, after all, believed I was a killer, and could be one of those pathetic, unaccountable groupies who find an irresistible attraction in known serial slaughterers. Not possible; she wanted only to reemphasize the deliberate unfairness of the program. The former murder had been brought up by the Westerlake police chief, Paula's namesake, and context made it clear he thought it pointed in other directions, but *Infamous Fugitives* had edited back to my face, and thrown a series of rhetorical questions in the vein of *Why does death follow in this man's footsteps?*

"But if this Chief Leahy has figured out that what you, and the Viennese lady, and Paula have in common is the people you worked for, wouldn't that mean he's in danger himself?"

A shrewd point, and I suppose having passed all her life in a world of acknowledged, actively expected ruthlessness made Fern here that much older than I, constantly having to rediscard the naiver assumptions of a childhood lived out before it all became conspiracy. If Leahy's small-town department was trying to probe into the odd association between Orbis Special Projects and violent death (and I'd like to see Laxitter's current personal file), odds on a long life for the chief would be not much different from mine, in those realms beyond the reach of actuarial tables. A point I'd raise if I lived to meet with John Battaglia.

That, if it could be accomplished at all, might take some days to arrange, and I was horrified to discover Fern's plan was to get Maretta started on the process, and then return here. This I vetoed absolutely; she'd said she could stay at the Preston ranch, where she'd be safe, as long as needed. Fern's gratitude for my concern over her safety was no better than grudging, but still she found pleasure in knowing a way to inform me if and when negotiations were a success. The ranch house, which was toward the north side of the property, was, on a clear day, somewhat questionably visible, if you knew where, from the summit of these heights, at a distance of nine or ten miles, but it had a tall flagpole, and the Prestons possessed a number of huge Japanese silk flags, poppy red and luminous yellow, said to have come from a Kurosawa film, and those could easily be seen from here, against the dark background of hills; the girls had used them in the past for signals, though hardly (I thought) to convey secrets they couldn't have more easily by phone. Giving me a bearing relative to two of the major mountain peaks beyond, Fern settled that if I gazed out tomorrow and saw the red flag it would mean the effort to contact Battaglia was under way, and that color would continue to fly until its replacement with the yellow signalled success; no flag would signify failure to reach the ex-senator, or his unlikely refusal to respond.

She said, "We should arrange somewhere for me to pick you up, the day after you see the yellow flag flying. How about right by your car — if it's still there; kids sometimes drive on that road. They could break in and hot-wire it. Anyway, that place?"

"Oh, it's still there, unless it's been towed somewhere." I'd brought the distributor cables away with me, and, with the thought of need for another getaway, had likewise guarded against somebody emptying the tank by syphoning off gas myself, into a gallon bleach-bottle, which I'd hidden not far from the car.

But worst possible venue for a rendezvous; the car was one piece of local evidence that could be certainly linked to me, and if the business-suited avengers from Brandsville, scouring the countryside in BMW's, should find it, they'd be sure to stake it out. Seeing my point, Fern, with a quick glance checking me for annoyance, again said she'd return here, but while I couldn't or wouldn't confide my recurring vision of her doing so to find me dead and *Azraël* coldly waiting, I once more said no. The spot where the ORV was now parked was still too close for me, and we compromised on another reasonably secure site she described, a patch of pinewoods where she'd camped in the past, and I could at need, six or seven miles to the northeast, hidden from, but not far off, the continuation of that rudimentary track I'd followed down into Brandsville in September.

Using a tiny round mirror Fern was trying to assess how middle couture had come through. "Maretta's going to think I spent the night — " she smiled complacently. "Exactly how I spent the night."

"That reminds me," just once more, when I stated my intention, still, of going down to collect my tent. "I left a rifle for you, up the Crow's Nest." She'd brought it with her on the expedition in the rain, when she'd decided, almost in sight of her goal, that being told about an appearance on *Infamous Fugitives* was inadequate to divert my wrath at her defiance of my ban (I have no idea how this Wotan-like Arthur Ames came to be invented). Not wanting to carry the weapon back, assuming I was the only one who'd come there to find it, she'd tucked it between twisted pine-roots on the southeast side. Thanking her, I promised to collect it so that it could be returned; of ways I might escape my predicament, shooting my way out, as I said, was least likely. So I would have bet.

Obvious good sense to keeping our excursions at a minimum, but now we'd run through every plausible reason for delay and there was nothing left but parting, I abrogated my own dictum, saying I'd go with her as far as the vehicle; despite her confidence in its concealment I wanted to be sure it wasn't being watched, wanted to see her safely on her way. I was conscious, as she surely wasn't, that there was next to no chance of our being together again as we'd been last night, not ever: if I lived and told my story it would mean going into hiding, and Fern had her own struggle to pursue. We went not-quite together, but in close succession, Fern leading, spending as little time as possible in exposed places. The ORV, when we came to it, was indeed well-hidden, an unhandsome little auto, in form somewhere between a dune-buggy and the flattened, starkly functional *Wehrmacht* equivalent of a jeep, as seen in WWII movies (*Kvick, you fool, after zem. Zey are Amerikan shpies!*).

Aboard, Fern regarded me with her great eyes, the color of which I still couldn't name, in this light a green-gold. "I'll see you in a couple of days. Be careful."

"You too. If van Muer shows up at the ranch, or anyone else, for the helicopter, no dramatic denunciations.

You don't know anything — tell Maretta, too. These are
desperate people — " a clunking cliché, of the genre I'd been
inducted into.

"Okay." She opened her mouth to say important
words, lowered her eyelids, pressed her lips together, and
began again at a less epic level. "I had the best time. It would
be great if we could have a whole week together — you know,
sometime."

"I'd like that, too."

"You know I'm lying," she said, and laughed. "I never
want to see you again. No, I want to be with you for ever and
ever. Do I get a kiss?"

She did; a serious kiss, but only itself, neither promise
nor, on either side, provocation. Describing its qualities by
subtraction I recognize all the errors I've made in the entire
account of Fern's sleepover: I wrote about Fern losing her
innocence, which emphatically she hadn't, although anyone
might be misled by the adopted Marettisms, imposed on her
own garden nature like plastic flamingos, and in our corrupted
world it couldn't be long before she lost — *reality*, I think it is,
a most astonishing reality, which made the world seem
unfamiliar by restoring it to right-way-up. Let be.

As near as could be judged due east of the cabin, I had
an idea of cutting across in the direction of the Watchtower,
and was reminded of why from the first this had been such a
good choice of hiding-places; in the bewildering jumble of
crags and crevices it was too difficult, perhaps impossible.
Following the way Fern had gone jouncing, down to tamer
slopes, I might be able to make a wide circle, and reach the
Watchtower in a five or six-mile journey; otherwise, the only
sure way was how I'd come, except for the last half-mile the
same cryptic route that took me back to Zack's stepped boulder
not far below the cabin.

Once there I noticed I hadn't heard any news today, and
returned to the cabin for fresh tea and a quarter-hour with the
radio; an earthquake in Turkey, a short piece on conjectured

cabinet selections by the President-elect, no mention of John Battaglia, a man in Saskatoon who said he'd found a cure for excessive yawning, which must be an endemic affliction on the Canadian prairie. Yesterday's midday temperatures had set records for this date in cities from Phoenix to Omaha, but for us the dreaded nor'westers were again bearing down, to bring forty-degree falls in temperature by late afternoon, with rain followed by freezing rain in the lowlands, snow higher, more than enough to send me scurrying for where not only my tent but a new supply of firewood was to be found.

Not far short of the hollow behind the Watchtower — by the place, it was, where I'd crawled to the rim to see if I could spot the droning helicopter — the descending slot made an abrupt drop, just too little to require a leap, though a comfortable step would miss the landing and jolt me down into the gap between. Here, briefly exposed to the right, hurry was always a good idea, and I noticed only in the middle of my looping stride the rock where that foot would descend was already occupied by a large, coiled diamondback rattlesnake, sunning itself. This late in the year, except for the unusual warmth, it ought to have been asleep, which might account for its being grumpy enough to strike but sufficiently below peak performance to make evasion possible — but it would be absurd to try to recount at once all the things that happened in the next fraction of a second, some of which as will be seen, rather than being directly experienced, yielded their secrets only to patient logical enquiry into what *must have* happened.

The snake lunged at me, and I twisted awkwardly, sole of my boot striking the edge of the level landing, so that I fell heavily on my right side, and scoured down into the gap between and partly under rocks, ripping pants and skin on my upper leg, and with my arrival banging almost simultaneously the other knee and my side just where the rib-cage ended. At the same time I'd been conscious of an inexplicable tweaking of the air near my cheek, and later I recalled a percussive, high-pitched whine from no particular direction, and other sharp, pattering sounds unconnected with my clumsy acrobatics.

My first concern, deferring agony, was the snake, but I could see no sign of it; probably the abrupt nature of my disappearance had bewildered that malevolent lentil-sized brain. Upward behind where I'd fallen from, I was puzzled to note markings on the rock-face that were surely new, a line of metallic-looking blots, exasperatingly irrational, as I began to feel the pain of my various wounds. Splashes of lead; I had been, O ultimate justification for all my absurd precautions, shot at with, as was the only answer satisfying all conditions, a silenced automatic weapon with a high rate of fire.

Shot *at*? Blood was already trickling down the outside of my thigh and darkening the edges of the rip in my jeans; slighter hole in the left knee was also secreting an ooze of red, and now back on the other side from where I'd crashed down on my ribs I felt a lot of cool wetness. Wedged as I was, I had difficulty sliding a hand back to feel, but it came away without color, and I found my plastic canteen, slung behind, had a neat hole on one side, and had been torn completely open on the other; entry wound, exit wound, the nomenclature came with a shiver, but my back was wet only with water. Shot at.

It came to me the rattlesnake, by provoking my violent evasive twist, had saved my life, barely. This, as with sole or scarce survivors of packed jumbo-jets that fall, might have been a moment of religious affirmation, except that if I could believe in a God concerned with my particular welfare, He'd demonstrate it by consistently arranging a world where I never got shot at, instead of resorting to vulgar displays of hairsbreadth beneficence. Besides, and despite the injuries of my fall, I had to think quickly about extending the life an unwitting snake had given back to me; the instinct to cower and tremble wasn't easy to condemn, but this, above all, was the prime moment for cool, rational consideration.

My first approach to a smile, wan and sour, came with
the idea my assailant, *Azraël* or other, to whom the snake had
to have been invisible, must think he'd hit me; what other
explanation would occur to him for my abrupt gyration and
fall from sight at the moment of shooting? Right, but fallen
isn't always dead, and the assassin wasn't going to assume I
was finished and go home, not without checking. At this
moment he must be approaching, weapon ready for a
murderous fusillade. No use lying here and playing dead; I
wasn't being stalked by one who'd be parsimonious over a
little redundancy.

I was largely on my back, in roughly the position, with
a skew to the left, of one whose rear has skidded from a low
armchair, shoulders still where the seat should be, legs largely
under the rattlesnake rock, which had considerable overhang.
Though there was a sharp, stinging pain *there*, a raw,
lacerating pain *there*, and throb of a heavier, deeper pain back
there, all my moving parts were working, and except perhaps
for cracked ribs nothing seemed to have broken. Biting hard
on my lower lip, I shuffled my legs back to work into a low
crouch, thinking it through. That the gunman — gunperson, if
you like, but I'd be astonished if it was a woman, or anything
but van Muer — had let loose his squirt of bullets from some
unknown distance, rather than closing in to where a miss
would be impossible, suggested I'd been a target of
opportunity for him, that he didn't yet know where my home
base was, and at the moment of firing had been unsure of his
ability to close the distance between us; this last was quite
plausible, since not far beyond the broken rim where I'd
scouted for the helicopter there was a narrow ravine, not deep
but steep-sided and formidable, which ran more-or-less
parallel to my route.

In the other pan of the balance, he would hardly have
fired without being certain who I was, and somewhere must
have had a longer look at me than the brief glimpse as I

emerged at that gap in the ramparts. That question could wait; right now he would be trying to find a way across or around to where he'd seen me vanish, which might take him half an hour or more, and which he couldn't do while at the same time keeping vigil. The conclusion was, I must get out of here, to do which my head would have to be raised to where it would be visible if I guessed wrong.

I might have remained paralyzed if I hadn't recalled and goaded myself with the words *completion bonus*, which occurred in *Azraël's* unpleasant note to Laxitter. A full-time Orbis employee would have no reason to work alone, and a pair of gunprimates could mean one keeping watch, weapon levelled, while the other (or others?) closed in, but van Muer with his pricey taste for clarets wasn't a man to split a fee if he could help it: if he was my adversary, he'd be alone.

There was a worrying amount of blood about; the torn pants leg had a dark streak all the way down, that sock was soggy and there were pools and brilliant spatters on the rocks; I instructed myself firmly it's a fluid that goes a long way; less than five centiliters dripping from a slightly sliced finger can make a kitchen look like an abattoir. The point with cutting off the flow was not that I was in imminent danger of bleeding to death, but I didn't want to leave a trail. I thought there might be a spare shirt convertible to bandages stuffed in my small pack, and when I slid the strap off my shoulder was dismayed to find signs two bullets had punched in and surged through the tough nylon pack. All my necessary evidence was inside, and if Judy's mobile disk had been hit the gunmammal had put me out of business almost as comprehensively as if he'd shot me.

Opening up in a panic, I found the bullets had passed through the lightweight waterproof anorak rolled on top, drastically reducing its usefulness in a rainstorm, but doing no damage to the irreplaceables beneath. Grabbing the shirt, I ripped off a sleeve and bound the gash on my upper leg, using the rest to do some crude blotting of excess blood, then stuffing it back in my riddled pack.

All the time listening, trying to assess how much my injuries would hamper me, I was ready now to test the logic of the single gunvertebrate theory, though to begin with it meant putting my face up to where the rattlesnake had been. Which way would I go? The wounded-animal syndrome had the cabin, my lair, beckoning to me, but the way there was less attractive, a long stretch in a narrow channel, with nowhere to turn aside. In the opposite direction, if I could get across the bare hollow, there were open woods with cover for me, but I expected my stalker to work his way around to the northward and approach from that general direction.

Here at last came to mind what any reader of this has been thinking of and shouting at me for several minutes: idiot, there was a weapon waiting not two hundred yards away and a scramble up the Watchtower. All I had to do was get there without being seen and shot.

And considering imagined reader, in trying to give here a representative selection only of thoughts that had been pelting through my mind since spotting the rattlesnake, I may have falsely extruded time: not altogether inappropriately; it could have been hours since the shots, but I should make clear it was by impersonal measure a very few minutes.

Still, I had to go swiftly. How many of you have ever had to rise from a squat with the possibility first of being eye to eye with a frustrated rattlesnake, and if that trial is passed, of having your skull instantly puffed by impact of fast-moving metal to a cloud of jelly and shards? Those who have know it calls for more resolution than could be summoned without the strongest inducement behind.

There was no snake, and my bitching body still worked. I clambered from my pit, and was still alive. In a crouch, I went like Lord Greystoke (less the grunts) down into and across the hollow, not looking anywhere but a few yards ahead. Reaching the base of the Watchtower, I clung to the rock, breathless from terror, not exertion. Interesting to note that none of the injuries suffered by violent contact with rock; gash, scrape or bruise, was handicapping me half as much as a wrenching pain at my groin, caused only by my contorted mid-step evasion of the snake.

By staying doubled over, I could scale the tower with minimal ostentation, but not minimum pain, at waist-high steps pushing myself up with my hands to come down hard on the injured knee, each thrust off my left leg a sickening jab at the hollow of my thigh. Near the level of the lookout I had to come out into the open on the northern side, and I did so with massive reluctance, though telling myself if the guncreature was on the move, it was too concerned with picking its own path to be gazing up at the heights. Emerging, I was struck hard by wind, and instantly conscious of being immersed in my own sweat, far more than could be explained by my exertions; as for other secretions said often to become involuntary under extreme stress, I had no wish to enquire into the state of my underclothing; more noteworthy was that weather at last was behaving as forecast; the sun was still unmarred, but the edge on that wind was unambiguous, and I shivered with pure chill.

Up, and sheltered by pines, I quickly found the rifle, in a heavy-gauge clear plastic bag with snap fasteners, a lovingly maintained weapon, clean, handsome leather sling, walnut stock pleasantly scented with linseed, scope sight, bolt-action, magazine-loaded, 30-06 — or at least I hoped so, since that was the ammunition of which Fern had given me a full box. I had more to learn about Professor Thomas; for a start he'd been left-handed; the hard-rubber cheek-rest was on the right side of the stock. Unimportant so long as the scope was centrally top-mounted, which it was, and for me the weapon couldn't have been better chosen; a type which, though in smaller caliber, I was thoroughly familiar with, and while it left me with a wide deficit in rate-of-fire, I wasn't planning to engage in a shoot-out, and knew of no automatic or semi-automatic weapon cockable without significant racket, whereas this breech could be eased open almost silently, action well but not excessively oiled. I was perhaps exaggeratedly concerned over noise, catching myself holding my breath, although wind was in the treetops below, and I saw nothing else moving.

Pressing the catch, I released the magazine and loaded it with eight rounds, the baleful bullets steel-jacketed, marksman's choice for a clean kill. Slipping the magazine back in, I didn't yet press it home, not till I'd breech-loaded one round and chambered it with a smooth thrust of the bolt, then snapping the magazine into place with a very slight click. Putting the rifle down within easy reach, barrel propped on tree-roots, I sat and considered my condition.

Physically, dented but functional, mentally over-alert, metaphysically, by my own pacific criteria, bizarre; I was waiting here hoping to shoot a professional who was trying to kill me, and that he was a hired gun with no animus against me put negotiation out of reach; there can be no conflict resolution where there's no conflict; those roseate civilized notions elide the existence of true evil, and its power to delegate; ignore, also, giant differences in power between oppressor and oppressed. If, eschewing armed response, I could *engage in dialogue* with van Muer's principal, Orbis as personified by Laxitter, the only *resolution* to avoid violence would be that of Czechoslovakia in 1938, my abject surrender and the triumph of bullydom — and by no means certainly would I have been able to keep my life, were I to give back my file-copies, and docilely promise never to tell.

I waited, seeing nothing, and grew cooler. With some careful scuttling I could keep intermittent watch over a broad arc of country, but found when gazing to the east I became certain my enemy would approach from the north; after a few rounds of that winless game I kept still. Van Muer, the fear occurred, might decide to scale the Watchtower for a quick survey, and I slotted myself between rocks, back against main pillar, rifle in hand with butt resting on the ground between my knees, a position from where I could watch the spot where his head would have to appear if he climbed up; to the right I also had a plain view across the tops of trees bordering the hollow of the place where I'd fallen; if the gunorganism had been firing from up here I wouldn't have survived, since he would have seen at once he'd missed me, and I would never have gone out of his sight.

Once or twice before I've confessed my majestic addiction to the trivial; that my mind drifted to Fern in lingering sensuality surely can't be considered an example, but it is embarrassing to confess I caught myself starting to doze on that reverie. I was very thirsty, mocked by the shattered canteen I hadn't discarded, and time was crawling on; an hour, an hour-and-a-half since the shots came, and like a trout at a mayfly, hope lunged for the idea he'd decided I was dead, and had gone home fulfilled. Tempting to swallow as a well-tied Coachman, and equally delusive; he was too professional for that, and I didn't think Laxitter would pay for a job so indefinitely concluded.

If, then, it was cat-and-mouse, with each of us casting the other for Jerry, he might have all the experience and natural aptitude for predation, but my patience had a motivation his couldn't: I *knew* he was alive and stalking me, and in the end he'd have to come and see. I massaged my neck muscles, shifted my left buttock for the eightieth time in attempt to ease the pain under the ribs on that side, yawned, and thought about that public benefactor in distant Saskatoon.

He came at last, first seen as he mounted out of the hollow into the trees, going just like the movies, in a stealthy crouch but with abrupt pirouettes, right, left, behind, finishing always in a shooter's stance, the weapon he levelled a nasty-looking contrivance, more like a caulking-gun than anything traditionally a firearm; it was slung over his right shoulder on a short, broad strap, evidently with some sort of secondary lanyard, which kept it level when his gloved left hand for a moment ceased to steady the gun. By his broad, blunt shape alone I could have confirmed it was the same van Muer I'd briefly met at Special Projects, dressed now for the field, soft hat, light jacket with baggy pockets over fatigue-style shirt and pants, desert boots I envied though probably made from the skin of some graceful veldt creature nearing extinction, all virtually the same shade and texture as his curiously matt complexion, which I saw as he made his final combative wheel before entering among the trees. Saw close up; by now I had him in my scope sight, cross-hairs briefly on his right cheek, but I wasn't trying snap shots where a miss would leave me deficient in firepower by at least fifty-to-one in the ensuing duel, and with a comparable shortfall in experience.

Emerging on the farther side of the trees, he went now with still greater caution, a catlike approach to where I'd fallen; I knew van Muer as a practised urban slayer, but he must have plenty of bushcraft, too, to have fixed the site so unerringly.

I'd been sighting in the classic sitting stance, elbow braced in the broad sling, but as he crept up the slope the trajectory became flatter, and I rolled and shuffled into the prone position, no comfort to my pulled thigh. Finding a new window among the bundles of pine-needles, tracking with him, I had three or four chances at a shot, but waited; I was confident at the range, and so long as the sight was accurately set I wouldn't miss.

The controlled breathing necessary for marksmanship incidentally creates its own Zen exercise, a LaMaze technique for delivering death, and I felt calm flood me like a drug taking effect, a physical sensation of unexcitable readiness. Van Muer circled the pit, pointing his weapon, staring down in what I judged to be disbelief at blood but no body. Carefully, he stepped up above the pit so as to see clearly under the overhang of rock-slab where the rattlesnake had sunned, and as he turned, without a jerk or tremble I slid cross-hairs to van Muer's temple, and kept them there as he stooped over where he'd seen me go down.

He was still, and by itself my forefinger took up the slack. The cross-hairs were perfectly steady above the right eye, and I could not squeeze the trigger. He was, I had no doubt, torturer and killer of Paula, killer of Hilde and of Bieman, prevented only by remote chance from being mine, alive a potent threat, and I couldn't kill him like this: face to face in a contest to see who could shoot first I would have fired without hesitation, and here I was, frozen by a squeamishness that was suicidal.

Doubtful a man of van Muer's experience had ever not been conscious of his exposed position, but as he satisfied himself of my inexplicable absence as corpse or cripple, I saw tension return to his posture; he rocked back into his crouch. My only chance for life was floating away from my fingertips: as his weapon swung left I moved my aim to the back of his remaining good hand, and fired smoothly.

I heard and cringed at his thudding grunt; he nearly toppled backward, but doubled over convulsively, and clattered untidily into the same pit where I'd fallen. His right hand was smashed, but as I might have anticipated the bullet had continued into his upper leg. Most of him was still visible from where I was; he'd either lost consciousness or found it best for the moment to be quite still; perhaps he thought he'd be shot again if he moved.

Instead of exultancy which might be appropriate to having outsniped the sniper, I felt nausea, and my instincts were those of a small child who, left alone, finds in horror he's broken the irreplaceable clock; I wanted to slink away from the mess I'd made, ready when caught to deny I'd ever seen a rifle. Cold wisdom would have dictated continued vigilance to be certain he was altogether disabled; softness has to confess I drew back from my vantage-point, and pressed the heels of my hands to my eye-sockets, while I shuddered wildly, released only now to experience additionally the physical shock of my own near-death.

When I could make myself try again, van Muer was sitting, his back against the higher rock, hat gone, eyes apparently shut, motionless, but he had been busy. The right hand was bound with what might be a kerchief in outdatedly patriotic blue, white and orange, now with additional blotches of scarlet, and he was using the gloved left hand to keep the bound one pressed to his thigh. In my self-indulgent fit of revulsion I'd possibly missed a gesture of surrender when he'd thrown his weapon aside; it was lying on the ground more than an armslength from him.

No avoiding confrontation; he had information I needed, and there was also a question of responsibility; whatever arbiter lays down the rules of etiquette for extreme cases discreetly advised it wasn't done to disable an enemy and walk away. Helpful if the same authority had supplied a booklet of correct phrases, *What to Say to the Man You've Just Maimed*, as it might be, and beyond social awkwardness there was the fact I was still afraid of *Azraël*, not knowing how deadly he might yet be. All too easy, so to take out a man with his *curriculum vitae et necis* and I didn't know, aside from his retirement from ambidextrous table-tennis, how much of the gloved hand remained from his Pretoria accident — enough, could be, to manage the small, genuine Italian automatic I was sure he was carrying.

Swiftly, before I could be immobilized by more reasons to sit and think, I went down the Watchtower, and crossed the hollow. Reaching the narrow belt of trees, I went upslope like a skirmisher, rifle at the port, and where cover ended remained fully two minutes, befriended by a supportive tree, aiming at where I could no longer see van Muer, wondering why I hadn't simply fired again from up above, this time to kill. With wounding, the sensibilities change sides and urge destruction — they do, I know, with creeping creatures we inadvertently injure, where the desire to be rid of what we've spoiled can masquerade as mercy. Too late now, or too soon.

At a sort of rapid limping tiptoe I went up the slope; van Muer was still as he was, but I scarcely looked at him before stooping to secure his nasty little automatic weapon, far handier for close-in work than the rifle, which I leant against the rocks well out of reach.

Van Muer's pale eyes came open as I bent over him. "Ames," he murmured as if half-asleep. "Ready. Ames. Fires! Bloody shit." He rested from that effort, and I with enormous distaste unsnapped the baggy pocket on the near side of his field jacket using my left hand only, reached in and at once found the expected pistol. While accomplishing this I noted there was very little blood from the wound in his leg, though the kerchief on the hand over it was a soaking mess.

"You're a lucky sod, aren't you," forced between his teeth, without his eyes reopening. I was worried by the trigger of the caulking-gun, a grip sculpted for three fingers, its pull unknown. Easy to say I could have fired a trial burst into the air; all this was new to me. After making sure the pistol was loaded, recognizing van Muer would stay put, I mounted to the broken rim leftward and taking the submachine by the snout, threw it whirling as far as I could, just reaching the ravine, where it vanished with a clatter. Van Muer came to life, and let out a stream of obscenities, remaining unmistakable when it diverged into Dutch, the *Taal*, and what he, probably, would have called Kaffir — there may have been others.

At our first bland meeting I'd made fifty the upper end of estimates as to his age, but now saw he could be ten years beyond that. Little lingered of that urbane, blazered, would-be distributor for Orbis products, but the diatribe had its focusing effect, and I startled myself with my own cogency by asking promptly, "Who knows you're up here? The Orbis people in Brandsville? — " a critical point.

He gave me a weary pout. "Fucking arse-lickers. If Spark tells me he's going to use his own dilettantes, I would have told him where he could stick his job. I don't need this. He knows I'll give my full cooperation, shit yes, share all intelligence, sure, with the bleeding boy scouts. What does he think, it's still 1970? That was a whole other scene, now it's just business, huh? Does Exxon share surveys with BP?"

He paused here on a grimace, body bending slightly over his wounds, leaving me to work out what had been said, and its import for me: though a mercenary, van Muer was, I adduced, or had been, a sincere anti-Communist, albeit in the widest sense of that umbrella term under which neo-imperialists, white supremacists, religion's brownshirts, art-loathers, arms dealers, apostles of unregulated greed, have all set up their stands: he might be all and was surely most of the above. In trying to murder me, however, as he saw it, he'd been serving only his income, and I'd speculate one who'd engaged and triumphed in who-knew-what deadly Cold War duels could extract a bitter irony out of defeat by a hopeless amateur in a venture where he had no doctrinal stake. Easy to show he was mistaken, because the success of Harness would enable corporate investors to extend control over enormous tracts of arable land in Asia, Africa and Latin America, and help keep the world safe for the kind of First-World rapacity his ideology embraced, but failure to perceive that might have saved my life: if he'd seen my death as part of the same old crusade, he wouldn't have disdained to collaborate with Laxitter's people, whereas in fact, with his completion bonus in mind, he'd apparently told them as little as possible. So I soon discovered.

Putting pain aside, he placated professional self-esteem with a tough grin. "Don't lose your beauty-rest over those guys, Ames. They couldn't find shit in a sewer. They haven't found out about your little lollipop, yet. Quite a lad for the jam-tarts, aren't you?"

I said nothing, but felt a guilty dread, just as when I read about Paula's death.

"Listen, laddie," voice not changing from the same flat drone, like reading from a booklet of boring instructions. "You can't have your little weaknesses and stay alive in this business. Anything I can find out about your habits, that's a handle on you. You're going to show yourself, buying your cigarettes or booze, you're going to ask somebody where to go for your hash, your coke, maybe your toyboys. Crumpet's the worst, there's not a tart been born who can live through next morning without telling some other bint who she screwed. If you can't keep old Simon in your jeans, keep him in your hand, boyo, you're miles ahead."

Advice, to be treasured indeed, sir, I was irritated enough by him, but too anxious about Fern to say, *coming from one who's been brought to this by his presumably blameless life.*

What followed was too desultory, too niggling, too diffuse to be recorded verbatim; though van Muer regarded this venture as a writeoff, he wasn't yet convinced he'd reached the very seamark of his own utmost sail, and work-habits acquired in the golden years made it a reflex for him to pull back and cover up whenever he caught himself talking about details of an operation, even one he no longer cared about. Also, he tired often, but by ruthless questioning I elicited that he'd spotted me this morning as I followed Fern, for whom he had a limitless catalogue of crude sobriquet and cruder metonymy, down to her ORV. Too distant for a shot, he apologized; he'd needed his binoculars to identify me, and by the time he'd managed to drive his own all-terrain vehicle near where he'd observed Fern's emerge and go bumping down to find the track, he was too late to see precisely where I vanished on my way back to what he supposed was the hideout described in my September notes.

Here, disjointed narrative was muddied more, as mystifying repetitions of the fact that his vehicle was right now standing in almost exactly the place where Fern's must have been left at last resolved into a weird proposition I use it to find some wealthy ranchers called the Prestons, and persuade them to bring me back in their chopper, to lift van Muer in the direction of competent medical treatment. In exchange, he offered to misinform his client, with absurd circumspection always left unnamed, that I was dead or had succeeded in escaping from this part of the country, if I liked, overseas. Van Muer himself would then vanish, and take no further part in operations against me.

That fine, flamboyant word *vertiginous* comes fluttering in to evoke my state. The effect was cumulative, chatting with an entity I could never have imagined existing, a human I had deliberately shot, who, having traipsed across half the country to kill me for a fee, was now asking me to save his life, to trust him.

"Have some sense," peevishly. "What can I do to you? You won. Going to take a year of surgery to give me just one hand that works again, if ever. It's time I packed it in. Once you start getting messy, you might as well."

After being unable to find the route I'd taken he'd let the lie of the land turn him northward, later catching a glimpse of me, it must have been as I crossed the stepped boulder, and recognizing we were on parallel courses. He deduced I might be heading for my tent, which he'd observed from the helicopter two days ago, with no idea what it might be for. Trying for a convergent route, he found himself wrong side of the "bleeding ravine" when I reappeared, but with the weapon he aimed should still have been unable to miss; how he'd managed to, and why I'd gone down remained mysterious to him, and I felt no compulsion to enlighten him.

A gloomy silence came, van Muer in pain, exhausted, brooding on failure. I too was sore and aching, and conscious as well of rapidly falling temperature. After a minute or two van Muer began a low muttering, words hard to catch, though it might have been centered, among renewed obscenities, on past triumphs of homicidal technique. Here, now, in a posture of acknowledged defeat, he still frightened me.

Once again he plied me with the relative nearness of his transport, and with directions to the Preston ranch, and now he recalled an additional inducement: "The gal there didn't look to me as if the elastic in her drawers was any too strong, streamlined little piece, just the way you like 'em, Ames, eh?"

"Why did you kill Paula?" I asked at last.

"Who?"

"In Westerlake."

"Oh, that. I had to kill her, had to. She would have known me. The whole thing was a wicked waste — you start with faulty intelligence, those things happen. They send me down there, she's the best one to know where you are, I get there, and right in front of her house, there's the car I'm looking for. Jesus! Shit-obvious, isn't it? you're there or else she knows where you've gone. Getting bloody cold."

Unflinching is criticspeak, a term of unquestioned approbation. Up to, well, the First World War, writing habitually flinched, was expected to; flinching, to spare the reader more than allusion to one's own most painful nightmares, was considered good manners, and as literature became more and more unflinching, the society it mirrored duly provided more and more to be unflinching about — I don't necessarily suggest a causal relationship, although there's always danger of implying aesthetic and intellectual sanction for all the nightmares with the art left out; precisely what seems to the critic and may occasionally be for the writer the courage to face explicit horrors may end by providing the lumpenconsumer with just the dash of tabasco his demonstrated relish for cruelty demands, certified literature, tabloid newsoid and cinema of annihilation all serving the same slavering appetite for gore.

As for me, I flinched then in not questioning and therefore denouncing on the subject of the torture Paula underwent, and flinch now from supplying details van Muer nonetheless volunteered: leave her at minimum the dignity of not providing soulless thrills for our legions of monsters.

Not that there was the least detectable voluptuousness in his flat delineation; nastily he droned about inflicting pain as another waste consequence of faulty intelligence, and (now I think of it, like those critics of their flinchless heroes) as an unsought, necessary duty. And then he had no choice but to murder poor damaged Paula.

I walked away. Somewhere, exhorting me to go for help, he'd asked rancidly, "Then what *are* you going to do with me?" and that question was made more complicated by his superfluous killing of Paula, and its ascription to me. A rap I could beat, surely, but one which would still lead to my arrest as immediate consequence of doing as he asked; authority quite properly doesn't simply say thanks very much and wave goodbye to persons who appear out of the wilderness to direct medical attention at gunshot victims, and whatever connection I was found to have to this new shooting would certainly add weight to the TV question about the violence that followed me like my shadow. As *Azraël* must know best of all, arrest was very likely my death-warrant.

To defer the problem, to demonstrate my injuries weren't incapacitating, and because the night was going to be cold, I went back across the hollow and down into the woods to strike my tent and load up with firewood. Not efforts requiring much thought, and by convention this should have helped me make up my mind, but my real-life experience has always been that while withdrawing from a question of recall or of pure reasoning may cause answers to float up from deep, hidden wells, with issues demanding decision, nothing happens except some time passes. When I came back, rifle slung, pistol awkwardly held in a hand under a weight of wood, van Muer was sitting more upright, and his light eyes were alert.

"This is stupid, isn't it?" he enquired, as I halted and put down my bundles. "If you meant to kill me, you would have shot to kill, or you could do it now. You're not going to just let me die."

"Why can't I? You killed Paula. You killed Hilde."

"Christ, laddie — " He seemed genuinely puzzled, offended, that I drew a parallel between my possible vengeance and his strictly business activities. "You can't let yourself get messed up with personal feelings in this game. In '68, when Prague got so buggered up, I had to risk my own skin to save this bloke in the Czech version of KGB before the Russkies got him. He was the same chap who'd killed two of my buddies, but he could finger every Soviet undercover in West Berlin. That's how it works."

That, as he'd said, slang appropriately dated, was a whole other *scene.* "Not for me," I said.

"Listen, then," he tried again. "You want to stay clear of awkward questions, I know all about that, believe you me. In the four-wheeler, I told you where that is, there's a two-way radio, channel one is boy scout headquarters. Leave the radio switched on. They can home on the carrier. All you have to do is tell them the lie of the land from the vehicle to where I am, then you can make yourself scarce. I haven't seen you."

He'd done the impossible, and outcuckooed what came before; expressions of incredulity would be wasted on a man who could utter such a bizarre suggestion. But aside from the major madness of asking me to summon his reinforcements (who, allowance made for his need to salvage pride, were surely more effective than van Muer's estimate), there were worrying illogicalities here. I said, "What did you use the radio for?"

He closed his eyes at the thought of more to tell, and I saw his focus, perhaps his being conscious at all, was a pure effort of will. "I'm supposed to check in with the boy scouts twice a day," he conceded. "I've been none too punctual, there's no telling when they're going to miss me."

A deficiency my use of the radio was meant to atone for. "But if you don't check in? What happens?"

"Nothing. Like I bloody told you, I been a bad scout."

"What's supposed to happen?" I amended.

"Bleeding alarm is supposed to go off. Panicsville."

"They would come after you?"

"Right, laddie. Well, after the vehicle."

Not right, couldn't be, if the radio had to be on to provide a homing signal. I *(a)*, agreed provision had been made for bringing him assistance, and his own contemptuous flouting of established procedure now had him worried his allies might not come for him, or would come too late, *(b)*, had no difficulty accepting he would have much preferred to find help without letting the despised Orbis crew know about his failure, hence the earlier suggestion I rouse the Prestons to summon medical aid. But *(c)*, could not believe the absurdity of an emergency system which would bring his backup people to the vehicle only with radio turned on, when its most urgent use would be if he were disabled, or separated from his transportation, or, as now, both at once.

You *bastard*, I didn't say aloud; this was indeed the wounded scorpion with the still-lethal sting. "You're wearing a homing device, aren't you," I stated rather than asked. With more energy, he might have managed scornful denial, but his quick reflexive movement inadvertently (and inexplicably) drew my attention to his watch, above the glove on the wrist of his top hand, chunky stainless-steel, very like one of the Russian-made ones that enjoyed a kind of antivogue in Western Europe a few years back. As I reached for that wrist he raised the gloved hand to ward me off, palm a sticky red jam. Part of the black vinyl glove was artificially stiffened, but while pushing it down I judged his games with explosives in Pretoria had left him an entire thumb, but cost the index-finger, and part of the middle finger. Also revealed to me was how much he was running on will-power; he was extremely weak, and I too angry and scared to be stopped by my revulsion for touching him.

It would need two hands, however; I had to step back and slip the automatic in my pocket. "Aren't we brave," he said, but scarcely resisted as I unbuckled the watch, surer than ever. It must weigh a quarter of a pound, fully three-eighths of an inch thick at the center. Besides the pull-out stem for setting hands, and smaller start, stop and reset buttons for stopwatch operation, the rim had little red plunger of no visible function. Pressed in, so I pulled it out.

Van Muer, watching with eyes like slits, said, "Can't be turned off once it's activated."

That obviously couldn't be right, but to be sure I unslung the rifle, set the watch up against the rock face, and shot once from a safe distance. The steel-jacketed bullet pierced and mangled the watch to shapelessness, but I scared myself again with the noise of the shot, which was tremendous down here among reflective rocks, and took seconds to echo away. Not knowing whether the electronic beacon had already guided enemies near, nor whether van Muer's bag of tricks had been emptied, I wanted urgently to get away from this place.

Mounting again to the broken rim I tossed the remains of the watch into the ravine. As I returned, van Muer said, "Not bad, boyo. I could have made something out of you."

He asked me to get his cigarettes, indicating left-hand pocket of his jacket. There I found a small bunch of keys including those for his ORV and a black leather pocket diary, both of which I appropriated, as well as a disposable lighter. and the cigarettes, an unfamiliar Continental brand packed in a flat, hinged metal box. I put one between his dry lips, but my attempts to ignite the lighter were defeated by the awkward angle and gusting wind; van Muer said, "Oh. Christ," more than once, and in the end I had to pocket the automatic once again, put a cigarette in my own mouth, light it shielding the flame in my cupped hands, and give it to him, an act of peculiar and instantly distasteful intimacy, for which I ignored muttered thanks. He smoked as a child sucks at a straw, taking air between gulps without removing the cigarette from his mouth. Not knowing whether he'd be able to work the lighter with the remaining fingers of his left hand, I put it, with the tin of cigarettes, on his lap.

"This is it?" he demanded angrily as, rather like loading a camel, I began deciding in which order to assume my various burdens; rifle, riddled knapsack, rolled tent, firewood. "What sort of limp-prick trick is that? Too fucking soft to kill me, and you're just going to leave me to die?" The cigarette in his mouth impeded speech, but conveyed its own parallel message, waggling in furious semaphore. "It's going to freeze tonight, bleeding freeze." Here, I noted that, taking advantage of my preoccupation, cold clouds had come with swift stealth to cover all the sky.

At that time I would have said I hardened myself to a tough decision by keeping in mind the torture of Paula, the shots placed in Hilde's already-dead body to simulate poor marksmanship. Principally, and this may be true for many uncharacteristic acts of calculated callousness, I was kept to my cold course by exactly the same weak and shameful terror that enforces suburban codes for dress and for lawn maintenance; *what will the neighbors think?* — wouldn't it be said I had no feelings for Paula, no sense of justice, no manhood sufficient to grasp this proffered vengeance, if I let a soggier instinct keep me from walking away? Moreover, there was no imaginable attempt to save shattered van Muer that wouldn't involve me in, at best, complicated inconvenience.

"Hoy, Ames." I hadn't gone ten hobbling steps when he called after me, "Hoy, *Ames*!" To achieve a shout he'd used gloved thumb and little-finger to take the cigarette from his mouth, an incongruous unmeant parody of affection.

"What?"

"Shoot me, will you. Have some bollocks. Shoot me in the head, once. Exposure's a rotten way to die."

Muttering angry words about Paula's death, I didn't do that, either.

Regaining the shack, I was in a condition of collapse. To say 'largely emotional' is illicit intellectualizing, a conclusion only reasoning can reach; the body makes no such distinction. Injured, sore, fatigued, shuddering with cold which time, altitude and my own condition had conspired to sharpen with every step, I dropped my burdens and dived into my jumbled bedroll, lighting a fire, heating up water only in ritual imaginings. The wind was whining, and I was more than ever conscious of deficiencies in weatherproofing; after a time also aware of a more soothing invasion, Fern. The smell of her, rather, clinging to bedding, more like a yearning childhood memory, such a fretful lifetime of unwanted experience divided me from that technically recent simplicity.

The Fern scent (*bracken*, my mind said, a silly pun) overlay the staleness that was mine, noticed now only by contrast, not a stink but a mustiness made diffident by familiarity, though others might find it less than pleasant. The symbol left dangling there can't be dismissed, merely for clanking too loudly; mine was a life gone rancid beyond retrieval, I was the soiled, unshaven, desperate fugitive of *film noir* who can't keep running forever, the fall guy, set up, railroaded, framed, glum, doomed, nothing but trouble, trouble with a capital T for you, kid.

And now, at last, a killer, if only by omission, but conscious omission; I couldn't achieve a nanosecond's self-deceit; I'd disabled *Azraël* and left him to die. A monster.

When I rolled off the bed-shelf to strip off my ripped pants and stand shivering in cold gusts to wash blackened blood from my wound, shrinking from the icy water, my mind was still with him, bleeding under the darkening sky, not far from where Fern at one glance had decided she could trust me not to be a murderer.

The comment was too apt; I couldn't do it. What, exactly, could be done for, or to, or with van Muer was unclear, but to be looking at my watch through the night, trying to calculate whether, a mile away, his heart had yet stopped beating, was not a tolerable option. After binding my wound I gingerly put on thermal underwear and the other pair of jeans, added a sweater, remembered I'd done nothing about my long-standing thirst and gulped down as much frigid water as could be endured, stuffed some dried apricots in my pocket to munch on the way, and set forth in the cold wind's wild lament, though unencumbered by wine, pine-logs or any flesh but my battered own.

On the way, I checked that the Beretta had a full clip: there was no proof I'd found and destroyed a homing device, still less the only one, and I might be descending into a wolf-pack; perhaps we'd leave the mountainside corpse-littered as from an amateur open-air production of *Hamlet*. Seriously, folks, I wondered whether van Muer's leg wound was altogether disabling; if no bone was broken he might be movable, with assistance. Maybe it was possible to get him up to the shack, where I could leave him, taking his vehicle and letting him inherit my supplies; with shelter he'd stand a fair chance of recuperating in time, but I'd be well away before he could give an alarm. Or if he couldn't be moved without more muscle, I supposed that would have to be summoned using the radio, but not tuned to the Orbis channel; he must know the frequency used by Sean Gomez's police department, or it could be discovered by experiment, and perhaps the Preston helicopter might yet be used to get him out. I'd report a hunting accident, and not obey instructions to stay where I was with the car, whose correct location I wouldn't in any event give; as with the first alternative, I'd spend the night somewhere in the vehicle, and then try to get in touch by phone with Fern at the Preston ranch.

All this contingency planning disintegrated on one hard fact: he was gone. Just as he had some hours earlier, but even more incredulously, I stared down at the empty space where a shot human should be, and just as with me no amount of staring could change his absence. The parallel was so complete I looked quickly up at the Watchtower in a clench of fear, while half-a-dozen mainly impossible explanations for his disappearance flicked through my mind.

Cigarettes and lighter were left behind, there were fresh daubs of blood on rattlesnake rock, and further smears indicated van Muer had gone down in the direction of the Watchtower. In the menace of growing dusk I followed warily, pistol ready, wishing now I'd thoroughly searched van Muer for additional weapons.

On the slope directly below the Watchtower to its eastward side, there was a knot of alien trees, the only mountain ash I'd seen in these parts. Leant against what must be the parent, its seed perhaps excreted by a transient bird asking what it could do for its country around the time of the Kennedy inauguration, I found him. His chin was lolled against his chest, shattered right and wrecked left hand still at his thigh, unconscious as I first thought, but permanently so, incredibly, completely dead. To be certain, I raised the head on its boneless neck, and in failing light the glint of a small fragment of glass was just visible, stuck to the lower lip. As the mouth came slightly open, the reader of country-house mysteries could identify the scent of bitter almond; cyanide. Since no one, not even in a Miss Marple, could be depicted sneaking up here to administer the fatal dose, it had been in a capsule which, like all good operatives, he carried with him for use in the last extremity. After my departure, he'd hauled himself out of the pit, and at incalculable cost in agony had tottered, sometimes (to judge by the state of his tan pants) crawled as far as he could achieve, roughly in the direction

---

he'd have to take to circle back to his car. Finding he couldn't go farther he'd obviously decided to decline the death, chiefly hypothermia, he'd called a rotten one. The wind now was gusting with surges of fine, cold rain, mixed with stinging grains of snow.

"You dumb bastard," offended in my turn he'd believed it when I walked away.

12.

Having come this far with my account I'm abruptly
illuminated with sympathetic understanding for novelists, their
perpetual state of war with their readers. Well, *war* may say it
too noisily, but it is a struggle between incompatible interests
for the territory of the mind, because a reader, naturally, wants
above all to know what happens next, which the writer,
whether of a real story like mine, or a made one, already
knows, and therefore finds least worthy of his attention: as
producer I find myself absorbed by what as consumer most
readily exasperates me, digression, elaboration,
embellishment, interpolated jokes, exhaustive exploration of
motive and feeling, not to say present reflection on those past
events. The highbrow reader should at least pretend to loftier
things than a vulgar obsession with plot, and it's true we're
more patient when it comes to retold classic tales, known
histories, opera — even an unfamiliar opera, where we
welcome an advance synopsis, which, loosening the tyranny of
what's next?, frees us to consider *how* the tale is told, enjoy
arias, ensembles, harmony and orchestration, the
ornamentation. But prose at its freest can only occasionally
approach the irrational splendor of music, and few nowadays
would bother to read a novel with (fine antique of a usage) the
argument set out in advance, to let reader and writer start
even: though sage and civilized, we still want to keep a bit of
the goggle-eyed, unbearable rapture from childhood — our
own, or of our species — when storytellers spun out their
unencumbered yarns; all else, beyond primitive
characterization, came later. Those bare recountings could
never satisfy our developed selves, but hooked us early enough
to create an ineradicable hunger; sophisticated as we've

become, *au courant* as we keep ourselves, we still want our music to sing, our poems to dance, and our stories to haul us along.

These thoughts somehow connect with how the time left to me in Zack's Shack became softedged, difficult to resolve in the viewfinder marked *reality*, beginning with an eerie waking to silence, unyielding cold, and an underwater sensation ascribable to the odd quality of the morning. Its quantity, too: for the first time I saw without help from my lantern the wrinkles and bulges in the rock ceiling overhead, and was dreamily conscious the light filtering through blurred windows was without its habitual downward slant. Unless a huge wedge of crag had been quietly excised to let earlier sun strike at a new, low angle, the only reasonable explanation was reflective snow.

A daunting amount of it, though measurement in inches meant nothing in this tormented and wind-worried terrain; a graceful curved ramp reached to the level of the knee I pushed against it on the other side of my door, but otherwise the rock shelf was mostly scoured bare, except for a knife-edged swell, rising to shoulder height, of stilled Waikiki surf sculpted by wind slicing through the westward gap. In sheltered spots rocks were crowned by smug cushions, but the soft beast had hidden claws, the going underfoot newly treacherous, sharp spurs blandly concealed, deep holes masked as innocuous pockets of snow.

Ally or enemy? my mind was already dizzied with the question of how close the neat-suited Orbis contingent might be to me, and whether staying put or making a run for it was the greater danger. Nothing van Muer had said could be accepted at face value, but his suicide must mean he'd *believed* the boy scouts had no idea where he was. Yet if they had only the vaguest idea of the country he'd been covering from helicopter and in his four-wheel drive vehicle, it would be in this direction they'd search, when his failure to check in extended beyond his habitual negligence.

Stupidly, I'd failed to ask van Muer who'd piloted the helicopter. He was very likely qualified himself, and yet to imagine the Prestons leasing the aircraft to a stranger on those terms was impossible. If there'd been a pilot, he or she could be questioned, and must know almost all van Muer had discovered from the air, would be able to point to the spot where they'd stooped to circle (as I surmised) my tent among bare trees, within a half-mile of where van Muer's body was propped against its mountain ash; that was three or four hundred feet lower than where I was; most unlikely there'd been sufficient snow down there to cover the body, though it might be enough to hide the spotted trail he'd dripped down, and two sets of superimposed bloodstains back at the pit. When, using a cautious hand to brush aside snow and make sure of footing, I climbed to my normal watch spot, flanks of the distant mountains were hard white wedges. but snow was the stipple of a leaky airbrush on the lower hills, and the intervening ground was dark; despite the bitter, still cold, where I was must be near the lower edge of the substantial fall.

My thoughts kept straying to van Muer's four-wheel drive, for which I had the keys, but it was a magnet for the very forces I feared were closing in — I needed to be an amoeba, a wraith, a wreath of mist to survive in this world of nightmare shape-changing, where dark-suited assistant-*nazgûl* could seamlessly morph into respectable Orbislings, able to ask for police assistance in tracking a private investigator, vanished after getting a lead on a known criminal. Such a full-scale search, with the predictable military assistance, could hardly fail to find me, but on the other hand, if I decided on flight, I might reach the vehicle and find it already staked out by my hunters, or else if snow made it impossible or too dangerous to drive, I would have achieved no more than to lay down a trail like a freeway from that place to this.

Once more, inaction won the debate; I stayed put, burning fuel parsimoniously, using the stove to make hot drinks for wrapping my numbing hands around. Temperature, as is now apparent to me, was part of what walled me off from the ordered world of cause and effect; easy to let the attempt to be warm obsess me, at the same time as my city-coddled self declined to believe in cold there was no escape from. In absolute terms, not such extreme cold; my water-supply never failed, though the source developed a jangle of glassy stalactites, and in the morning I'd had to break a slab of ice on the inside cistern, so restoring the flow beneath the latrine; by mid-afternoon my eaves were a cascade, sun fretting the topmost fringes of snow on the rocks into scintillating lace (World Copyright). It was so when I made my second careful clamber to the lookout post, and in the direction Fern had told me to look for the Preston ranch house, discerned a tiny alien patch of lucent color, the poppy-red flag flying to inform me there was progress in reaching John Battaglia.

Inside, I put up my tent again, and took away some of the chill by carrying inside big stones warmed in front of the infrequently-burning fire. I dozed and made hot beverages, read and dozed, worried. Fresh light dustings of snow appeared twice overnight on the hard refrozen crust, while in the middle of day the noises of thawing, dripping, the sharp crack of ice breaking, sudden splashing spurts as an ice-dam gave way, over and again all sounded remarkably like the inadequately surreptitious gathering of enemies, readying themselves to storm in through the door, and their repeated failure to do so did nothing to lessen the illusion. But my fear was oddly ineffectual; half-dozing and convinced this time I really had heard the shuffle and clatter of feet, I did nothing, and the curiosity I felt about my own prostration was at an equally inattentive level, although I can see now the beginning of a passivity still entangling me like miles and miles of tacky spider's thread, a layered dread of any action, easily traceable to the distasteful results of my one sortie into decisiveness.

I'd been keeping both loaded rifle and van Muer's automatic ready beside me in the tent, but someone, not Fern, Judy, perhaps, said I should give *Azraël* back his gun.

"He's dead."

"Right, and you've got the gun. The police are going to come storming in here — " and the police, or some menace, did come, but not really here, more like my apartment. Though being arrested, I was very cunningly preventing them from going downstairs where van Muer's body was, but they took my gun, his gun, and ballistics revealed —

"Give it back. Put it in his pocket."

"I'll go no more: I am afraid to think what I have done; look on't again I dare not."

"Infirm of purpose! Give me the weapon — "

No, that was *Macbeth*. "That's *Macbeth*," aloud, jolting myself to full waking, and recognition I'd been dreaming sense: while there'd be no reason to connect the automatic to past crimes if found on van Muer's (probably not to be identified) body, taken in my arrested possession it would be, the adverb is inevitable, automatically tested; once matched to the bullets that killed Hilde and Paula, there would be great ingenuity expended in assailing my alibi, and it would be hard to find anyone to believe a word I had to say on any subject: *Double murder suspect Arthur Ames claimed today that both killings were part of an Orbis Corporation coverup... Due, police say, to lack of evidence, Ames has never been charged with either crime, although the weapon in his possession when apprehended has been identified as...* No.

In one sense it mattered less, now the killer was dead, that to destroy the only hard fact to connect him to the murders meant they would be unsolved, my innocence never established beyond rumor, but since I couldn't make myself revisit the cadaver, and couldn't have if there hadn't been snow, no gun was better than my being caught with it; I dropped the excellently-made weapon into the unfathomed crevice next to the box of my latrine, and quite a long time passed before I heard it strike anything. Gone.

After that, time went flaccid, and its only fixed markers were the four times each day I emerged and climbed to look out, until the noon when the small, distant spark of color had changed to yellow.

As I emerged from the ring of pines, Fern, face perilously bright, came running to hug with a small cry, I heard as joy. She was trembling, and after some moments I noticed she was determinedly not weeping.
"What's the matter?"
"I was scared," instantly. "I got certain I'd never see you again."
Consoling soon brought vivid physical reminiscence of our night together, and avid Fern murmured, "We should have thought of this before you struck your tent." She was, by the way, in her Subject To Inspection By Maretta mode, hints of pigment at lip and cheek, red leather driving cap, lush black turtleneck, probably cashmere, possibly borrowed, undebatably becoming. Unable to function in verbal ambiguity, I'd decided on *clouded amber* as the usual and dominant color for her eyes.
"We have to get out of here. It's dangerous," I reminded, and began humping what baggage there was into the low back of her utilitarian little set of wheels. I'd unloaded the rifle, but when it was handed to her, being a well-trained ranger, she threw open the breech, and saw instantly it had been fired. "I hope it was useful," laconically, but the anxiety came back to her tautened lower lip.

"Does Sean Gomez know you have a 30-06 rifle?"
Only now it occurred to me there was a bullet in the right thigh
of a cadaver that could be traced to this weapon.

"Oh, sure. He's hunted with it — the ammunition is
his, I think. Why?"

"You'd better lose it. Tell Gomez it was stolen from
the cabin while you were away."

"Okay," without discussion. "He gave me a lecture
about leaving my door unlocked, with all the strangers there
are in town." I had to wait to find out what about that amused
her. She wrapped the rifle in a threadbare piece of blanket, to
stuff it under an accumulation of clothing and camp equipment
in the back of the car, remarking she could report it as stolen,
and hide it out at the Preston place. Later, it could be
recovered, and then she would notice it had been fired, was
that okay?

"We'd better get moving," I repeated.

"I know," wistfully, setting herself behind the wheel.
"Maybe we can get some sack time out there — " this with a
sidelong look. "But Maretta will be back."

"And?" deferring the question, back from what?

"You're going to want to make it with her. She said
she's going to seduce you."

That, beyond dispute, settled the question for Fern, but
my imagination failed in the attempt to construct talk between
friends, one probably in love, where the other could make such
a threat. Seeing my eyebrows, Fern became defensive: "Every
one of her lovers is always the biggest and best, she's been
telling me about her fucking marathons since I was twelve. It's
my own fault. I couldn't help it — " there was a devastatingly
tender gesture to go with this, a beseeching hand lightly
touching my mouth and alighting on my forearm, so I needed
only one guess: present passion and past patronization had
combined to exaggerate my prowess in the telling, and kindle

either Maretta's connoisseurship or her competitive urge, or both.

While, as a collector myself (Hilde), I — what am I doing with all this coupling stuff? Hilde was dead, Paula was dead, their killer dead, Orbis was loosed upon the world, and I had yet to hear about my attempt to meet with a former senator, future cabinet-member. Still, there was nothing trivial about Fern, then or now: I told her it took two to achieve a seduction, and notwithstanding her sad, knowing smirk which seemed to confer irresistibility on her friend, despite also that universal greed always pricked into life by news of willing hectares yet unplowed, I genuinely doubted Maretta was for me; the echoings of her in Fern's mouth, together with van Muer's word *streamlined*, made her sound like one of the women who remain for me no more than visual experience, or most theoretical of fantasy; they become, as I paraphrased for Fern, incidents in erotic biography, and presumably, with films, undressed commercials, random sexual references, the entire glossy landscape of masscult titillation, part of the process by which the testicular batteries are charged for real service.

At once, she was interested, with the academic air that could camouflage deep feelings. "You mean, when you make love, it's kind of an *anthology* of all the women, everything that turns you on?"

"To some extent, I think so, yes." We were moving now, her eyes on the notional road, while I sprawled as low as possible on my spine, reducing slightly the chance of my being spotted by an unobserved observer, but doing nothing to diminish the unease I felt at letting her risk association with me.

"For me, it's like just the opposite," this with an approach to romantic self-satisfaction, but my admission was too complex to have only one opposite: of available antitheses,

I was reasonably certain it wasn't that she expressed her excitement with one man by making love to many.

In retrospect, my conclusion about what she did mean is hardly a modest one; at the time I returned to easier puzzles. "Back?" I said, her word for Maretta.

From the state capital, and her TV station, and there was a story in this that made Fern giggle in advance. Told about the suited searchers who'd descended on Brandsville, Maretta had mischievously decided to see how they'd react to the bright lights of publicity, in this case absolutely literal, as shouldered by members of the mobile camera-unit she'd called in, telling her station there might be a big story simmering here. She'd obtained plenty of typical probe-show scenes of men having nothing to say, ducking away from cameras, slamming the door of their big camper in her face, and her persistence had evidently routed the dapper contingent, the lot next to Tony Arkle's trading emporium being empty when she came back for another try. That was two days ago, and might explain why I'd remained untroubled by any follow-up to van Muer, but this morning Maretta had left in the helicopter, summoned by her station-manager, who nursed the quaint notion a preexistent exposé story is needed to give interest to *no comment* footage. Maretta, by Fern's report, was cheerfully unconcerned about the conference: she came in with the unfair advantage of having neither financial nor emotional need for her job.

Maretta's return had a bearing on my future, since I was to be helicoptered to my meeting with Battaglia, at his home, in the adjacent state, but not much more than a hundred miles from here. Maretta, who'd set up the appointment, had wanted Fern to emphasize from the start that Battaglia had agreed only to *meet* with me, implying no kind of commitment. "Politicians," Fern offered sagely, "always have to cover their asses, even when they're nice ones." She noticed the ambiguity, and, grinning, let it sit there.

Fittingly the passive voice comes stealing into my
history, the point becoming what was to be done with me, not
what I did. Dismay at the consequences of action had made
me surrender my will, and the question I was contemplating,
while hardly an original one, has to be dealt with in some way
by everyone who comes to that place (as faced by my father's
generation in the One Just War): can the good (i.e., in this
case, me) defeat a ruthless and brutally competent adversary
without giving up what's being defended, without *becoming*
the enemy?

Some of this must have gotten into what was meant to
be a flat, factual account of how the rifle came to be fired,
because Fern said, "What would have happened if you hadn't
disabled him, then?"

"He would have killed me." That one was easy; if I
hadn't pulled the trigger it would have become a stalking
game, and van Muer was better armed and better at it than I —
that doesn't make him a superior all-round specimen; on my
own turf, well, I'd seen a sample of his prose style, and knew I
could have run rings around him in a punctuation contest, or
with tricky subject-verb agreements. But only a one-in-near-
infinity chance had produced the snake at the precise moment
to delude him he'd shot me, and so create that moment of
vulnerability; there would never have been another such
opening. Next day, or the day after he would have done the
job right.

"Well, that's it, then," Fern summarized. I loved her
for it, and only wished my nightmares could be filed away so
conclusively.

The Preston spread possessed an inner enclosure, a
stone-walled citadel entered through a high wrought gateway
where the name, *RANCHO FELIZ*, surmounted an arch line
from a once-beloved song, WHERE JOYS NEVER CEASE. The
spindly iron letters had been given small twig-spurs to
simulate rustic wood, but remained a distressing reminder of

the notorious *Arbeit Macht Frei* at Auschwitz, and about as likely to be true. Beyond this portal was material enough for a separate novel, perhaps decades of *daytime drama*, dealing repetitiously with the tensions and power-struggles behind a bland facade of insouciant wealth, and beneath a tall flagpole with a large square of yellow silk flying. The facade itself, and the house as a whole, were no more than mildly irritating in their folksy pretentiousness and vague-minded melange of Western themes: outpost primitive with jutting and in this instance non-functional timber balks, the stucco and glazed tiles of pseudo-mission as seen in Southern California railroad stations, and a determined thrust into the mid-fifties suburban ranch style, picture windows and breezeway-connected garage. Also a hint of Old Seville, with a stone archway between wings leading to a paved courtyard with plants and central fountain.

This muddle of manners had resulted from years of accretion; as I discovered, the coyly frontier-fort portion, with optimistic gate, had been put up by the original Everett in 1922, when his grandson, present head of the family, was born. Middle Everett gave a sinister twist to the motto with his highly fashionable suicide in 1929, but his (still-living, now ancient) widow, with less volatile wealth of her own, kept adding to the place, as did Everett III, especially after his marriage; the final intrusive *Andaluseria* supplied in a late spasm in 1972, so the building, for scandal fans, spanned the entire half-century from Teapot Dome to Watergate.

We halted under the *Ran* banner, and Fern did an unconscious physical quotation, leaning back gripping top of the wheel with one rigid hand on a stiff arm, like a ghetto stud profiling. "Anyway," she said, or prayed. "After... "

That panicked me — I don't mean fear of commitment or any of that fashionable zombie-talk: it's absurd to speak in those terms when, no matter how things went with Battaglia, I was going to remain a casualty, or what I used to call my life was, of this Other Just War. And she was sixteen, which ought to have let me off the hook, but I still felt guilty, and that irritated me: how had she a claim? when she'd been the one to insist on our carnal congress, had decided unilaterally to be in love? Fine, but she was, in another tone of voice, *sixteen*, her pain was real, and while I wasn't remotely in love with her, I felt, what? — a vast tender responsibility for her. Sentimental self-aggrandisement, no doubt.

As gently, as objectively as I could, I said, "There isn't any future for us, Fern."

"How do you know?" a response so hair-trigger she must have been waiting for my pronouncement. "You don't know — seeing Jocko Battaglia could change everything. This is the only time I was ever in love. Let's go."

Rigid-jawed, defiant Fern in the lead (I was still limping from the pulled muscle), unforbidden by a coffered oaken front door designed to intimidate, we came to an ambiguous space, entrance hall expanding with no break into a vast all-purpose prairie lapping into doubtful distances, areas designated for sitting, dining, doing office things, main stair with massive banister descending somewhere amidships, low steps down to more remote colonies, glass slabs opening on ferny or palmy courtyards, while a great deal of money had been spent to add discomfort if not actual danger by flooring the entire expanse with annoyingly convex tiles of glazed terra cotta where the foot rocked precariously, and small hand-woven rugs waited to go glissading under an unwary tread. As I was to learn, this expanse, which had required gutting the existent conglomeration of structures, was the contribution of Elise, mother of Everett IV, a native of Pasadena, to which climate its unenclosed vistas would have been better suited; here, east of the Rockies and north of the 38th parallel, its winters were, to quote Graham, a bitch to heat.

I have no key to how or for what shifting reasons the family divided itself among three principal dwellings, this and another subsidiary address handier for Bloomingdales and the

Metropolitan Opera, and the ur-domicile with readier access to the Preston International offices and Niemann-Marcus. Neither Everett III nor Elise was currently here, and of his offspring, Everett IV only because of a complicated dispute with suppliers concerning some inadequate bovine sperm.

He didn't smile when I asked whether the cows had been writing letters to *Cosmo*. Knowing him a nascent winemaker, I'd expected some boyish glint to reflect from his enthusiasm, but he was tall, dour, alarmingly desiccated at 28, with dull brown eyes and permanently pursed lips. When I say he made it clear to me I wasn't welcome I don't mean just the frigid courtesy of his quasi-greeting; no, he drew me aside into a small room or large alcove to say, "Let me make it clear, Mr. Ames. As far as I'm concerned, you're not welcome here."

"I'm here only en route to meet Senator Battaglia."

"Okay, but if I understand your status, you may be involving this family in a serious felony, harboring a fugitive. I have business interests to consider."

"I understand." The disadvantages of my twilight legal standing, my dependence on Preston goodwill, and my scruffy appearance were exacerbated by inability to ask this swine whether a tissue was available, and consequent anxiety over the droplet I felt sure would soon adorn the end of my nose; scarcely another physical condition is so fatal to aplomb.

"I don't care whether you understand or not. I want you out of here as soon as possible, and I want you to forget you were ever in this house. If you claim you were ever here, it will be totally denied."

After my ironic bow, he capped himself by saying I would be billed for use of the helicopter, adding somewhat contradictorily that it was ranch equipment, and he wasn't running a taxi business.

I suggested the cost could be deducted from whatever his sister's station paid me for their exclusive interview. A

mistake; Everett IV said icily his sister's actions and
transactions had nothing to do with the Rancho Feliz, and he
wasn't cold at all, he was trembling with anger, the grinding
frustration of a man, who, despot over an Oregon winery, was
bullied here by his younger sister's connections to the media
and to a prospective member of the incoming cabinet.
Outside, under the flagpole, it had come to my mind betrayal
(of Fern, as well as me) was not out of the question, and now I
was sure only Maretta's insistence on her *scoop*, and his own
desire to avoid adverse publicity, had stopped Everett IV from
having platoons of police waiting for me.

A very few minutes later his younger brother was
telling me not to mind what Ev said: he was especially touchy
right now about the chopper, lease of which he had at first
denied to the stranger who'd come and presented various
credentials, including a valid pilot's license. Within thirty
hours Everett III, Dad, had called from Texas to instruct his
humiliated heir that the visitor, a distinguished academic
author (Laxitter must have been behind this), was to be
permitted use of the helicopter *for nothing!* Not surprisingly,
he was neither van Muer nor anything Dutch; he was Alfried
Starkus, a German historian of the American West, though
described as having "some kind of British or Aussie accent."
(My research has since turned up a genuine Alfried *von*
Starkus, born in 1885 at Memel, a kind of mirror-image to
Azraël's counterfeit, who wrote a chest-drumming account of
German *eastward* expansion from 1200 to 1917, the *Drang
nach dem Osten*, which one might call 'How the East Was
Won.' In a charming historical irony, this scholarly Teutonizer
was killed in the Nazi bombardment of Danzig in 1939.) I
wondered idly about the passport, if any, to be found among
Azraël's effects; surely it wouldn't be in the name van Muer,
which had been bandied about too freely at Special Projects.

Not expecting to, I liked Graham. He'd provided the
college buddy, remember, who took Fern to (and in) Santa Fe,

and then, evidently stimulated by his friend's report, had himself achieved those "no big deal" beddings with her. But none of it could have been knowingly schemed by this diffident, uncomplicated young man, boyish for 22. Having taken me over from his repellent brother, he found me, oh blessed rescue, a box of tissues, asked if I wouldn't like a bath, and contrived not to suggest the thought came from standing downwind of me. Much my size, Graham conducted me to a spare bedroom and gave me the freedom of a closet filled with clothes he said were his castoffs, though most appeared brand-new. After I'd luxuriated half an hour in a vast sunken bath, my regretful decision to shave a beard still too scrubby to trim into an adornment revealed the new angularity of my cheekbones, and a digitally flickering scale stammered that I'd found about fifteen pounds to lose from my normally spare frame. Still, swathed in wool-silk blend with a shirt miraculously laundered to be at the same time crisp and soft, my newly civilized appearance brought a whistle from Fern when I came back downstairs. In yet another area uncertain whether to be a separate room, this one down three steps from the main tiled acreage, food was brought for us both by a short, olive-skinned, heavy-lidded woman Fern called Tía; the meal, however, was determinedly *yanqui*, cold roast beef, very rare, warmed onion rolls, various garnishes, no *salsa*. The wine was terrible, a nasty cabernet produced from young vines by a winemaker trying for Haut-Brion first go; a spurious size, chemical oakiness and an undertaste like cherry-flavor cough-syrup.

"Oh, God, they gave you Domaine Elise — " Graham observed my involuntary grimace. "You don't have to finish it, you've done enough to satisfy family honor."

"What are you, the *mater dee*?" Fern said. "Quit hovering." She treated him with a familiar rudeness, given edge by her continued desire for time alone with me, but Graham was swinging back the door of a massive ultra-Spanish armoire, dark as the Escorial and ornate as the

Alhambra, revealed now as a cabinet storing serried bottles of wine.

"How about Côte-Rôtie?" Very soon I was filling my mouth with a rich, silken Rhône, and dazedly trying to identify the precise mechanism in my instant change of condition, as if I'd twisted upward through that vortex, a ghostly inverted drainpipe, by which El Greco transfigures common clay, or perhaps been seized by some visually similar, yet vulgarer Spielberg special effect, sucked up as vile vermin to emerge on the other side as a pampered guest. The ease of this transition could turn all my running and hiding into paranoid fantasy, but for the blood, *Azraël*'s, too sticky not to be real, the twitch of his bullets near my face.

Fern kept watching me, trying to make me complicit in her plot, and soon she had a new hoverer, a boy of about twelve with moist brown eyes and no neck, Paco, the nephew of whom Tía was the *tía*. There was a side-table with coffeemaker, and Paco darted there to fill cups as soon as eating subsided and our glasses were empty; he watched like a cat at a mousehole while Fern drank a very milky half-cup, and the rattle as she returned it to the saucer was his cue.

"¿Now, Fern?" The boy had the set face of one who's inured to disappointment, but never reconciled, still hurtable by odds that were always against him.

"Oh, Paco — "

"But you *say*... "

She turned to me imploringly. "I promised to shoot baskets with Paco." Agony for her, caught between commitment and desire, with the added fear of my disappointment, although in fact I was relieved; I would have found it hard to say no to what was really a wildly irresponsible idea; here, among many potential witnesses, was not the same as Zack's Shack, another felony for Everett IV to be upset about.

"I did promise," Fern repeated, anxious, with all the rest, that I know she'd much rather be making love with me. I murmured I had to make some notes about what to say to Battaglia, and she predicted it wouldn't be long. "Just twenty-five points," she told Paco, and for certainty, "*Veinte y cinco.*"

"*¡Cincuenta!*" The glum face was now radiant with joy. He was the second passionate adorer of Fern I'd found here, but while that "no big deal" couldn't be true on the other side, Graham didn't appear to know how crazy about her he was; if a case of *He Never To-ho-hold His Love*, it was not so much reticence as inability to discard cool and casual assumptions to te-he-hell himself. Fern's cruelties to him, then, were completely unconscious, part of an established pattern; she treated him like a familiar friend who can be ignored or deferred for more pressing concerns, told to get lost, while his reflexive need to avoid humiliation came near reinventing courtly love; suffering became a prize.

A good time for a look at the black leather pocket diary I'd taken from Scudder, *Azraël* I mean, but it had no name written inside, and was singularly uncommunicative, all the entries I could find consisting of nothing but AM or PM times of day, with nothing but crosses or check marks to indicate what they might refer to. After some minutes of this, the heavy slapping bounce of a basketball on paving set me wandering to find the right window. The court was a canyon between house and garage, which must have space for about nine Rollses; the house faced almost due east, and late-afternoon sun was behind the free-standing hoop, casting a long gallows shadow on the pinkish flagstones.

Even the lower total set by Fern was going to take some time to attain; the standard of play was abysmal. Fern had good hands and moved nimbly enough, but the hoop was a long way above her head, and she did too much laughing to set herself properly for a shot, while Paco, large around the middle, short-armed, with unreliable reflexes, was as easy to decoy as a trusting puppy — in those terms, the contest was between an excitable terrier and a St. Bernard too new to know just where its feet were, and yet, and yet; there was the soft golden light in Fern's avid face as she watched her shot flirt with the rim, all that youth on the other side of the glass; my veins were alive with a wonderful wine, but I wasn't smiling. Graham was there after a time, a sideline referee ignored by the blithe players, except when he called Fern for a double-dribble, and she stretched to bounce the ball off his head.

At my ear a voice said, "You don't look much like a mountain man." Maretta, unmistakably, with rather less resemblance to her twin than ordinary brothers and sisters share, but dressed to assert her journalistic identity, the Platonic perfection of a belted field-jacket, if Plato (and why not?) had sat beside the likes of Bill Blass and Calvin Klein at the feet of Socrates, a work-shirt Marie Antoinette would have enjoyed, soft linen masquerading as tough gabardine, olive-grey chinos — but could they be, it is fitting to ask, only chinos? dexterous as they were in tracing the intricacies of slender thighs, and then their long frontal span; falling with a faint sheen and the ripe fold of Renaissance drapery to blouse faultlessly over soft umber ankle-boots, tops rolled just enough to reveal fleece from a lamb which had shared a single (and its sole) experience with magical Macduff.

"I could be a dead man on the mountain, if you hadn't panicked the hunters," in awkward thanks.

She brushed away both gratitude and the need for it. "I've just been catching hell over that," imperturbably. "You and Fern have to be wrong about those guys. That was some high-level shit that hit the fan — they must be on some government project."

I knew otherwise; it was simply their paychecks came from the same source as hers. "I hope it wasn't too bad."

"Comes with the territory," she said, nearly sang. "They know me by now. If they want Cokie Roberts, they should hire her." A distant, not unpleasant threat of sulking echoed in the overtones of her voice; the career of managing men had begun early, and by now acquired patina.

Still, *streamlined* was wrong — I'll come back to that; in our next minute, before there was time for assessments, she was interviewing — or, since she made no notes, and wasn't using a recorder, it would be more accurate to say, auditioning — me.

From Fern, she had what must be an annoyingly anonymous story about a giant corporation and its hugely dangerous process, and she went straight to questions about how that connected to the murder of which I'd been accused. So far, so cogent, but I'd hardly begun an answer, which required a light sketch of my troubled relationship with Paula, when the news-magazine's *feckless irrelevancy* made its appearance.

"You've never been married?"

O Muse, of worlds I sing, and many painful deaths. "Not yet."

She wrinkled her forehead. "Do you think you're afraid of making a commitment?"

"Not at all," I said. "I've made dozens of them."

Wide blue eyes tried to unperplex a sexual innuendo from this nonsense-answer, while I went on to tell how my car had come to be standing in front of Paula's house. We were back in focus until I came to where Judy's computer skills allowed me to break into the private files of (unnamed) Laxitter.

The pretty pucker returned. "Are you a man who feels threatened by a capable woman?"

"Only if she's holding a gun." Outside, the requisite number of points to placate Paco had been achieved; Fern bounced the ball to Graham, who, with a casual loop of his arm, sank a basket from thirty feet or so, and this side of the glass Maretta sought in vain (and unfashionably) to find a phallic metaphor in my reply.

More than once in this untidy narrative, I've indicted myself with sexual distractibility, but I was and am a model of ascetic singlemindedness in comparison with Maretta; again when I told how Hilde had known about falsified results of (unnamed) Bieman's research, the question that came to Maretta's mind was: "Did his wife know about his relationship with this Hilde?"

Seldom is it exactly true to say one is dumbstruck, but here it went beyond a mere figure of speechlessness; my tongue clave behind my bottom teeth: I simply couldn't form words to cope with one who went so unerringly to the least significant element. But she wasn't stupid by any standard measure, on a scale of sophistication at least a century older than her twin; and I'm not sure to this moment the earnest flibbertigibbet wasn't, well, let's say, sixty percent conscious parody, a partial put-on she found dangerously compatible, and often useful; clearly she'd worked the airhead play in deflecting the wrath of her employers. My uncertainty about whether she was laughing up her sleeve was disconcerting, and she was much — how can I say this; her appearance was far less prepackaged than I'd expected; though immaculate, she registered as unstudied. Oh, I know, and knew then it was an effect, art that transcends artifice, the caramel-color hair and fresh skin made softly natural with patient skill; even so I was wrong-footed by the simulacrum of vulnerability, at absolute odds with the tough-broad portrait presketched by Fern's quotations — authenticity of which I never doubted. Those recollections must have been what forestalled spontaneous attraction; I was fascinated, but distantly, as by an ingenious riddle, one of those exquisite false-perspective tricks by Escher where men-at-arms eternally trot *down* the steps to reach the topmost level of the castle, the observer's mind, trapped in visual convention, unable to reconcile the inconsistencies.

In a swift transformation she appointed herself my handler, continuing with only a brief preoccupied glance to mark Fern's arrival; "You should level, I mean totally, with Jocko Battaglia. He's a guy who responds in a positive way to straight shooters, and you better cool it with the snappy comebacks, you know?"

How can they do it? From the gnarled wisdom of near half the ordained span of a man's years, I'd been reticent about offering sane and unthreatening advice to a sixteen-year-old, and here was this, this *post-deb*, airily instructing me, survivor of deadly duels, prophet of doomsday, as if I came hat in hand. In keeping with my new passivity, and because I needed Maretta's conduit to Battaglia, I clamped down hard on a snappier comeback than any so far, but Fern didn't fail to note and identify my outrage, and said, "Jeez, come on, Maretta — it's not like Arthur is trying to put something over on him. He's giving Battaglia a chance to save a whole bunch of lives, not selling snake-oil."

Maretta turned, and stretched forth an exploratory forefinger to touch beneath Fern's eye. "After you shower, don't forget to use the moisturizer I gave you."

"Don't bullshit."

"It's total merchandising now — " outfaced Maretta abandoned her sleight. "It doesn't matter — if you were Lincoln, you'd have to have spin control for the Second Inaugural; St. Paul would go on the talk-show circuit and register the Cross as a logo — "

"You're *quoting* Jocko Battaglia," Fern protested.

"It never hurts to be prepared," Maretta, lamely, and it came to me that for herself she had absolutely no opinion on anything I'd told her, which must entail the eerie possibility it was all the same to her if she was helping an actual murderer.

Thoroughly committed Fern, meanwhile, having won a round, appeared to regret her temerity, and meekly asked her friend to explain again about the damned moisturizer: she'd been brave, I was touched to perceive, only on behalf of her threatened man; for her own sake she behaved with a saddening deference, wry illustration of the Maretta-Battaglia thesis, the ascendancy of style over substance. Nothing about Fern's intense reality was remotely concerned with image, except in her enthrallment to Maretta's specious glamour, inexplicable (everything is inexplicable), but, given her history, not mysterious: old Buckwheat Thomas (Dad) must have thought all he needed to know about a girl was that you bought her jeans in steadily increasingly sizes, till one day she was old enough to pick out a dress for herself at J.C. Penney.

AMES BETRAYS FERN, CITES `PRUDENCE'
That happened when Fern headed for her post-basketball shower, her swivelled eyes telling me she'd meant to have me join her there, if Maretta hadn't arrived. At top of the three steps, she turned to ask, "So: when are we leaving for Battaglia's?"

"You're not," Maretta stated.

"I have to come."

"Uh uh. You know I can't do that to Jocko. He's taking a big chance here as it is."

A stricken silence, Fern pondering the further implications of Maretta's sentence. "I'd just *be* there," she submitted. "He wouldn't have to know anything." Her plea gradually tracked from Maretta to me, but what was I in this but a package Maretta was forwarding?

Besides, I agreed with her: added to the array of criminal charges and suspicions already against me, a sixteen-year-old paramour in the offing would be no asset in reassuring Battaglia as to the political wisdom of adopting me, or in convincing him personally of my entire uprightness — I could prophesy a time, moreover, when my character might be a larger issue, and every corner of my life ransacked by a prurient press; it may sound like megalomaniac fantasy to say that whether Arthur Ames was known to have slept with a legal minor could conceivably decide if Orbis would be allowed to poison and pollute on a global scale, but those who've experienced or been part of the homivorous orgies stirred up by TV's piranha-trainers know a man who'd *violate a child* (who should, no question, be castrated forthwith) is capable of any monstrosity, from the torture of Paula to wild and slanderous fantasies about Orbis, one of our most environment-conscious organizations (*We have with us here in the studio Mr. Frank Lupin to speak for the Orbis Corporation — are these charges which need to be addressed, Mr. Lupin? or you may understandably feel they should not be dignified...*).

As I did conspicuously nothing, Fern tackled me direct. "Don't you want me to be with you?"

What use is the replay function if nothing is ever changed? if no editorial emendation can ever take effect, so that after ten thousand reviews, I'm still the same criminal lout who doesn't on the instant take Fern in his embrace? There is no inventable atonement or compensation for such missed moments, tides in the affairs of men, frozen to become monuments in the mind, not just of human failing, but of failures as human, at being human. Small, shabby excuse, but I did mention I hadn't become in love, didn't I? and that from the start she'd been warned not to expect any such development? Nor was there a chance of my countermanding Maretta's veto; where I was going Fern couldn't go, what I had to do, dee-dah, dee-dah. Even more than before, when I sent her away from our first meeting, I owed her the reassurance of clarifying distinction between preference and necessity; that time I'd omitted to say the right words; now, with our interaction transcending the verbal, no words were the right ones, and like — like an *endtable*, I didn't act.

I did say, "Of course, I *want* you to — "

The emphasis was enough clue for Fern, who said, "Oh, God." Not an expletive, not a *cri du coeur* — most like

the interjection, quasi-conversational in tone, when, dicing
carrots, you see the darker welling of ruby red, or, getting up
after having tripped or slipped, feel an abrupt alarming failure,
and know this time it's worse than a nick or a twist, the
startled, exasperated, somewhat ashamed recognition of
serious injury, hushed by underlying fear. Oh, God. That was,
you see, when she first had to give full force to the bleak idea
of *no future*; one might speak loftily of her "growing up," but
if maturity is to depend on such dreadful instants, may a
kindlier life preserve most lovers as adolescents; the price is
too crippling. Fern couldn't've been comforted to know I'd be
leaving in the company of her standard for desirability, who'd
vowed she'd seduce me.

"If you need underwear — " Maretta prompted,
nudging her toward her shower.

13

Perfect peace was mislaid at Rancho Feliz, and leisured progress toward our departure fast-forwarded, when family disagreement erupted into noisy war; left alone for a moment I heard angry voices, two male, one female, rising to the level of strident ultimata, defiant clattering feet, and shortly Graham came to find me and ask, in the tensely contained manner of one putting best face on necessity, if I would be ready to leave almost immediately; he, I gathered, was to be our pilot.

When, not much later, we leapt into that kindly sky, he was still muttering. "That bastard," not a bid to displace Ev as legitimate heir. "He was threatening to call the state police."

"Shit, he's gone over the edge," Maretta, up front, confided to her brother. "He has to be a dozen logs short of a full cord. What is he going to tell them, my sister invited home this known murderer? — " She twisted to look back over her shoulder. "No offense, Arthur. I mean, Dad's going to be tickled to death if he gets me arrested."

"He always resented us," Graham, sententiously. At the time, I smiled, thinking he was indulging in parody, but perspective convinces me Graham was producing a genuine original insight, perhaps, his lifetime's first stab at psychological analysis.

Fern opened her mouth and closed it, and I knew she was thinking she too might have been swept up as a minor on the run; the state police was outside the influence of her friend Sean Gomez.

Yes, we included, after all, indomitable Fern, who'd come back just before the quarrel broke out with damp, flattened hair and a compromise: why couldn't she join the flight, if she stayed in the helicopter with Graham and was never seen by Battaglia? I doubt Graham had necessarily meant to stay with the aircraft, but he made no complaint about having Fern all to himself for an indeterminate period,

while as for me, I might still need Fern again: I didn't know
where I would spend the night — properly seasoned trigger-
men shouldn't preoccupy themselves with these domestic
details, but this could determine my survival: Battaglia might
listen to my tale, yet decline to give me asylum, the waspish
acting laird of Rancho Feliz had put down his purple-stainèd
foot, but resourceful Fern came forward with a contingency
plan whereby the returning helicopter could let me off at some
distance from the ranch house, and she would collect her
ORV, and pick me up for smuggling unseen to her waterside
cottage.

    Mootest of points if Everett IV, having carried out his
extreme threat, told the police where the fugitive could now be
found; I had hopes of persuading John Battaglia not to turn me
in, but with the police at his door the political risks would
obviously be too great for him: **LOMAX APPOINTEE
HIDES WESTERLAKE SUSPECT**, not exactly the bold new
initiative the President-elect had promised.

    Fern had begun in a state of exaltation over her
reprieve. Thought of the police sobered her, on her own
account as well as mine, but she soon recovered high spirits —
and still my sense of fitness revolted against this spasmodic,
installment-plan parting, which couldn't do other than
encourage her to think impossible things; better if we'd said a
one-piece farewell and she could have her tragic catharsis, the
sooner to resume her own saga. But life seldom achieves a
consistency to sustain tragedy, which, like religious ritual, is
an artificial imposition, a doomed attempt to give solemn
order to reality's irrepressible weakness for messy slapstick; an
actual Queen Gertrude would do a spit-take on the poisoned
chalice-from-the-palace, and Brünnhilde's noble end be
delayed by trouble with a disposable lighter — or consider
how the catastrophic payoffs of (e.g.) *Romeo and Juliet*, or
Rigoletto, flirt with the precipice of farce, so that just to *think*
of the one word `*Whoops!'* tips us over into the world of

Monty Python. As for *Oedipus* — but, something too much of this, as the little seamstress says to Sydney Carton. For me, needless dilution of purpose, just when I should be converting myself into a single-pointed instrument of justice or retribution, to which nothing mattered but exposing and thwarting Orbis.

      Battaglia's home was near his old college town; his attendance at Homecoming Game that very day was responsible for his not being in Washington. (Oh, shit, *Homecoming! for me, a garotte of nostalgia, Ann Arbor clogged with bulging horsepower, but elsewhere the sharp, lucid autumn air blued with the more fragrant smoke of burning leaves, while pleasant melancholy recalling the splashing joys of summers yet to come mingled with grantable dreams of snow inexhaustible, of Christmas; Homecoming, oh shit! The specious, heart-filling self-congratulation of inland America, happy us, better than all the rest: Hail to the victors valiant!*) We'd crossed the state line in failing light when Fern offered that I might, after all, have a chance to sample some of her venison. I answered carelessly I *hoped* I wouldn't be coming back — well, you know what I meant; Battaglia was my prospect of repose, end for a time of hiding from pursuit; but when you go through the world as scant-armored as Fern, an unintended dart may any time pierce through to an indispensable organ; after a minute I was astonished and dismayed to see she'd quietly begun to cry. Gathering her hands in mine I held on, and silent tears still came, Fern still and small, giving no room to murmured clarifications, would-be comfortings. Altitude had undammed my logged sinal cavities, and now with no hand free for tissue work, I was obliged to sniff often, absurdly like supplying a soundtrack for Fern's moist mime. Not ducking my own clumsiness, what I honestly believe (folks) about that fit of weeping is that in the shifting shadow world where emotions wait for their assignments, the prospect of loneliness had connected to loss of her father, thus far inadequately mourned — a thesis Fern would have angrily rejected.

I risked, "Who won the shoot-out?"

"*I did!* — " the tone consigned me to uttermost dumbbelldom, and she disengaged a hand to give mine a sharp little slap. Then, rather primly, damp face reorganized: "Paco needs reassurance, but letting him win would be no good for his self-esteem, long-term."

"Cheez, I thought it was just a friendly one-on-one." (The subject is, was still, *basketball*.)

After consideration: "That's how it began, but you know me." (not true) "I have to turn everything into fucking *Lord of the Flies*."

A coy but at the same time lumbering allegory of life, i.e.?

I had seen us fluttering in to touch down on Battaglia's lawn in a wild tornado of dead leaves, but instead we came to land at a country-club kind of airport, among the Pipers and Beechcrafts, a scattering of biplanes still garishly colored in the twilight, the workhorse de Havilland, a restored Me-109, the sleek inevitable Lear. Forewarned, Battaglia had himself come to meet us, and was waiting in a black Mercedes.

Kissing now dry-eyed Fern, I muttered the conditional farewell mandated by circumstance; "If I don't see you later, I'll try to be in touch. Thankyou for everything."

"Sure, any time." The jaw was firm, gaze level. Resiliency, youth, me no guilt, some hopes.

On a rolling half-acre of savannah dotted with what in the dim might be laurel and lilac, a solid Victorian house, oddly European so far west of Greenwich; colored glass above the door, checkered tiles in the hallway. In a high-ceilinged, book-lined room furnished in ponderous oak, where the word *barrister* came readily to mind, John Battaglia held court, half-sitting on the massy desk before a curtained bay-window. While the ex-Senator had been making a quick phone-call,

Maretta and I had been conducted there by a looming, fortyish
man hailed Barney, who functioned as a kind of major-domo,
but whose shiny, slab-soled oxfords and watchful mien
suggested security and proclaimed, recruited from the police.

"Hold on a sec, Barney; I want you to hear this."
Battaglia leaned up straight, and spoke in carefully portion-
controlled phrases, making only glancing eye-contacts. "I'm
still licensed to practise law in this state, so, as an officer of
the court, I want Mr. Ames to understand that if, as I've been
told, he has felony charges outstanding against him, my formal
advice is that he avail himself of competent legal counsel."
Here, he put up a hand to forestall an interruption I never
considered making. "My understanding," going on in the same
annunciatory voice, "is that Mr. Ames maintains he's innocent
of all and any crimes. Now, I am in no position to represent
him, and this communication between us will not be covered
by privilege, but any responsible attorney would advise him
that his only proper course is to surrender himself immediately
to law-enforcement. Only a duly-constituted court can decide
guilt or innocence."

My turn, evidently, but I wasn't expected to get up and
go looking for a mouthpiece on the instant, and could easily
recognize a disclaimer. "Understood," I said. "Perhaps, after
you've heard my story, you'll be able to recommend an
attorney." Wordlessly, Battaglia not so much assented to as
approved of my opener; on one point Maretta was right; there
was a lot of merchandising involved in this.

She was eager to speak, but waited till taciturn Barney
had been given his leave. "Okay, Jocko," she then said. "But
it's still my story, okay? No Washington Posties or Sixty
Minuteses till I get the chance to break it, deal?"

"That's between you and, it's Arthur, isn't it?"

"Well," she demurred. "If you like what he has to say
— which I haven't heard yet — I have no way, no physical
way to stop you undercutting me, and calling a news
conference, and that kills my lead time, makes it anybody's

story." She luxuriated in the Lois Lane jargon, but watching her I wondered whether, in the eyes of an observer — of Fern — she'd been as relentlessly flirtatious with me, the flicking eyes, subtly proffered shoulder. "All I'm asking for," not quite caressing Battaglia, "is the guarantee of an exclusive interview, and enough time to get it on the air before anybody else can break the story."

No longer speaking for the record, and infinitely more human, Battaglia grinned. "We can work that out. Arthur?"

The craziness of it began to exasperate me. "Sir, shouldn't we save the world first, and then work out the movie rights?"

This unconsidered imprudency was crucial, or rather that Battaglia chose to be pleased by it. Shortly, Maretta too was banished (at my insistence, not happily), and he gave me the half hour he had before his mandatory appearance for a speech at the Homecoming Banquet, where Eugenia, his wife, was, he said, holding the fort.

I'd never let go of my small, bullet-holed pack, although vigilant Barney had swiftly checked it for weapons, but before I could produce the disks full of evidence Battaglia said, "You were at Orbis Special Projects? You know, Hilde, um, Konwitschny? wrote me a letter the week before she was killed, bringing up all the old rumors about the Harness thing again? Boy, maybe it is only coincidence, but there's sure been a lot of sudden death connected with that project."

"Sudden loss of seats in the Senate, too," I said, not without some strategic purpose. He must already be aware his persistent challenge to Harness had been a factor in that defeat, but not how massively Orbis had intervened. "They were funneling money to five different PACs," I told him. "The negative commercials were produced at Special Projects. They hired a private investigator to find somebody you'd dated in law school, and persuaded her to come up with the acquaintance rape story — "

"Angie Godwin," Battaglia, despondently, with a Mediterranean sigh for sanctimonious Nordic treachery. "As she was then."

"Orbis set up *WOLSAC*, and paid her *support money* through that."

"Do I know *WOLSAC*?"

"Women Opposed to (a Statute of) Limitations in Sex-Abuse Cases," I supplied. Though cynically spawned by Orbis, the group had been embraced by an alarming number of passionate volunteers, including a candidate for the House (narrowly defeated).

"Oh yeah. They were also against *habeas corpus*, bail, the right of confrontation, and the presumption of innocence — they were out to repeal Magna Carta. *Were*? still are, no?" Orphaned by Orbis, the group had gone on hysterically existing, advocating penal mutilation, on, it must follow, mere accusation.

Appropriately reminded of his own obligations, he made a partial revisit to the formal manner. "These are pretty serious allegations you're making, Mr. Ames. Two points — " he held up that many fingers: "What do you have to substantiate your story; what's the connection to your own problems?"

"The evidence I have," rummaging in my pack and producing the single floppy and the mobile disk, "is itself the cause of my troubles; Orbis knows, and they want it back."

When I told him what the disks contained, he was briskly dismissive. "We had a tip before about computer records for Harness, but when I had it checked out, there was nothing you could call evidence of wrongdoing. In fact — "

"That was a plant — " amused, if anything, by what amounted to his cool admission of permitting a raid on the Orbis files. I explained the fake file created solely for leaking; it was my deliberate choice to avoid dispute at that time, not telling (or perhaps reminding) him access had come via *Ilium*, Helena Smitt. She had, after all, been beside Battaglia in the President's election campaign, and he would find out about her for himself when he saw the real files.

Some of the more lurid contents of which I now sketched for him; the disastrous unsuccess and catastrophic side-effects of the Jastrebarsko adventure, the pragmatic decision to murder Bieman, and subsequent campaign of lies, bribery and intimidation. As rumor or conjecture, none of this was very new to Battaglia, but I was certain he'd never expected to have documentary evidence, times, places, people, amounts. He was darkly frowning as I told him there was unambiguous evidence of how Laxitter had plotted Hilde's death, but because I was concentrating mainly on what the files showed — no, that's disingenuous; if I said only Paula's murder was, logically, part of the attempt to silence me, and didn't mention how that deduction had been confirmed, it was because I couldn't yet entirely trust Battaglia. Not that he wouldn't believe my tale of the encounter with *Azraël*, but his opening speech was still in my mind: the self-proclaimed officer of the court could hardly be expected to turn a collusive blind eye to an unreported gunshot wound in an unexplained cadaver, not, that is, till I could convince him of the danger there was for me in letting myself be arrested, no less if only to be exonerated. Something was making him retreat from the hardheaded guesses he'd made three years ago about Orbis and the Harness Project, yet the very qualities that had first driven his solo crusade argued a degree of naiveté; now, long after the engineering of his electoral defeat, I was sure he would without a trace of satire proclaim *the system works*, that flagwaving shibboleth of the desperate optimist; patriotism can also be last refuge of disappointed decency.

He was warier now: "The question that comes to my mind, Mr. Ames, is, why me? If these files are all you say they are, why are you a fugitive, why didn't you simply turn them over, lock, stock and barrel to the FBI, or get them to the *Washington Post* — both at once, if you wanted to be sure?"

"The answer to that is in the files themselves," rapping the mobile disk with a knuckle. In terms as dispassionate and far from paranoia as I could attain, I tried to convey the ramifications of Laxitter's Briarean reach, his self-evident ties to CIA, probable influence with the FBI, lease-purchase arrangement with many elected and appointed officials, leading to my conclusion that for a chance of safety, I'd had to hope for a change of Administrations. But a lame duck could be dangerous, and, as I said, the Lomax inauguration still wouldn't bring safety, with corporate money working like yeast throughout federal agencies and on both sides of the legislative aisles —

"Hold *on* a minute," Battaglia protested. "This is getting to sound a little like the Grassy Knoll."

The tone in which the last two words are spoken give a reliable litmus-test of ultimate faith in government, and Battaglia emerged true-blue, though certainly not base. But to be on the Warren Commission side of that controversy was much the same as insisting Bieman was killed by Palestinian terrorists. "It's all in the files," again using a knuckle to indicate the mobile disk. I reminded him of how the chairman of the Senate committee on Harness, a senior member of his own party, had blocked his attempt to enter evidence about cancer in Yugoslav workers, for which, again, the thoroughly corrupt reason could be found in Laxitter's file.

While it's embarrassing now to recall my temerity in instructing the professional politician, subsequent events support what I told him, that only with the help of outraged public opinion, fuelled by revelations in the press, could the power of Orbis be overcome; and that key witnesses (me) would need the protection of anonymous invisibility until the principal criminals were convicted; perhaps beyond that.

Battaglia was neither offended nor entirely convinced. "I can see you've given this some thought." He checked his watch. "Look, can you stay? There's a lot of ground to cover here. I don't know what your plans are."

After all, I didn't have to beg asylum. With my purely symbolic permission, he scooped up the disks and put them in a small safe lurking behind false morocco bookbindings; it says a lot for the trust his manner inspired that I felt no more than a twinge of unease at giving up all that authenticated me as more than a criminal on the lam.

On his now chauffeured way to the banquet, he was to ferry Maretta back to the airport, and I asked if his driver could collect my larger baggage from the helicopter. Maretta reminded me I was still hers for the breaking of my story, and with a suggestion of irony asked, "Any message?" For Fern, she meant.

"Will she be staying with you?"

"She knows she can."

"Take care of her."

"She's right," with a quick glance to be sure Battaglia was out of earshot. "You are sexy. Sensitive is sexy."

This season, I thought, like the What's In column between the celebrity gossip and the tampon ad. Battaglia's last word was that he expected to be back late, and faithful Barney would show me where I'd be sleeping. "You understand, I can't make an openended commitment at this time to shelter you. But I had it checked out during the week; they'd still like to talk to you in Westerlake, but you're no longer a suspect in the murder."

I was, however, still wanted on a garland of lesser charges, beginning with the trumped-up ones I'd always known there'd be from Orbis, specifically to do with misappropriation of large sums in connection with ORBISCARD travellers' checks, followed by a ruffle rather than a wave of crime in southern Illinois, which I guessed would come to include further offenses to do with use of my ORBIS/Orbiscard plastic, but which for now reached only as far as the theft of property valued (and overvalued) at $10 from the Happy Haven Motel, to wit, the guest register, which I was able to show John Battaglia, giving the reason for its abstraction.

I'd had a long wait for clarification of that offhand revision of my standing with the law; a restless night in what objectively was a perfectly comfortable room, and an irreproachable bed, where with a sheet alone my icy feet kept me awake, and addition of a light blanket had me braising in my own sweat in minutes; slight noise jerked me from near-sleep, silence kept me warily wakeful. Breakfast, still early for a Homecoming Sunday, was with Eugenia Battaglia, also an attorney, tall, aquiline, long upper front teeth, her manner gracious but somewhat distant, while her husband was with his computer, going through the highlights disk I'd dubbed *Laxitter's Greatest Hits*. The fruited table was joined mid-muffin by the eldest of their four offspring, soph in college here, the short but burly and surprisingly tough-guy Giovanni (do please note the march of sociological history herein, unalloying of the melting-pot: Battaglia's father, Marco, in the homogenizing post-war forties, anglicized his son, but the ethnic seventies reversed the process); after asking me if I had business with his "fader," he entered into a complicated wrangle with his mudder about living expenses, needlessly protracted by his refusal to abandon the double-negative, and her insistence on didactic misunderstanding ("Oh, then that must mean you *do* have *some* of that money left."). Giovanni had evidently been receiving a small salary for token efforts during the Presidential campaign, Eugenia money, not Elect Lomax money, and thinking we all understood his supposed duties were no more than a cover story, was aggrieved to find his stipend coterminous with the electoral process. Truce, or tactful silence, was attained when he grudgingly offered to "come to Washington and sit behind Dad at his confirmation hearings," and Eugenia capitulated, less, I think, in justice than to avoid further discussion; John Battaglia had not so far been publicly offered a post in the new Administration.

Giuseppina, called Josie, the fifteen-year-old, joined us in a shiny hyacinth wrap over a frilled nightgown, and after brief exposure to her languid eyes I was relieved at the arrival of shirtsleeved and gritty-chinned John Battaglia, who refilled his outsize coffeecup, but after a very short measure of quality time retreated again to last night's Rumpole room, taking me with him.

Already there, either recently-arrived or too preoccupied to think of taking off his tan all-weather jacket, was a short, slight man near my age, who might been snatched from an early round of golf; pseudo-tartan shirt, sandy moustache.

"Is what I've seen typical?" hungrily. "Can you authenticate it? How much more of this stuff is on the mobile disk?"

"Steve Lang," Battaglia, answering my glance. "Who's a hell of a researcher, and can hear anything I can hear."

"The unexpurgated record of Harness-Stirrup from its start up to last month. Laxitter's entire confidential file, covering the same period; every contact with a government agency or individual official, complete records of all undercover disbursements — everything. It authenticates itself." My highlights, I underlined, had concentrated on shorter documents, and plain texts; the ur-file, with graphics and facsimile originals of translated documents, was altogether more convincing, virtually impossible for anyone to have faked.

Steve said, "Jesus."

"The weakness, as you well know," Battaglia, seated now behind his desk, struggling, so it seemed to me, against irresistible belief. "Is that by now all these records, if genuine, will have been destroyed, or put out of reach — but with this kind of detail, you can dig up independent corroboration. Some of these names — you confront them with this kind of evidence, in an intimidating context, there's going to be plenty of people ready to cop a plea."

He was reliving past triumphs; his political start had come from sudden fame as the prosecutor who'd quarterbacked a successful investigation into what came close to a comic-book ideal of villainy, a complex conspiracy of fraud and kickback making giant profits supplying inferior school lunches in his state; fascinating to see his doubts being swamped by relish for the process. "You dangle immunity in front of them like a stripper's garter — oh, yeah; I can see why they'd be ready to kill to keep this out of sight. You're going to have to show me how to hook up the mobile disk; I've got some of my people coming in so's we can get started analyzing what's here. I may need you for a while yet."

A question. "I can help with some of the code-names. I'm not going anywhere, if you're not going to turn me in."

A puffing noise of dismissal, and then I learned not only what charges were still outstanding against me, but how I'd been dropped as a suspect in Paula's murder. Just as Fern had adduced from the *Infamous Fugitives* show, it was Chief Leahy in Westerlake who'd led the way.

Steve had talked to him on the phone a few days ago, when Maretta had first called to say the Westerlake Monster wanted to come in from the cold (pardon the punchy style). Two points occur; one, Fern had exceeded her brief in what she'd told Maretta about me; two, Battaglia wasn't quite as guileless as I'd begun to buy. "He didn't like you for the job after the first five minutes," Steve recounted. "Some people next door to the victim — Hasty, something like that — "

"Hastings," I corrected, remembering their yapping dog and adamant upstairs daughter.

"They said your car had been standing outside for a week before the killing. Leahy was pissed, because it was his case, but the state police came charging in, and the FBI — an interstate crime, so they said."

"Yeah, but that's not out of line, when you're dealing with a small town," Battaglia put in. "Police department with limited resources."

"Your friends at Orbis," Steve resumed. "Were more than cooperating; they turned over every scrap of information they had on you. Afterwards, Leahy, who is pretty shrewd, figured they were pushing you as a suspect, not necessarily because they thought you did it, but because a murder, with that kind of publicity, gave them a better shot of bringing you in on their boring little embezzlement. If that's true, they did themselves in, because another Orbis division had reported a positive ID of you, license number of your rental car and all, when they brought a complaint you vandalized a company vehicle at the Tri-State Mall, way down near St. Louis — either there was some missed communication, or they just didn't realize it gave you an unbreakable alibi on the murder — the incident was just a few hours *before* the killing, and that dovetailed with the motel evidence; there was no way you could have driven to Westerlake, and been back at Happy Haven early that same evening. You stopped being a serious suspect before you knew you were one."

Before, that would be, hysterical headlines depicted me as a blend of Gilles de Rais and Heinrich Himmler, long before the "dramatic re-creation" on *Infamous Fugitives*.

"I'd have to see the tape," Battaglia commented succinctly. "Those slimeballs are usually pretty careful, but if you think there's a case, I can put you in touch with an attorney who'd be delighted to sue their asses. But it could be Leahy didn't try too hard to convince the media you weren't their man. Sometimes the real perpetrator gets careless when he thinks somebody else is prime suspect. Hell, I worked that myself when I was DA."

Back with his notes, Steve chuckled. "You almost made it back to suspect. Leahy began to think the Orbis name was coming up too often, and somewhere he heard about the

Konwitschny killing. He started out as a detective in your fair city, so he used his contacts to get hold of the ballistics report — it was him, not the FBI, who showed the two women had probably been killed using the same .25 caliber handgun."

I resisted giving make of the pistol, or its present whereabouts. Remember what I said about guile, and note that all the Leahy information *plus a letter from Hilde* indicting Orbis was in Battaglia's hands before I said my first word to him.

"Steve tells me," Battaglia said. "Leahy did a double-take when he found you'd allegedly been with victim two at the time victim one was killed, medical evidence. That's very Erle Stanley Gardner, huh? Suppose the killing in Westerlake was because she was the only one who knew you weren't really there when the Konwitschny woman was killed?"

"But that wouldn't fly," Steve neatly resumed; association with Battaglia must go back to his adolescence for them to work so well together, but while Steve often took the verbal lead, deference was plain in the posture of his body. "The next-door people saw you trying to start your car the Saturday afternoon of the first murder, no doubt about it. The ticket-clerk at the station, who knew Paula Leahy by sight, remembered selling you a ticket in a hurry that same day."

"So, here's one gun — " Battaglia again — "But two totally different murders — one apparently a screwed-up robbery, the other like some kind of ritual killing. I'd have to see those ballistics pictures for myself, but Leahy started thinking, professional hits, disguised. Right now, he appears to be going on the lines of industrial espionage, maybe an Orbis rival; he wonders if there's some project for Orbis all three of you were connected with, Hilde, the girl in Westerlake, you — he thinks that would explain your disappearance, if you were afraid the same guy was after you. Like Steve says, he's nobody's fool."

"He's in danger himself," I said. Fern had suggested the same when we discussed his ambiguous participation in the *Infamous Fugitives* episode, but Leahy was much closer than I would have anticipated to the truth.

"Oh, come *on*," Steve said, an exact echo of Battaglia's *Grassy Knoll* skepticism. "He's a police chief with big-city experience; he can take care of himself."

"Wouldn't hurt to give him a call, Steve," Battaglia said, moved, I thought, more by the urgent tone of my voice than by reasoned conviction. "Just advise him to be careful what he says around Orbis."

"Sunday."

"They'll give you his home number, won't they? Use the secure phone." The last might have been some sort of standing joke, but Steve nodded, and left for the room where the computer was.

"I'll tell you, Mr. Ames, in my position I can't afford mistakes." Here, I recognized Steve had been deftly sent off-stage, though I didn't know why.

Battaglia shuffled the jottings he'd been making throughout. "Three years ago," he said. "I *knew* I was onto a mother-lode with the Harness thing; it had the same smell as the school lunch scam, but worse. As you know, it went nowhere."

"Read the files," I urged.

"Last night, I talked to somebody on my Washington staff who has experience in common with you, but eventually came to some very different conclusions." He looked at his watch. "Helena should be with us soon, if she made her connection in Minneapolis."

"Helena *Smitt*?" And why not Helena Smitt? if Battaglia had been so pleased with how *Ilium* had misled them all during the Lomax campaign, why wouldn't he hire her for his own staff? As an original part of the Harness Project, she'd be his resident expert, and I saw that well beyond feeding him the access code for the false file, she must have been influential in moderating his views on Orbis.

"Her position is that while Harness might have been an instance of criminal mismanagement, there was no knowing criminality."

"Not surprising, since she's never stopped being an Orbis employee."

"That's not possible."

"Read the files." A pity, but he had to know the full extent of *Ilium*'s loathesomeness, and I went on to outline everything I could recall; pseudo-resignation and continued undercover payments through an Orbis-owned insurance company, her hawking of the DIRTYSPY access code for the ersatz file, and keeping Orbis informed from within the Lomax camp, so Vice-President Hardy was prepared and primed for the Harness questions at that early so-called town meeting — this was particularly poignant for Battaglia, who'd worked on those questions with Bill Elderbush, his former speech-writer. It would have been tactless to mention who'd prepared the Vice-President's pony for that occasion.

"She set up Hilde Konwitschny's murder," and I heard a final digit of that combination click in; I'd believed the birthday-party meeting where Hilde spoke about her desire to go public to be fortuitous, but now I saw it wasn't so. "You showed Helena the letter from Hilde, or told her about it?" Of course he had, just as now, when I showed up, she was consulting authority on Harness. And had made sure Hilde was invited to the party, drawn her out about what she knew, and then, by promising a contact with Elderbush, kept her quiet long enough for the murder to be arranged.

Battaglia's face reflected the vertiginous process of reviewing a whole chapter of experience under drastically altered light. He shook his head slowly, and began, "I always wondered — " but Steve Lang came back in, draped in a solemnity that demanded and received attention.

"Mike Leahy was killed in a car-crash Friday night or early Saturday morning. I just talked to the acting-chief. Leahy left Westerlake Friday midday with an appointment to interview some people at Orbis Special Projects, which apparently he did. Nobody is sure what time he started back, but the state police say he must have fallen asleep at the wheel; he drove into a culvert at sixty miles an hour, and there was no sign he ever hit the brakes, no skid marks."

The cliché, *grim satisfaction* carries a built-in apology for the pleasure we feel at terrible, prophecy-confirming news; I'd truly begun to like Chief Leahy for his spirited intelligence, but I can't deny gratification with so dramatic a proof my fears weren't exaggerated; I didn't expect to hear more about surrendering myself to the evenhanded security of the law.

I asked, "Has there been an autopsy?" Surely, Leahy had been drugged, it might have been with a friendly cup of coffee in Mark Worth's office.

Steve gestured unknowing, and when I asked if it could be checked Battaglia made me the give-me-a-break look, and began to explain there were limits as to how far vaguely-defined influence could take him, and barriers of discretion to his use of official channels.

Big-boned Barney tapped and poked his head in at the door to say Helena Smitt was here. "Hold on, I may want you," Battaglia told the security man, and Barney came fully in, stepping aside to admit a woman of indeterminate age: a sturdy, fatless frame, and one of those low-relief Germanic faces, slow to show aging, for more than a century the model for every china doll. If Steve had been interrupted at golf, she could have been snatched from her early pew, except she was hatless; blue skirt-and-jacket, frilled but unfrivolous off-white blouse, and severe shoes were the epitome of devotional stylelessness.

"Hi, John," cheerfully.

Ilium! In this chronicle I've tried to keep faith with my feelings of the moment, carefully indicating modifications brought about by later reflection, and yet it's hard to admit the ridiculous choke of terror this arrival brought me, not less than if a resurrected *Azraël* had come smiling into the room — I suppose it was the abrupt penetration of what had come to seem a circle of safety that made for such panic; not crouched in the hole after my simultaneous avoidance of rattlesnake and chattergun had I felt so despairingly the jig was up.

Headlong flight, however, was not an option, nor bruising battle, and it's more cheering to report the bypass circuits functioned, and what would have been congestive overload for trapped muscles swiftly converted to furious and more useful intellectual activity. If a showdown, this was a mismatch, because unless Helena was packing heat under her two-piece, I had all the weapons; I knew one browse through the complete files would demolish her, notwithstanding first-name terms with Battaglia. Reaching that point, I could see her tension was not less than mine, quite likely more. Again, why not? She was aware how precarious her position was, had made the long journey here in a fret about how much I knew and could prove, things her real employer would hardly have told her. The tight smile was deepening the horizontal crease beneath high, rounded, front-facing cheeks, to make it an extension of the straight mouth with its planed upper lip, so her whole flat face looked as if it could be folded in half, chin to forehead.

"Helena — " and I would never have imagined Battaglia's voice could be so devoid of its characteristic warmth. "I told you about Arthur Ames on the phone." The way he drew back just a little after making the introduction put me in mind of a referee, having delivered the pre-fight litany and arrived at *shake hands now, and come out fighting.* But he didn't wait for the bell: "According to Mr. Ames, you're still being paid by Orbis."

"Oh, sure," harshly ironic. "They love me."

"He says you were an accessory in the Hilde Konwitschny killing."

"John! That's ridiculous. How? The last time I saw Hilde Konwitschny was in Vienna."

Steve, who'd been trying get some grasp of events, said, "But you told me you'd seen her at your friend's birthday-party. You said she was drinking too much, and you wouldn't rely on word one she had to say about Orbis."

"That was my understanding." Battaglia sounded genuinely wonder-wounded, although he could surely never have credited me with such an Homeric feat as inventing the saga of *Ilium*.

"John, you're taking the word of a known felon," Helena said, meaning me, and as if her own self-contradiction had never been noticed. "What does he have to lose by making irresponsible accusations? For all we know, he may have killed poor Hilde. How come he knows so much about what she was doing?"

Does criminality, I wonder, have a hidden evolutionary role? As surely as chameleons can change their colors, and squids squirt ink, a striking number of the vocationally guilty have the capacity to make an accuser's head swim with the brazen illogic and monumental irrelevancy of their counter-attacks; only the suggestion I was a threat to national security was needed to make Helena's a classic specimen.

No use: Battaglia, with a light touch which made it more impressive, proposed his own agenda. Apologizing for usurping her weekend, he told Helena he had some files to go through, after which he'd ask for her comments. "How long do I need?" he asked me.

"You can get through them in three hours."

"Skimming."

"That is skimming."

"All due respect, John," Helena said. "I didn't drop everything at a moment's notice, and make this trip on a Sunday — "

"You'll have to bear with me, no?"

"Well — there's some phone calls I can make — "

"I think they can wait." With a look at Barney, Battaglia turned this into an order, then with sudden inspiration told her there was a small job she could do; he had the final printout of contributors within the state to the Lomax campaign, which needed collating with the existent list of Battaglia's own past supporters, a menial job, but somebody had to do it. In anger, the bland Smitt face became more foldable still, lips whitening with pressure when Battaglia, saying it went better if one person read names to another, incontrovertibly suggested she could work with Barney.

This, with a smile and a massive courtesy, was effectively a kind of citizen's house-arrest, but when Helena and Barney were gone, Steve (displaying, I thought, remarkable adaptability to startling new circumstances) pointed out she couldn't be held, just as I was wondering where melodrama went when really needed: it would have been sweetly convenient if *Ilium*, as in a whodunit stuck with an unprovable case, had clutched her throat and expired in a guilty seizure, or produced a pistol and gone alone and meaningfully into the nearest equivalent of the conservatory, or been loser in a shootout with Barney, anything to prevent her carrying tales back to Laxitter.

"Well," Battaglia said. "Let's see what evidence we have. It may be time to lean on her."

I wasn't allowed to see that, though it consisted, so I was told, of Battaglia warning her Laxitter and all his Special Projects circle were going to be indicted and convicted, and holding out the possibility of a deal for her when that happened, if she began cooperating now, by keeping him informed about Laxitter's intentions, instead of the reverse.

She had been first of many subjects we discussed after far more than three hours with the Laxitter files; Battaglia, Steve Lang and I sat at the kitchen table constructing sandwiches from what was in the refrigerator, helping them down with Mexican beer, and trying to think of ways to neutralize *Ilium*. Though eventually indictable, it could only be as part of a complicated conspiracy: the police here, Battaglia said, wouldn't take her into custody on the remote chance of a future extradition, and the FBI had no interest in Hilde's murder, still officially a botched local burglary.

Battaglia, after what was for him a nightmare journey through names and offices for hire by Orbis, many of them people he'd admired, or worked closely with, or both, was far less gratified to be judged incorruptible than distressed to be counted as a freakish exception. With no doubt now about the power, influence or *covert capacity* (his term) of the Orbis conspiracy, he was to my mind cavalier on the question of personal safety — for himself, for others, for me. Perhaps more justly, his focus was otherwise: it's excessive to say for him it was all politics, but all his calculations had a political factor.

"You were right," he allowed. "Nothing comprehensive can get started till after the inauguration — or at least till we've got some of our transition people in place. Maybe Christmas time."

"Without protection, I can't last till Christmas."

"Officially, my advice to you would still have to be, give yourself up. The illegal conversion wouldn't come to trial for months, and by that time, Laxitter and his little group will be blown out of the water. You'd be acquitted."

"Posthumously? It'll never come to trial; they killed Leahy, they'll kill me. Laxitter could be blown out of the water tomorrow — release this to the press, give them some time to go to work on it. By January there'll be such a furor,

Lomax will have to promise a full investigation as part of his inaugural address."

This earned me a full-scale lecture. "You know," patiently. "Orford Lomax won by six-tenths of one percent in the popular vote — "

"Head-to-head," Steve elucidated. "Throw in minor candidates, and he polled less than forty-six percent — that's of the fifty-one percent who bothered to vote — about seventy-four adult Americans in every hundred *didn't* vote for him. He won by fourteen electoral votes; in the end California did it for him by about three thousand votes, with under forty-four percent — "

"Yeah," Battaglia, drily, implying *enough, already, with the statistics.* "When we were going over the figures the day after, he said, `You know what Jocko? Nobody won, Hardy just lost worse than I did.'"

"He'll be the one taking the oath," I said, not clear about where this was going.

"The perceived political strength or weakness of the President," Battaglia said. "Conditions his effectiveness at every level — whether he can get the kind of changes he wants at CIA, the FBI, any agency, the Pentagon, how well he can bully Congress. Do you happen to know what the biggest Lomax negative was in all the exit polls? He beat Hardy hands down on *integrity* and *has the right ideas to solve our problems* — "

I did know. "*Leadership qualities.* Rightly or wrongly, he was under fifty percent, even among people who voted for him — that's not a fact, of course."

"The exit poll is a fact," Steve said. "We're talking perceptions, here."

Battaglia: "But with Presidential power, perception translates into reality; the White House doesn't really have a headsman with an axe, it just has to look that way."

My face, evidently, asked a question.

"I'll tell you," Battaglia replied. "What it has to do with how we handle this affair; we're not going to begin the first hundred days with the President *reacting* to a scandal in the press; if there are going to be leaks from Justice, this time it's going to be on stuff where the Administration is already taking action. Sure, we're going to use the press to get public opinion behind us — behind us, not out front; the media are going to have to run like hell to keep up with what we're doing; we're not going to be followers in any way, shape or form."

Reluctantly recording that last exasperating redundancy obliges me to admit I've edited out a number of others from the speech of John Battaglia; the greater my admiration and actual liking, the more I wished one of his advisers would try and cure him of resort to such hollow echoes from empty minds: *in this day and age, first and foremost, without rhyme or reason, hope and pray —*

"But why does it have to be leaks?" If I (too) slipped easily into conspiratorial habits, there was some excuse in my recent experience, and I was always aware these were a dark mode of thought which the snap of a light-switch could dispel. If not just one newspaper, fed with surreptitious hints, but all of them and all the networks, together in a shadowless glare, were given the story, supported by some documents and by Battaglia's reputation, the game would be over. "They'll go on killing as long as they think they can still get the cork back in the bottle. Why not smash the bottle into pieces?"

The reply to this sounded more Presidential than I ever heard Orford Lomax achieve. "In case you haven't noticed, we as a country are in trouble; this Orbis thing is bad, but it's like a secondary or tertiary symptom of the real trouble we're in; we're making the wrong stuff in the worst conceivable way, and using public money we can't collect to help obsolete industries pretend they haven't failed — we can't stop making superbombers for attacking an enemy that no longer exists, because we're afraid somebody will have to learn a new job.

We've got the biggest GNP in the world, the biggest negative balance of trade, biggest corporate profits, most illiteracy, the highest-paid execs, the richest doctors, and enough poor people with untreated diseases to make a separate third-world country the size of Ethiopia, while just the interest payments on the deficit paralyze our good intentions — as Lomax said at the convention, you're not going to turn this around by fine-tuning a failed system; we need a new beginning.

"So you see," he said. "There's a method to my madness. We want to stop Orbis, yes, and bring the perpetrators to justice, but for that we have to have political strength — and this could turn out to be just what we need to pull the country together behind a new Administration."

A pause, in which I failed to stop wondering what would become of me, and then he became confidential: it was no secret he'd hoped to be Secretary of the Interior; over and above, he said, all other questions, he was concerned with the state of the planet and of our water, soil and air. Now, Orford Lomax, while leaving him that option, had offered the far more generally influential post of Attorney-General, a choice Battaglia had been debating, though now it seemed the chance to prosecute the garland of Orbis cases had made up his mind for him.

"Maybe I can accomplish as much or more for the environment at Justice," he reflected. "We need new legislation, sure, but we can do a lot of cleanup with strict application of laws on the books right now. I told Lomax, if I take it, the way Hoover had a task force on subversion, and Bobby Kennedy took off after organized crime, I'd want a whole new unit to concentrate on industrial crime, pollution, toxic waste, enforcement of safety standards, liaise with Commerce, Interior, Labor, get the EPA up off their asses. He said, go ahead, but be sure you get the facts right, otherwise they'll say we're anti-industry."

Steve: "They're going to say that anyway."

"I told him, or anti-jobs. You know how it goes; the guys on the other side will say, like Hardy did, hands off, this is a great American company, a national treasure, and the guys on our side in the House will say, no, that's wrong, they're obscene, they're polluting the air and poisoning our water, our people are getting cancer, our babies are born deformed — *but don't stop them doing it in my district*, we need the jobs. Shit, it's like an addiction, where everybody's ready to just say no for everybody else. That's where this Orbis affair can put us over the top; if we can get these facts out, and put some people in jail, it's going to send a message to friends and foes alike."

He was, dare I say, aroused by the prospect, eyes like embers, and having said hard things about his weakness for empty cliché, I'd like to hold this as my truest recollection of our meeting, the man of passion struggling to shake real conviction loose from the tacky strands of rhetoric, decency *in extremis*, in a time that's left us very little language for saying what we mean.

The President-elect wanted an answer from Battaglia immediately after Thanksgiving, which was four days away: for either job he was going to face a political battle over confirmation, but while Lomax was reconciled to a revival of all the old slanders, and had accepted his appointee's word there was no fire and therefore no smoke to the innuendo about dope, and the date-rape story was (despite display, two years ago, of a blouse allegedly torn twenty years before that), made up out of whole cloth, I understood why Battaglia was nervous about newer charges: an Attorney-General of the United States didn't consort with and abet a fugitive from justice.

"There'll be media people out for dirt on all the Lomax appointments," Battaglia pointed out. "Anybody at Orbis can call in an anonymous tip, and they'll be here with the lights and the cameras, and staking out the Georgetown place."

Patently, he still wished it could be done by the book, but Leahy's death and his traversal of the files had made my case, and after frowning consideration he spoke of a hideaway, a kind of ski cabin he owned over in Wydaho — I may have the state wrong; possibly he said Uvadah, but it certainly wasn't his own home state, where we were. That, and his extreme reluctance to speak of it, made me think it might be a place where a playful senator or aspirant to office could explore unfamiliar slopes unobserved by tabloid sports analysts. He described it as a modest place, up seven miles of meandering private road, if not yet, soon and till April to be reachable only by snowmobile or helicopter.

With its own generator and water-supply and a stocked freezer, it approached self-sufficiency, and sounded like Zack's shack with hot baths, but Battaglia promised me company, a couple of his best security men, while Steve Lang, who'd get me there, would shuttle in regularly with news and supplies; there was a phone, but it would be reserved for utmost emergencies, and I wouldn't be able to write letters. Send any, that is.

"Maybe we can find a friend for you up there," with a grin, giving me my cue to ask counsel in the case of an equally unnamed friend, a minor seeking emancipation.

Pressed for more detail, I identified her as someone known to Maretta, and he said, "That's not the little girl, the biologist's daughter?"

"Botanist."

"Oh, yeah. *Fern.* They had dinner with us at the Rancho Feliz one time."

"The botanist is dead."

About to ask where I came in, he changed to a long, ruminative look, and I watched his expression progress from the quizzical, not unfriendly recognition of exactly what had happened between Fern and me, to the purely political assessment *Oh, Christ, this is just what we need! Let's get her out of here!* As I'd expected him to, he suggested this was his wife's area of competence. This, now, was after his lean-on meeting with Helena Smitt, who was being driven to the airport by Steve Lang, a man passionate about loyalty, deeply offended by a colleague's duplicity, who managed at the same time to be a cool pragmatist, unflustered on the subject of, in molespeak, *turning her around.*

Eugenia Battaglia, as was well known, had abandoned fully half her lucrative practice of corporate law to *coordinate* (a pleasantly vague term indicating no imaginable real activity) the efforts of various individuals and groups dealing with women's legal issues: this cohort in his corner, by insuring Battaglia against the now-standard media blitzkrieg (*She said it, therefore he did it!*), armored him against the rickety rape rap.

She said, "Where is the girl now?"

"Maretta knows how to get in touch with her."

A barely perceptible pursing of Eugenia's lips, while John-Jocko wondered if he was developing a hangnail.

"Does she live there, Brandsville?"

"Sacramento," I recollected.

Eugenia was unruffled. "Rachel Levi-Ybarrondo runs a support group there," she reminded her husband. "Trouble with the stepfather, is that it? What, does he beat her? Sexual abuse?"

"As far as I know, he's just boring," disappointingly. "He's Swiss. But she can't stand her mother."

A gap; dogma, I knew, minimizing the bickering which, over three thousand years, from Electra or Salome to Lizzie Borden and Joan Crawford, had occasionally erupted, preferred mothers and daughters to be invariable pals.

Having assured Eugenia the girl wasn't pregnant — the question surprised me, but she said it was commonest reason for seeking emancipation, and for Eugenia a source of mixed feelings, when the girl wanted to be free to marry the unfortunately virile creep her parents very properly forbade her — I undammed a flood of legal terminology by mentioning, in a manner as uncreeplike as I could command, Fern's fear she'd be preemptively transferred, like illicit funds, to Switzerland: I gathered an *interlocutory injunction* was the talisman to defeat such a hijacking.

"Okay," John Battaglia looked at his watch. "The move is to put the girl in contact with — in Sacramento?" There was a brisk, arbitrary feeling to all this, and I hoped Fern would know my motives weren't identical with Battaglia's.

"Rachel Levi-Ybarrondo," Eugenia resupplied. "I can call her today, fill her in."

"So, I'll, we'll get in touch with Maretta," like making sure the back door is locked, and I realized I was the one about to be spirited away, right now.

When Eugenia had vanished and my baggage was heaped in the tiled entrance-hall, Battaglia gave me the revised timetable. Early in December the President-elect would use a policy speech in Miami as cue for a ten-day working vacation in the Keys, itself an excuse for serious strategy sessions with his major appointees, removed from the glare and rumor of Washington. Now "practically certain" he was going to opt for Attorney-General, Battaglia would use the opportunity to brief Lomax on the forthcoming Orbis scandal, and would begin putting together his team for the case, which would be heavily represented among the first transition staff to move into DOJ, able to make certain there was no wholesale destruction or abstraction of files on Harness-Stirrup.

Though still without formal authority, by that time the influence of impending power would let him have me declared a protected witness, to which local charges of embezzlement (and vandalism) would be coerced to defer; he saw me coming secretly to give grand jury testimony authenticating the files and telling what else I knew; "we" would find me a good attorney; he suspected I'd eventually have to testify in murder trials in two separate states, although the conspiracy which included those killings would be part of the federal indictment. That was just the main feature; spinoffs would include a special prosecutor for implicated officials, and widespread bribery and influence-peddling to be dealt with by House and Senate, if either could find enough untainted members to constitute an ethics committee. But for my part, he ruefully predicted a severely circumscribed lifestyle for the next six months or so, touching lightly on what he called "monetary compensation," reasonable expenses, which I was never, never to think of in terms of payment for my testimony.

Not to teach him his job, I tentatively suggested that of all Special Projects people, the one who knew the most was also the least actively culpable, though certainly guilty of conspiracy by silence; Fena Keller, I thought, would grab at an offer of immunity, and could put the genuineness of the files beyond rational doubt. Having ventured so far, I was moved to remind him Helena might well have briefed Laxitter before coming here, which would make him, Battaglia, as much a worry to Orbis as dead Bieman, dead Hilde, dead Leahy or endangered I had ever been; his own safety, and that of his family should not be skimped. He thanked me, and said he was used to that; during the famous school lunch prosecution he'd had more than fifty death threats, six of them traced to a man whose entire income derived from heat-sealing plastic flatware, packets of sugar, salt and artificial sweetener, foil squeeze-packs of ketchup and mustard, and little paper napkins, none of which he made, inside transparent sleeves, which he purchased. "Boy, there's a cause worth killing for, huh? What an epitaph."

14

Steve Lang was a formidable intelligence, his personality benignly doomed by its entry, eight years ago, into the Battaglia orbit, a captive satellite. During the first leg of our journey, house to airport, he asked me how I'd come to seek out John, told me how he'd first heard John speak, had volunteered for John's initial Senate campaign, and was still sure John had more to offer this country than any other current political figure. The thing about John was that, through triumph and tragedy alike, he'd never lost his essential — I think Steve wanted to say, his ineffable Johnness.

Extraordinary to me that the De Havilland was waiting out on the small, somewhat tufted runway, a pilot in place; not two minutes after parking the car we were airborne, for a three-hour flight to a similar landing-place somewhere in the state of Montoming. During this longer stage, as we left the Battaglias farther behind, John's name began to fade a little from Steve's talk, and he told me a few things about his own law-school, legal research and law enforcement days, but a highly conditional blossoming, like Simon telling of his youth in the fishing business before he got a new name from his destined leader.

Along with his regrets over Chief Leahy's death he supplied some additional detail; the coincidence of names, Steve conjectured, had helped turn the finding of Paula's killer into a personal crusade, and Leahy had been irritated to the limit of endurance by the FBI's continual attempt to fit me to the crime.

"Did John brief you about Guadalajara?" and then Steve told that from Leahy he had the story a young woman came and insisted on giving a sworn deposition to the American consul there.

"Judy?" I said numbly. "Judy Fine?"

"Yah. It related to the Westerlake murder, or that was the intent; she'd read you were a suspect, and apparently thought she could give you an alibi. Actually her timeframe was off, and nothing she said covered the time of the killing, but she confirmed some of Leahy's thinking by saying you were on the run from killers yourself. It also went to your state-of-mind; it was obvious the last thing you were planning was a jealousy-revenge thing. Nobody, by the way, thinks that's you at all; John says, this guy may not have killed anybody, but if he ever gets into politics, he'll be murder."

"Meaning me?" Most of my thought was still with Judy's surfacing, not, I judged, with Michael's approval — you remember Michael? The chocolate chicken man. If they were that far south in Mexico twelve days ago, they were somewhere deep in the patchwork serpentine continental coupling by now.

"The way women are ready to go to bat for you," Steve expanded. "Another gal, a receptionist at Orbis, told Leahy nobody there believed you could have done it, you were a real teddy-bear, but that science woman of theirs you see all the time on the tube — the gorgeous black gal — "

"Dionne Theobald?"

"Yeah, Dionne, she had said pretty much the same thing on local TV, and Orbis had to come out with a formal disclaimer, it wasn't the corporate position, they had no special knowledge one way or the other, they were cooperating fully with law-enforcement agencies. Then, there was Maretta, who said you had to be okay, because *her* girlfriend said you wouldn't hurt a fly — "

That explained the long, whimsical look Battaglia had given me when I spoke about Fern, as well as the sidelong one Steve was employing now. Since any comment could only diminish an unearned reputation, I decided to remain an enigma. The alert reader will also have adduced, correctly, from this unamended assessment of my non-lethal character that I hadn't spoken to Battaglia about my encounter with *Azraël*, though the unmasking of *Ilium* had been an obvious cue, and I'd come close half-a-dozen times after that, always unsure of whether he might decide, after all, that failure to report an orphan cadaver with gunshot wound held too great a potential for political embarrassment.

The efficiency of the operation, worthy of a head-of-state on the way to a photo-opportunity, continued when we touched down in southern Idahana: a helicopter snatched us up, and we skimmed in the direction of snow-clad mountain scenery. Our destination was some nine thousand feet above sea level, and our pilot, Rod, in his terse Western way, confirmed the upper four miles of access road were under a whole heap of snow, adding for Steve's benefit the dude information there was plenty of fresh powder on a packed base.

Yet to call Battaglia's hideaway a ski cabin was in defiance of sense; except for a short clamber above the treeline to a peak scoured bare, it's true everything was downhill from there, but there was no practical way of getting back up after a reckless run. On the western side, where the slopes might be fairly negotiable, you could, I suppose, ski down and then trudge across four miles of valley to where a pseudo-Swiss chocolate village nestled beneath a quite-famous winter sports venue.

From the helicopter as it edged in, the most conspicuous features of the house, aside from the neatly cleared landing pad, were the large satellite dish and a windmill generator set on a shoulder nearby; for the dwelling itself, fieldstone and dark timbers, wide roof snow-covered, slotted back into the rock-face, but with a great sweep of window across the front, my first quarrel with nomenclature was not misleading *ski* but belittling *cabin*, and the interior was no less opulent, with flagstone floors and bricklined walls coffered with mellowed wood, great dark beams overhead; an open stair of golden oak led up to a dormer bedroom, and there

were two further symmetrically distributed sleeping-places on
either side of the one major space, with its baronial dining-
table, wrought-iron chandelier, and vast stone fireplace, for
which at least two cords of logs occupied an open-front shed
next to the garage, where a purring generator supplemented the
wind-powered one. A large fuel tank and larger one for water
were recessed into the hillside.

For me, there was a mental shrug over all this, the
property of John Battaglia, the unbribable. He was only
twelve years older than I. His father had run a modest import
business (pasta and prosciutto), and the future senator had
needed a job to get through law school; since graduating he
had spent a very few years in private practice, five more as
assistant and full DA; two terms in the House had led to six
years in the Senate, and since then he'd been a consultant,
accepted speaking engagements, and worked for the election
of Orford Lomax. His wife, too, was earning, but had been
away from her profession for most of the decade in which
children were born and attained school age; nowhere could I
see a family income equal to maintaining the home-state
domicile, the Georgetown house, and this mountain retreat,
not to say the network of logistical support to which I'd been
exposed. John Battaglia, as I hope is established by now, was
conspicuously honest among public servants, and yet we've
come to accept without question a sort of superstar standing
for office-holders, friendships with wealth and celebrity,
extreme good fortune with investments, a Mandarin rank; as
with all aristocrats, some benign, others malignant, but all the
exact opposite of the citizen-legislator once admired, whether
or not he ever existed, as backbone of our republic.

Having touched us down, pilot Rod was converted to
one of two security men, Steve taking over the controls and
promising to return on a milk run — not a figure of speech —
on Thanksgiving eve. We had been hailed at the landing pad

by somewhat grizzled Robb, trying to be discreet about the
Uzi slung at his waist, shorter but more large than Rod, with a
similar economy of speech, though I did learn early on he was
Canadian in origin, and when his hair was still unmixed
auburn had served with the RCMP, but had been with
Battaglia since the crime-busting days. As I was to discover,
Rod and Robb took their mission in conscientious earnest;
there was no time when both slept, and when awake I was
practically always in sight of one or the other. They made
regular patrols around what they called the perimeter, and
were armed with beepers and walkie-talkies as well as their
sidearms.

     At my departure Battaglia had told me to make a list of
any additional books, movies or music I wanted. Low
bookshelves along one sidewall displayed a selection of the
mandatory, from Plato and More to Theodore White and
Barbara Tuchman, but also a swathe of boyishness, which
shouldn't have been unexpected, uniform editions of Walter
Scott, Stevenson, Dumas père, Conan Doyle, with Jules Verne
oddly in Italian, *Affmo.* a present from Pappa on John's twelfth
birthday.
     At the opposite wall, Rod showed me where large-
screen TV lurked behind a sliding door, and told me the dish
"pulled in" about two dozen channels. In offering me movies,
Battaglia had cautioned, "No skinflicks," explaining he
couldn't risk having them purchased: as soon as he was named
by Lomax there'd be many varieties of snoopers scrutinizing
his life down to the brand of toothpaste he used. I told him
accurately I had no interest in peer-and-leer, but noted now
that if the snoopers could penetrate to this fastness, they'd find
an existent cache of cassettes portraying unlikely adventures of
cheerleaders and airline employees, which, let's allow, might
be there for the singlehanded stimulation of Rod and Robb or
their equivalents; otherwise the film library was the normal

jumble of established classics (Welles, Houston, Lean, Kubrick) with more recent big-budget action hits, from which the production values and special effects were visibly rotting away to leave internal emptiness gruesomely exposed.

Music: CDs covered the standard Italian opera repertoire, and among LPs were some warhorse orchestral reissues (beethoven, brahms, mozart, wagner) all unfortunately but predictably conducted in very large capital letters by a ferociously efficient, brisk, inexplicably idolized northern Italian martinet; the remainder of the large black disks were classic jazz, with a small clutch of Beatles, Rolling Stones, Dylan, perhaps in memory of marching student days, ca. 1967 (was it possible the faint taint of teargas still lingered?).

Shortly after making this inventory I was introduced to the housekeeper, a small, brooding, fierce-nosed woman named Loima, said credibly to be mixed Estonian-Dakotah; a resident, but I never found out where she slept; she might have had an apartment over the garage, or a wickiup in the woods. Mostly monosyllabically, she kept offering to prepare food, but the ethnic background was gastronomically ominous, and her coffee unspeakable; I cooked for myself and for any who wanted to join me, finding porterhouse steaks, loin lamb chops, cleaned trout and several sorts of fowl tidily organized and labelled in a closet-sized standing freezer, though Rod's delight was to microwave a frozen pizza, and Robb subsisted mainly on cheese-spread with jalapeño peppers, corn chips and rocky road ice cream; neither blenched to begin the day with cola and cookies but either would accept scrambled eggs as if reminded of some long-forgotten rite of the ancients.

As in the self-contained world of a cruise ship, within thirty-six hours I had both a routine and a hierarchical ranking; in absence of Battaglia or his surrogate, Steve, I was clearly the resident gentry, with exclusive dibs on program selection for radio and television, and use of all facilities, including the kitchen, where my cooking was to be seen as a diversion of the leisured class not a descent into proletarian utility, though at the same time I would be expected to obey instructions relating to my security, as when I was reprimanded by Robb for going out to explore without calling for artillery support. I did a great deal of random reading, tried to limit my browsing among the temptingly various available TV diversions, and used a little laptop computer to write unsendable letters to Judy, my parents, my sister, and to make detailed notes which would have been helpful in compiling this account, if I'd had access to them.

The arctic outpost, the space-station illusion, was emphasized on Wednesday by how anticipation quickened and skies were scanned for the expected advent of Steve, although in reality our connection to the large world wasn't entirely severed: the garage contained two small snowmobiles and a big snow-crawler, in the operation of which I was given a lesson by Rod-of-few-words, while Robb rode shotgun; it was on this expedition, winding down the snow-choked road, that I observed the adjacent valley and cuckoo-clock village, with the ski-lifts and tramway above.

Steve, on the eve of Thanksgiving, brought eggs, a gallon of milk, the news John Battaglia had informed Lomax he would accept the post of Attorney-General, a written list of queries about details in the Laxitter files, a small turkey (cooked) and regrets none of us would be able to enjoy the traditional family brawl.

On the holiday, having tucked away the turkey for staff snacks, I was thawing what the label said was a cock pheasant when a flurry of excitement was created by the unforewarned descent, amid fresh snow squalls, of the fat yellow Preston helicopter. I more than half expected Fern to emerge, but Maretta was pilot and sole occupant. She'd obviously been here before, and though mildly criticized by Rod for not making radio contact first, was *persona* very much *grata*, no trouble persuading the two men to unload her cargo, while she presented herself smiling to me, and giving a childish salute reported that, having checked with John before coming, she'd therefore brought everything else to accompany the bird, some of which would need rewarming. When I expressed surprise she wasn't at the ranch with her family she told me they were all clumped in Dallas, where she'd gone yesterday, making her escape on the pretext of an important TV show.

"And Fern?" I asked, and was told she'd flown to Sacramento, might be staying in a women's shelter there, sent love. None of my contrasting emotions can be called disinterested; I was relieved for her, no longer a fugitive, and for myself, free of that fragile burden — but a sharp disappointment came first, when the helicopter disgorged only Maretta, than whom Fern was far better company.

A verdict unaltered by subsequent diversions. In the kitchen, where space, inadequate in the original plan, had been turned into a cramped slot by the restaurant-sized fixtures, we unpacked the store-boughten transfiguration of Thanksgiving fare, stuff the colonists, even with the justifying recollection of that famished winter, 1620-21, would have found a sybaritic peril to their thin-lipped souls, smooth, luminous sweet-potatoes the size of pigeon's eggs, glistening newborn corn, green salad with the dreamlike glamour of a vintage Sam Goldwyn musical, a chiffon pie that achieved the laudable ambition of all pumpkin pie by suppressing every memory of pumpkin, sauces and candied fruits, with jellies soother than the creamy curd, and lucent syrops tinct with cranberry, nuts, and dates in argosy transferr'd from Fresno. All this she arranged for reheating, chilling or serving with a swift competence that, with her piloting of the helicopter also in mind, was utterly unfair; having discarded a down jacket and camouflage overpants, she was in a close-fitting burnt-orange jumpsuit of soft, affectionate jersey with a couple of big splashes of gold-and-enamel trinketry; stylish as well as celebratedly scatterbrained, she wasn't supposed to be able to

do things. I'd been drinking a quite ordinary red Chilean wine
from a stock in an open rack, but Maretta now showed me the
real liquor supply, lurking behind an undetectable panel door
in the short passage to the kitchen, and I was soon furnished
with an 18-year-old single malt, while she mixed herself a
margarita.

In the big room by the fireplace were two further soft
zippered bags, and from one she produced small presents for
Rod, Robb and Loima; not for me, and I deduced this was
something one did at Thanksgiving for the menials. Rashly
after several sips of memorable scotch, I said, "What's in the
other bag?"

She laughed slyly, while doing the eyelid business.
"Gift-wrapping, mainly."

"For what?"

"For me. I'll show you, after dinner."

Naively, as it now appears, I'd assumed her *bonne
dame patronesse* act would last no longer than it took to dine;
an unplanned stopover, if margaritas and wine made piloting
inadvisable, wouldn't have been astonishing, but that she'd
brought clothes with her was, and that they would consist
almost entirely of what the stores where she shopped would
call *intimacies* (not sex-shop stuff, just tasteful middle-class
provocation), altogether outside my imagining. Let's note, in
our scholarly way, that the indomitable male simple-
mindedness that would help her keep a promise made to Fern
goes back at least to *Lysistrata*, she who escalates the pressure
of her play-action by advising the women to exhibit
themselves, not tauntlessly naked, but draped in diaphanous
gowns of shining saffron silk — I seem to be defending myself
for the excitement Maretta kindled and maintained, assisted by
her rainbow of airy paradox, but there was no reason to
exclude enjoyment from exile, and I could foresee no reunion
with — anybody.

Not a revisionist afterthought; we sat down four to
dinner, Loima not explicitly declining but vanishing in panic-

stricken retreat when confronted with gift and invitation, and
it's clear my mind was already made up. We'd found and
lightly chilled two bottles of Alsatian gewurtztraminer, but one
remained unopened; I limited myself to a glass-and-a-half, and
at the end declined what looked like a noble Armagnac.
Maretta might have interviewed Jacques Cousteau and (as
legend asserted) never mentioned water, but a point like the
gist of my abstinence didn't escape her; throughout the meal
she'd been flirting generally, but always with reference to me,
a punctuating glance like asking my approval, vowing I'd be
sole beneficiary when all this hormonal bombardment resulted
in a sustainable reaction, a look itself stimulating and, yes,
dammit, flattering; great lingam of Siva! but it's humbling to
regard the puttying power of a woman who knows she's
desirable; we simper like caressed cocker-spaniels if she but
smile on us.

　　After Thanksgiving dinner, time for a time lost its
retaining force, and some days slipped away; breakfast could
come at teatime and a champagne brunch at midnight;
wonderful with what tact (or experience) Rod and Robb faded
into sentinel shadows, unobtrusive and apparently incurious,
so long as my gambols with Maretta didn't go wallowing out
into the snow-choked forest. Before I'd met Maretta, I tagged
her *intriguingly corrupt*, which, after six millennia or so still
turned out to mean she was good at finding fruits old Adam
felt uneasy about enjoying, causing me to learn some infantile
aspects of my own intense delectation I remain not altogether
at peace with in cool blood. She had a genuine if narrow
dramatic gift, probing into my hoarded fantasies, and sweetly
incorporating them in the plotlines of agreeable playlets, but
even if I'd never heard Fern reciting her friend's pragmatic
sexual creed, I would have known by touch that a patronizing
contempt for men and how easily, as she believed, they were
controlled by pleasure, underlay Maretta's gambits. In which
she was inevitably checkmated by her own surrender to

enjoyment, provided her subject wasn't going to fall in love or in simple addiction with her.

As I wasn't: *she must be great in bed* is an explanatory cliché that fails at every level, cynical without being on-target: in all my experience of erotic thralldom (including mine), I've never known a heterosexual man (including me) who could honestly ascribe his obsession to quality of orgasm; that's one of those desperate fables that try to sort some rational sense out of utter unreason.

STORY TAKES TURN INTO POMPOUS; come *on*, we're only talking about an extended romp with esurient Ms. Preston. Forgive my clarity, captivating Maretta or any in her corner, and understand I was grateful for world-class diversion — but on your side, too, it was wonderfully impersonal, like performing in a mirror.

On Tuesday, when, quite abruptly, she decided to leave, there were the first wrinklings on the surface of our mutual inches-deep amiability, signs of the inadequacy of unmixed venery to sustain a connection between two people with not much to say to each other; in certain arch, still-smiling near-taunts it became apparent Maretta was developing a petulance over my failure to be anguished over our parting. She nevertheless promised, with adequately tender arabesques, to be back quite soon. After the yellow bird had lifted, I was restless for a few hours, not stricken, and soon content to be back with books and boredom.

Steve came again at the end of the week, and his theme was damage control: the morning John Battaglia's new job had been made public Steve had taken calls from an Elvis-spotting tabloid, two real newspapers, and a TV network (not the one in which Orbis has a major interest), asking about a rumor the Attorney-General designate was "shielding" a suspect in the notorious Westerlake killing.

"Battaglia met with you, and believes in your innocence. But advised you to retain counsel. Period."

"What about if he's asked whether he knows where I am now?"

Steve shook his head. "We should be okay on that one — Helena Smitt has much more information than she should, but she's through blabbing. No way she could ever know about this place."

Still skeptical about *Ilium*, I asked how Steve could be so certain she'd been neutralized.

"John put the fear of God in her. He told her, if he found she was still giving information to Laxitter, he'd leak her name to the press, and say she was cooperating with the investigation. Better than anybody, she should know what Laxitter would do about that."

Okay, hardball, but as I didn't say, her fear of Laxitter right now could be enough to keep her on his side.

Another of the tabloids had called about a story, linking the former senator to a popular young TV interviewer, "but they haven't had the balls to go with it yet. They collared Maretta outside the studio. She told them, John and Eugenia Battaglia are dear friends of her family, period."

"Did Helena know about Battaglia and Maretta?"

"Oh, shit, yes; she and I discussed it." Here, some stored bitterness over the treachery of *Ilium* boiled up like battery-acid, but from rancor Steve passed on to the proposition plenty of people could have guessed; "For one thing, Maretta did her goddamned show with him, and asked her famous question. Shaking up Maggie Thatcher is one thing, but, Christ! She was in this black lace shirt thing, doing everything but rip off his clothes right through the interview — " (I must interject here that, floating pronoun aside, it was *Maretta* whose dress and behavior Steve described). "When she asked him how he felt about garter-belts, an idiot could see she already knew the answer, and loved it. Actually," Steve

smiled proudly. "John did a great job fielding it; he related it
to the Second Amendment."

"Sorry?" Garter-belts and gun-control failed to link up
for me.

"Emotive symbolism, going way beyond the original,
intended function." Besides, loyal Steve asserted, Battaglia's
sex-life was nobody's business, so long as it wasn't some
Mafia babe he was fooling around with (a reference to a
former Administration), the less so when his wife had known
about and condoned the affair. Having seen Eugenia's lips
tauten on mention of Maretta's name, I wasn't sure *condone*
was precisely the word, but couldn't dispute the basic thesis,
that for any Attorney-General the discharge of his duties and
his semen were, so to speak, quite separate issues, with the
latter seldom a legitimate public concern. According to Steve
at least thirty full-time print and television prospectors were
digging for paydirt on Battaglia: so far, Orford Lomax had
named some dozen cabinet-level appointments, and if Steve's
estimate was reliable, and could be extrapolated, investment in
the hope of scandal went very quickly into the millions, and
could be justified, in business terms, only by a massive,
disheartening popular appetite for mindless gossip and prurient
self-righteousness. It might be best, he said, if Maretta was
besieged by press, to bring her here for an indefinite stay. He
guessed (sidelong query, ignored) I wouldn't have much
problem with that.

I agreed, but felt the first twinge of an anxiety I was
reluctant to confront more squarely: all praise to Maretta's
infinite variety, and scarcely troubled by my hurt thigh, I'd
performed prodigiously, and exulted in it, but like Roger Maris
in that one fateful year could create debilitating pressures on
myself to duplicate or surpass a phenomenon: we weren't, as
I've made clear, soul's siblings who could modulate to other
sharings. Strange worry, when on an intellectual plane
Maretta's opinion of me meant nothing, but confinement
narrows vision; jailed overlords of crime may fight to the

death over possession of a comb, and to astonish Maretta was, together with small triumphs in the kitchen, among the few victories still within my reach. An indefinite stay, and all the time I'd only be as good as my last box-score.

Meanwhile: "I still wish Battaglia would go public with the files."

"He will, when it's time to," testily. "Don't worry, you're safe."

"It's not just me. You're in danger, Battaglia himself, Maretta, maybe Fern, we're all at risk, so long as knowledge of the files is kept within a killable number of people. As soon as it's out in the open, the danger's over: they can't kill the whole press-corps."

"If it comes out too soon, the lame-duck people we've got at Justice still have time to botch it up with bad indictments. Besides, you have to let John have something. This last two years — shit, he was unquestionably the best first-term Senator this century, can you imagine what it was like losing out for reelection? He's the man who got Lomax elected, but Lomax couldn't make him official campaign manager; still a political liability, according to some of his midget handlers. Shit, John should have been the *candidate*."

For the first time I recognized what this chance at resurrection meant to one whose career, before he took on Orbis, had been all palms and hosannahs, and how inextricably ambition and his idealism intertwined.

"Besides, John has called a news conference, for right after he briefs Lomax down in the Keys. He'll announce formation of the industrial crimes unit, and drop some hints about the Orbis thing, without getting too specific. How many of these clowns trying to find out where he buys condoms will cover that story? Policy doesn't sell papers."

All this was prelude, *background*, as Steve would have said, to a fresh interrogation of me, to guard Battaglia against unpleasant surprises out of my past. "You've never been

married? Single and straight, that makes life easier — John
has a great record on discrimination, I'm here to tell you, but
— you are *straight* straight, huh?"

I assured him that while it might not consistently
amuse Queen Victoria, there was nothing in my coupling
biography that could (*rim-shot, please*) be held against me.
There was no absolute defense against invented histories, but
the Orbis people might hesitate to produce the astonishing
coincidence of yet another long-dormant case of sexual
assault, particularly with the evidence for the first fabrication
in Battaglia's hands. My financial and business dealings were
of a probity that was practically quaint, and the only yet-
unrevealed problem (just barely worth bringing up, my tone
suggested) was that this chap I'd shot in the hand and upper leg
and left to die had subsequently swallowed poison, none of
which I'd reported, the body still remaining to be discovered.
Perhaps worth noting, the man was certainly murderer of
many, including Bieman, Hilde Konwitschny, and Paula, and
had been trying to add me to his bag.

"Christ," Steve said. "You are kidding, aren't you?"

It took fully ten minutes, much of it repetition with
emphasis, to convince him — not of the facts, those he soon
inured himself to; the singular fact of my not speaking sooner,
and the validity of my reasons for not doing so were the hard
part to sell. Steve, angry on Battaglia's behalf, said "Shit"
many times and in various shades of exasperation and
contempt, and I didn't regain his respect till I stopped trying to
placate, and told him bluntly I hadn't been sure how far I could
trust his boss. Battaglia had no personal investment in my
wellbeing, and if he'd thought the case against Orbis would be
damaged by doubts about my actions, he'd have been justified,
from his standpoint, in cutting me loose, to let me take my
chances with the law. But (I swore) I'd always known he'd
have to be told, and, to avoid just the sort of late-popping jack-
in-the-box Steve feared, had decided my best time to do so

was right after he informed the President-elect about the Orbis case, when my value as a witness was highest.

"Jesus," Steve, in all-at-once amused outrage, when my point was plain. "John's right, you are a born politician; if only you had some charisma, you'd be a bitch of a candidate. You wanted to make sure he was committed to you with Lomax."

"I want Orbis stopped. I'd also like to survive."

Only incidentally trying to make me feel like an ingrate, Steve again gestured at all that was being done by Battaglia to make that happen. After the accident to Leahy, he said, there'd been no chance John would turn me in and trust the police to keep me safe.

Without committing his chief to the idea of sidestepping the law, Steve moved our discussion to practical questions: how soon the body might be discovered (unknowable, snowfall a factor), and how, when it was, it could be connected to me. Describing the scene, the pit where cigarettes, lighter and ample spilled blood, ejected brass from rifle, splashes of lead on the rock wall, automatic weapon and smashed watch in the ravine nearby, were all left for the finding, I could very nearly achieve a smile over the forensic puzzle a thorough search and battery of tests would pose, beginning with gunshot-wounded but poisoned body, which, I was sure, would have no antecedents, no next-of-kin to provide a name; the pocket diary I'd taken was anonymous, and I'd be very surprised if there was a passport in the name of van Muer; that name had been used too freely at Orbis Special Projects. What his official nationality had been, what name he lived under in Suriname (if that was where he lived) — none of that was known to me, and I was sure apart from the evidence I'd given Battaglia there would be no trail leading back to his former association with Hurd Laxitter, CIA. Two rifle shots, one from the Watchtower, the other beside the pit, a brass-strewing burst of automatic weapon fire from the far side of the ravine; make up your own story. All this assumed the mobile Orbis crew from Brandsville hadn't already found the site, where they could have altered or removed anything, including the body.

If not, Steve asked what there would be to identify me as the missing rifleman. I'd had plenty of time to think that one through: if the finders were conscientious enough to do DNA tests on bloodstains at the pit, they'd be startled to come up with two different price codes, the other of which could be matched to me, just as fingerprints I must have left all over Zack's shack would match those on my various abandoned rental cars, my own car in Westerlake, and complete sets which by now the FBI must have lifted from my apartment. There was, as far as I could see, no way to *prove* an occupant of Zack's shack had anything to do with a shooting two miles away, but it would be assumed, especially if Orbis, in the person of Hurd Laxitter, had enough audacity to supply the deceased with a milder identity, let's say of an unarmed private investigator, looking for me solely on the embezzlement charge.

To this Steve tried fitting the rest of the evidence, saying I must have fired at him from above with the rifle, hitting him in hand and leg, and also smashing his wristwatch, then, instead of finishing him off at close range, using my submachine gun to fire at him from across the ravine, missing him completely, then dumping automatic weapon, reloaded with full magazine, into the declivity. Then, I watched him stagger and crawl to where the body was found, and perversely used the rifle to force him to swallow poison. "Where is the rifle now, by the way?"

"I don't know. I gave it back to Fern, and she got rid of it." This was true as far as it went; I didn't know where *on the Preston ranch* Fern had secreted the weapon, but thought it inadvisable to worry Steve with the idea that **RIFLE LINKED TO MYSTERY SLAYING** might connect up to both **"JUST GOOD FRIENDS" WITH BATTAGLIA, SAYS TV**

BEAUTY, and *DID A-G CHOICE SHIELD TORTURE-MURDER SUSPECT?* — Rancho Feliz as wild card in a nasty straight.

Not for the first or last time I regretted failing to place the Beretta automatic with the body, but Steve agreed what I'd done with it was better than either leaving it up at Zack's shack or bringing it away with me, and that was a windvane for me; he was thinking in terms of inaction. With the habitual disclaimer about his inability to speak for John, he thought it best to let events take their course; any manipulation of evidence by Orbis or its allies could be countered by material from the Laxitter files, and he, Laxitter, must know that as Attorney-General with the President's ear, Battaglia stood a fair chance of getting CIA files to show the *Azraël* connection; somewhere there must be a dossier on the man, very likely including fingerprints. For this reason or another, quite possibly the body would never be found, or never be associated with me. "Rule forty-seven. Don't get so far out front you're denying accusations they wouldn't dare make."

Steve, who would accompany Battaglia to the Lomax audience, left, and Maretta did return, but on her own impulse, this time charming the men into carrying flowers she'd brought to brighten the scene, while she handed over to me, honorably unopened, a letter enclosed to her from Sacramento.

Beginning with upbeat news about legal prospects, and how the Swiss consul from San Francisco had been allowed to interview her, patriotically siding with Miki and naturalized Lenore, abruptly having to defend himself against firebrand Rachel Levi-Ybarrondo, who blamed him personally for his countrywomen not getting the vote until 1971.

From there, with only a dash for punctuation, Fern, still in the same firm, even handwriting, turned to extravagant, trusting, touching, appalling devotion, founded in a

preposterously inaccurate evaluation of my virtues and
severely limited experience of grown-up love; what can be
more gratifying to ego or dismaying to shopworn heart than an
intelligent woman's comprehensive surrender to a glad and
generous fallacy: without Orbis and how it was dictating my
associations, without feelings that continued to grope
southward over desert, through jungle, amid lunatically bad or
desperately striving regimes, to locate a battered VW and
dismiss its psoriatic driver; with my life fully functional and
no one to love but Fern, I still wouldn't have been able to come
near the specs implicit in her rash purchase of all I wasn't —
like being relied on for a transcending *interpretation* of the
Schumann concerto when my fingers couldn't cope with more
than half the notes, and I loathed myself for finding, no less,
some pride in the misplaced admiration a more plausible
Doppelgänger had inspired. I'd achieved the supreme male
ambition, completely snowing a class chick, and the
accomplishment tasted like earwax.

  Though preoccupied, Maretta read my face. "Don't
you hurt her," she warned. "She's my buddy, and you better
not hurt her." Cruel to record that Maretta was at the same
time dangling and shimmering for my approval in front of her
fully-clothed body a newly-acquired, nearly non-existent, pale-
blue chemise.

  John Battaglia — I truly apologize for this
juxtaposition, but it exactly represents how the shock came —
John Battaglia was assassinated at 2.30 PM (EST) on
December 6. I almost wrote "as everyone knows," but in
history, the name of John Battaglia, Attorney-General
designate, will be a footnote to a bungled attempt to kill the
President-elect, Orford Lomax, and only a few of us know the

assassins made no mistake. A single armor-piercing incendiary projectile from a shoulder-held launcher, fired from cover off the Florida Turnpike, struck the black, bullet-proof Lincoln sedan supplied by the Secret Service, instantly killing its occupants, who also included security-man Barney Weber, driving, aide Steve Lang, and midwestern journalist Bill Elderbush, who'd just resigned from the *St. Louis Post-Dispatch* to handle public information at the new DOJ. In Palm Beach, Battaglia had spent five minutes in private meeting with Lomax, far longer being photographed in various groupings as part of the Administration-to-be, but was making his way south for what was called a strategy session in the Keys with the President-elect.

On a phone tip, if it matters, an arrest was made before teatime in Pompano Beach. The man, Josip Milanovic, a small, seedy Serb, though thought to have been acting on orders, remains sole detainee; the support of Orford Lomax for the EEC position on borders for the independent states of Croatia and Bosnia-Herzegovina is the accepted motive. Milanovic was in the USA ostensibly on business, but apparently as an agent of the irregular Serbian militia, trying to buy arms to defeat the embargo, a quest that led him to the Coalition for a Democratic Cuba in Florida, who might be persuaded to resell some of the weapons generously supplied by a government deeply committed to reestablishment in Havana of freedom, prostitution, gambling, drug-dealing, and an offshore conference-center for American businessmen with similar interests. Though Milanovic, by way of sample, did acquire a portable anti-tank weapon with a case of projectiles, that it was ever fired is in dispute, and his firing the fatal shot requires his leaving a Juno Beach bar where he was drinking ("establishing a phony alibi") and covering 56 miles in a maximum of 45 minutes with no spare time for setup, leaving the scene immediately to show up at a package liquor store 25 miles back along his trail by no later than 2.58 PM, at which time exactly, again developing his alibi, he purchased a bottle of rum, the time being printed on the register tape. The clerk, after hours of interrogation by the FBI, finally recalled him as "extremely nervous and distraught."

Apart from a demand, as a reserve major, to be treated as a prisoner-of-war, Milanovic's sole interesting statement has been stolidly translated as, *the true perpetrators have used me as a catspaw in their schemes*, which I, with no knowledge of Serbo-Croatian, render more idiomatically as, yes, *I was the patsy*.

As for the error in victims, true, the President-elect had originally intended to drive, or be driven, the 150 miles from Palm Beach to his vacation-spot in the Keys, but his wife's well-publicized allergic reaction to the air-conditioning in the limos had brought about a change of plans — not quite last-minute; their boarding of the helicopter had been covered live by local and filmed for network television, but the maladroit conspirators were seen as disdaining accurate information as to the whereabouts of their intended victim; the presumed conspirators, I should say, noting Belgrade had been prompt to disown Milanovic.

Yes, yes, I am evading my own more immediate reality. Where was I when I heard Battaglia had been killed? Watching a rebroadcast, with its host, of Maretta's interview with an alleged composer responsible for numerous tuneless chants on and off Broadway; she let out an incensed, "Son of a *bitch*," when it suddenly vanished from the screen, but after five long seconds of dead air a nervous local anchorwoman got our attention by telling there had been an attempt on the life of Orford Lomax, that details were as-yet unclear, but the President-elect hadn't been harmed. At once we were whisked away to the network where a more celebrated but equally harried newsman gave the entire story up to arrest of a suspect, with mistaken-identity theory already firmly in place. The loss of *Azraël*, I noted, hadn't crippled Laxitter's capacity for elaborate attributions.

With fatuous chatter and sillier video of locales where nothing was now happening, the busy screen was foreground to a profound silence, till Maretta said, "No. *Jocko*?" in a voice like a very distant scream.

In anger, I stood up, and said, "Those bastards. Those fucking bastards."

She looked at me. "You don't believe they were trying to kill Lomax, do you? Does this have something to do with your thing?"

With crushing conviction I told her she didn't want to know, mustn't ask, should forget the anonymous generalities I'd given her, forget anything else she'd heard, overheard or deduced, must absolutely not so much as hint at it on her show, or around the station. The death of Battaglia, as was immediately apparent to me, meant the quest to confound Orbis was over, and all that could be saved was other lives. My own was much worse than doubtful, a loose end for tidying up, with nothing now to protect me, but I was going to try to go on living, and surely do what I could to prevent deaths by association; as an intimate of both John and me, Maretta would need all her reputation for light-minded inattention.

"A great loss," Orford Lomax said, squinting in latening sun, and fenced in by hand-held mikes. "To my Administration and to the country. Senator Battaglia — our hearts must go out to his lovely wife and his children — "

Question: *(inaudible).*

"I can't comment on that," said the President-elect. "It may have been, but I'll leave that to the enforcement people. In any case, this is a mindless, senseless crime, which — "

"I'd better wake Robb," I said. Security demands of Battaglia's trip had reduced my sentries to one, Rod leaving to take Barney Weber's place with Eugenia and the family. I'd been given electronic gear and a quick course in Uzi, and was my own sole guard during Robb's six hours of sleep, afternoon to evening.

"Always controversial, a fighter for his beliefs — " having finished with Lomax, the network had gone to a hastily-cobbled capsule biography of Battaglia, with some highly miscellaneous film-clips, not always appropriate to the text, finishing with a ten-year-old still, captioned with name and dates. *" — first and last, an A-*murr-*ican, John M. Battaglia."*

"Ba-*TAHL*-ya," Maretta, automatically. He really was dead: the announcer had said B'*tag*-lee-uh.

Plans formed in a numb and desultory way; whole eras had dragged by, twilight had come to Florida, but here it was still mid-afternoon. Eugenia would have no need for most of her husband's support staff, and the future of the ski cabin itself was in doubt. Though the media informed us the widow was flying to Florida, Robb thought he should join Rod at the Battaglia home, and Maretta offered to make the side-trip on her way back to Rancho Feliz, where she also proposed I return, footnoting that her unpleasant elder brother had returned to his Oregon winery. Once more I tried to hammer in the lesson of Battaglia's death, the reality of near danger.

"You said. But it's not right — if you give in to them, John will have died for nothing."

I can't really endorse the idea of past lives remembered, if only that the present population of California by itself would use up all available souls from the entire world of Cleopatra's day,: there'd have to be a lot of sharing, like the roomful of Bonapartes in the psych wing. Yet here we'd plainly regressed into the Frank Capra era, to the mandatory don't-let'em-getcha speech of helpmeet Jean Arthur, Barbara Stanwyck, Donna Reed; too tedious to explain how, in real, unwonderful life,

our shambling hero is just another feckless, failed S & L
speculator.

"Whatever else happens," obstinately. "I'm going to
rerun my interview with Jocko, and take out the intro so's I can
do a new one saying, maybe his death wasn't a mistake — "

"You are *not* — " sole instance in all our exchanges
(outside the scripts of collusive fantasy-drama) that I'd issued
anything like an order, and it took her by surprise; she actually
tossed her head, a move I thought had gone out with Mary
Pickford, if not Nell Gwynn (*La, sir, you do presume too much
upon our brief if busy acquaintanceship*).

"Why am I not?" was her real-life defiance.

"Quite apart from the pain it might give Eugenia
Battaglia," I said with some cunning. "Because it can't do any
good." John Battaglia, I told her, had some chance of stopping
the nebulous Them; she hadn't, and her death would truly be
useless; they wouldn't hesitate now, having chanced so much.
They'd begun the killings for the sake of perhaps a billion
dollars in profit, but the murders themselves had so upped the
ante nothing they now did could increase the risk, and if they
had to blow up an airliner with three hundred people aboard to
silence one, they'd do it without a single ordinally-numbered
thought. "Hell," I said, "they'd nuke a whole city to get one
enemy."

"You can still get your story out. Okay, nobody takes
my show seriously, but I could maybe get you in touch with
one of the network news magazine shows."

"Too late." If Battaglia, strategy be damned, had used
his prestige to call a general news conference before Orbis
could act on Helena Smitt's report, had handed out copies of
some of the more lurid pages from the Laxitter files, he might
have annoyed Lomax by handing a coup to the outgoing
Administration, might have blown his chance for a cabinet
position this time around, but he'd surely still be alive, with
Orbis shuddering under a far worse media siege than Steve had

feared for Maretta. Whereas I, without evidence or standing
— I could make myself very angry over how Battaglia, for the
sake of political advantage, had gotten himself killed, and
three other good men, and probably me, except you might as
well blame a lioness for hunting, a spider for making webs; if
John Battaglia hadn't made a life out of political ambition, I
wouldn't have had him to go to. Besides, I'd liked him.

My assumed pessimism, while it depressed me, had, as
far as I could tell, the desired chilling effect on Maretta, and
she retreated to "maybe there'd be a time" when she could talk
about Jocko's murder. With no one who could countermand, it
was accepted that I (and the seldom-seen Loima) would stay
put; disposition of the ski-cabin would scarcely be near the
head of Eugenia's priorities, and I had not the ghost of another
plan. It kept running in my head how close we'd come; at the
moment fiery death had arrived, Battaglia, Steve Lang and Bill
Elderbush must have been discussing how to present the case
against Orbis, first to Orford Lomax, then to the public. I
supposed they had printouts of the Laxitter files, and wondered
where the disks were now, whether they'd been returned to
Battaglia's safe. For a moment I was resolved to go with
Robb, but I didn't know how to open the safe, and if I had,
wasn't likely to be given a chance to. The Battaglia home
would be under surveillance by the ghoulish press if nothing
more directly lethal: I would certainly be recognized,
especially after the rumors linking the Attorney-General
designate to the Westerlake Killer, so instead I puzzled Robb
by asking him to get me the name and phone-number of
Battaglia's attorney. He informed me pityingly both Battaglias
were attorneys, but I managed to convince him that where
that's true it's still normal for well-off and prominent people to
retain the services of yet another lawyer for the drawing up of
contracts, purchase of property, the making and guarding of
wills. In Battaglia's case I would expect it to be a personal
friend as well, who should be warned about the lethal content
of the disks, and the dangers in taking charge of them, but if he

(or she) could be persuaded to forward them unexamined to a major newspaper with an explanatory note, it might be that even now, with the talisman of Battaglia's authenticating name, Orbis could be stopped. So, when it's too late for the governor's call, must the condemnee hope for a power failure.

Shall I record the multiple layers of unreality in Maretta's farewell? With some vigorous brushwork and jaunty resumption of tailored combat dress, she was again the ace war correspondent, ready to share designer chow under picturesque bombardment with the chic infantry, and asked if I hadn't had a good time, forgetting for an inattentive moment that everything now was supposed to take a mournful coloration from Battaglia's death. Recollecting, she shook her head in genuine grief, but still (here it is) there was room for a final Marettism: "Maybe after you and Fern get married, she won't mind if we get together and play, once in a while."

Of phones, the blue one might have been quite normal, but it didn't ring and was never used while I was there. Except for displaying no number, the two beige phones, one in the living-room, the other a cordless usually in the main bedroom, also seemed ordinary, but I'm still not sure how they connected to the world; Maretta said they functioned as an extension of the line to Battaglia's home, some hundreds of miles and a state-and-a-half away. When you called that number you got a beep, and could either press zero, which made it ring in the usual way, or another, very confidential, three-digit sequence, which connected you to the ski cabin. She was sure the procedure was known to a very few, possibly not including Eugenia Battaglia, so it was a reasonable assumption on my part when the phone sounded late that evening — a soft buzz rather than a ring — that I'd be talking to one of the inmost circle.

"Arthur Ames?"

"Who's speaking?" A voice I nearly knew; Robb? Rod?

"Hold on." A low mutter, and another phone was picked up.

"Is that you, Arthur?" Of that smooth voice I had no doubt, and knowing it, recognized the other; Frank Lupin had placed the call for Hurd Laxitter.

"Arthur?" *Laxitter*! I jumped as if he'd come into the shadowed room, and very nearly slammed down the phone, prevented only by counter-panic, which shrieked at me that to let terror show would be fatal.

"We need to have a talk, Arthur," and I heard the click as Lupin's phone went off-line. "We've been very concerned about you. You're having a terrible run of luck — another loss close to you today, I understand."

"Four losses — " paradoxically a little cheered by Laxitter's revealed need to attempt what in fact he'd accomplished just by existing. In the midst of tremulous curiosity about how near he might be, I could still achieve the calculation he wasn't a wasteful person, and if he was trying to frighten me, couldn't yet have the immediate power to reach out and crush me.

"I think we need to meet, to discuss our differences."

"Fine," after a struggle. "I'm here; you can drop in any time." Outside, it was snowing heavily, and by me I had an Uzi and a lavish supply of ammunition. The helicopter touching down, Laxitter emerging; front door invitingly open, me crouched by the bedroom window which jutted enough to command the porch, and if I kept middled in my mind the deaths this dapper monster had caused, most recently the missile crashing into the Battaglia car, easy to feel myself squeezing the trigger, cutting him down with half a magazine of bullets. He'd never come alone, and his escort would have weapons, but I'd have cover and surprise on my side; I could kill or disable them all, and cripple the helicopter, then use a snowmobile for my getaway, perhaps, after making sure

Loima was out of the way, set fire to the cabin to add to the confusion...

Get off it, Laxitter wouldn't come. He didn't want a talk, but to eliminate me, and most likely arrival would be a combat team with orders to kill. Or if there was still some unguessable point where he required information, to capture me, but either way he wouldn't venture here himself, no more than Adolf Hitler rode in Guderian's vanguard, or LBJ personally napalmed Vietnamese villages; our modern Richard Crookbacks don't ramp around the battlefield, bidding extravagantly for a mount.

He said, "I think it would make more sense for you to come to me."

"Why?" banally. "The weather's nice here."

"I'm sure it is — " and his tiny hesitation had confirmed my suspicion: *he didn't know where I was.* From unneutralized *Ilium* or by some other means he'd discovered how to reach this place by phone, but not its whereabouts. That couldn't last; with his resources he'd be able to trace the installation, but right now it meant he was not keeping me pinned down on the phone while his commandos surrounded and crept into the house. That he'd made this call without first doing the research indicated some urgency on his part.

He said, "There were important documents destroyed by fire today — our documents."

"Not the only copies," instantly seeing how to exploit what worried him.

"We've now secured the original copies. A mobile disk and a set of floppies."

"Oh?" I contrived to parry, while fighting off internal dismay: the description was adequate proof Laxitter wasn't bluffing; with Eugenia and the rest of the family on their way to Florida, no doubt accompanied by what was left of the security force, it would have been relatively easy to achieve a break-in at the family home, and Helena Smitt, perhaps, knew the combination to the safe. The end of my fleeting fantasy with the family lawyer saving the day, but clearly Laxitter didn't know he'd won, and there was faint hope for me in that.

Based, I suppose, on memories of childhood conspiracies, it's notable we automatically respond in kind when addressed in the allusive, we-know-what-we're-talking-about style Laxitter was using to defeat the possibility of wiretap or recording; it takes a huge conscious heave to wrench the discourse over into the brutality of plain statement. Making that effort, I said, "Breaking and entering must be a minor consideration, for people who've arranged so many murders. How much did it cost you to have Battaglia's car attacked? More or less than *Azraël* charged you for killing Emil Bieman?"

Emptiness stretched out so long I thought he'd silently disconnected, till a forced chuckle came. "Your paranoid fantasies are getting the better of you, Arthur. We can find treatment for you."

"As you did Hilde Konwitschny? How many people connected with Orbis Special Projects do you think you can get away with killing? If Chief Leahy was getting close to the truth, others will get there, too — and some may not be as easy to kill as he was. You've been on a roll so far, but you didn't kill the new Administration when you got Battaglia; someone else is going to associate all these untimely deaths with the Harness Project." My object should be plain; to make Laxitter's imagined tape as detailed and damning as could be.

"Speaking of Harness," Laxitter said. "Or Stirrup, as it now is, thanks in part, as I'm the first to admit, to the splendid work you did before your breakdown, we'll be pressing ahead with marketing in the new year. We don't anticipate fresh problems with authorization."

"Then your lost documents don't really matter all that much."

"Well, you see, they're complete fabrications," Laxitter belatedly informed the phantom eavesdropper. "We would like to know where they are now; it's not good to have such elaborate forgeries in circulation."

I began to make up in my head what should have been done, and was close to convincing myself. "Before the disks were turned over to John Battaglia," I lied. "Several complete print-outs were made. You already know about the one sent to the FBI; it was intercepted. Other copies went to three major newspapers, and one was placed in a bank, a safe-deposit box. How many copies Battaglia made, and what became of them, I can't say. Several, I would think."

"What newspapers?"

"They'll be calling you for verification, I'm sure — or you could watch the headlines."

"Strange, none of this is showing up in the news; before you met Battaglia, you say? That's more than three weeks now, isn't it?"

"They're quality newspapers. They like to do some research before breaking a story like this. Be patient."

Here I saw this was more than an empty game to tease Laxitter with. "There was definitely some skepticism," I said. "They were very polite, but, well, skeptical. Of course, I told them you were trying to kill me — "

"*Of* course," Laxitter cooed soothingly.

"And that you'd try to make it look like an accident, or maybe suicide. So that if something did happen to me, they'd be more inclined to accept the whole story."

"I really think we ought to have a talk," after another unbreathing silence. "I'm in Des Moines. Could you meet me tomorrow at Orbistran, the Administration Building? It's out, not far from the Drake Observatory — "

"I'm very comfortable here."

"We can arrange transportation, if that's a problem."

"You specialize in things that blow up, don't you? No, I think I'll stay put."

If he bought my story about the print-outs (and the intercepted one for the FBI was, I thought, a touch of artistry), we had the makings here of a classic standoff, and it's legitimate to enquire, What, then, ever caused me to come down from my mountaintop? and meet, eventually, with Laxitter in a room like the Galactic Admiral's impersonal quarters in a zip-and-zap film, the building itself a metallic extrusion of Orbistran Aerospace technology.

Sentimentality, for which, we've told, there is no place in today's dog-absorb-dog commercial world, a proposition Laxitter handily disposed of; its place is secure, as the killer weapon of the emotionless, back-pocket derringer in a contest with foils.

He didn't have to say much, simply, "Have you heard from your little friend since she went to Sacramento? It's a worry — there's a lot of crime there, nowadays."

I was too sickly enraged to find out then how Laxitter knew about Fern, and he wouldn't have told me on the phone, but face-to-face where any bugs were his own he told me elliptically that *Azraël*, by contrast with his contemptuous refusal to cooperate with the contingent of Orbis men, had sent regular reports to Laxitter, in the final of which, written on his last evening under a roof, he described at length his observations and deductions about the "little underage piece *Alias* could be poking — " this was, as we now know, before he'd certainly verified my presence near Brandsville. In casual chat with Sean Gomez he'd found out where Fern's cabin was, and with this information Laxitter inadvertently gave me the joy of knowing by disabling van Muer I'd very likely saved Fern from the kind of visit he'd paid Paula in Westerlake; it acted on me like the fastest, safest, gentlest of all-natural relief; my residual guilt over the death flushed away, leaving me briefly euphoric.

That still didn't explain how Laxitter had known where
Fern was now, but that, too, was simple; before flying to
Sacramento, Fern had insisted on visiting the Brandsville
cabin to pick up clothes and one or two indispensable
treasures, and had been waylaid there by Sean Gomez, at last
aware her father was dead and she a technical fugitive. With
their ancient friendship, he was wheedled into rounding up the
usual suspects, Fern promising to contact the Sacramento
police as soon as she was safely under the Levi-Ybarrondo
wing. But by now, one would venture by adroit flattery of the
small-town cop, the chief of Laxitter's Brandsville contingent
was a confidant of Gomez, who spilt the story over the second
or seventh beer at Sourdough Sam's Roadhouse: ORBIS touches
every life; Sacramento, Seoul, Sikkim wasn't far enough.

But I'm not going to posture as some romantic martyr;
the threat to Fern brought me to where evil offered me its
truce, but I would, obviously, have accepted for the sake of my
own life if I'd never met her. Coming to Des Moines, entering
the hard and echoing building, I felt inadequately shielded by
my ramshackle story, expected death moment to moment, and
would have made any shabby deal to extend my life by an
hour.

Nor do I want to overestimate my importance; the
enemy had won with the successful hit on Battaglia, and I'm
alive (so far) chiefly because I never mattered all that much —
because like Egmont in Goethe's odd play I might in death
display a trace of the effectuality so conspicuously absent from
my life. Or so Laxitter feared. He very much wanted the
names of the newspapers in possession of the files, my last
defense against vanishing, and looking back it's puzzling, and
perhaps surest sign of my small-potato status, that he never
told me he had *vays* of making me talk; the only coercion,
aside from the inherent, crushing pressure of Orbis triumphant,
was further reference to Fern's vulnerability, but, beaten as I

was, it remained evident to me one way I couldn't make her safer was by giving Laxitter the chance to find out I'd been lying. As he remarked, the number of plausible newspapers was very limited, and as I replied, knowing which ones had the print-outs wouldn't necessarily enable him to forestall publication. Here, our standoff was on a tightrope, with Laxitter weighing the relative dangers to his cause of yet another Special Projects death (slash, disappearance), against my continued availability to give evidence.

Tamely, I agreed in the end to plead guilty to two counts of misappropriation and felonious conversion from the Chinese-restaurant menu of charges sworn against me, entailing, a brusque corporate lawyer warned me, "some" time in prison — the conviction at the same time establishing for future reference my prejudice against Orbis, and allowing Laxitter the luxury of knowing exactly where I'd be during months critical for the commercial foisting of radiation-enhanced agriculture. The frameup had gone into such detail as big back-dated deposits to an account under the name of Albert Kevin Ashford (it being a well-established habit of name-assumers to retain their original initials), whose signature, though carefully unlike mine, would yield to the ever-dubious science of orthographic analysis, so I was told, twenty-six traits of resemblance: I wasn't gratified to learn my pseudoshadow controlled assets approaching the quarter-million mark. My trial, then, hard by Christmas, was a mumbled affair without jury, where tufted and garrulous justice (like a blanched phoenix), calling me a hitherto-immaculate citizen tempted by prospect of effortless riches, fated me to eighteen months of minimum security confinement, eligible for parole in about two hundred days.

My own attorney, call him Solomon Sisserow (his true name is in the public record), a saintly figure haloed with silver hair, wouldn't withstand a rigorous conflict-of-interest probe, supplied as he was by the Clarence Darrow Group, wholly supported by the Orbis Foundation for Social Justice.

Laxitter had warned me against "flights of fancy" if questioned
on the Westerlake murder, for which my alibi was incidentally
embedded in the Orbis evidence at my trial, and in the event
Sisserow took from me a bland deposition concerned only
with how my car had come to be there, and how (but not why)
I wasn't. Neither Laxitter nor the law has made mention of
mountainside poisonings, and with silence, to this point, I've
survived.

In the whole process, the one brief flash of spirit I
displayed was at that Orbistran meeting, when I asked Laxitter
why, with his own lofty position and handsome income secure,
why, with profits cascading in from thousands of Orbis
ventures, why, when he must know the Harness-Stirrup
process would in time be blamed for devastating ills, why he
fought so ruthlessly for something no reasonable intelligence
could endorse. I'm always unpleasantly fascinated by the
apparent, impossible sincerity of self-serving conviction:
cheered by his constituents, quivering with passion, a House
member champions, for defense of our nation and the entire
free world, an aircraft, rejected by the Pentagon itself, and it
seems only a side-issue that the plane would have been built in
his own district: at the brink of tears, unable to gain a
conviction, an alleged victim falters that this isn't *about* profit;
her sole desire is to *send a message* to men, as she announces
a civil suit for the price of many millions of stamps: the
chairman of a pharmaceutical company warns with true,
religious fervor of the deadly dangers to the public inherent in
the idea that some conditions might be better treated with
vitamins (readily available, unpatentable, immorally cheap).
To struggle hoof and antler, claw and maw, for our own patch
of habitat is forgivable; but not to delude ourselves the fight is
for humanity, or truth, or abstract justice, or any damned thing
else but natural acquisitiveness: as old Sam Johnson said, we
must clear our *minds* of cant.

Laxitter was not less than one cynical step beyond that stage. He reexamined me with those chilly eyes. "The process will improve," he said. "It's bound to, once it can pay for itself. In the meantime, we're not a charity, not dedicated to pure science, and we're absolutely not a debating society: there has to be a place where we draw a line, and say, that's it, we're not going to have government bureaucrats or environmental evangelists micro-managing an international corporation. My responsibility is to the shareholders, and it's not my place to tell them, oh, let's not do this or that project, Orbis is big *enough*, we're profitable *enough*, the dividends are good *enough* — when I do, they'll very properly find somebody else to represent their interests.

"I'll be sixty-one next month," flat lips edging into a frigid near-smile. "The one thing I've learned is that doomsday is always further off than you think."

"So is justice."

"I don't know justice. I hear it as a slogan, a weapon the weak use to shake down those who've worked and struggled for what they have. What I do know is winning."

I was silent then, not knowing a language for talking with the dead.

15

Being a state, not a federal institution, this *facility* I call
home lacks some of the country-club atmosphere reputedly
enjoyed by naughty traders and the occasional elective
scapegoat, but is still more remote from the Big House as
portrayed in dark and sweaty films (metal cup on the bars, shiv
in the laundry-room); leisure time is generous, and though
tennis and handball courts are still under packed snow, there's
ping-pong in the games lounge, basketball in the gym. Chess,
and, wry comment on the activities that brought most of us
here, Monopoly, are popular pastimes, cards are dealt, socially
or solitaire, but no one picks and warbles *Oh, mah luhv, mah
darlin'* into the long, empty halls of night. White-collar, so
they name our species, but we could as readily be called
college criminals, wolves with sheepskins; in my weeks here
I've met only one inmate, a union official irresistibly drawn to
pension funds, lacking a degree; MBA's are as common as real
education is rare, and though I learn much more than I ever
expected to know about escrow, it's necessary to gloss the
most ordinary allusions to — well, even nursery rhymes or
pre-Disney versions of childhood tales; Shakespeare might as
well be an obscure Etruscan poet; there is as elsewhere a
strange and alarming discontinuity with our human past, as if
only techniques and methods are passed on, wisdom and hope
forgotten, the mindless functionalism of a community of
super-ants able to improve its mushroom-growing or aphid-
herding, but not remember why it began. Though my liking
for books and solitude is well-known and unpopular, no day
passes without my being instructed in how to invest money,
take advantage of tax breaks, become an entrepreneur, find
capital, buy real-estate, use a computer to my profit. With
music, I've become shy about my authentic lifelong love for
Mozart, so chic an emblem has the name become, a caste-
mark: my Rolex, my Porsche, my Burberry, my Mozart, but

when doors are left open to living quarters (there are no *cells* here), or there's occasion to go visiting, I never catch a neo-Salzburger furtively freebasing *Così fan tutte* or the *Sinfonia Concertante, K.364*; it's always the same pounding, puerile tribal mock-music, transmuting tin ears of the many into wealth for the androgynous few.

      I do use a computer, a tiny notebook, mainly late at night in my own quarters; this record of my defeat exists only as magnetized molecules on disks the size of wrapped teabags; what becomes of them and how I conceal their existence needn't be told: I know one of my fellow-felons must be here only as the eyes of Laxitter.

      Leading candidate is Gregarious Jack, credit-card virtuoso, backslapper and recounter of lubricious adventures with models, starlets and large-breasted civilians; it's a howling absurdity to say he doesn't ring true, but how could a fraudulence so self-advertising have succeeded long enough to earn his sentence? He, therefore, was the one I asked to take the message, I wasn't seeing any visitors, when word came that a Ms. Thomas had made the long, bleak, wintry journey here to see me; the haunting report that she didn't leave, but sat stoically in the waiting area till told the hours were over, was worsened by his unsought evaluation, she was unexpectedly sexy, for a girl with small tits. Persistent Fern has also sent envelopes that hum and quiver with the life and rash emotion they enclose, returned unopened. Cruel, yes, and I lack the ultimate romantic-novel courage to make her stop with a curt note feigning acquired dislike; I couldn't bear to think of her believing that (or, worse, disbelieving it), but can think of no way but silence to convince my watchers Fern is no danger to their enterprise, and can be allowed to live. My own life is extended, day by day, on sufferance; minimum security works both ways, and I'd feel less vulnerable in a lost dungeon, like Dr. Manette, brought to heel in the bowels of the Bastille, or you there, Cristo-to-be, in the lowest circles of the Château d'If...

Because any time, with the myth of Battaglia's mistaken murder firmly established, Laxitter may decide, either that I lied about additional copies of the files, or that whether or not, he can nonetheless risk my erasure, if it can be plausibly ascribed to accident, food poisoning, or one of those swift prison illnesses so opportune all through history for Caesars, Plantagenets, Texans. All I've bought is time to write down my story, to no effect, and the place of selected radiation in agriculture is "increasingly accepted as the new and decisive element in the population/food supply equation" (*New York Times* article by Gerhardt Fiori, widely reprinted). As you say, more than one way will do to balance an equation, but the regulators remain at best phlegmatic; with no Battaglia, the first hundred days of Lomax have been much like any DC season; the other day the adipose chairman of a Senate committee made profuse apology to the same Dr. Gerhardt Fiori for "submittin' you good folks from Orbis to some kind of instant *ree*play — " i.e., for doing, however torpidly, his job.

An ineffable moment caught on television; sets are ubiquitous here, and not less than three are always on in the main lounge — which accounts, throughout these pages, for a more intimate familiarity with the ikons of *Lumpenkultur* than might have been the case a few months ago; commercials, *daytime drama*, talk-shows, sitcom, sports have all been background to my recollection, and have irresistibly seeped into the substance of my Odyssey — the parallel is pretentious, but while for me, unlike the great commuter, Nausicaa preceded Circe, we have in common the force and character of the women our wanderings embraced. I'm grateful, but at the same time puzzled about the great gap, most of all in generosity, between the women one actually encounters and notional women of current culture, such as the asp-tongued campus book-burners, who celebrate their new-won individualism by expressing, word-for-word, precisely the same angry opinions on every subject — which are, indeed, all one obsessive subject.

When I was still small, expressed hostility against a whole sex embarrassed and angered me; whether the charge was knowing perversity over beer or permanent immaturity with the coffee and cake, I was conscious early of how vulgar such partisanship is, like all vulgarity a threat to any hope of civilization; there may be differences in the power to effectuate one's prejudices, but there's nothing to distinguish among the shoddy souls of those who ascribe all their dissatisfactions, all troubles of the world to blacks, or whites, or men, or women, or Protestants, Moslems, Catholics, Jews...

In which light, the rabid bait-show audiences I witness are to the sisters of the poison-ivy league as the beerhall bullies of Nuremberg to Aryan theoreticians, mindless hostility given sanction from above, hatred made societally acceptable — instance; the studio crowd that gave a heroine's ovation (I'm not making this up) to a young woman, piped in from prison, who, tiring after six married months of her husband's parsimony, shot him dead, or another audience's equally rapturous approval for a mother in deadly earnest advocating castration for her son-in-law, who'd committed the unimaginable crime, uniquely evil in all human history, of sleeping with his wife's younger sister. Or those who support lynch-mob organizations like the one Orbis sponsored — while the shrill accompanying rhetoric so deafens the debate that I have to make plain what shouldn't need saying: to be against conviction without proof, judicial mutilation, any kind of murder, doesn't mean I'm in favor of rape, adultery or even spousal penny-pinching.

Once, as a sophomore in college, I was literally shouted down at a party for maintaining, against the party line, that there were innate differences between men and women, but since then, without a word of acknowledgement, truth has altered: there are differences, but all to be interpreted as female superiorities, although at the same time we're ordered

to admire women who imitate ill-bred men at their offensive
worst: great Brummell's shade! I don't willingly associate with
men who yelp at strippers, or who loudly assess or worse, grab
at the buttocks of chance-met women, or who deliberately
humiliate their partners by belittling their sexual performance,
and I decline to let television bully me into viewing the same
bad manners in women as admirable instances of burgeoning
self-confidence.

At such times, and more intensely, perhaps, when the
anointed opinion-makers, exploitive women or pandering men,
grant weight of observed fact to the newest tendentious
allegation of male perfidy or phantom discrimination, I despair
— but then I remind myself how unquestioningly Judy gave
her help, Fern her trust, and begin to believe the Final Solution
may be delayed yet a while — or more seriously, that we
haven't yet poisoned every chance of plain dealing, friendship,
mutual help, between men and women. Not quite yet, but
these things take time.

You'd have liked to arch into a happy ending, here in
the deadly century's last decade? Ladies! gentlemen! euphoria
without reason is nothing but a buzz; the examples you watch
and cheer, as soft and crushable individual miraculously
vanquishes the steely, impermeable corporate mind, are
themselves manufactured, precision cast by exactly the sort of
juggernaut organizations whose daydream defeat they depict,
situations consumer-tested, dialogue vetted by accountants
who calculate how many tickets each ennobling sentiment will
sell; how else could they get distribution? Visions of niceness
triumphant: back-projected scenes of the open savanna, to
quieten the declawed, tethered felid, and if real victory were
possible over the keepers, we wouldn't want it, not at the price
of losing all-new, state-of-the-art, fun-filled Edenland, the
comfy and toystrewn theme-park they provide.

I can't force the fairytale finale of film or novel: life is
more jealous of its integrity than was Mr. Maugham, grafting

on an MGM ending to mar his middlebrow masterpiece, like image-conscious Dickens, who'd acceded to an even falser sentimental coda for *his* tale of human bondage.

Oh, if you're incurably hooked on fable, there still exists, or did exist, another set of the Laxitter files, those floppies I made after the first set was taken from among my towels, before I knew Judy would give me her mobile disk. She kept them.

My previous attempts to protect others from danger by contagion have not been a great success; criminal to draw attention to Judy, one whose existence Orbis seems till now to have entirely overlooked: they knew nothing about our friendship. When they killed Leahy, an attempt to get at his files would have risked spoiling the picture of random accident, so there's no reason for them to know about Judy's impulsive Guadalajara attempt to provide me with an alibi; nor would that sworn statement, generous but off-target, figure in a reopening of the case. So far, so consoling, but I'm terrified when she returns from Latin parts Judy's going to try to get in touch with me, and since I'm certain all my one-a-day calls are monitored, my letters intercepted, it's hard for me to forestall her attempt (e.g., by getting in touch with roommate Vickie, or with Judy's suburban parents) without bringing about what I want to avoid, and the same is more perilously true of an enquiry about present whereabouts of the disks. They may still be at the apartment, although there'd been some inconclusive talk of Judy saving money, and giving Vickie the chance to find, like, a new sharer (*'nkay?*), by moving out all the Judy-belongings, which would cram the disks among whole crates of stuff, out at her parents' northside house. Or she thought it safest to take them south with her; their weight and the space they occupied was negligible.

Patience; to make fantasy acceptable takes extra attention to humdrum detail. I mentioned cards, and this place, with one or two dour exceptions I avoid, is filled with astonishingly bad poker-players, sandbagging, bluffing big, willing to speculate, draw-and-pray, on the inside straight, doubling bad bets, always out for, rarely pulling off, the big killing — heaven-sent, like a steady supply of plump missionaries to the cannibals, for a boringly prudent, untemptable player like me, who regards the odds, and never confuses staying in a hand with retaining his *cojones*. Provided the game lasts long enough for the probabilities to take hold, I can always finish with a modest profit.

In theory we're not allowed to have more than a few dollars at a time, but the rule is hopeless to enforce so long as our guardians can handsomely supplement their modest official incomes in the luxury-smuggling trade; for twelve-year-old scotch or the ever-superseded epitome of enchanted athletic footwear, going price is just double retail, and I've been told by those who care that coke (neither oven-roasted coal, nor a beverage) is, in times of scarcity, murderously high. In any event, no one pays attention to loose change, and I accumulate amazing quantities of dimes and quarters.

Two further points: we become eligible for a weekend furlough, Friday afternoon to Monday roll-call, after thirteen weeks of blameless inertia. This, for me, should closely coincide with the moderation in weather that makes it possible to take up my volunteer duties as a gardener in the genteel surrounding landscape.

Dream Sequence

A late-April day on the northern prairie, cooler than it looks or the heart feels, sea-foam snow in sheltered pockets scintillating away to nothing, the air with the serene pale gold of Frascati. Friday, and having judged to a precarious instant the time when Judy is back, but hasn't yet made an attempt to reach me, I've applied for and been granted a furlough. After lunch, I go to the so-called checkroom, show my ticket, and am permitted to take some of my own clothes. Having made sure my two roomies, Gregarious Jack and Moody Paul, will be absent, I go to the room, and put on slender jeans and a high-necked sweater, but instead of what all weekenders do, killing time in the main lounge till the four o'clock bus loads up, I put back my uniform denims over my own togs, and after picking up a rake and trowel from the shed, wander out into the grounds, and make for fairly dense evergreens in the direction of the highway, where, earlier, I have concealed a small flight bag containing a few useful items. Masked by shrubbery, I down tools, take off my prison blues, stuff them in the bag, and having legged it over the low chainlink fence, more demarcation than a serious barrier, I quickly cross the highway — all this part, based on the notion Laxitter's people will try to keep me under surveillance on my furlough, may be over-elaborated; perhaps I simply wait for the bus, and go off in some unexpected direction after its forty-mile trip to where real buses, trains and infrequent, zig-zagging planes can be found. Whichever, I get to a payphone carrying a plentiful supply of coins, able to make as many calls as it takes to reach Judy, with very little risk of being overheard, at the old apartment, her family home, if necessary, Michael's.

Here, the dream stubbornly bifurcates, ignoring its duty to follow the best-case scenario: in a disappointing sub-routine I've miscalculated, and Judy isn't yet back from down there, but I take the opportunity to ask Vickie or a parent when she's expected, and leave the curious but adamant instruction she is not to make an attempt to get in touch with me; I'll call her, which should mean the preferred path (below) is no worse than delayed.

One, two rings. *"Hello? — "* the familiar, bright voice, then, when I speak, a joyful *"Arthur!"*

A brief period is allotted for purely personal
interchange; she's happy to be back, didn't have a terrible time,
has decided to break off with Michael (?), has been worried
and wondering about me, is dissatisfied with my vagueness as
to present whereabouts, a natural bridge into the ostensible
purpose of my call.

Do I trust my reasoned guess her phone is still secure,
and speak openly of the files? I can say `*you remember what
we were so concerned about when I last saw you*,' and so forth,
but if there's a third hearer, it isn't a stupid one, and as noted
several centuries-worth of experience ago in the case of Hilde,
anything cryptic sounds the same alarm-bell.

"*Do you still have the floppies we made?*"

"*Well, sure —* " and my instructions now are simple, to
airmail the disks, anonymously or pseudonymously, but with a
note giving provenance, to the *Sunday Times* or the *Observer*
—

"*I could copy them, and send a set to each —* " in
England, where, though Orbis is still a force, it hasn't attained
its North American omnipresence. There (understandably, in
view of our greedy Windsormongering), they love to exploit
an American scandal, and publication should let loose an orgy
of investigation: the Jastrebarsko disaster, cancer and residual
radiation, are subject to a corroboration independent of the
files, and so is the original, untenable tale of Bieman's death.
Above all, the many bribes must have left tracks, and some
bribees, faced with indictment, are bound to tell what they
know; whether the result is the death of Harness-Stirrup and a
slew of convictions, or that Laxitter, throwing a few minor
shipmates to the sharks, outrageously succeeds in a counter-
campaign of rogue-element confusion and brazen denial, once
it's all in public domain, I become less than a bit-player, a
walk-on whose death would accomplish next to nothing. No
certainty I won't be murdered, when desperation sets in, and
one killing more or less makes little difference, but that's also

the moment when minions start putting a priority on their own survival, and arch-criminals find it increasingly harder to get things done.

All this, but for an excess of fear, could have been achieved too many deaths ago. Meanwhile, after that weekend, I come back here for Monday roll-call, any irregularities in my furlough, if noticed, explainable by muddle-headedness; I missed the bus, didn't know I had to be on the bus, got distracted by my gardening. Having impassively served out my sentence, I emerge when Yugogate or Harnessgate has become a national sport, resulting in a climate of skepticism about Orbis and all its works, where in time I can have my conviction reversed, so to resume my life unspotted by felony. The world restored in a nearly convincing mask of innocence, the sun sets in golden, Straussian C-major (*twelve* velvet-throated horns, as in the opulent Dresden years), and squinting I amble hand-in-hand by the burnished water with lovely — well, this is your fantasy more than mine.

This proleptic dream, you see, depends on the intact existence of some small and eminently destructible disks, which may be stuffed — and from time to time, restuffed – in a duffel-bag, under the frontal wing-case of a disintegrating VW, jolted over execrable back-roads, subjected to fierce, warping heat, mildewing moisture of the rain-forest, daily and nightly possibility of theft. Most of the smart money is still on Orbis.

THE END

www.ingramcontent.com/pod-product-compliance
Lightning Source LLC
Chambersburg PA
CBHW020823180626
46814CB00001B/86

* 9 7 8 0 9 8 6 3 8 4 8 5 1 *